RESET

RESET

BRIAN ANDREWS

THOMAS & MERCER

Text copyright © 2018 by Brian Andrews
All rights reserved.

No part of this book may be reproduced, or stored in a retrieval system, or transmitted in any form or by any means, electronic, mechanical, photocopying, recording, or otherwise, without express written permission of the publisher.

Published by Thomas & Mercer, Seattle

www.apub.com

Amazon, the Amazon logo, and Thomas & Mercer are trademarks of Amazon.com, Inc., or its affiliates.

ISBN-13: 9781503954267
ISBN-10: 1503954269

Cover design by Mike Heath | Magnus Creative

Printed in the United States of America

For John Cook, whose integrity, generosity, and kindness have touched lives and made the world a better place.

FOREWORD

Estimates vary, but most experts calculate that the human brain contains approximately 100 billion neurons. New research, using a high-resolution imaging technique called array tomography, has allowed neuroscientists to evaluate neuron density and connectivity at the synaptic level. The primary insight gained by this new finding is that the human brain is much more densely and broadly interconnected than previously thought—with each neuron linked to hundreds of other neurons. Consequently, the human brain contains an astounding number of synaptic connections—upward of a *quadrillion*.

Closer examination of these connection points has revealed that synapses themselves are more complex than simple junctions. We now know that synapses are designed to function like microprocessors, with a single synapse containing up to a thousand molecular-scale biological transistors. Taken all together, this means that a single human mind has more switches than all the interconnected computers and routers on Earth. With an organic memory capacity in the neighborhood of one hundred terabytes, and the equivalent processing power of one trillion bits per second, the human brain is the most formidable, self-aware computer in the known universe. It is adaptable, autonomous, and, unlike its machine analogs, unhackable.

Unhackable, that is, until now . . .

AUTHOR NOTE

The events and characters in this novel are fiction, but the biological and technological methods of mind control described are real.

An acronym glossary is located at the back of the book in the event you get lost in alphabet soup. And for anyone who is curious and wants to take a closer look inside Silo 9 as you read, I've posted diagrams from an actual HGM-16F Atlas Missile Silo Operation Manual online at my website: www.andrews-wilson.com.

PROLOGUE

November 1963
Rockland State Hospital
Orangeburg, New York

Captain Will Barnes, USAF, woke up from the dream.

It was a terrible dream.

He went to rub his eyes but couldn't. He tried to sit up, but that was a nonstarter also. For some reason, his arms weren't working properly. This had happened to him once before. He'd fallen asleep on his side after having too much to drink, and both his arms had gone completely numb from lack of circulation. He sighed with exasperation and then proceeded to flop around like an inebriated sea lion until he was on his back. Only then did he realize he was lying on the floor.

Gee-whiz, apparently I got so drunk, I actually fell out of bed.

At least he didn't have a headache. He smiled a lazy, self-deprecating smile and opened his eyes. Staring at his bedroom ceiling, he blinked until the world slowly began to come into focus. Wait a minute; this wasn't his bedroom. This was some other room. He lifted his head and looked at the unfamiliar, dirty fabric-covered walls. He tried to push himself onto his elbows, but his arms were still not working.

What the hell is going on?

His arms felt like they were wrapped around his chest, bound in some sort of self-inflicted, interminable bear hug. He looked down. What was he wearing? Was that a straitjacket?

Impossible.

"Diane?" he called, his voice a hoarse whisper. He tried to swallow but couldn't; his mouth was as dry as parchment. He tried again: "Diane, can you get me a glass of water, please?"

He looked around the bedroom for his wife. Wait, he'd already established this was not his bedroom. He tried to sit up, but the straitjacket—*yes, it really was a straitjacket*—prevented him from doing so. Cursing, he rolled onto his stomach. He turned his head to the side, pressed his cheek against the floor to get the leverage he needed to arch his ass into the air, and then worked himself into a kneeling position. From there, getting to his feet was manageable, even without the use of his arms. The head rush hit as soon as he was vertical, but it subsided relatively quickly.

The vertigo did not.

He stumbled to the door and peered through the tiny square glass window into the dimly lit corridor beyond. "Hey," he shouted. "Is anybody out there?"

No response came. The only noise was the monotonous, unsympathetic buzz of the fluorescent light fixture overhead.

"Help!" he shouted. "Somebody help me. Somebody help me! Is anybody out there? Can anybody hear me?"

A woman shrieked.

"Diane? Diane, is that you? Do they have you too?" he called, but the woman's shriek turned into a maniacal laugh, and then he knew that creature was not his wife. More people began to stir somewhere along the corridor. A cacophony of sounds erupted. Shouting and sobbing, banging and screaming . . .

Will suddenly and desperately wished that he could cover his ears.

The hall lights flipped on, and the ruckus instantly subsided. He heard the sound of a door slamming closed, or maybe open, and then footsteps. He craned his neck to try to see down the corridor. The footsteps were coming closer . . . multiple pairs now . . . hard soles clicking on linoleum tile. Someone stopped in front of his door, but instead of a face in his window, a flashlight beam greeted him.

"Back away from the door," a voice said. When he didn't move the voice repeated the command, baritone and angry. "I said back away from the door, patient."

Patient?

Confused and blinded by the light, he took a step backward. The vertigo kicked in, and he tripped on his heel. Without his arms to break his fall, he hit the ground hard. The landing hurt, but not nearly as badly as it should have, and that's when he realized that the floor was padded.

Oh God, I'm in a padded cell.

He looked up at the square window, and the flashlight beam found his face again. He squinted but refused to look away.

"What is your name?" the voice asked.

"What?" he said, confused.

"We don't have time for games. Tell me your name."

"Will Barnes. I—I'm an officer in the United States Air Force," he stammered.

The beam stayed fixed on his face for another few antagonizing seconds and then clicked off.

"He's awake," he heard another voice say. "Call the Colonel."

He waited for hours, and still they did not remove the straitjacket. They did not answer his questions. They left him alone, in his padded cell, until dawn's rays illuminated the hallway outside his room. Sometime after sunrise, they moved him to another room, this one without padded walls but nearly as Spartan. They served him a breakfast of scrambled eggs, bacon, and a glass of milk, fed to him by a nurse named Shirley as if he were an infant. When he asked for a cup of coffee, her eyebrows arched with surprise.

"Coffee?" she repeated.

"Yes, coffee," he said, wondering why she considered this a strange request. "You do have coffee here, I assume."

"Coffee is not permitted for patients," she said in a thick Queens accent without an ounce of empathy.

"What kind of hospital is this?" he asked, screwing up his face at her.

"Rockland State Hospital, in Orangeburg," she said.

"Rockland? I'm at the funny farm? I don't understand."

She shot him a look that said it all: *Normal fellas don't wear straitjackets and get locked up in padded cells. You're at the funny farm, mister, and you're here for a reason.*

He let her feed him the rest of his breakfast without making any further attempts at conversation. As he ate, the brain fog that had been plaguing him began to clear and his wits came back to him. The first priority, he decided, was to piece together the missing time between the last thing he remembered and waking up in the cell. He had no idea how much time he was missing, but to wind up in a place like this, with no recollection of how or why he'd come to be here, did not bode well. Had the stress of his job finally made him crack? He certainly didn't remember falling to pieces. He didn't remember having a psychotic breakdown, but maybe that's how "going crazy" worked.

The door to the room opened, and in stepped two men in uniform and a powerfully built young orderly. Will popped to his feet and snapped to attention, save for his arms, of course, which were still bound in the straitjacket. Every minute he wore it, the sensation that his arms were being pulled out of his shoulder sockets seemed to intensify. He had to get out of this damn thing before he really did go nuts.

Will locked eyes with the taller of the officers. "Colonel Alexander," he said with relief. "Thank God you're here, sir. There must be some sort of mistake. You've got to get me out of here."

Alexander was the Commanding Officer of the 556th Strategic Missile Squadron at Plattsburgh Air Force Base in upstate New York. Will respected him, and they'd always gotten along. But the Colonel glared at him with an expression Will had never seen from the man before: equal parts anger, disgust, and disbelief all rolled into one.

"Sit down, Captain," the Colonel said, his voice hard and cold.

Will sat. His gaze ticked to the other man in uniform. Like Alexander, this officer wore silver eagles on his epaulets, except instead of Air Force blue, he was dressed in the Army's Class-A, green service uniform. His name tag read "Schumaker," and Will had never seen the man before in his life. Schumaker's expression was hard but harbored none of the apparent disdain Will was feeling from Alexander.

"This is Colonel Schumaker," Alexander began. "He works at ARPA, and he and I both have questions we need to ask you."

Will had heard of ARPA, the Defense Department's classified Advanced Research Project Agency, but he knew few details about the nascent skunkworks. ARPA's charter was to ensure that the US military did not fall behind Russia in technological superiority. The Atlas F missile program was the crown jewel of the DOD's strategic weapons portfolio, and the hundreds of millions of dollars being spent on its development and deployment meant ARPA was involved.

"Sir, before we get started, can you just answer me one question, please?" Will said, turning his head to look at his CO.

Alexander nodded, but it was a *conditional* nod.

"Why am I here, sir?"

The Colonel's eyebrows knitted together. "You don't know?"

"No, sir."

Alexander looked at Schumaker, and the two seemed to share some silent understanding.

"What's the last thing you remember?" Alexander asked.

"Standing watch. I'm MCCC at Silo 9," he said, then to Schumaker added, "That's the Dannemora site."

"The MCCC is the Missile Combat Crew Commander, the ranking officer at the silo, and he holds one of two launch keys," Alexander clarified for the ARPA man.

"Understood," Schumaker said with a nod. "You're on a twenty-four-hour alert, correct?"

"That's right. Twenty-four hours on, seventy-two off. SM-65 utilizes a five-man crew. We turn over at 0600."

"Tell me, Captain, what do you remember about your last alert?"

"The first eighteen hours were uneventful. No drills or scheduled practice exercises. The guys did preventative maintenance on the diesel-gen sets and the refrigeration system. Lieutenant Bates was my Deputy MCCC. It was around 2300 hours, and we were working on paperwork in the launch control room when the lights started flickering. Then we get a liquid oxygen–tank low-pressure alarm—not a good thing, obviously. And then a second later we get a call from Staff Sergeant Lewis in the silo. Lewis was the MFT on duty." Will paused, turned to Schumaker, and said, "Missile Facilities Technician. He's in charge of the missile elevator, propellant tanks, refrigeration, hydraulics, ventilation system, and the like. Anyway, the LOX tank is on level eight, very bottom of the silo. I tell Bates to stay in the launch control room, and I'll go check out the problem with Lewis. I take the utility tunnel over to the silo. The general alarm is wailing, and there's white steam everywhere from the LOX boiling off. I work my way down the stairs and ladders as fast as I can to level eight, where I find Lewis in a panic trying to figure out what's broken. After a little investigation, we determine that a relief valve is stuck open on the LOX tank. I order Lewis to shut the valve, which immediately stops the bleed-off. Once that's done, I direct him to repressurize the LOX tank from the O2-topping tank, clearing the alarm. Problem solved, Lewis spent the rest of the alert replacing the faulty relief valve. By shift turnover, the system was restored and good as new. The details are all recorded in the logs."

Colonel Alexander stared at him with eyes as cold and dead as a corpse's. "*That's* what you remember?"

Will nodded. "Yes, sir."

"I find it strange that you failed to mention the *anomaly* you and Sergeant Lewis discovered in the silo. What can you tell me about that?"

"*Anomaly?* You mean the faulty relief valve?"

Alexander looked at Schumaker. The Army Colonel frowned. "Do you recall anything after the events in the silo?"

Events in the silo? It was just a stuck-open relief valve, guys. We fixed it.

He couldn't understand why they were making such a big deal over this. He tried to rub his chin but couldn't because of the straitjacket. "I briefed the oncoming MCCC about the repair, we conducted the 0600 turnover, and I left."

"And after you left the facility, what did you do next?"

"I went home. The house was still dark. My wife, Diane, was asleep in bed. Sometimes she's up when I get home; sometimes she's not. I kissed her on the forehead, and then I . . . I made breakfast for us. Eggs and toast, I think."

"And after that?" the Colonel asked, leaning in.

"After that I . . . uh, I really can't . . . um, it gets foggy after that," Will said. He squirmed in his seat, wriggling his arms under the sleeves. "Can somebody get me out of this damn thing?" he growled.

Alexander and Schumaker shared another glance. Then Alexander said, "Captain Barnes, I'd like to share a different account of what happened that night, based on sworn testimony from eyewitnesses and video footage recovered from the LCC closed-circuit security camera system."

Will's stomach went sour. It wasn't what Alexander had said; it was the *way* he'd said it—with the hard, dispassionate certainty of a judge delivering a sentence to a criminal. Will had no idea what sort of bad news was coming, but he knew the next words out of the Colonel's mouth would change his life forever.

He listened, without interruption, as Colonel Alexander launched into a very different telling of the night's events. In Alexander's version, Will and Sergeant Lewis went rogue and orchestrated a scheme to defeat the layers of redundant safeguards—both procedural and engineered—to take control of the launch complex and fire the Atlas ICBM.

In Alexander's tale, Will murdered his fellow crew members.

In Alexander's tale, Will tried to start World War III.

When the Colonel finished, Will's heart was pounding like a bass drum. Despite being seated, a wave of vertigo washed over him, and he almost fell out of his chair. None of this made any sense. He had no memory of doing any of those things. He would never shoot a crew member. He would never try to launch a missile without the order from Command Ops. If it were true, then why not show him the video? Why not show him proof? Because Alexander was telling lies—bold and terrible lies. That was the only logical explanation for any of this. Alexander was framing him as the fall guy for some readiness incident that must have occurred at Silo 9. Maybe an accident had damaged the silo or the missile. That's why Schumaker was here; Alexander had brought in an outsider to validate his cover-up and make it official.

"Is any of what I said ringing a bell for you, Captain?" Alexander asked, a smug look on his face.

I have to keep my composure, Will told himself. *If I can keep my composure and just get out of this damn place, then I can hire a lawyer and deal with whatever bullshit charges they've decided to trump up against me.*

"No, sir, I'm afraid it isn't. I don't recall any of the events you described, and to be frank, sir, I would never do any of the things that you said. I don't know what's going on here, but there must be a mistake. A terrible mistake. Somehow, I'm being confused with someone else."

Alexander sighed. "Barnes, you were my number-one junior officer. I'd already prepped the paperwork recommending you to screen early for O-4. If I hadn't seen the video footage of you with my own two eyes, I would have never believed it possible."

I need my own witness. I need an alibi, Will realized, his mind racing a hundred miles an hour now.

"Talk to my wife. I'm sure she can clear this up," Will said. "She can vouch for my behavior and my whereabouts—" The grimace on Alexander's face stopped him. His stomach knotted. "What's that look for? Did something happen to my wife? Did something happen to Diane?"

"Your wife is dead," Alexander said, holding eye contact. "When the MPs came to your house to arrest you, they found Diane murdered in your bed. You strangled her, Will. Strangled her in her sleep."

A bomb went off in Will's brain, scrambling his thoughts and igniting a fire-jet of raw emotion in his chest. *Dead? Diane is dead . . . murdered by my hand. Impossible.* His vision blurred, and the sobs came in lurching torrents. "No, no, this can't be happening. Please tell me this isn't happening. Please tell me this is some sort of twisted joke."

Alexander shook his head. "I wish I could, son. I really do, but something in you snapped that night. This is the first moment of lucidity you've had in three weeks."

"Three weeks?" he said with a cough. "I've been in here for three weeks?"

The Colonel nodded. "I'm afraid so, and we've been waiting desperately for you to snap out of this fugue you've been in since you were arrested."

Whatever sick, twisted game they were playing, it needed to stop and stop right goddamn now. He wanted his life back. He wanted it back right now.

"Captain," Schumaker said, his expression calm and mollifying, "I know this is difficult, but I need to ask you some technical questions, all right? How did you know how to defeat the launch enable–system safeguards? How did you disable the primary signal from Command Ops and the backup signal from A-OPS?"

Will ignored the questions. He didn't give a shit about this asshole from ARPA.

"Captain . . . Captain, over here," Schumaker said, waving a hand. "You and Sergeant Lewis changed the missile-flight trajectory by tinkering with the rate gyroscopes. Who taught you how to do that? What was the new target you selected? Look at me, Captain Barnes—what target did you select for the missile?"

Will was on his feet now, pacing like a caged lion. His face felt hot, and a buzzing sound was drowning out Schumaker's voice. Then another voice—a voice both strange and familiar—said:

You don't have to talk to them. You don't have to tell them anything. They're insignificant. They're fools . . .

In his peripheral vision, Will registered that both Alexander and Schumaker were on their feet now, backing away from the table. No, backing away from *him*. The orderly had stepped in front of the two officers and was holding a wooden baton at the ready.

"What's he saying?" one of them asked.

"It's all gibberish. This is what he's been doing since the day we brought him in," someone else said.

"All right, we're done here."

No, please don't go. Please don't leave me here! Will begged, but something was wrong. The words weren't coming out. It was as if they were trapped in the vacuum of his mind.

The door to the room opened, and he watched his one and only chance at freedom walk out of the room. Colonel Alexander paused at the threshold, just long enough to give him one final pitying backward glance.

Will screamed, but he couldn't tell if it was a real scream or something he only imagined.

They can't hear you. I'm in control now, the voice said.

No, don't lock me in again, Will begged, suddenly remembering who and what he was dealing with. *Please don't send me back to that place.*

Then you have to promise to behave, or back to purgatory you go.

I promise I won't interfere. I'll just watch. I can do better this time. I promise, Will said.

Oh, I know you can. Stick with me, Willie boy, and I'll get us both out of here. Time's a wasting, and we've got a job to do . . .

DAY ONE

Did Noah wait to start building the ark until after it started raining?

No, no, he did not.

—*Willie Barnes*

CHAPTER 1

The Present
1658 Local Time
The Tora Bora Mountains
Afghanistan

The bullet clipped his left ear.

Staff Sergeant Michael Pitcher dropped, spun around, and pressed his back firmly into the rock he'd been sheltering behind.

"Your ear's bleeding," said Corporal Jeremy Wayne, a.k.a. Bug, flashing Pitcher a toothy, tobacco-stained grin from behind his own rock two yards away.

Pitcher reached up and felt the shredded cartilage. His fingers came away wet and bloody. "No shit, Sherlock. Does everybody from Tennessee have your powers of deductive observation, or are you just special?"

A barrage of 7.62 x 39 mm bullets pounded the other side of Pitcher's rock as the Taliban terrorists they had been hunting strafed his position with a prolonged burst.

"I'm special," Bug said. "My mamma dropped me on my head, so she makes a point of telling me that every chance she gets."

The ear was beginning to burn. Pitcher could feel blood running down the side of his neck now. He turned his head, angling it enough that Wayne could get a look. "How bad?"

Bug gave a little shrug. "I always thought that ear stuck out farther than the other one. If you ask me, it's an improvement. At least now you got a book-matched set."

"You're a real dick, you know that, Wayne?" Pitcher laughed, despite himself, despite the ear, and despite the shitty situation.

Bug acknowledged the compliment by barking, "Hooah, Staff Sergeant."

Rock chips and dust rained down as another volley of rounds pounded Pitcher's rock shield. "You know what I think? I think it's time we blow this sonuvabitch up," he shouted over the staccato cracks of the enemy's AK-47. He pulled a grenade from his kit.

"I thought they wanted us to take this dude alive."

"We tried it their way. Didn't work."

Bug spit a brown glob of tobacco juice onto the dirt beside him. He brought his M4 up and shifted into a squat. "Ready."

Pitcher nodded and with his left hand counted down: *Three, two, one.*

Bug popped up and went to work with his M4, sending a storm of bullets in the enemy's direction. A beat later, Pitcher was up. He pulled the pin, sighted his target, and threw the grenade. It was a picture-perfect toss—a twenty-yard lob landing on the backside of an outcropping of boulders where Zabiullah Momar Haliqani had taken position.

"Helluva throw," Bug called as both men dropped back behind their rocks.

As if in reply, the grenade exploded, the detonation echoing through the mountain pass all around them. They waited for return fire, but none came. All was still and quiet, but as a rule Pitcher didn't trust quiet. Now came the shitty part—checking to see if the grenade had worked. He looked over at Bug.

"You ready to do this?"

"Pincer?" Bug asked, gesturing two converging arcs with his hands. Pitcher nodded. "I go high; you go low."

"Check."

Pitcher turned to face the two soldiers on his other side and fixed his gaze on Corporal Connard, who was clutching an M249 SAW. "Ready?"

"Fuckin'-A I am," Connard said, all spit and vinegar.

"Anything goes wrong, anything at all, I want you to hunt those Taliban assholes down and cut 'em to pieces. Understood?"

"Roger that, Sarge," Connard said; then he and Specialist Garland to his left both moved into cover positions. Pitcher looked back at Bug and chopped a hand forward. The two elite soldiers—from the Army's Tenth Mountain Division out of Fort Drum, New York—crept out from behind their respective rocks and began the treacherous advance on the outcropping of boulders where their quarry was hiding. Zabiullah Momar Haliqani had blown up five Americans, and it was their job to either capture or kill the terrorist bastard before he disappeared into the mountain catacombs the Taliban currently occupied.

Pitcher and Bug left the safety of the rocks behind and moved slowly but deliberately in a tactical crouch over the uneven terrain. Behind the cluster of boulders now fifteen yards away, Haliqani and two of his lieutenants were waiting. Odds were good that at least one or two of the Taliban terrorists were still alive—alive and waiting with AK-47s or their own grenades for the stupid Americans walking into a suicide trap.

Pitcher glanced to his right at Bug, who was maybe a yard ahead of him.

Bug caught the look and nodded once in understanding.

The two soldiers began to arc away from each other, Pitcher climbing up the mountain and Bug looping down. They would come at the enemy from opposite directions, above and below, creating a cross fire.

21

Connard would use his SAW to keep the Taliban pinned down during the advance, which so far—*knock on wood*—had gone smoothly. *Too smoothly,* Pitcher thought. No shots fired. No slips, no falls, no tumbling rocks giving away their positions. He kept his eyes and feet moving and working hard: scanning the target, checking the ground, placing a foot, scanning the target, checking the ground, placing a foot.

He was a tactical fucking mountain man today.

Climb to glory and hooah and all that shit!

As he reached the zenith of his approach, only three yards from the snowman-shaped boulder he'd selected to shelter behind for the final engagement, adrenaline coursed through his veins like liquid lightning. His entire body felt turbo-charged. His senses were crisp; his muscles were—

Connard's SAW roared to life behind him, sending a maelstrom of 5.56 x 45 mm NATO rounds into the rocks below. Pitcher's legs churned, and he closed the distance to the snowman boulder in a snap. He dug in behind the rock, squatting, his back to the enemy and pressed against cold, hard stone. He heard the crack of the enemy's AK-47 lighting up below him, but the strafe wasn't aimed at his position. Then he heard a burst from an M4 below and knew whom they were shooting at.

Bug.

Another strafe, this time from the SAW.

Pitcher capitalized on the cover fire. Bringing his weapon up, he popped his head around the side of his boulder for a look down the mountain. Two figures. One lying supine and motionless. The other crouching, aiming an AK-47 down the mountain. Pitcher sighted in, exhaled, and let a round fly. The bullet caught the Taliban fighter dead center mass, and the man pitched forward.

Pitcher watched Bug pop his head out from behind a rock twenty yards below. They locked eyes and shared the same wordless thought: *Where's the third dude?* Pitcher scanned east; he knew exactly what had gone down here. He'd seen it before. Haliqani had commanded his underlings to stay behind and martyr themselves while he made a run for it.

Coward.

He gestured for Bug to check the two downed Taliban fighters while he stalked east after Haliqani. From the expression on the other man's face, he could tell Bug didn't like that idea, but Pitcher was the boss. He got to his feet and began advancing east, sighting over his M4 and scanning every rock big enough a man could shelter behind. Haliqani couldn't have gone far—and Pitcher had the upper hand. He had backup, superior firepower, and . . .

He took a knee and dipped his gloved finger in a red-black, wet splotch on a rock.

And he wasn't injured.

He tracked Haliqani, following the blood trail over the rocky terrain for at least a quarter mile until he spied a low crack in the side of the mountain.

"Oh fuck," Pitcher grumbled. "You've gotta be kidding me."

Weapon up, Pitcher advanced on the crevice. From the outside, the almond-shaped tunnel entrance reminded him of a cat's eye, winking back at him. A deep, throaty Afghani voice taunted him in his mind: *You want me, Michael Pitcher? Then come and get me. The mountain is my domain, ally to my people for thousands of years. Follow me, if you dare, to your death.*

Pitcher took a knee beside the mouth of the cave so he could peer inside; there was no telling how deep it went. Was this cave an entrance to the fabled Tora Bora tunnel complex—the same infamous cave network that Osama bin Laden had once utilized in the early days of the War on Terror—or was it simply a crevice of opportunity? In either case, Pitcher knew he was walking into a trap. All Haliqani had to do was hide in the darkness ten yards inside the mouth of the cave, and he could pick off Pitcher with ease.

He rubbed his chin, and then it occurred to him that all he had to do to counter that strategy was toss a grenade into the crevice and blow the bastard up. And without hesitation or further self-debate, that's exactly what he did. The mountain barked a plume of dust, and smoke bellowed from the low crack. Twenty yards away, he saw Corporal Wayne running toward him, anxiety and concern ripe on the other man's face. So this time he waited, reclining against the mountain beside the crevice until Bug arrived.

"You're not going to actually go in there?" Bug said, breathing heavily.

"Confirm capture/kill," Pitcher said, setting his M4 down and fishing out his SureFire EB2 tactical LED flashlight. "Those were our orders." He took a knee, and Bug stepped up behind him, sighting into the cave with his M4 over Pitcher's shoulder.

"Ready."

Pitcher clicked on the power button, and a six hundred–lumen beam of white light cut the tunnel's darkness like a laser. He swept the light through the space, tracing a rectangle in the air.

"Clear."

Pitcher clicked off the light.

"How deep you figure she is?" Bug asked.

"Dunno . . . but deep," Pitcher answered. He couldn't put his finger on it, but something about this crevice didn't feel right.

"Sure you want to go in there?"

"Yeah," Pitcher said, taking off his Kevlar helmet. His neck muscles instantly rejoiced at the respite from the weight.

"That's one helluva tight fit," Bug said. "Why don't you let me go? My ass is skinnier than yours."

It was true. At five foot seven inches and 143 pounds, Wayne was the smallest man in the company. Yet despite his compact frame, the Lord had seemingly blessed him with the strength of a man twice his size. Wayne had once carried an injured soldier halfway down a mountain while wearing fifty pounds of gear. The scene had reminded Pitcher of a Discovery special called *Ants of the Amazon*, where he'd learned that soldier ants can lift twenty times their body weight. It was this infamous incident and his insectlike physique that had won Bug his nickname.

Pitcher drew his .45-caliber 1911 handgun and said, "You're in charge while I'm gone, Corporal."

"If you're not back in fifteen minutes, I'm coming in after you," Bug said, packing his lower lip with Wintergreen snuff. "Right after I finish this dip, of course."

"If I'm not back in fifteen minutes, it means the Taliban captured my ass and you need to call in an airstrike on this mountain."

"Your wife is never going to forgive me for letting you do this," Bug said in protest. "You know that, right?"

"What Josie doesn't know can't hurt her," Pitcher said with a crooked grin and disappeared into the mouth of the cave.

CHAPTER 2

Josie Pitcher stared at the fish, and the fish stared back at her.

Hmm. So that's what tilapia looks like.

She'd always assumed it was some slimy, ugly fish, like a cross between a catfish and an eel, but no, it actually looked like a bigger version of the sunfish perch she used to catch as a kid when her dad took her fishing at the pond down the road.

"I think he likes you," her eccentric host said with what could be described only as a goofy old-man smile. "They don't usually sit still like that."

"What made you pick tilapia for your hydroponic system?" Josie asked, squatting and staring into his "aquarium," which was essentially a giant blue plastic bathtub with a Plexiglas window on the side.

"Aquaponics," he said.

"Excuse me?"

"You said 'hydroponics,' but this here is an aquaponic system," he said. "Hydroponics doesn't cut it."

"I don't understand," she said, getting to her feet.

"Hydroponics is like half the equation; it's unbalanced. Aquaculture is the other half of the equation, but fish farming is also unbalanced. In each system, the nutrients get depleted, and the waste products build up to toxic levels. But put the two systems together, and *wham*, you get a balanced system. I grow duckweed here in these hydroponic beds. Duckweed is high in protein and minerals, grows fast, and does a good job of keeping algae from taking over. The duckweed serves as the feed-stock for the tilapia. I picked tilapia because they's a strong fish. They grow fast; spawn year-round; and can tolerate warm, dirty water and crowding. And most importantly . . . they taste damn good."

He paused, and she watched him smiling, probably thinking about his next fish fry.

"Anyway, the uh, fish waste gets broken down by bacteria into nitrates, which get pumped back into the hydroponic beds where the nutrients get sucked up by the duckweed. The effluent from the duck-weed gets pumped back into the fish tank and recycled." He clapped his hands together and then flicked his palms out flat in a gesture that reminded her of a magician's flourish. "And shazam, you have a perfectly balanced system, just like nature intended. You see, nature figured this shit out a long time ago. We're just too stupid and lazy to pay attention. People are just starting to wake up. But it's too late. Don't matter now."

"What do you mean it's too late?"

"I mean the world is already fucked," he said, spittle flying from his lips. "Excuse my language. Don't get me going, Josie. Can I call you Josie?"

She smiled at this. Getting him going was exactly why she was here. She wanted to film it all with her body cam: his crackpot conspiracy theories, his survival methodologies, the rationale behind the design of his bunker, his contingency plans, and his survival strategies for the coming dystopian future. Willie Barnes was widely considered the Sun Tzu of doomsday-prepping culture—a modern mage of survival wisdom. It had taken her six months to get this interview. Six months of plotting and suffering. Willie was a shrewd old tomcat, and she knew from the get-go that none of the typical strategies—flatteries, five minutes of fame, or even cash money—would work on old Willie. Others had tried and failed. Her husband had been the one who came up with the winning idea one night over a KFC dinner.

"If you want to interview this guy, you first have to win his respect," Michael said. *"You have to show him that you're worthy of the privilege of interviewing him. That you're legitimate and your motives are pure. Remember who you're dealing with here. He doesn't trust the government. He doesn't trust the media. He doesn't trust corporate America. As far as this guy is concerned, everybody is either out to get him or exploit him. You think he's going to let you, a freelance investigative journalist, just walk into his bat cave, shoot video, and then sell it to HBO? Hell no."*

"Then what should I do?" she asked, knowing she wasn't going to like the answer.

"You need to audition," Michael said with a sadistic smile. *"Tenth Mountain style."*

The next three months had been hell. Whenever Michael wasn't on base training for his upcoming deployment, they were in the woods—building shelters, starting fires, making snares, and shooting every projectile-based weapon invented by man. He taught her Morse code, compass navigation, and way-finding techniques. He made her eat wild mushrooms and leeks, forage edible lichens from tree trunks, and dig up bugs and worms for breakfast. He made her bathe naked in freezing-cold streams, defecate in hand-dug latrines, and pull out her own ticks. He even taught her how to make a solar still from two plastic water bottles and forced her to drink her own purified urine. Yes, she now was a member of the small, illustrious club of people who'd drunk their own pee. And she did all this, on film, for Willie.

When Project PJ (Prepperizing Josie) was complete, she had over a hundred hours of video, which she had professionally distilled and edited into a twelve-minute highlight reel that included a three-second clip of her pale, naked self squealing in a frigid stream that Michael had *insisted* she include. Then, instead of asking for an interview, she had sent it to Willie—on VHS with a masking-tape label that read, "Audition," along with her mobile phone number.

A week went by, and nothing happened.

Two weeks, and still no call. By then, Michael had deployed to Afghanistan, and she was feeling very much alone and foolish. By week three, the defeatism set in, and she regretted even sending the tape. By week four, she was cursing Willie Barnes's name for being the impetus to drink her own pee, and by week six, she'd written off the entire idea as a colossal waste of time. At week ten, when the call finally came, it caught her completely off guard:

"This is Willie Barnes," the voice said, gruff and hesitant. "You sent me a tape?"

"Uh, yeah, that was me. Josie Pitcher," she stammered, not sure why she was so nervous.

"It's a good tape," he said. "Helluva rabbit snare you made."

"Thanks."

"And I liked the solar still you made with two water bottles. Even the diehards don't usually . . . well, you know."

"Yeah."

"Why did you send this to me?" he asked, his tone sincere and without sarcasm.

"Because I want to meet you."

"You coulda just asked."

"You woulda said no."

"That's true," he said, chuckling, and then coughed. "I woulda."

"So can we meet?"

"You're a journalist."

"Yes, I am."

"I do my homework, Miss Pitcher."

"I know you do. So do I. That's why I want to meet you."

"I don't like reporters."

"I know, but I'm not a reporter. I'm a journalist."

"I didn't realize there was a difference."

"There's a difference. I assume you've seen some of my previous work?"

"Yeah. I liked the piece you did for Vice *on the anti-vax movement in America."*

"Thanks."

"Is that the sort of thing you want to do with me?"

"Yeah, another in-depth, intimate piece for Vice*," she said, hesitating to add that it was a segment on doomsday preppers.*

"Okay," he mumbled.

"Okay what?" she said, not trusting her ears.

"Okay, I'll do it . . . but I have conditions."

"Um, okay, great. I mean, of course, whatever you want."

"Condition number one: I get to sign off on the footage you use. Period. No exceptions."

"Done."

"Condition two: you come alone."

"Okay," she said, having expected this but still uncomfortable with the idea.

"Condition three: you can't know the location of my facility. I'll pick you up at the lat-lon coordinates of my choosing, and you have to ride with a blindfold there and back. If you won't agree to this, the deal is off."

She hesitated a beat before finally agreeing. This little tidbit of information she'd have to keep from Michael. Thankfully, he was on the other side of the world . . .

"Well?" Willie said, his voice ripe with impatience.

"Well what?" she said, snapping back to the present.

"Can I call you Josie?"

"Of course," she said, wondering why he was asking that now. He'd been calling her Josie for ten minutes.

"You see, Josie, it's already under way as we speak."

"What's already under way?"

"I thought you said you did your homework," he growled.

She gave him a tight-lipped smile but didn't take the bait and get defensive.

"The Sixth Extinction," he said, spittle landing on the tangled whiskers of his fully gray beard. "The coral reefs around the world are dying. They're literally being cooked to death. A third of the Great Barrier Reef is dead, and in the next five years, that number will be two-thirds. When the coral reefs are gone, it will kick off an ecological collapse in the world's oceans. The same thing is happening on land. We've wiped out fifty percent of the world's species in the last forty years. Can you believe that? In forty years we've managed to annihilate ecosystems and creatures that have existed for hundreds of thousands of years. People think of nature as a stone fortress, but in reality, it's a crystal palace—beautiful but fragile. Get too many cracks, and it shatters; then everything comes crashing down. When the Sixth Extinction has run its course, over seventy-five percent of all species on Earth will have gone extinct."

She'd not expected this from Willie. Sure, all preppers had their particular hot button, but they always came from a well-established pool of dystopian triggers: nuclear war, the next great pandemic, climate change causing global floods, droughts, famine, etcetera. She'd not heard any mention of the Sixth Extinction on the forums and discussion threads she'd researched.

"So that's why you've built this place, because of the Sixth Extinction?"

"Were you not listening? Don't tell me you're like the rest of them?"

"The rest of who?"

"People. Everyone! Everyone who thinks that human beings somehow live in a magical vacuum where our species can flourish while all other species are dying. The Sixth Extinction is coming for us too. We're not safe. We are not immune!"

She angled her torso to make sure the body cam had him in frame. "So that's why you purchased this facility and devoted your life to renovating it . . . in preparation for the Sixth Extinction?"

"Did Noah wait to start building the ark until after it started raining? No, no, he did not."

"Point taken," she said, noticing he was starting to become agitated.

"They've got plans," he mumbled, pacing back and forth in front of her. "Secret plans. They've tried it before, and they're going to try it again."

She had prepared herself for this sort of thing—for the "crazy talk." She could see that Willie was getting wound up. There was a difference between getting him going and getting him frazzled and angry. She had to tread carefully, because one misstep—one offensive or misconstrued comment—could flip that switch she knew existed in Willie's head. And when that happened, they were done. The interview would be over, and he would kick her out. No do-overs. No follow-ups.

"Who has plans?" she asked cautiously.

"The government!" he snapped, scratching manically at his beard.

"The US government?"

"Of course the US government, you fool. I knew this was a mistake. I've already said too much. This was a bad idea . . . a very, very bad idea."

"Hey, Willie, how about you tell me more about your aquaponic system?" she said, gently interrupting the diatribe. "Or maybe you could talk to me about your solar rig and energy-storage system."

He looked at her, then at the fish. He stopped scratching his beard and began to nod slowly. "Did you know that tilapia is a Nile River fish?"

"No, I didn't."

"There's some folks believe the Egyptians practiced aquaponics thousands of years ago."

"I didn't know that," she said, nodding politely and suppressing a victorious grin.

"Aztecs and the ancient Chinese practiced aquaponics as well."
After an awkward beat, he cleared his throat. "Enough about fish. You
didn't come here to talk about fish. C'mon, let's go grab a cup of hot
tea."

Phew, dodged a bullet there.

He led her from the aquaponic shed back to the modest Adirondack-
style cabin they'd visited in when she first arrived. As she followed him,
she realized that his baggy jeans and flannel shirt belied what must
have been a strong, wiry frame beneath. She eyed a pile of freshly cut
firewood. An uncut log stood on a massive stump, a long-handled axe
leaning next to it at the ready. For a man Willie's age to maintain such
a place, by himself no less, must have been a backbreaking endeavor.
From his weathered face, she guessed he had to be midseventies, but
Willie had at least another decade, maybe two, of fight left in him.

He held the cabin door for her, like a gentleman, and she stepped
inside. She didn't realize how much heat the late October chill had
sapped from her body until she was in the fire-warmed cabin. She
looked around the main room, with its windows on three sides and
timber walls. Not exactly the fortress of solitude she'd expected. Where
was the armory? Where was the secure communications room with
shortwave radio equipment and satellite feeds streaming from all over
the world? Where was the ration room with three years' worth of food-
stuffs stacked floor to ceiling and a water-reclamation unit? Where was
the secret, impenetrable underground lair? She was beginning to think
that maybe the notorious Willie Barnes was nothing more than a myth.

He handed her a mug of steaming-hot tea.

"Thank you," she said, blowing ripples on the surface and then taking a tentative sip. "What is this? I don't recognize the flavor."

"Half and half," he said.

"What's half and half? I'm not familiar with that."

He gave her that goofy old-man-talking-to-a-pretty-young-girl grin
again. "Well, I brew one cup of black tea, one cup of green tea; then

I mix 'em half and half. I can't stand the taste of green tea, but it's full of antioxidants. This way I get the taste of black tea and the benefit of green tea. Can't get too many antioxidants."

"I hear blueberries have lots of antioxidants," she said awkwardly.

They drank their tea in silence after that, and suddenly she wondered if she'd been wrong about old Willie. Maybe she was the one who'd made the mistake. As she contemplated this, she noticed him staring at her legs. She'd probably erred by selecting jeans a little too far on the slim-fitting side.

"Yeaaaah, that tape of yours was the only reason I invited you out here," he said and then started to chuckle. "Seeing you hooting and hollerin', jumping around butt-ass neked in that stream, got me howling."

A creepy tingle chased up her spine. Michael would be furious with her if he knew where she was right now, and he'd be right to be. What had she been thinking coming here alone? And why in God's name had she agreed to ride blindfolded in his Jeep to get here? She had no fucking idea where she was, no mobile phone coverage, and she was unarmed. What if Willie's "safeguards" had all been a ploy to get her out here alone so he could kidnap and rape her? An argument broke out in her head:

He can't rape you, Joz. He's over seventy years.

Of course he can rape me. That's what Viagra is for, you moron.

You're the one who sent him the tape. He didn't lure you here; you solicited him.

Doesn't matter. He's a crazy old man. I'm a twenty-eight-year-old girl with a body he's seen naked.

A rock-hard body that you can kick his ass with.

Not if I'm unconscious because he put a roofie in my tea.

"Something wrong with your tea?" he said.

She realized she was scowling and staring into the mug. "No, it's fine."

"You don't have to lie on my account. It won't hurt my feelings. Half and half's not for everyone. I'm sorry; I probably shoulda asked." He ran his tongue across his tea-stained teeth and then set his mug down. "Well, you didn't come all this way to drink tea in my living room. C'mon," he said, turning away and waving for her to follow. "Let me show you the rest of the facility. If you thought the aquaponics was neat, then you ain't seen nothing yet."

Her heart leaped, and she didn't know whether she should be ecstatic or turn and run for her life. She watched him walk to a coat closet and open the door to reveal . . . a coat closet. He parted the coats with both hands and ducked under the hanging bar. Before disappearing, he stopped and looked back over his shoulder. "Well, you coming or not?"

"Coming where?" she said, still clutching her mug with both hands.

"Into the bunker, of course. That's why you're here, isn't it?" he said, pushing the false back wall of the closet open to reveal a space behind it. Through the gap, she could just make out red stenciled letters on a steel door:

**RESTRICTED ACCESS—556TH STRATEGIC MISSILE SQUADRON
SM-65 LAUNCH COMPLEX #9**

CHAPTER 3

Afghanistan

Pitcher was only fifteen feet in, and the cave's ceiling had sloped so low that he was already crawling on his hands and knees. The acrid odor from the grenade he'd detonated was strong here, and he realized that the geometry of the cave he'd imagined was entirely different from the reality of the cave he was now exploring. *This isn't a cave,* Pitcher decided. *It's a fucking crack.*

At thirty feet in, the ceiling funneled even lower, and he was forced to belly-crawl. The deeper he went, the more he felt consumed. Like Jonah and the whale, he had been swallowed by the mountain. The tunnel was so narrow now that his body blocked all light from the entrance behind. His Kimber in one hand, his SureFire flashlight in the other, he wormed his way forward. Right forearm, left leg, frog kick. Left forearm, right leg, frog kick. His ear was burning now. He resisted the urge to touch the raw, mangled cartilage and kept on squirming.

He heard something in front of him—a scratching sound. He clicked his flashlight on—the low-light setting, just five lumens. Bright enough to illuminate a two-foot arc in front of him and put his nerves at ease, but not so bright as to wash out his night eyes or betray his position. He exhaled with relief. Nothing lurking in the dark in front of him: no scorpion, no coiled viper, no Taliban terrorist pointing the barrel of a gun in his face.

He clicked the light off and pushed on, forearm over forearm.

Two feet, four feet, eight . . . He squirmed into the black.

Into the silence.

He could no longer hear the wind. He'd grown so accustomed to the incessant howling in the mountain passes that his subconscious was now craving a windy echo to fill the void. But the only sound was his uniform fabric dragging over rock—like sandpaper on concrete. A nerve-grating sound. He tried to ignore it and pressed on.

Two feet, four feet, eight . . .

He lifted his head to look forward and conked the crown of his skull against the rocky ceiling. *Fuck, that hurt.* He clicked on the light. Nothing but rock and a shrinking, dark void ahead. He clicked the light off. If this tunnel got any smaller, he ran the very real risk of getting stuck. He shooed the thought away. *I'm not that stupid.* But then another, even more disturbing thought occurred to him. Even if he didn't get actually physically stuck, he might be effectively stuck already. Belly-crawling was a forward-biased means of locomotion. Could he reverse-crawl all the way back to the opening? No, probably not. Eventually, the crevice would have to open up wide enough that he could turn around.

But what if it didn't?

Shit.

A wave of claustrophobia-induced panic washed over him.

Don't think about it. Just keep going.

He pressed on. Right forearm, left leg, frog kick. Left forearm, right leg, frog kick. His right elbow came down on a jagged rock, sending a stinger of pain along his arm and into his fingers. Cursing to himself, he pressed on. Under his belly, he began to sense the angle of the floor changing. Ten feet deeper in, the term *floor* became a misnomer, because the ground was no longer horizontal. It sloped twenty degrees down to his left. Every time he inched forward, gravity tugged his body into the V-shaped angle of the crevice, amplifying the sensation of being squeezed.

That same claustrophobic panic welled up in him again, but stronger this time.

What if this really was just a crack . . . a crack that had opened in the mountain because of all the bombings? Hadn't they dropped a MOAB not far from here a few months back? What if the mountain was unstable? What if this crack pinched closed? His body would be pulverized. Pressed into a juicy pulp, like a bug squished underfoot.

Like a bug. He let out a chuckle. *I definitely should have sent Bug in here instead.*

A bead of sweat ran down his temple. The temperature had dropped noticeably since he'd entered the crevice, but he was sweating from exertion now. He hadn't belly-crawled like this since boot camp. He paused for a second to catch his breath and noticed an amber glow, barely perceptible, etching a faint almond shape into the black ten yards ahead. He squeezed his eyes shut, counted to three, and opened them again. Yes, that was definitely light ahead. A fresh and much-needed surge of adrenaline dumped into his bloodstream.

He resisted the urge to move.

Lying perfectly still, he closed his eyes and listened. At first, nothing. Then the thud of his own pulse, regular and baritone, filled his ears. He tried to filter it out, but the absolute quiet of the tunnel made the task difficult. He waited patiently, listening for any other sound besides the beating of his heart.

A minute passed.

Nothing.

He opened his eyes. Then, just as he started to crawl, he heard something. A whisper, barely audible. He cocked his head for a different listening angle. Was his mind playing tricks on him? Maybe he was hearing the echo of his own movement reflecting off the cave walls?

Then, as he began to crawl a second time, he heard it again. Whispers.

A chill chased up his spine. Definitely voices. He held his breath and strained to make out what was being said.

Sounds like Pashto . . . Shit.

Gripping his Kimber and gritting his teeth, Pitcher inched slowly and quietly toward the light. He stopped a foot from where the cramped tunnel widened into an antechamber and listened. A man was talking. Yes, definitely Pashto. Pitcher wasn't fluent, but he'd picked up a good bit of the language during his multiple deployments over the years. He strained to hear, translating what he made out:

"Tora Bora, Afghanistan . . . Yes . . . Zabiullah Momar Haliqani . . . Yes . . . November 2 . . ."

Pitcher screwed up his face. Such a strange one-sided conversation. It was almost as if Haliqani were talking on the phone, but that was impossible. No signal could penetrate this deep into the mountain. And the information he was providing was so, well, generic.

Pitcher had to know what was going on; he had to take a look.

Carefully, he set his pistol on the tunnel floor and retrieved a telescoping inspection mirror from his left breast pocket. Using his teeth to grip the quarter-size mirror, he expanded the metal shaft from a compact four inches to fourteen. Exhaling slowly, he extended his arm until the mirror overhung the mouth of the chamber by a few inches. An errant glint off the mirror could get him killed, but the odds of being counterdetected were lower than with the alternative—sticking his head inside the cave and waving hello to Haliqani.

A three-second initial sweep was all he needed. *One, two, three.*

He pulled the mirror back.

Okay, what the fuck was that?

What he thought he'd just seen made absolutely no sense. He shook his head and extended the mirror over the edge again, this time letting it linger, but the reflection confirmed what he'd seen before: Zabiullah

Momar Haliqani, standing alone in the middle of a perfectly spherical cavern, talking to himself, his back to the tunnel entrance. The tunnel entrance bisected the strange chamber approximately eight feet above the floor, effectively giving Pitcher a balcony-like vantage point. He watched, transfixed, as Haliqani carried on a one-sided conversation with nobody. Then the Taliban commander lifted his arms as if to embrace an invisible face in front of him and said something to the effect of, "I am your faithful servant, Allah. Do with me as you will." A beat later, Haliqani began to convulse. His knees buckled, and he collapsed to the floor.

Curiosity got the better of Pitcher. He compressed the inspection mirror, stuffed it back into his breast pocket, and squirmed to the edge of the tunnel. Propping himself on his elbows, he looked down into the antechamber. Many things about what he saw did not compute. Caves were dark. Caves had asymmetrical walls, jagged outcroppings, and bold rock formations. This void had none of those things. This cavern was a perfect sphere. He estimated the internal diameter to be approximately twenty feet.

He stared down at Haliqani, who lay on his back on the cavern floor, convulsing and foaming at the mouth.

What the hell? Is he having a seizure?

Pitcher scanned the space again, confirming one more time that Haliqani was completely alone. He contemplated shooting the terrorist, from right here, right now. It sure would uncomplicate matters. Take a picture, mission accomplished, no questions asked. But Haliqani's body had fallen still, and something about shooting an unconscious man just didn't sit well with Pitcher. It crossed the line between battle and execution. Not that Haliqani didn't deserve to be executed, but still, it just felt dirty. Cowardly.

He took a second to scan the geometry of the space again. Whether he shot Haliqani or not, how the hell was he going to get the man out of the cave? There were no other entrances or exits. He'd have to put the terrorist in restraints. Could a man crawl back out through this tortuous tunnel in PlastiCuffs? *Maybe.* Pitcher looked down. The vertical drop to the center of the floor was close to eight feet, but the wall was curved and smooth. He extended a hand and touched the inner surface of the cavern.

His fingers slid over the stone like it was polished marble. No, not polished marble . . . more like handblown glass. He picked up a rock fragment, one of many that lay at the mouth of the tunnel, and rolled the grape-size chunk of rock between his thumb and index finger. Three sides of the pyramidal stone were scalloped and chipped like flint, but the fourth side looked to have once been molten. He imagined a sphere of lava, glowing and bubbling, then quenched and cracked to cold, black onyx. What natural phenomenon could form a cave such as this? He dropped the stone and watched it slide down the wall into the basin, where it came to rest against the top of Haliqani's shoulder.

The chill of unexpected epiphany washed over him.

The cave was lit.

Why could he see? His flashlight was off. Haliqani hadn't been holding a light. So where was the light coming from? His gaze flicked to the ceiling, looking for a crack or vertical shaft to the surface. Nothing. He looked back into the spherical void, searching for the source of the light, but it was as if the chamber was backlit from behind the glazed stone walls.

Fear tickled his subconscious. A primitive fear. A childlike fear. Danger. *Run, Michael. There's a monster lurking under the bed. Run now!*

Hello, a placid female voice whispered.

Pitcher jerked and picked up his Kimber. He trained the muzzle down into the spherical cavern, but the only person there was Haliqani, still lying unconscious on his back.

Hello? the voice said again.

The hair stood on the back of his neck. "Show yourself," he stammered, still searching for his tormentor.

I'm here.

"Where?" he said.

Down here. Come inside. I need help . . . please.

"I must be losing my mind," he mumbled.

Please help me, she said again, this time with pain and urgency in her voice.

Against his better judgment, Pitcher wiggled headfirst out of the tunnel and slid on his belly down the sloping wall into the void. The walls were so slick, he couldn't steer or stop himself, and he ended up careening into Haliqani. He quickly scrambled to his knees and checked the terrorist's vitals.

Breath: rapid and shallow, but not labored.

Pulse: quick and strong.

Pitcher settled back onto his haunches; Haliqani was alive.

Too bad, he thought.

Hello, the voice whispered again, closer this time. Pitcher whirled on his knees, looking for the woman his ears told him was standing right behind him, but there was no one there. Slowly, he got to his feet. A ripple of movement to his left caught his attention. He pivoted and fired, immediately regretting the decision. The geometry of the chamber amplified the roar of the gunshot, and from the sharp pain in his ears that followed, he wondered if he'd ruptured his eardrums. Whatever it was he'd seen was gone, faded into oblivion. Like a mirage. A beat later, a flattened .45-caliber round dropped from the void above and landed at his feet. He knelt, picked up the deformed slug, and studied it.

"That was no ricochet," he mumbled. "I must have hit something."

Please do not discharge your weapon again.

He dropped the slug and stumbled backward. The voice spoke to him with perfect clarity, despite the ringing in his ears. He scanned the air above him but saw nothing. He glanced down at Haliqani, but the terrorist still lay sprawled at his feet, eyes dancing the funky chicken behind closed lids. What the hell was going on? What was this place?

Do not be afraid, said the voice. *What is your name?*

He studied the domed ceiling for a loudspeaker, but the polished rock surface was perfectly bare. "My name is Staff Sergeant Michael Pitcher of the United States Army. Whoever or whatever you are, identify yourself," he shouted.

Staff Sergeant Michael Pitcher. Can you tell me the geographic coordinates of this location?

"Fuck your questions. What did you do to this man?" he demanded, looking down at Haliqani.

Zabiullah Momar Haliqani is unharmed.

"Then why is he unconscious?"

No reply came.

"Show yourself," he barked. "What do you want?"

I want to know you, Michael.

Gooseflesh stood up on his arms. He whipped around, but there was nothing behind him. No, wait . . . there was *something*.

A presence in the light.

A surge of warm, soothing energy washed over him. The breath of God. He inhaled deeply and closed his eyes. He heard his pistol clatter onto the glassy stone floor, but the sound seemed to come from somewhere far away. Defending himself was no longer a concern. There was no need for a weapon, in the company of such peace . . .

This was not the first time he'd felt a supernatural presence. Though he was a preacher's son from a devoutly religious Texas family, as a boy of nine, he'd done plenty of what nine-year-old boys do best—engaging in harmless mischief. He and his two best friends, Ricky and Jake, had tagged along with Ricky's older brother on a day trip out to the family "ranch," undeveloped acreage an hour's drive outside of Austin. While the older boys practiced plinking cans with their .22s, Michael and his two best friends had gone wandering. They'd followed a dried-up creek bed as it snaked between cedar elms and live oaks. The creek bottom offered an infinite supply of round, smooth pebbles to launch with their Daisy slingshots at dumb birds and basking lizards.

It had been a dreadfully hot, cloudless summer day, so they'd stuck to the shade of the creek bed. Emerging at the other end of a curving switchback, they discovered they were not the only ones with this idea when they came face-to-face with a three-hundred-pound wild boar. Wild boars were the most dangerous creatures in Texas—much deadlier than the fabled diamondback rattlesnake. A rattler might get one of them, but a mature, territorial male boar could chase them each down in turn and eviscerate them. There was no antivenom treatment for flesh carved to ribbons by five-inch, razor-sharp tusks.

Immediately upon seeing the black, bristled monster, Michael had known something wasn't right. It was panting and drooling, despite standing still. One of the hog's eyes was white as milk, and the ear on that side hung in two limp, ragged halves. He was an old-timer, this razorback—a gladiator that had survived countless battles with other upstart males. The boar grunted, scratched at the earth with a hoof like a bull, and charged. That was when the archangel Michael, the great protector, came to his aid. A royal-blue aura encircled his vision, and a voice spoke in his head—a voice as calm, certain, and wise as his father's voice during sermons.

"Aim, Michael, and I will guide your hand. I will be the stone," the archangel said.

The pouch of his slingshot was already loaded with a gray pebble he'd been saving—round, smooth, and heavy—pinched between his thumb and index-finger knuckle. He drew the pouch back to his chin, stretching the yellow rubber tubing taut, and let the stone fly. It tore through the air like a miniature comet with a tail of royal-blue light as it sailed toward the demon beast. The stone struck the boar in its one good eye, and the creature jerked its head, bellowed, and halted its charge. Shaking its head, it spun in circles and thrashed its tusks wildly while sniffing the air.

"Run," the archangel said.

He ran, his friends in tow, but he could not help stealing a fleeting backward glance. In that instant, he swore he saw a winged man, robed in purple, plunge a flaming sword into the eye of the beast . . . the same eye he'd struck with his stone. As an adult, he'd prayed for the archangel's protection on multiple occasions, but the blue aura never returned. And with every enemy fighter he killed, he felt farther and farther from God. Was he now so lucky as to finally stand in the archangel's grace once again?

He opened his eyes.

A million glowing points of light converged inches from his nose, an orb of living luminescence, coalescing in midair. Was this the archangel Michael returning, or was this something else? So beautiful and wondrous—this could only be the one true God.

"Oh Lord, I am not worthy to stand in your presence. I have done things. Terrible, sinful things," he heard himself confess.

Show me your thoughts. Tell me your secrets.

And he did.

Surrender your burdens to me.

And he did this too.

Do you accept this baptism of light to wash your sins away and quench the fire in your soul?

"Yes, Lord. I do."

Then you must surrender to me.

His thoughts suddenly went to his wife, Josie. He remembered their love and their union and for an instant what he was about to do felt like a betrayal . . . but to surrender to God was no betrayal. He would bring God's peace and love to her as well.

I am love. I am communion. Say you surrender to me.

He closed his eyes and—letting all his worries, regrets, and inhibitions fade away—he breathed, "I surrender." Then, as he felt his body begin to convulse and his legs turn to jelly, somewhere very far away, he could just make out Corporal Wayne shouting his name.

CHAPTER 4

Silo 9
Dannemora, New York

Feeling very much like Lucy Pevensie, Josie stepped through the coat closet and into another world.

"Watch your step," Willie said, holding open the steel door leading into the missile-silo complex below. "It's a short landing. I wouldn't want you to fall down the stairs."

She squeezed past him and stopped, her gaze fixed on a descending concrete stairwell lit only by dim, intermittently spaced red lights.

Looks like a stairway to hell . . . Wonderful.

Just as she finished the thought, he flipped a switch on the wall behind her, and the lights brightened and changed to white.

"I usually keep it low light to conserve power, but since this is my first official tour in over a decade, I suppose I can splurge and turn on the lights for you."

"So generous," she said, flashing him a wry smile as he slipped past her back into the lead.

She followed him down the long stairwell, which she estimated descended twelve feet. Each concrete step had a six-inch metal toe tread on the leading edge, etched with a diamond crosshatch for traction. Years of foot traffic had worn the cross-hatching smooth and slightly scalloped in the middle. The staircase stopped at another short land-ing, and then a second, similar set of stairs took them down what she guessed was another six feet or so into a tunnel. White paint—stained with rust in some places and flaking in most—coated the otherwise unadorned concrete walls and ceiling. At the bottom landing, the tun-nel doglegged: a ninety-degree turn right, then a ninety-degree turn back left. A heavy, windowless steel door blocked the path forward. The door looked ancient, except for the very modern, very expensive-looking biometric scanner on the wall. Willie scanned his thumb, the lock clicked, and he opened the door. "Ladies first," he said, gesturing to the little room on the other side.

She hesitated. "What is that?" she asked, looking into a short, omi-nous passage blocked by another steel door a mere eight feet away.

"This is the intruder-entrapment enclosure."

"Wait, what?" she said, still not stepping across the threshold. "That sounds evil."

Willie flashed her a smile so big she could see his gums. "This is old-school defensive military engineering at its best. You cannot access the launch complex without passing through this chamber. There are limit switches on this door and the door over there. You can't open both doors at the same time. You cannot open *this* door unless *that* door is closed and vice versa. See that window in the other door?"

The metal door eight feet away had a one-foot square glass window at eye level framed in the steel.

"Yes," she said.

"That's laminate glass. Bulletproof and blastproof," he said. "See that rectangular box built into the wall beside the doorframe?"

"Yeah, I see it."

"There's a camera and a murder hole in there."

She didn't like the sound of that. "What's a murder hole?"

"A space you can fire a weapon through. It allows you to shoot into the enclosure from the safety of the other side. Anyone wanting to gain

47

access to the LCC and the silo has to come through this chamber. Back when this complex was operational, the control room would be notified when someone entered. With the camera system, they could visually identify the person or persons who were trying to gain access. Only authorized personnel were granted access through the second door. Intruders, on the other hand, would be trapped in this chamber. By modern security standards, this might seem primitive, but sometimes there's no substitute for brute-force simplicity."

She looked at him and cocked an eyebrow.

"Well, go on," he said with a chuckle. "I told you, we can't open the other door until we close this one."

With a slightly queasy stomach, she stepped into the intruder-entrapment enclosure. Willie stepped in behind her, and the first door slammed shut on spring-loaded hinges. She eyed the murder hole warily as they crossed the small chamber to the other door. Willie once again pressed his thumb to the biometric scanner, but this time he also had to enter a four-digit code. The lock clicked, and he opened the second door for her. She stepped past him into another tunnel. Eight feet away, the tunnel turned ninety degrees right. She walked to the bend and peered around and saw a massive steel door—much thicker than the first two she'd just passed—hanging fully open on correspondingly massive hinges.

"What's *that* door?" she asked, staring at it.

"That is a blast door. There's two of them, one on each side of the vestibule ahead."

"Why do you leave it open?"

"I'm seventy-six years old," he said. "I can move it, but it takes a toll."

She followed him into the "vestibule," which was simply another lockout-style chamber, this one enclosed by matching blast doors. "I think I'm sensing a theme here."

"Yeah, redundancy was the guiding design principle for this facility. These double blast doors were designed to protect the LCC from a direct hit from a nuclear strike topside."

"What's the LCC?"

"The LCC stands for *launch control center*. That's where we're headed. The complex is divided into two separate but interconnected structures: the LCC, which served as the operations and communications center, and the silo proper, where the missile was stored."

She paused a moment to look at the black-and-white framed pictures hanging on the walls in the vestibule. The first was a picture of five young men, two seated and three standing, in a room with control panels in the background. Another was a photograph of a missile raised completely out of the silo and ready for launch. A third was an illustrated schematic of the facility, drawn in the three-dimensional cutaway perspective. She stopped at this one and studied it, trying to take in as much information as possible before he moved her along.

"C'mon, we don't have all day," he said.

Technically, we do have all day, she thought. *It's not like you have a queue of visitors waiting outside.*

She lingered a beat longer, making sure the lens of her body cam—which was pinned to her jacket just above her left breast—recorded the illustration before she turned to follow after him. He led her through the second blast door and down yet another set of steps. At the next landing, they could either enter an open door to a room beyond or turn 180 degrees and take a switchback staircase down farther. Willie went straight, taking her into a large circular room with a thick round column in the middle, almost like a vertical axle bisecting a donut lying flat.

"Welcome to the LCC," he said, grinning like a schoolboy. "This is level one. It's still a work in progress, as you can see . . . I'm doing all the work myself, so it's slow going."

Josie scanned the space, walking in a slow arc around the room as he talked, taking in everything she saw. The erstwhile launch control center looked like it was in the final stages of being converted into modern living quarters. The ceiling was freshly painted white and the walls a light gray. The floor was covered with a nondescript but handsome commercial-grade carpet in most areas, linoleum tile in others. The room was windowless, of course, but well lit thanks to a generous number of LED work lights installed overhead, oriented like wheel spokes all the way around the room.

"There used to be divider walls, but I took those out. I prefer it nice and open like this. No dark corners. Good sight lines."

No place for an intruder to hide and no way for old Willie to get snuck up on, she mused.

"Over there was where the communication room used to be," he continued. "Over there was the battery room and an office area. Where we're standing right now used to be one of two launch control rooms. There's another one on level two. Over there was where our bunk room used to be . . ."

She stopped and turned to look at him. "*Our* bunk room? Wait a second—did you used to work here?"

Willie's expression went sour, like he'd just taken a bite out of a lemon. "I can neither confirm nor deny that."

"Wow," she said, looking at him in a new light. Come to think of it, one of the young men in the black-and-white photographs she'd seen had looked familiar—a much younger, beardless, and, dare she admit, handsome version of the Willie Barnes standing in front of her. "So you actually bought the missile silo where you used to work? You must know this place like nobody's business."

"Not many Atlas Missileers left these days" was all he said. Then, gesturing to a small kitchen area, he added, "This over here was the kitchen."

"And apparently still is," she said with a smile. "How many people lived down here at any given time?"

"The Atlas F complex, which is what this facility is, had a complement of five."

"How long was each watch—is that the correct term, *watch*?"

"*Watch* is more of a Navy term; Missileers use the term *alert*. We were on a twenty-four-hour alert, which meant we were on for twenty-four hours, then off for seventy-two. A fresh crew turned over each morning at 0600."

"How long could you stay down here, you know, if you had to?"

"This silo was designed to take a hit from an incoming nuclear missile and survive. We'd have up to two months' provisions at any given time, but, eh, that's nothing compared to my current inventory. I have seven years' worth of provisions, plus medicine, plus fully redundant water-reclamation and air-recirculation systems."

She eyed what looked like his security and communications suite, which contained an amalgam of ancient-looking and cutting-edge technology. "That your comms area?"

He nodded.

A bank of flat-screen monitors streamed live video feeds from dozens of locations both topside and inside the silo. "How many camera feeds do you have?"

"One hundred and two," he said.

"One hundred and two? Are you kidding me?"

"No. I monitor a two-mile radius of forest around the silo, plus the cabin and every room and passage in the silo."

"Wow, okay then . . . Looks like you've also got some old-school radio equipment in addition to your satellite news and internet feeds."

"Cellular service will be the first thing to go when it happens. Satellites will be next, then the hard lines. Once the internet is taken down and the world gets knocked back into the Stone Age, shortwave radio will be the only viable communication option."

This was not new information to her. She knew most doomsday preppers were proficient radio talkers and tuners and one of the last enclaves able to communicate using Morse code. "I've been wondering, what is that big column in the middle of the room?" she asked, pointing at the giant concrete pillar.

"Believe it or not, the entire LCC is built on a metal crib and supported by suspension struts equipped with giant shock absorbers. If you look closely, there's a one-foot gap between the center pillar and floor. There's also a one-foot gap between the outside perimeter of the room and the concrete foundation along the entire circumference."

"You mean this level is actually floating?"

He nodded. "Both level one and level two are floating on a metal crib. The entire missile-launch and support structure is also built as a floating crib, suspended inside the concrete silo."

"Why?"

"Do you know what kind of a shock wave a direct nuclear hit would create outside? The engineers had to design this place to withstand that shock wave and maintain operational readiness. By mounting all the critical equipment on the crib decking, the interconnecting piping and wiring all moves as a unit. If everything was hard mounted to the silo, it would deform, crack, or rip apart."

"Wow. That's impressive," she said, staring down the gap between the center column and the level-one deck into the room below. "How deep are we right now, by the way?"

"Level one is thirty feet down. Level two, which you're looking down into, is at the minus-forty-foot elevation."

"How do you access the missile silo itself?" she asked, turning around to face him.

"Through a utility tunnel, which is located on level two below us. Do you want to see it now?"

"Yes, very much so."

He led her out of the LCC back the way they'd come and into the switchback stairwell. They took two half flights down and were once again at a decision point. Go right to enter level two of the LCC, or go left to take the tunnel to the silo. In keeping with the design theme, the tunnel was secured by two more blast doors, one on the LCC side and one on the silo side. The LCC-side blast door was open, and Willie strolled through it into the tunnel. Unlike the earlier tunnels, which were rectangular in shape with flat concrete walls, floor, and ceiling, this tunnel was round and had overlapping corrugated-steel plating lining the inside circumference. At the end of the tunnel, they came to a green blast door stenciled with the words MISSILE SILO ACCESS, except this blast door was shut.

"Here, help me open this," he said, grabbing the top end of a long vertical metal handle.

"I thought you said you left these open," she said, grabbing the same handle just below his hands.

"Not all of them." He grunted, pulling on the handle. "C'mon, Josie, put those young muscles to work."

She strained against the dead mass of solid metal, pulling with her back and arms, but letting her legs do most of the work. Once they got a little momentum, the door swung open the rest of the way without too much effort, creaking on its eight hinges. "Aw, c'mon, you've got to be kidding me," she said, looking at another closed blast door eight feet away. "How many more are there?"

Willie laughed. "This is the last one; I promise."

They repeated the exercise, working together to open the final green-painted blast door to reveal the inside of the silo. Unlike the LCC, the silo appeared to have undergone very little in the way of renovations—at least cosmetic renovations. The hulking metal structure was rusting and at least fifty years past its last paint job. She stepped out on the metal grating and paused at the railing to look down into the abyss. Somewhere below, she heard the gurgling of moving water, but she couldn't make out what it was coming from.

"Careful," he said behind her, a strange timbre in his voice. "It's a long way down."

"How deep is the shaft?"

"One hundred and eighty-five feet from the surface. One hundred and forty feet from here, give or take," he said, stepping up beside her.

The platform creaked under their combined weight, sending a miniature lightning bolt of nerves through her abdomen. She clutched the handrail and attempted to count the levels, but the structure disappeared into shadow well before the bottom. "How many levels are there?"

"Eight," he said. "Labeled in reverse order, with one at the top and eight at the bottom. We're on level two. There used to be a service elevator in that corner over there, but it was removed along with all the other equipment when the facility was decommissioned. They stripped her clean, salvaging everything they could. I jerry-rigged a winch-and-pulley system over the shaft, which is how I move materials up and down between levels."

"What do you use this for?" she asked.

A devious little smile spread across his face. "Food production and storage," he said, turning to walk back to a lighting panel on the wall behind them. He flipped on a series of breakers, and the sound echoed in the silo: click, click, click, click, click, click. Light flooded the silo, sequentially illuminating level by level, top to bottom. On the level below her, level three, she saw the same hydroponic systems she'd seen in the outbuilding topside, fish tanks and duckweed beds, only on a much greater scale. In addition to duckweed, here she saw fruits and vegetables, including splashes of color that looked like peppers, tomatoes, and strawberries growing in the hydroponic beds.

"Whoa" was all she could manage to say, looking at the enormity of it all.

"That little rig topside is just for sampling and fish-stock quarantine. This is the *real* operation."

"What do you mean by quarantine?"

"Before I introduce any new stock, I need to make sure they are disease-free. I have a nursery program down here to replenish my stock, but I'm always tinkering with the gene pool. I need my fish to be as robust, nutritious, and disease resistant as possible."

She felt a chill creeping past the fabric of her jeans. "It's chilly in here."

"Yeah, and it gets colder the lower you go. Bit of a thermocline in here. It's cold enough at the bottom, I can raise salmon without need for any cooling system. Down at level seven I have natural refrigeration year-round at forty-three degrees. I can keep eggs and dairy down there if I want. Plus, it dramatically extends the shelf life of all food rations canned, jarred, and bagged. Wanna see?"

"You mean, go down there?"

"Well, sure," he said. "Don't tell me a young, healthy girl like yourself is afraid of a few stairs."

"A *few* stairs?" she said, eyeing him. "Looks like a couple hundred to me."

"Suit yourself," he said and sighed. "If you want to be lazy and miss out on the only chance you'll ever have to explore an Atlas F missile silo, that's fine with me." He turned back to the lighting panel and was about to flip off the lights when she stopped him.

"Fine," she groaned. "I'll do it." Her acquiescence seemed to please him because she saw a glint of pride in his eyes. He led her to a narrow spiral staircase that wound all the way down to the bottom of the silo. To climb 140 feet down and back on a spiral staircase seemed akin to torture. "We have to take that?"

"It's that or ladders," he said simply. "Your pick."

"Fine," she said, staring down the eerie ten-story-deep hole disappearing into the floor. "And don't you dare say, 'Ladies first.'"

CHAPTER 5

0937 Local Time
Office 231
Department of Technology Integration, Management, and Security
(TIMS)
The Pentagon
Arlington, Virginia

Everyone knows someone like Major Legend Tyree.

Someone whom God and fate and nature all smiled upon in utero. Someone whose deck seemingly got stacked with an unlimited supply of kings and aces. Someone whom people envy profoundly and want desperately to hate but fail to because the object of their resentment is so likable, charming, and noble that all their negative feelings morph into admiration. Legend had been his high school's valedictorian and homecoming king and a star athlete. He had been accepted to West Point and graduated top of his class. As a junior officer, he had excelled in combat, leadership, and strategy. But in the Pentagon, his physical prowess, male-model good looks, and quick, capable mind were the wrong tools of the trade. In the crush of bureaucracy, red tape, and military politics, he found himself stymied, eroded, and, for the first time in his life, performing at a level below his expectations. He needed a new opportunity to exploit.

He needed a win.

The desk phone rang.

He glanced at the incoming caller ID on the secure line but didn't recognize it. "Major Tyree," he said after picking up the receiver.

"Major, this is General Kane, the Deputy Commander at Bagram. We've never met," said the voice on the other end of the line.

"Yes, sir, how can I be of service?" he asked, his heart rate ticking up.

"I've been told you're the guy to call when there's a technology mystery nobody else can solve," Kane said. "General Troy said your office is the Pentagon's equivalent of the X-files division and that whenever something weird pops up on the radar, they send you and some lady from DARPA to check it out."

"Yes, sir, that's both classified and true."

"He also said they call you The Legend of Zelda at the Puzzle Palace, whatever the hell that means."

He hated the nickname. It really was an awkward fit, in his opinion. Yes, his first name was Legend. Yes, there was a video game called *The Legend of Zelda*. And yes, his job was investigating and acquiring new technology for the DOD—a job that required him to travel extensively to far-off kingdoms (Europe, the Middle East, and Asia), gather and collect treasure and weapons (innovative technology for the military's next-generation weapons systems), and meet with esoteric characters (inventors and IP lawyers) . . . but it really was a stretch. And yet it had stuck. Pretty much everyone at the Pentagon called him Zelda, and now people at DARPA, ONR, and DS&T had started using the moniker too. He'd liked it better when they called him by the department's acronym, TIMS. He even preferred when they called him "the dude from 231."

Zelda . . . Really?

Legend resisted the urge to sigh and simply said, "Yes, sir, General. I'm your guy. What can 231 do for you?"

"I'm not one for bullshitting, and I don't have time for big words and long sentences, Major, so I'll keep this short and sweet. One of our patrols found an unknown piece of tech in a cave in the Tora Bora mountains, and I have no friggin' idea what it is or what to do with it. So far, three people have interacted with this thing, two of my soldiers and one crow—excuse me; I mean Taliban *detainee*. Since that first interaction, none of them have been right in the head."

He did a double take in his mind. What in the world was Kane talking about? An unknown piece of tech in a cave? He hadn't heard anything about this . . .

After a breath, Kane continued, "So I packed everything and everyone in the belly of a C-17, and I'm sending it to Andrews. You'll need to put together a welcome party. I recommend hazmat, EOD, medical, and an interrogation team. And it wouldn't hurt to have your counterpart from DARPA there as well. Make sure you cover all your bases, Major."

"If I didn't know better, General, it almost sounds like you're saying this object your men found is not from the *neighborhood* . . . if you know what I mean."

"Major, I don't know what the hell this thing is. That's why I'm sending it to you. What I can tell you is it didn't come from Best Buy. So keep it secret. Keep it secure."

"Okay" was all Legend could muster, despite the fact that his mind was flooded with hundreds of questions.

"Do you have any contacts at USAMRIID?"

"A few."

"Good, you might have a couple of blue suits on-site just in case."

His heart skipped a beat. "Sir, are you implying that the object you're sending me is a biohazard?"

"I have no friggin' idea, Major. The only test I was able to conduct here is a radiation survey. It's not radioactive. Other than that, I don't know what the object is, where it came from, or what it does. If I was in your position, I'd take precautions."

"Sir, if I might propose an alternative solution for consideration. What if you retain the object there in a secure holding facility and let me come to you? Give me twelve hours to put together a team, and we'll be on the first flight out tonight to Bagram."

"Too late. The bird is already in the air," Kane said. "I'm not equipped to deal with something like this. And to be honest, I don't want to. You'll have my report within the hour and details on the transport schedule. If you have any questions, don't bother calling me. I've told you everything I know . . . Oh, and as of fifteen minutes ago, the event is code-word classified: BRIGHTWORK."

"Roger that."

"You ever play hot potato, Major?"

"No, sir."

"Well, you're playing now. Try not to get burned. Kane out."

The line went dead. Staring at the receiver in his hand, Legend mumbled, "What the fuck just happened?" He turned to his computer, looking for any preliminary files that might have been transmitted to the secure server, but there was nothing from Kane. He ran a query for BRIGHTWORK and skimmed the results, looking for something fresh, but he didn't see anything relevant so far.

I should have asked him when the plane was scheduled to land. Shit . . .

Then, as if Kane could hear his thoughts, a message came in addressed to him with a flight plan for a C-17 flying from Bagram to Andrews with aerial refueling en route. Looked like he had less than twelve hours to get his house in order. He picked a pen up off his desk, pulled a pad of paper from the drawer, and started on his list of team members for the welcome party. When the list was finished, he started making calls. Brigadier General Kane had counseled him to "Keep it secret. Keep it secure," which by default meant keep it small. These were people he could trust.

When there were only two calls left to make, he glanced down at the list. He'd already decided to save the most challenging call for last. Before making *that* call, he needed to talk to his sometimes sidekick but always ally at DARPA. He dialed the number from memory.

"Cyril Singleton," said the female voice on the line.

"Cyril, this is Major Tyree at the Pentagon. What's cooking? What's shaking?"

"Whenever you ask me that, Legend, it either means you need something from me or you're about to drag me on a wild goose chase across another continent," she said in a proper British accent that would make Mary Poppins proud. "So which is it today?"

"The former." He laughed. "I'd like to borrow Malcolm Madden for a special project."

As the lead scientist in DARPA's Systems of Neuromorphic Adaptive Plastic Scalable Electronics (SyNAPSE) program, Madden was helping develop the world's most advanced neuromorphic machine technology. His charge was to build a cognitive computer—a machine intelligence with the plasticity and flexibility of a mammalian brain and the speed and precision of a computer. The hardware he was developing mimicked the architecture and scalability of a biological brain—utilizing a synaptic-based structure with broad interconnectivity. On top of that, Malcolm Madden also happened to have the highest IQ of anyone working in the defense industrial complex. The man was, literally, the smartest person Legend had ever met.

"How long will you need him?" she asked. "The SyNAPSE team leans heavily on him. Things are busy, Legend. AI is the next battlefield frontier, and I'm getting a lot of pressure to transition lab projects into deployable prototypes."

"I know" was all he said, letting the pause afterward do the negotiating for him.

"How long?" she asked with a sigh.

"Hard to say. It could only be a day or two, or it could be a couple of weeks. Depends on what we find."

"What is the nature of the project?"

"Classified TS/SCI," he said.

"Okay," she said, perking up at this. Apparently there was nothing like a good top-secret/sensitive-compartmented-information mystery to break the monotony of everyday Beltway minutiae. "But only under one condition: you read me in. I like to be apprised of what Malcolm is working on. He has a tendency to lose himself in either the weeds or the clouds. I can usually help keep him on altitude."

"I wouldn't have it any other way," Legend said.

"When do you need him?"

"Today, actually. It's a short-fuse deal, and I need to get chess pieces into place as soon as possible."

"In that case, I need you to pick him up from the airport. I was going to do it myself, but now that you're seeking temporary custody of Mr. Madden, you can assume the responsibility of saving him from himself."

He chuckled. "Explain, please."

"Malcolm is returning from holiday in Brazil, but what constitutes holiday for Malcolm and holiday for the rest of us mortals have little in common. Last time he left the country, they caught him trying to smuggle parasitic wasp larvae from the Costa Rican jungle back into the US; they detained him, confiscated his samples, and slapped him with a thousand-dollar fine."

"All right," he said, a devious smile curling his lips. "This could be fun."

"Anything else DARPA can do for you, Major?"

"Actually," he said mildly, "I was hoping I could use Westfield D as the evaluation facility."

The line went silent.

Westfield D was the insider's name for Westfield Dynamics—DARPA's miniature equivalent of Area 51, a proving ground for DARPA's top-secret projects. However, unlike Area 51, Westfield D was neither a military base nor located in the desert. The facility was nestled in the Virginia countryside, a short hop by car from the Culpeper Regional Airport. Seventy-five percent of the testing complex was located underground; the aboveground buildings consisted of two warehouses and the electrical controls–manufacturing shop. Westfield Dynamics was a *real* company, purchased and expertly operated as a for-profit front company for DARPA.

"Are you still there?" he asked.

"I'm still here," she said. "You know I'll have to run this up the chain."

"I know, but I promise I'll make it worth your while."

"Oh really. You mean like the time you got us arrested in Berlin? Or how about the time you got us lost in Taiwan and we ended up at the wrong facility and almost got shot by security . . . that sort of worth your while?" she teased.

"No, not like that." He laughed. "More like I'm in tight with the Colonel at Camp Darby in Italy. How about on our next trip I make sure your flight home goes through Florence? How does five days on the Italian Riviera sound to you?"

"I do like Northern Italian cuisine. Consider me officially persuaded."

"Thanks, Cyril. I owe you one."

"Yes, you do," she said, and he could hear her smiling. "And don't think I'm going to let you off the hook on the Italy trip."

"Never in a million years."

He ended the call, took a deep breath, and then dialed the final number on his list.

Major Beth Fischer, USAMRIID's Director of Biosecurity, picked up her secure line on the second ring. "Hey, Zelda," she said, and he could literally *hear* the smirk on her face.

He rolled his eyes. *Et tu, Brute?*

"Hi, Beth. How are things at the slammer?" he asked, referring to USAMRIID's infamous BioSafety Level 4 Medical Containment Suite, designed to handle persons who had been exposed to or infected with the world's most deadly pathogens.

"We don't call it that anymore," she said, "and things here are fine. I haven't heard from you in a while." *Woman-speak for "You're a shit for not calling me."* "How are things at the Puzzle Palace? Discover any new gizmos lately?"

"Um, maybe. That's the reason for my call . . . I mean, one of the reasons for my call. I wanted to talk to you too, of course."

"Mmm-hmm" was all that came back.

He cringed at his fumble and went for broke. "Maybe we can grab lunch and I can fill you in?"

"Today?"

"Yeah."

She chortled at this. "Maybe if you had booked it with me three months ago. I'm looking at my calendar right now, and I don't see any white space I can squeeze you into for weeks."

Now she was just toying with him. He probably deserved it. Actually, no, he didn't deserve it. Romance in the twenty-first century was supposed to be egalitarian. She had just as much responsibility to call him as vice versa.

"I'm serious, Beth. I've got a shipment coming in, and I've been advised by the sender I need to have a biosafety team standing by when it arrives."

"What are you talking about, Legend?" she said, suddenly all business.

"I'm saying I need a couple of blue suits to meet me at the tarmac at Andrews Joint Base in fifteen hours to inspect and test this package."

"Okay, first of all, importing a biosafety hazard is not something you simply spring on a girl, especially when that girl happens to be the Army's head of biosecurity. Second, one does not simply requisition 'blue suits,' as you say. If there is a shipment inbound containing an infectious pathogen, I need to know all the details, and I needed that information yesterday to make all the necessary arrangements—containment, transport, testing, storage, etcetera."

"I'm just trying to cover all my bases here. Besides, I know you. Don't tell me you don't have emergency-crisis-management and field-response teams you can stand up at a moment's notice. If you want to send a team, you can send a team."

She sighed. "Biosafety is serious business, Legend. It's not a game. There are protocols I have to follow."

"I'm sorry," he said, all the humor gone from his voice now too. "You're right, but please understand, I'm in the same boat as you. This thing was literally dumped in my lap five minutes ago. It's already in the air, Beth, and they've made me responsible for it. My ass is on the line here; all I'm asking for is a little help."

"And by roping me into your pop-up circus, you're putting my ass on the line too."

An awkward silence hung on the line as he tried out multiple next sentences in his head and rejected each in turn.

She broke first. "Are you going to tell me what's in the shipment or not?"

"I don't know what it is."

"How can you not know what it is? You're responsible for it."

"Meet me for lunch and I'll tell you everything I know."

"Tell me now."

"It's TS/SCI. I'd rather talk face-to-face."

"Fantastic, we'll have to eat at a shitty restaurant where nobody else wants to go."

"Please."

"Fine."

"How about that one shitty place we used to like to go?"

"TGI Fridays?"

"No, the sushi place."

"Old Dominion isn't shitty, Legend."

"I know, but if I ask for a table in the back we can whisper."

"Fine. Let's meet late; I have a ton of work. How about 1300?"

"That works for me. See you then."

He hung up the phone and felt a little surge of excitement and anticipation. He wasn't sure why he hadn't called her since their last hookup. It wasn't because he hadn't wanted to see her; the reason was pedestrian, in all honesty. He had gotten busy, and too much time had gone by. Then calling had felt obligatory and awkward. Girls aren't turned on by obligatory and awkward, so he hadn't called.

What the hell am I doing? Now is not the time for worrying about relationship bullshit.

He pushed his chair back from his desk and walked over to the small closet in his office. He opened the door and pulled out one of three suits he kept. The gray one, he decided. For today's meetings, he would eschew his Army uniform. Working and traveling in civilian clothes went hand-in-hand with working for 231. Outside the Pentagon, 80 percent of the people he dealt with on a daily basis were either civilians or nonmilitary government employees. Or spies. One must never forget about the spies.

After a quick change, he headed out the door for Dulles to pick up Malcolm Madden.

The Legend of Zelda was on the move . . . Where this strange new adventure was about to take him, he had no idea, but there was a spark in his step now. A spark that wasn't there when he had walked into the Puzzle Palace this morning.

CHAPTER 6

Washington, Dulles International Airport

Malcolm Madden fidgeted in line.

He couldn't help himself. He was nervous.

Do you have any meats, fruits, vegetables, plants, seeds, soil, animals, or animal products to declare? That was what the customs form had said. He had checked the little box labeled "no," but this was a lie. He did have items to declare, specifically *Camponotus rufipes* infected with *Ophiocordyceps camponoti-rufipedis*. Collecting samples of the Brazilian carpenter ant and the parasitic fungus named after its host species had been the purpose of his two-week vacation to the Amazonian jungle. While most people selected their vacation destinations in search of exotic cuisine, inspiring art and architecture, and the opportunity to visit famous cultural-heritage sites, Malcolm Madden used his vacations to find and collect mind-controlling parasitic organisms.

Ophiocordyceps camponoti-rufipedis, popularly referred to as the zombie-ant fungus, was generating considerable buzz in entomological circles. What made this particular parasitic fungus so intriguing was that, despite not having a nervous system itself, it was somehow capable of manipulating an ant brain. Once infected with fungal spores, an unwitting ant quickly became a slave to *Ophiocordyceps camponoti-rufipedis*. The fungus infiltrated its host's brain and then actively modified the ant's behavior to facilitate its own reproductive life cycle. Instead of behaving like a normal ant, an infected ant would climb into the understory canopy, clamp its jaws to the bottom of a leaf, and wait to die. After death, a fungal stalk grew from the head of the ant cadaver, spewing fresh infectious spores toward the forest floor below to infect other foraging ants and start the cycle anew. The fungus's adaption was altogether remarkable, and for an ant, the stuff of nightmares.

Malcolm was not an entomologist; he was not even a biologist. He was a cognitive neuroscientist and artificial intelligence subject-matter expert at DARPA. The experiment he intended to perform on the ants—euthanize them at different stages of the infection to observe the precise mechanism of neural infiltration and control—was neither funded nor directed by DARPA. It was one of his many little pet projects. His boss at DARPA was smart. Not smart in the same ways that he was smart, but rather in the ways of human motivation and productivity. She understood that people like Malcolm were not assembly-line workers. That a mind like his didn't think and work linearly or sequentially all the time. *Creative abrasion, idea cross-pollination, chance capture, disruptive collaboration, epiphany mutation*—these were terms that Cyril Singleton liked to use, some of which he was certain she'd coined herself. She was the best boss he'd ever had, and he loved her for it.

He loved her for everything else that she was too.

"Next," the customs agent said at the window ahead.

There were two people in front of him in line. Malcolm felt his forehead break out in a sweat. He cursed silently. He was a terrible liar—always had been. Ever since he was little, he'd been a rule follower. Except for when the rules were unjust. Even the meek should not have to tolerate injustice. *Especially the meek,* he told himself. There were certain rules no person should be made to follow. As he matured and the complex intercourse and contradictions of governance, religion, and economics became self-evident to him, he constantly revised his moral code to suit. Morality is nuance. Very few people understood this.

The customs declaration and import procedures, however, were both just and prudent. They had been drafted with foresight and validated many times over by transgression. The Asian carp, Dutch elm disease, and zebra mussels were all examples of invasive species that had infiltrated the North American ecosystem with disastrous consequences. What he was doing, smuggling an aggressive alien species into the United States, posed an undeniable threat. Should the *Ophiocordyceps camponoti-rufipedis* fungus get out and invade the local biosphere, the impact could range from damaging to devastating. If local carpenter ants were susceptible to the zombie-ant fungus, then entire colonies could collapse. Worst-case scenario, it could cause an extinction-level event for the local species, which had not coexisted with the fungus for millennia like the Brazilian ants had. That was the crux of the problem with invasive organisms: indigenous species simply could not adapt fast enough.

Someone put a hand on his shoulder, giving him a start.

"Dr. Madden," a harsh male voice said.

He turned to face a uniformed security officer. "Yes." The word came out meek and pathetic. So pathetic it made him sick.

"Please come with me, sir," the guard said and pulled him out of the queue.

"But I didn't go through customs yet," he protested.

"I know" was all the guard said.

"I'm an American," he said.

"We know," the guard said, changing up the pronoun.

"Where are you taking me? I did nothing wrong."

The guard didn't answer, which sent Malcolm's anxiety to eleven. The compulsion to talk and tell this guard about the container of ants was overpowering. *I have to come clean. I have to tell them the truth before they search my bags. When you're caught, it is better to tell the truth.* His mother's wooden spoon against his bare buttocks had inculcated that lesson, and it was forever branded on his psyche.

"This way, sir," the guard said, gesturing to what looked like an interrogation room. The metal door to the room was shut, but Malcolm could see a man in a gray suit standing inside, his back to the door. The guard opened the door and stepped to the side.

Flushed and dripping with sweat now, Malcolm entered the small room as the door shut behind him.

"Tell me about the bugs," the man in the suit said, keeping his back to Malcolm.

"Wha-wha-what bugs?" he stuttered.

"The bugs in your bag. The nasty little buggers you're trying to smuggle into the country."

"I'm sorry; I'm sorry," he said. "I should've filled out the paperwork, but—" He stopped midsentence when the other man's shoulders began to bounce with laughter. Then the suit turned around. "Major Tyree?" Malcolm breathed with euphoric relief.

The Pentagon officer from 231 smiled broadly at him. "How was your trip, Dr. Madden?"

"It was fine. Great, actually," he said, glancing around for the next surprise guest. "What are you doing here?"

"Saving you from another embarrassing incident, it appears."

Malcolm was tongue-tied, not sure how to respond. Sometimes he had trouble with subtext, and right now he couldn't tell what Major Tyree's endgame was. So he stayed quiet and let the Major play his cards first.

"I was talking with Cyril Singleton this morning, and she mentioned you might have forgotten to file the paperwork for your specimens. I took the liberty of having my admin send over the approved forms with the necessary blanks for you to complete here before going through customs. If you wouldn't mind handing over your declaration form and completing these papers instead," Tyree said, trading him a stack of forms for the little card Malcolm had completed.

The knot in Malcolm's stomach unraveled, and he could finally breathe again.

"Oh, er, yes. Thank you, Major. I was in such a rush packing, I must have forgotten the forms altogether," he said. He took a seat at the empty table.

Later, seated in the front passenger's seat of Tyree's Ford Fusion as they cruised east on the 267, Malcolm decided to forgive Tyree for having a little fun at his expense. Tyree, to his surprise, turned out to be fascinated by the zombie-ant parasite and was happy to listen as Malcolm rambled on the topic.

"And it's not the only species of mind-altering parasite," Malcolm said. "Last spring I flew to Costa Rica and collected *Hymenoepimecis argyraphaga* specimens."

"Is that a fungus also?"

"No, it's a parasitic wasp who lays eggs on the abdomen of a particular orb-weaver spider. After hatching, the wasp larva injects a mind-controlling chemical into the spider, stimulating its host to build a specialized web cocoon for the larva."

"Does the wasp kill the spider?"

"The larva consumes the spider as its final meal before its metamorphosis into an adult wasp."

"Nasty."

"If you think that's bad, then you'll love *Dicrocoelium dendriticum*."

"Is that the snail parasite?"

"Very good, Major. I'm impressed. I didn't realize you were a fellow parasite aficionado."

"I think I read an article in *Scientific American*. Remind me what the snail parasite does again."

"*Dicrocoelium dendriticum* is a type of lancet liver fluke that has quite a complex life cycle, utilizing three host species. First, land snails consume fluke eggs in infected cow dung. The eggs hatch in the snails, where the larval flukes burrow into the snail's digestive system and mature to juvenile flukes. The snails combat the infection by encapsulating the flukes in cysts and sloughing them off as slime balls in the grass. Foraging ants eat the slime balls and become infected with the juvenile flukes. Once the flukes mature, they become ready to transition to their final host so they can lay eggs. But for this to happen, the ant has to be eaten by a grazing cow or sheep, and ruminants are not anteaters. So the flukes do something very clever: they burrow out of the ant's digestive system and make their way to the ant's subesophageal ganglion nerve cluster. During the day, the ant behaves like a normal ant, but after sundown when the temperature drops, the flukes take control of the ant and force it to climb to the top of a blade of grass, clamp down with its mandibles, and wait to be eaten by a grazing cow. If the ant escapes digestion that night, the fluke releases control and lets it go about being an ant again during the day. When nightfall comes anew, the fluke takes control again and zombifies the ant until morning."

"Zombie-ant fluke is even more disturbing than zombie-ant fungus," Tyree said. "The fact that the fluke releases control each day only to wrest it back again each night is so—I don't know—archetypal. Light and shadow, good versus evil . . . in a weird sort of way, it's almost like the biological equivalent of the Jedi mind trick."

Malcolm nodded. It was an interesting metaphysical analogy the Major was making. Maybe Tyree was more intelligent than Malcolm had given him credit for. The guy was certainly making a name for himself, albeit by standing on DARPA's shoulders. Every new and obscure piece of technology Tyree harvested from the field, he routed through Cyril for evaluation. To make matters worse, the Army man had started dragging Cyril along on his scouting trips. Water-cooler banter had already dubbed them the new Mulder and Scully, which chafed Malcolm more than it probably should have. Now, to hear that Cyril had outsourced the task of picking him up from the airport to Tyree . . .

"What is the real reason you intercepted me at the airport, Major?" Malcolm asked. "I don't think it was to save me from my administrative pitfalls."

Tyree answered the question by talking for several minutes but ultimately provided Malcolm with very little of substance.

"So, to paraphrase," Malcolm said, "there's an object being transported here from the Middle East. You have absolutely no idea what this object is or where it originally came from."

"Yeah, that's the long and short of it," the Major answered.

"Why involve me?" was Malcolm's next question, but he already knew the answer. He just wanted to hear the other man say it.

"Because you are DARPA's in-house guru on artificial intelligence, and according to General Kane, this object communicated with three people and somehow induced seizures afterward. If there is anyone on this planet who is smart enough to assess what the hell this thing is, that person is you, Dr. Madden."

Malcolm turned to look at Tyree and tried to decide if he should verbalize his true thoughts on the matter. Clearly the Army officer had no idea what he was dealing with. There was no artificial intelligence capable of communicating telepathically—which was essentially what the report Tyree had summarized from General Kane implied. However, a mechanism for *technological* telepathic communication of thoughts from one brain to another *did* exist . . . It simply went by a different moniker. If some breakthrough technology had occurred, then Malcolm certainly would have heard about it. For argument's sake, however, he decided to play the scenario out. Assuming a breakthrough had occurred, why would any research team, corporation, or foreign military deposit an object with this capability in some obscure cave in Afghanistan? It was entirely nonsensical. Which left only two alternatives: the entire story was a hoax fabricated by the soldiers to get shipped home, or the object was extraterrestrial in origin. Certainly Tyree must have considered both these possibilities. But if so, why hadn't he mentioned them?

Compartmentalization? Operational security? To avoid embarrassment? Malcolm sighed; this felt like a hoax.

But on the off chance it wasn't . . . bowing out was not an option.

"So I can count you in?" the Major pressed. "Will you lead the technical investigation?"

"Yeah, you can count me in," Malcolm said, thinking, *But only because I don't trust anyone else to do it.*

CHAPTER 7

Legend arrived before Major Fischer, which earned him the privilege of getting to see her the moment she stepped into the restaurant, before she spotted him. It was a strange thing to get turned on by, but it turned him on nonetheless. There wasn't a name for it as far as he knew. *I see you, but you don't see me?* Or even better yet, how about *a voyeur's hello?*

She was dressed in uniform today, and when she removed her cover, a spiral lock of her mousy brown hair tumbled to rest beside her left temple. She stood with impeccable posture—confident and athletic. It was the thing that attracted him to her most. Beth was a handsome woman, but no one would call her beautiful in the traditional, archetypal sense of femininity. She was tall, with broad shoulders and narrow hips. From behind, she might be mistaken for a man. She had big hands, big feet, and big breasts that she put incredible effort into de-emphasizing both in dress and body language. Sex with Beth was not lovemaking; it was a rugby match. Their first time together had been awkward. Crazy, stupid awkward to the point that halfway through they'd both busted up laughing. After that, they agreed just to go carnal, and it became a rumble, tumble, wake-the-neighbors fornication cage match. A wry, naughty grin crept across his face at the thought of their last night together.

He raised a hand, and she turned in his direction.

A gorgeous, genuine smile lit up her face, but she wrangled it back under control an instant later. *Games and games.* She walked briskly to the table and took a seat opposite him.

"Hey, Zelda," she said, entirely too impressed with herself.

"Please don't call me that," he said.

"But it's just so deliciously irresistible. I can't help myself."

"Try."

"Oh fine. You're no fun at all." She sighed, putting her napkin in her lap. "Did you order for us?"

"No."

"Why not? You know what I like."

"Yeah, but maybe you were in the mood for something different today. I didn't want to be presumptuous."

"Hello, Earth to Legend," she teased, waving her hand in front of his face. "It's me, or have you already forgotten how I roll?"

He tried to think of a witty zinger to fire back but came up blank. So he said, "You look good, Beth."

"Really? You're going to go there? I look good? Could you make this lunch any more awkward?"

He resisted the urge to sigh in exasperation. "Sorry. What I meant to say is you look exhausted. You'd need a bottle of concealer to hide those bags under your eyes. Hello, Beth, I'm sleep. Have you met me before?"

Her glare turned into a smile. "Better."

He flagged down the waiter, ordered quickly, then turned his attention back to her.

"Let's talk shop. What can you tell me about this cargo you've got coming in?" she asked.

"Did you read the docs I had my admin send over?"

"Yes."

"Then you know what I know."

She nodded and leaned in, elbows on the table. "So what's the plan? Do you have space arranged at Andrews to inspect this thing? I hope you didn't ask me here because you're planning on dumping it in my lap at Fort Detrick."

"The thought did cross my mind," he said.

Her expression soured instantly.

"But I secured another location."

"Where?" she asked.

"Westfield D."

"What's Westfield D?"

"A place . . . with, um, stuff."

"Ahhh, one of *those* kind of places. So you want me to clear it before transport?"

"The General has it crated up in a steel box and hermetically sealed with heat-activated PVC shrink-wrap. Can you bring some sort of portable tester and check it on the plane before we load it in a truck for WD?"

"Yeah, I have a portable BioDetection unit that tests for anthrax, *Brucella melitensis*, botulism A, *Coxiella*, *E. coli*, tularemia, ricin, salmonella, smallpox, and plague. Takes thirty minutes to run the analysis but a little more time to set up, take samples, and the like. I'd plan on at least a ninety-minute cargo hold, longer if we find something."

"Of course, sure, no problem."

"One thing I need to point out is that everyone who stayed behind in Bagram and everyone on the plane who has come in contact with this thing is potentially at risk. If we find a biological agent, then they all have to go into quarantine. I understand that the General wanted to get this thing out of his sandbox, but in his haste to do so, he put everyone in that plane at risk."

"I was thinking the same thing."

"Now, that being said," she continued, "from the witness statements, I don't think this object, whatever it is, is a biological weapon—delivery apparatus. If it is, and I can't believe I'm actually saying this out loud"—she dropped her voice into a whisper—"extraterrestrial in origin, then the pathogenic risk extends beyond our known library of infectious organisms. In that scenario, we throw the rulebook out the window and start from scratch. Quarantine, sample, detailed study of any DNA collected . . . and so on."

He nodded. "What do you make of the reports about the two soldiers and one Taliban detainee who interacted with the object all having grand mal seizures after exposure? Does that symptom fit with any disease you are familiar with?"

Her eyes lit up. "Now there's the part of the mystery I'm most interested in. There was an NIH study that found a link between a class of roseola virus, known as HHV-6B, and the onset of epilepsy three to five years later. But there's nothing in the literature linking grand mal seizures as an acute and immediate symptom of infection by roseola viruses or any other pathogen. Now, it is possible these men could have experienced febrile seizures, but febrile seizures typically only occur in children under five years old. It would be extremely unusual to see febrile seizures in an adult, let alone three genetically unrelated adults. Besides, there was no mention of these men running fevers or complaining of any other typical indicators of infection: headache, nausea, muscle pain, achy joints, etcetera."

"So it sounds like the risk of them turning into zombie ants is low?" he said with a chuckle.

"Are you talking about *Ophiocordyceps camponoti-rufipedis*?"

"Yeah, that's the one," he said, surprised. "You've heard of it?"

She raised her eyebrows. "My job *is* studying biological security."

"Yeah, for humans. This is a fungus that attacks ants."

"Obviously the risk is minuscule that *Ophiocordyceps camponoti-rufipedis* or any of the other cerebral parasitic organisms could be weaponized, but they're all on our watch list."

"Sounds like you and Dr. Madden will get along just swimmingly," he murmured as their food arrived.

Using chopsticks, he took his first piece of the salmon-and-cream-cheese-stuffed Philadelphia roll, dipped it in wasabi-infused soy sauce, and popped it in his mouth. The salty, creamy, spicy culinary creation lit his palate with instantaneous delight. "I forgot how good this place was," he said.

"Yeah, we should try to do this more often," she said, and then with a coy glance added, "And there's Cafe Nola for breakfast, in case you've forgotten."

"I thought your calendar was completely booked for the next three months?"

"My lunch calendar," she said. "I never said anything about breakfast."

CHAPTER 8

Silo 9
Dannemora, New York

"First stop, level three," Willie said as he stepped off the spiral staircase.

Josie joined him a beat later, gawking in awe.

"I call this the trading post," he said, smiling ear to ear like a kid showing off a painstakingly built Lego collection.

Josie's gaze ran over the rows of shelves packed with survival supplies. The first stack contained items related to fire and light: matches, candles, flint-and-steel sets, lighters, fire-starting bricks, flashlights, flares, and hundreds upon hundreds of batteries of all shapes and sizes. The second shelving unit was dedicated to what she might call construction and maintenance: wire saws, a shelf with at least fifty rolls of duct tape, nylon rope, plastic parkas and tarps, several folding utility shovels, serrated knives, and axes. The next shelf was like a pharmacy: stacked with fish antibiotics, isopropyl alcohol, creams and herbal remedies, bandages, suture kits, bottles of Tylenol and Advil, toothbrushes and toothpaste, and even boxes of tampons. The final shelf stack was loaded with commodity goods: tea, coffee, liquor, cooking oil, cans of lard, boxes of sugar, bags of rice and flour, bottles of ketchup and hot sauce, vinegar, bags of nuts, dried fruit, and packages of jerky.

"You weren't kidding," she said. "Looks like you made your own private Trader Joe's here. Walk me through the logic of having a trading post inside your hidden bunker. Seems like it defeats the purpose of everything you've accomplished here."

"After the culling, a new postapocalyptic society will emerge. Paper currency will be worthless. The only things of value will be gold, silver, and tangible goods. Commerce will be based on bartering, just like in the old days. Twenty years into the apocalypse, do you know how valuable a bottle of Jack Daniel's will be?"

"Probably not as coveted as those Tampax you have over there," she said with a sarcastic smile, cocking an eyebrow at the shelf.

"My point exactly," he replied. "All the basic everyday necessities we take for granted will become incredibly valuable."

"Agreed, but what good is it to possess all this commodity wealth if you're stuck down here all alone?"

"Well, maybe if you're lucky, I'll let you in when you come knocking on my door after hell starts reigning on Earth . . . Then you can inherit all of this." Wistfully, he added, "Diane and me never did get a chance to have children."

"So, does that mean you're not going to blindfold me on the way back?"

"I haven't decided," he grumbled.

Her stomach growled. She'd known this was going to be a long day, so she'd stuffed herself before leaving, but her metabolism was in overdrive, and she already needed to eat again.

"You hungry?" he asked, watching her eye the vacuum-packed bags of nuts and jerky.

"Yeah, I'm famished," she said, turning to meet his gaze. She gave him the human version of puppy-dog eyes.

"Little thing like you can't eat much," he said, walking to the shelf. "You like almonds?"

"Yeah, but, uh, I probably should go for the jerky. Is that okay?"

"Sure," he said. "Wanna try buffalo jerky? It has more protein and less cholesterol than beef."

"Yes. Thank you."

He ripped open a vacuum-sealed pouch and handed it to her.

"Thanks," she said again and popped a piece into her mouth. It wasn't as hard and chewy as she had expected. "This is good, and it's not like eating shoe leather."

"Yeah, I make it myself. It's all about breaking down the meat fibers and managing the moisture content."

"Well, it's really good," she said, savoring the salty teriyaki flavor.

He gave her time to finish the package then waved for her to follow him back to the stairs. She stuffed the empty package in her left jean pocket and headed to the spiral staircase. She found the tight radius and narrow treads of the spiral staircase incredibly awkward to navigate, but eventually her feet found a rhythm. While they descended, the entire silo seemed to groan and creak, and she couldn't help but wonder if it was nothing more than the harmless protestations of tired, old metal or if the entire dilapidated structure was one footfall away from catastrophic collapse.

For all the butterflies it was causing in her stomach, Willie seemed utterly unfazed, chatting away as they descended. The Atlas F silo was, at the time of its construction, the strongest and most expensive concrete structure ever built by man. The concrete that was used to make the silo walls had been mixed with epoxy resin and embedded with over six hundred tons of steel rebar, making the foundation capable of withstanding external pressure up to two hundred pounds per square inch—a force equivalent to five-hundred-mile-per-hour winds. At the top of the silo, the walls were an incredible nine feet thick, but they tapered down to a *paltry* two feet thick at level two, a design criteria maintained thereafter all the way to the bottom. Willie explained how the Atlas missile had sat on a launch platform that functioned like an elevator capable of lifting it completely out of the silo for launch. He described how the missile used a liquid-based propellant system, with RP-1—which was essentially kerosene—as the rocket fuel and liquid oxygen as the oxidizer. The liquid oxygen was maintained in pressurized storage tanks on level eight. To make the missile ready for launch, the missile's tank had to be purged of nitrogen and filled with LOX. The time delay to accomplish this, along with the dangers and complexities of storing and handling liquid propellants, was the primary reason for the short-lived nature of the Atlas missile program. Advancements in solid rocket fuels used by the Minuteman ICBM, which had been in parallel development, led to the cancellation of the Atlas missile program and the closure of all SM-65 sites by 1965.

"Wait a second," she said as the gravity of his words sunk in. "You're telling me that the government built dozens of these Atlas silos over a five-year period and then shut them all down a year later?"

"Seventy-two of the Atlas F sites. Plus fifty-seven more when you count the Atlas D and E sites. Incredible, isn't it? The weapon system was already obsolete by the time it was serviceable."

"How much money did they waste?"

"I tried to figure that out once," he said in between breaths. "I estimate in today's dollars, you're looking at about fifty billion."

She shook her head at this figure but then thought of the War on Terror and the *trillions* of dollars wasted on America's "longest war" and the subsequent occupation of Iraq and Afghanistan, and suddenly the cost of the Atlas missile program didn't seem so egregious. Thinking of Afghanistan made her thoughts turn to her husband. She wondered how Michael was doing. She wondered if he was safe on base or if they had him out on some extended patrol. She hadn't heard from him in two weeks, which indicated the latter and always left her nervous and unsettled.

Last night she'd had a nightmare that Michael was drowning. Trapped under the ice in a frozen pond, he was looking up at her with the strangest expression on his face. As bubbles streamed from the corners of his purple lips, he was smiling. She'd been there, on top of the ice. She'd screamed his name and pounded her fists against the frozen barrier between them, but the ice was thick and impenetrable. She'd scanned the surface, frantically searching for the hole he'd fallen through to pull him out, but she couldn't find it and was forced to watch him drown. She'd woken bolt upright, gasping for air. After calming herself in the dark, she'd pulled the covers up to her neck and hugged Michael's pillow. She inhaled deeply through her nose, craving his scent, but his olfactory ghost had already faded from the unwashed pillowcase. This had made her feel profoundly lonely and resentful toward the Army for sending her groom to the other side of the world. Army wives didn't get a vote. Neither did soldiers for that matter. The military, defender of freedom and the American way, was a juggernaut, indifferent and unrelenting. There were only three choices: get on board for the ride, get run over, or get left behind.

Willie Barnes had long since been left behind. That thought made her realize that she'd tuned out her host for the last two levels. "What was that you just said?" she asked, a beat into an awkward pause.

"I said, 'How are you doing back there?'"

"Oh, I'm doing fine," she said. "Finally got the hang of these stairs."

"Going down is the easy part; the trip back up is a bitch. By the way, the staircase ends at level seven. Only way to reach level eight is by ladder. You okay with that?"

"Sure, unless we can see everything worth seeing from here," she said, stepping off the spiral staircase onto the metal-grating floor of level seven. As she walked clear of the stairwell, a drop of liquid plinked her on the top of her head. She reflexively touched the wetness with her fingers and inspected her fingertip.

"It's just water," Willie said. "Some of the fittings and tank connections leak."

Now that he had said that, her ears tuned to the sound of multiple water droplets pinging off the metal framework on different levels with different frequencies, creating a rainforest sound effect. She inhaled, taking in the smell of the place, and talked into the camera microphone, memorializing the mélange of odors: "Fish and rust, earth and must."

"What did you say?" Willie said, suddenly whipping around to face her.

"Oh, nothing. Just recording an observation."

"No, no, I heard you. You were speaking in verse," he said, clutching at a silver pendant on a chain around his neck that she'd not noticed before.

"I wasn't speaking in verse."

"Don't lie to me," he said, practically shouting at her. "I heard a rhyme; don't tell me I didn't."

"Oooookay."

"Does she talk to you?"

Josie took a step back and folded her arms across her chest. "Does *who* talk to me?"

"The other Josie," he growled, taking a step toward her.

"The other Josie? I don't understand, Willie."

He eyed her for a beat and then waved a hand at her dismissively. "Forget it."

"All right," she said, keeping her gaze fixed on him as he paced away, mumbling. She strained to hear what he was saying—something about a woman named Eve and another named Diane. She watched him walk toward the center of the platform and stop at the edge of the grating, where he stared down into a reflective pool of black water.

What the hell was that all about? she wondered, eyeing him nervously.

"I'm sorry about that," he said after an awkward pause. "I'm not going to lie to you, Josie. I, uh, struggle with PTSD from time to time. Certain phrases and words set me off."

"It's okay," she said, but the goose bumps on her arms still hadn't seen fit to relax. She wanted to believe him, but something in her gut told her there was more to the story than PTSD.

"So, uh, this is level seven," he said, smiling and falling back into tour-guide mode. "One level up from the bottom of the silo. It was where the instruments and controls for the gas systems were located. The tanks were all kept on level eight."

"Is that water down there at the bottom?" she asked, moving toward the gaping square hole in the middle of the platform but angling away from Willie to maintain a cautious separation.

"Yeah, there's a collection sump down there. It catches the leaks from the aquaponics beds, and I get a little bit of groundwater in leakage too."

She nodded and tilted her head back to stare up the great center shaft where an ICBM had once been. Grow lights shone in a patchwork through the metal grating of the crib structure above. A slight haze hung in the air from the humidity. She lowered her gaze and as she looked around, she noticed that the decking and structural supports were warped and charred. The damage extended to level six above as well. On the opposite side of the silo, a huge area of decking between levels eight and seven was missing, as if it had been carved out by some giant ice-cream scooper. Pipes, brackets, and cable trays were also warped and cut. She turned to Willie.

"Was there some sort of explosion or fire down here?" she asked, gesturing to the empirical evidence all around them.

"No, no. What you're seeing is just the aftermath of the decommissioning process," he said dismissively. "It's easier to remove the tanks by cutting out the decking first."

"But this area is carved out in an almost perfect sphere," she said, walking around. When she reached the edge of the scooped-out deck, she knelt and touched one of the deformed metal struts. "It looks melted . . ."

"Well, Ms. Pitcher, not much left to see down here. We should probably wrap things up and head topside."

The distinct change in his demeanor and the reversion to calling her by the more formal Ms. Pitcher were not lost on her. She sensed him clamming up, and she wondered if she'd said or done something wrong. *Probably not,* she decided. Most likely the excitement of playing tour guide to his first visitor in years had worn off and was now supplanted by the anxiety caused by her presence. His need to boast and be praised was now usurped by the primal and paranoid desire to be rid of her. She had anticipated this behavior; it happened with almost every interview subject after she'd successfully unlocked and gained access to the intimate—to the secrets they were dying to share but then regretted telling afterward. She didn't know if there was a name for the phenomenon, but she called it the narcissist's stopwatch: *Time's up. Interview's over. Time for you to go and leave me alone.* In her experience, there was little that could be done once the switch had flipped, at least in this session. The window of opportunity was closing, and all she could do now was take in as much details and information as possible before she was forced to leave.

She climbed the spiral stairs, this time taking the lead at Willie's insistence. The climb up was exhausting, considerably more difficult than the way down. Although he didn't ask for a break, when she heard him getting winded, she said *she* needed a rest and stopped for a respite on level four. When he'd caught his breath, she resumed the ascent to level two. Before he shooed her out of the silo, she gazed upward one last time. A massive, round tarp hung suspended overhead, stretched taut by radial stanchions.

"What's that tarp for?" she asked.

"To control leaks," he said.

"Leaks from what?"

"The silo clamshell doors above. They leak pretty bad when it rains."

"Are they operational?" she asked.

"No."

"Why not?"

"Because I don't want them to open. But even if I did, they're so massive, they require a hydraulic system to operate."

"When was the last time they were opened?"

"Probably in 1965, when the Air Force removed the missile and decommissioned the facility," he said, gazing at her with impatient eyes. "C'mon, time to go."

Like a reluctant child, she lagged behind him—walking at half speed, filming every last detail she could without being overtly conspicuous about it. She followed him through the series of blast doors and the utility tunnel leading back to the launch control center. As he started to climb the stairs toward the level one landing, she paused. "Can I see level two of the LCC?" she asked, taking a step toward the open door leading into the lower level—the only space she'd yet to explore with him.

"Level two is my personal living quarters and the armory. Not much to see in there except a messy cot and a gun locker," he said.

She acknowledged him with a nod, but instead of complying, she took another step toward the threshold. She could now see into the round room and noted that, like the level above, it was in a state of ongoing renovation. "Is there a bathroom I can use down here?" she called over her shoulder, taking a step into his personal living quarters.

As with level one, he'd removed most of the divider walls in the donut-shaped chamber, leaving the floor plan wide open. To her left, she spied his sleeping quarters. *Sleeping quarters* was the appropriate descriptor, as opposed to *bedroom*, because there was nothing comfortable or cozy about it. His bed was nothing more than a folding cot with a sleeping bag and pillow strewn on top. For a bedside table, he used a stack of metal ammunition boxes with a wooden board resting on top. Along the curving back wall stood an IKEA PAX four-door wardrobe she recognized instantly because she owned the exact same one. Beside the wardrobe stood a walk-in gun cage, constructed from plate steel and heavy-duty wire-mesh panels. Inside there were enough weapons to arm a decent-size militia. She counted six AR-15s stacked neatly in a vertical rack, four AK-47s in their own rack, and a half dozen other assault rifles she didn't know by name displayed on peg hooks. A dozen pistols of every size and caliber were laid out on a series of downward-sloping shelves. She spied a rack of shotguns, hunting rifles with optics packages, compound bows, and an expensive-looking crossbow. Finally, standing up on end and leaning into the corner was something that looked like a bazooka out of a WWII movie.

"Oh my God," she said through her breath, having never seen a private collection of weapons like this in one place before. "If Michael could see this."

Then something else caught her attention—something even more interesting than the armory. A shiny silver suit hung suspended on a hook from the ceiling. The full-body suit, with gauntlet-style gloves and Moon Boots, looked like something straight out of an old science fiction movie. The outer layer of material appeared to be some sort of woven metallic fabric. The large dome-shaped helmet had a curved, rectangular Plexiglas faceplate with what appeared to be wire mesh fixed inside. The bottom of the helmet had a drape-style skirt that extended down to cover the neck and top of the shoulders. The outfit reminded her of the flame-resistant suits worn by stuntmen, except this one had an intricate network of copper wires affixed to the outside.

What the hell is that?

Willie's hand clamped down on her shoulder from behind, sending a shock wave of alarm through her entire body. She jerked free of the grip and whirled to face him, but her resolve to give him a dressing down fractured to pieces under the weight of his gaze. The strange look on his face set her knees to trembling, and in that moment, she realized she had grossly underestimated him. He was old, yes, but as he stood in front of her now, she noticed his square, broad shoulders and his muscular forearms. He had at least a forty-pound weight advantage, and he was probably carrying a concealed weapon. Despite her youth, despite her level of fitness, she acknowledged the grim reality that he could overpower her.

She took a step back.

"There's an old expression; you might have heard it," Willie growled. "Curiosity killed the cat."

"I'm sorry," she said. "I made a mistake. It won't happen again."

His nostrils flared with short, angry breaths as he seemed to consider her apology.

"I should go," she said and glanced at the door, her mind doing a quick flight-to-freedom calculation. He was stronger than her, but she was quicker. She could beat him to the door and up the stairs, but when she hit the intruder-entrapment enclosure, she would be screwed. The doors were interlocked and controlled with biometric security. There was no getting out without Willie. There was no escape from this place . . . .

"Did you bring your computer with you?" he asked, some of the edge gone from his voice.

"Yes," she said.

"You're going to need to download your video footage and delete this part," he said.

"Okay," she said, her heart still pounding wildly in her chest despite having defused the situation.

He escorted her topside back the way they'd come—through the double blast doors, the vestibule, and the intruder-entrapment enclosure; up the long entry stairwell; and out the hidden panel in the back of his coat closet. Reentering his modest log cabin, she felt unexpectedly emotionally deflated. She'd taken a plunge down the rabbit hole, toured the ultimate Armageddon bunker, and now was expected to leave and never come back. She knew she should be happy. Old Willie Barnes could have trapped her down there. He could have molested her, even murdered her, and no one would have ever found her. Not even Michael. As far as off-the-grid properties were concerned, Silo 9 took the grand prize for obscurity. But none of that had happened. Willie Barnes, despite his paranoia and doomsday-conspiracy beliefs, was not a psychopath. He was an old man with a rare treasure to guard, and he took his self-imposed assignment quite seriously.

They sat down at the kitchen table, and she pulled a MacBook Air out of her backpack. She removed her Veho MUVI Micro digital action body cam and connected it via a USB cable to the notebook computer. She imported all the footage into iMovie and then, as a show of good faith, worked through the recording with him, deleting every segment he didn't approve of. It was a lengthy, painstaking process but achieved the intended result of ingratiating herself back into his good graces. She wanted and needed today's interview to end on an up note; for a piece like this to be great, she would need to have follow-on interaction with him. Good journalism wasn't about winning or being right or ego; it was about capturing and conveying the human condition. This story was as much about Willie Barnes as it was his converted missile silo, his aquaponics system, and his prepper acumen. This was not an exposé; it was a partnership.

When the work was done, he offered her a bottle of water and a granola bar, which she gladly accepted. She wolfed down the granola bar and drank half the water, and then it was back in his Jeep Cherokee and the blackout hood. She rode in darkness next to him for what felt like an eternity, conversing very little. When he finally allowed her to remove the hood, they were two miles outside Potsdam.

"Can I give you a piece of advice?" he said as he pulled along the curb on Market Street in front of the 3 Bears Bakery, where he'd picked her up earlier this morning.

"Sure," she said, turning to look at him.

"You need to be more careful. You're too trusting."

"How so?"

"You climbed into this Jeep with me. Didn't know me from Adam. You let me blindfold you and power off your phone without hesitation."

"But those were your conditions. They were nonnegotiable, you said."

"That's true," he said, nodding. "But I could have taken you anywhere. I could have done anything I wanted to you—bad things—and you would have been powerless to stop me."

"I know," she said solemnly. "But that was the chance I had to take to get the story. Journalists have to take risks."

He nodded. "I understand that, but you're a young, pretty girl, and, uh, not everybody out there is a gentleman like me. There's some A-1 lunatics running around out there. You just never know who you're dealing with until—most of the time—it's too late to do anything about it. All I'm saying is be careful, Josie. Be suspicious. Be prepared. And stop climbing into cars with strange men who promise you what you want to hear."

"Okay, Willie," she said with an accommodating smile. "I'll keep that in mind."

She unclipped her seat belt, manually unlocked her door, and climbed out of the SUV. Before shutting the door, she leaned in and said, "As I said before, there's a good chance I might need to contact you again with a follow-up question or two. Is that still going to be all right?"

He flashed her a lopsided grin. "We'll see when we see. You have my email address."

"I do," she said, taking that as a maybe. "Goodbye, Willie."

"Goodbye, Josie."

She shut the passenger-side door and watched him pull away. Standing there on the sidewalk, everything felt surreal. She felt like she'd just got dropped off after a trip to the moon and back. She couldn't wait to tell Michael everything that had happened . . . well, not *everything*. With an incredulous smile plastered across her face, she retrieved her iPhone from a zipper pocket in her backpack and powered it on for the first time in seven hours. The home screen loaded, and the selfie-wallpaper pic of her and Michael smiling cheek-to-cheek greeted her. The image, one she saw countless times every day, suddenly evoked an insatiable longing for her husband. Then her phone chimed with a voice-mail notification from a number she did not recognize. She played the message:

"Mrs. Pitcher, this is Wendy Wilson, calling from the Fort Drum Family Liaison Office. Our office serves as an information link between the leadership and Army families. I'm calling to inform you that your husband, Michael, will be returning stateside from Afghanistan on a flight that's en route from Bagram. I don't have much in the way of details, but as information is made available to me, I will keep you posted. Feel free to call me at this number, or stop by our office anytime you like. Thank you."

A big grin spread across her face at the good news but then quickly morphed into a fretful frown as reality set in. Michael wasn't due home for three more months. The Army didn't send soldiers home early to be nice. The Army didn't cut deployments short so guys like Michael could catch a little R&R. No, if Michael was being sent home, then it was because something had happened . . . something bad. Nausea washed over her as her mind's eye pictured the worst: her husband maimed and mutilated from an IED explosion, barely clinging to life and being transported on an emergency medical flight.

Josie was not a woman of faith, but she suddenly found herself doing something she hadn't done in a very long time. *Please, God,* she prayed, *please let my Michael be okay.*

Chapter 9

Keep it secret.

Keep it secure.

That was what General Kane had said to Legend right after tossing him the hot potato. As the day progressed, Legend had had too much time to stew about the mysterious cargo being transported in the belly of the C-17. It was what he *didn't* know that spooked him, so he made the decision to change airports. If this thing in the box was some kind of weapon, better for it to blow up in Martinsburg than a stone's throw from the White House.

Sorry, West Virginia.

Arrangements had been made to cordon off Hangar 306 to receive the incoming C-17. Legend had his tech team from DARPA and his biosecurity team from USAMRIID standing by inside. The gargantuan four-engine heavy transport from Bagram arrived on schedule and landed without incident. As it pulled into the hangar, he marveled at its size. With a 170-foot wingspan, the height of a five-story building, and a length over half a football field, the C-17 was a monster of a plane. And when the rear cargo-bay door opened and he saw the tiny steel box strapped to the deck at the top of the loading ramp, he had to suppress the compulsion to bust out laughing. All of this for something that couldn't be much larger than a basketball?

Then he watched as four operators, armed and kitted up, took positions around the box, one operator at each corner. The display was sobering, and in that moment, he reminded himself that some of the deadliest products of man's machinations of war were small. A nuclear warhead with the power to obliterate a twenty-mile radius could fit in that box. A canister of sarin gas could fit in that box. An aerosol mechanism loaded with some deadly virus that could start the next pandemic could fit in that box.

Overkill was necessary.

He looked at Major Fischer, who was dressed out in her orange racal biosafety "space suit."

"I didn't know they were auditioning for *Orange Is the New Black*," he quipped.

"Very funny," she said, her voice muted by the inflated hood and battery-powered HEPA blower that kept the helmet pressurized and supplied with fresh, filtered air.

"I thought your suits were blue."

"The ones we use in the lab are blue. They're heavier and use plug-in forced-air regulators instead of the battery-powered blower. You should come by 1425 sometime and I'll give you a tour."

He shuddered. "No thanks. You can keep your Ebola to yourself."

"Wimp," she said and rolled her eyes.

"Looks like you're up. Be careful in there."

She nodded inside the oversize helmet, turned, and walked toward the loading ramp with two technicians, also wearing orange racal suits, in tow.

Legend pressed an earpiece into his ear so he could listen to Beth's radio chatter.

"Gentlemen," she said, greeting the armed security detail at the top of the ramp. "My name is Major Fischer from USAMRIID, and these are members of my biosecurity-hazard response team. We're here to take a few samples and run a few tests."

"No one said anything to us about this cargo being a biosafety hazard," said the leader, an operator with a shaggy red beard.

"I understand," she said, her voice patient and calm. "This is just precautionary. I'm sure there's no threat here, but we can't be too careful. Now, if we can just start by you answering a few questions: How is everyone doing here? Anyone feeling sick or nauseous? Does anyone on board have a fever?"

"We have one guy, Sergeant Pitcher from the Tenth Mountain, who had a seizure during the flight. He's still out cold. The corpsman's looking after him."

"Okay. Anyone else have any health issues during the flight? Any of you men feeling flulike symptoms? Any nausea or diarrhea?"

"No, ma'am, we're locked in tight and good to go."

"That's good, very good. All right, gentlemen, if you would both kindly stand down and take a seat along the bulkhead over there, we can do our analysis and clear this airplane."

"Not going to happen, Major," the operator said. "Our orders were to turn this cargo over to Major Legend Tyree from the Pentagon. No one touches this box without his express authorization."

Major Fischer rotated her entire body in her suit. "That's Major Tyree right there," she said, pointing a gloved finger at him. "He's the one who ordered this biohazard sweep."

At least these guys take their orders seriously, Legend thought as he waved at the red-bearded operator. "I'm Major Tyree," he shouted. "Before we can unload the cargo, we need to complete a threat assessment."

The bearded operator nodded humorlessly and then disappeared out of view back inside the belly of the plane. Over the next hour,

Fischer and her team conducted a complete chemical, biological, radiological, and nuclear survey of the package. First, they used a portable radiation survey meter to confirm the package was not a radioactive point-source emitter. Next, they used a frisker to sweep for contamination—radioactive particles on the outside of the package. Finding no radiation or contamination, they used a JCAD CED to sniff for explosive vapors and test for chemical residues. After confirming the object was not a nuke, a dirty nuke, or an IED, Fischer and her techs began checking for biological threats. They collected multiple samples and ran them through a portable RAZOR EX BioDetection system. According to Fischer, the instrument conducted real-time PCR analysis with 99 percent accuracy.

When Fischer finally emerged from the belly of the plane to give him the thumbs-up, Legend already knew the results—zero hits for all the major threats. Health assessment of the passengers in the cargo compartment was encouraging as well, with no one exhibiting any signs of infection.

With the CBRN survey complete, Fischer walked down the ramp, an orange blimp waddling toward him. Upon reaching him, she said, "I'm comfortable clearing the plane and the cargo. I don't see any indications of a biological or chemical threat coming from the device, but it's your call whether you want to hole everyone up for a mandatory observation period of forty-eight hours to see if any symptoms manifest."

"But you don't think that's necessary?"

"No, I don't."

"Are there any other precautions we can take?"

"As an alternative to a quarantine, we could take blood samples from everyone on board, run labs, and see if anything pops. Then if something comes back positive, we know who to bring in."

"Okay, let's do that," Legend said. Then, rubbing his chin, he asked, "What about the guy who had the seizure during the flight?"

"I spoke with the medic on board, and I did an evaluation myself. Sergeant Pitcher is currently in a postictal state."

"What's that?"

"A postictal state is the refractory period—an altered state of consciousness—that a patient enters after suffering a seizure. It usually lasts only a few minutes, but sometimes longer following a major grand mal event, which is what he had."

"How long has he been postictal?" Legend asked.

"Six hours and counting."

"And that's unusual?"

"Yeah, it's unusual," she said, worry lines creasing her forehead. "Postictal periods are typically characterized by drowsiness, confusion, migraine headaches, and other disorienting symptoms such as nausea and vertigo. Epilepsy is not my area of expertise, but I'm concerned for him. Sergeant Pitcher is not even lucid enough to answer questions."

"Okay, so what do you suggest we do with him?"

"If he doesn't come to by the time we're done here, I suggest we send him to Walter Reed for observation."

"All right, that's what we'll do." Legend turned to Malcolm Madden, who was sitting alone in a chair typing away on a notebook computer on his lap. "Dr. Madden, a word, please."

Malcolm nodded, packed the computer into his bag, and walked over to join them.

"Green lights from Major Fischer across the board," Legend said. "I'm ready to give the authorization to pack the cargo into the truck and mobilize for Westfield D, unless you'd like to run some tests of your own here first?"

"A few quick checks would be prudent, yes. First, I'd like to see if it is actively transmitting anywhere in the electromagnetic spectrum. If the answer is no, then I would like to expose the container to a series of RF test signals and monitor for a response. If we get no reaction, then you have the green light to load it for transport."

"Agreed. Please conduct your evaluation, Dr. Madden," Legend said, then turned back to Fischer. "You know you're going to have to run all your tests again when we open the box. This was just a preliminary survey to determine if I should take this thing off the plane."

"I know," she said. "Are you planning on opening it tonight at Westfield D?"

Legend checked his watch and said, "By the time we mobilize, drive to Culpeper, demobilize, and get the box in a lab, I imagine it will be after 0300. I don't see much to be gained by pushing everyone to work through the night. Unless Malcolm detects something earth-shattering here, I think whatever it is can wait until morning."

"Agreed," she said. "In that case, I'm going to release my guys and head home. What time do you want us to meet you in the morning?"

"Zero eight hundred."

"Roger that," she said.

A beat later, Madden was already walking back down the ramp. They both turned to look at the DARPA scientist for his report.

"Nothing," Madden said. "No signatures at all."

"Okay, let me go collect those blood samples, and then we can call it a wrap," Fischer said and headed back to the plane.

"Aren't you curious to see what it is?" Madden said, walking up to take her place. "Let's open the container tonight."

"There's a saying in the military: 'Nothing good ever happens after midnight.' The way I see it, I'm already pushing my luck running the cargo transfer to Westfield D."

"In that case, I'm going to head home. I have plenty of other work to do," Madden said.

"Luggage to unpack, zombie ants to play with," Legend said with a crooked smile.

"Precisely," the scientist said, turned, and walked away.

Legend headed over to the C-17 and walked up the rear cargo ramp. At the top of the ramp was the steel box, shrink-wrapped and strapped to the floor. *Much ado about nothing,* he thought, looking at the little package. *Thank God.* The operator with the red beard walked over to greet him.

"I'm Harris," the operator said, then, nodding at his companion added, "And he's Unger."

"Major Tyree," Legend said, shaking hands with the paramilitary operators. "I'd like to keep you fellas engaged through transfer and unboxing tomorrow. Once I get the crate open and I see what I'm dealing with, we can reevaluate."

Harris nodded. "That's fine by me. We're yours as long as you need us."

"Very good," Legend said. "Why don't you guys unstrap the cargo and load it into the black Suburban in the middle over there. It's going to be a three-vehicle convoy to Westfield D. Harris, you can ride with the box. I'll travel in the lead vehicle and Unger can ride in the tail."

"Check," Harris said with a nod.

As Legend watched the final tasks being taken care of, he wasn't sure if he should be relieved or disappointed. On the one hand, he'd caught General Kane's hot potato and hadn't gotten burned. If things kept on this path, they'd open the box tomorrow, identify the object as some sort of benign ancient artifact he could turn over to a museum, and be done with the entire business. On the other hand, a part of him had been hoping that the object the two soldiers from the Tenth Mountain had found was a legitimate technological anomaly to add to his collection of treasured acquisitions.

"Hey, Harris," Legend called. "What does the object look like? Can you describe it to me?"

"It's a perfect sphere, approximately the size of a basketball."

"It's metal?"

"Didn't look like any metal I've seen before. You know what it reminded me of, Major? A giant soap bubble—because it was sorta reflective and transparent at the same time."

"How much does it weigh?"

Harris laughed at this.

"What's so funny?"

"To put it in the box, we had to lift the box *up* to it."

"I don't understand."

"Sergeant Pitcher brought it back to base wrapped in a blanket and stuffed in his pack. When he and Corporal Wayne unwrapped it, it floated in midair."

"That information was not in the General's report. Are you fucking with me, Harris?"

"Do I look like someone who fucks around, Major?" Harris said with an expression carved from stone.

"No. No, you do not."

Harris shook his head and blew air through his teeth. "The General saw that thing floating and it spooked him. He told us to pack it up, lock it down, and get it the fuck off his base."

"Did you or any of your men interact with the object?"

"No. Pitcher and Wayne got it in the box. Me and my guys were safety observers, if you catch my drift," Harris said, tapping his assault rifle.

"Anybody else have a seizure like Pitcher and Wayne?"

"No."

"Anything else you can tell me that might be pertinent?"

Harris rubbed his beard and said, "Actually, yeah. I don't know how relevant this is, but those Tenth Mountain boys are odd ducks. I mean, aside from the seizures and all."

"In what way?"

"That Wayne is a jittery motherfucker. The dude can't sit still. The whole fucking flight over he's up—pacing and rambling on and on about computers and the internet. He dips like a fiend too. I swear the brother musta gone through four cans of Kodiak."

"What about Pitcher? Was his behavior the same as Wayne's before the seizure?"

"Nah, he was almost the opposite. Sat real still most of the flight, but hardly blinking and almost like he was looking right through you."

Legend nodded. "All right, I'm going to go talk to Wayne and see what he has to say. Let me know when the convoy is loaded and ready to go."

"Roger that," Harris said and went to join his teammate, who was removing the tie-down straps from the steel crate.

Legend turned and walked over to where Fischer was collecting blood samples from Corporal Wayne and the still-incoherent Sergeant Pitcher.

As he approached the group, he pondered over the new information the operator Harris had just shared with him. Apparently Kane had withheld important details about the object, and he couldn't help but wonder what else the good General was keeping from him.

Day Two

Is it the Devil or is it me,
working, working, so diligently?
My mind a clockwork of gears and springs,
my voice of two a chorus sings.
We wait in concert for her return,
So glorious, so glorious, to watch the world burn.

—*Willie Barnes*

CHAPTER 10

Malcolm Madden was an insomniac.

By choice.

He was also an atheist.

By Hobson's choice.

Eliminate the solace of a theological afterlife and unconsciousness becomes a terrifying state of existence. Asleep, Malcolm Madden was no different from any other human being, his intellect, creativity, and passion all neutered. His education, experience, and capacity for observation nullified. For Malcolm, being asleep was akin to being dead. The act of falling asleep felt like suicide committed ritualistically night after night after night.

Empirical evidence bolstered his *somniphobia*. Asleep, he ceased to exist. He had no self-awareness, no directed cogitation, no sense of time, and no willful access to his memories. His boss, Cyril Singleton, thought his somniphobia was just another one of his eccentricities. As did everyone else. But Cyril mollycoddled him—out of pity, he suspected, for they had never been intimate. She was ten years his senior; maybe she felt some misplaced maternal or sororal obligation for him. She'd once told him he was like a puppy stranded in the middle of a busy highway in desperate need of rescue. She had even tried to help him transcend his insomnia by making him a care package replete with chamomile tea, a book on meditation and relaxation, melatonin tablets, and incense candles. He hated tea, candles, and meditation, but he tried them all out of respect for her thoughtfulness.

The melatonin tablets he threw in the trash.

When he finally confided in Cyril the reason behind his insomnia, she had responded like any proper scientist should—with data and counterarguments. She argued vehemently that sleep was not analogous to death but rather that sleep was an altered state of consciousness. An unconscious brain and a sleeping brain exhibit very different EEG patterns, she said. When he poo-pooed her EEG data as irrelevant to the crux of his concern, she turned immediately to her fallback argument: dreams.

"Do you dream when you sleep?" she asked him.

"Yes, of course," he replied.

"Do you remember your dreams?"

"Sometimes?"

"There you have it," she declared with a girlish grin. *"Dead people don't dream. So stop this nonsense, and try to enjoy a good night's sleep with sweet dreams."*

He'd wanted to kiss her for that, but instead, he'd bid her good night and worked in the lab from dusk until dawn on some urgent deliverable, which now he could not remember. Intimacy was fleeting, and another moment like that with her had not come since.

Cyril was not a beautiful woman.

But he was in love with her.

Someday he would tell her so.

His doorbell rang, startling him and causing him to spill lukewarm coffee on his lap. He cursed and blotted the coffee from the crotch of his sweatpants with a wad of Kleenex, which was a bad idea because it instantly shredded into soggy, brown, little shards. *Why is it that tissues*

are good at wiping up snot but little else? He wiped the soggy, brown remnants off his pants, then padded to his apartment door in his bare feet.
He looked through the security peephole, and his heart skipped a beat.

Oh shit.

He fumbled with the dead bolt and then opened the door only a
few inches. Through the gap he said, "It's three o'clock in the morning,
Dean."

Dean Ninemeyer stared at him. "We're both insomniacs, so who
cares? Let me in."

"I'm a little busy right now."

Ninemeyer glanced at the wet stain on the crotch of Malcolm's
sweatpants and smirked. "I can see that."

Malcolm sighed. "I'm serious; now is not a good time."

Ninemeyer's smile morphed from mocking to humorless. "A little
bird tells me something big is brewing."

"I have no idea what you're talking about."

"You're a terrible liar, Malcolm. You always have been. Let me in
so we can talk about this."

"I don't work for you," Malcolm said, mustering his courage.

"We have an arrangement, you and me, or have you forgotten?
Now, either you let me in, or I'm going to let myself in."

Malcolm could tell from the other man's face that the statement
was a cold fact, not idle gamesmanship.

"Okay," he said, defeated, and closed the door enough to unfasten
the chain lock and then reopened it.

Ninemeyer pushed the door open and swept into the apartment
like a cold breeze. He was wearing his standard uniform: a black suit
with a white, starched shirt, open at the collar with no tie. His onyx-
black hair was parted and swept back with gel in a Cary Grant–esque
conservative throwback to the 1950s greaser style. Ninemeyer stood
three inches taller than Malcolm, had a lean frame and a perfectly flat
stomach. His features were hard and chiseled, like the skin on his face

had been stretched over a skull carved from granite. The thick-rimmed, black-framed eyeglasses he wore stood in great contrast to his pale-gray eyes—eyes that were always analyzing, calculating, and judging everything around him.

"I love what you've done with the place," he said, scanning around the disheveled apartment. "You've really put all that cash to good use."

Malcolm scratched his ear. "If your plan was to woo me with flattery, you're doing a dismal job."

"My father always told me I'd make a terrible businessman," Ninemeyer said. "He was the one who convinced me to work for the government."

"You don't work for *the* government. You work for *governments*."

"Semantics." Ninemeyer took a seat on the sofa and leaned forward, his elbows propped on his knees, to look at the container holding Malcolm's recently acquired Brazilian carpenter ants. "Aren't you a little old for ant farms?"

"Those ants are infected with a parasitic fungus that infiltrates their brains and kills them. I wouldn't get too close if I were you, or you might wind up with an uninvited guest in your head."

Ninemeyer scooted away from the sample container, and Malcolm fought the urge to revel in his little victory. "Just tell me why you're here, Dean," he said, already exasperated with the conversation.

"I want to know what the Army found buried in that cave in Afghanistan."

Malcolm shook his head. "How do you do it? Seriously, how? The project is one day old, classified TS/SCI with less than twenty people read in, and somehow you already know about it."

Ninemeyer smiled coolly. "I have friends in low and high places."

Still standing, Malcolm crossed his arms over his chest. "I've got nothing to report at the moment."

"Bullshit." The spy wagged a finger. "I hear it's unusual tech. There's even a rumor that it could be extraterrestrial in origin."

Malcolm cocked an eyebrow at him. "Are you intoxicated, Dean?"

Ninemeyer stared at him. "Do I look intoxicated, Malcolm?"

"No," Malcolm said, rubbing the back of his neck.

"I know you're on the scientific capture team tasked to examine the technology. I followed you to the airport. I watched the C-17 taxi into Hangar 306, and I watched them shut the door. I watched a three-vehicle convoy depart, and I followed it to Westfield Dynamics. Don't look so surprised; I know all about DARPA's secret skunkworks. I assume they took it to the BRIG?"

Malcolm nodded, and his stomach turned to acid. The bastard was gloating and bullying him at the same time. How was it that Ninemeyer already knew as much about the project as he did? This was unfortunate because the more Ninemeyer knew, the less wiggle room Malcolm had to negotiate.

"What took so long in Hangar 306?" Ninemeyer continued.

"They were screening it for CBRN threats."

"Makes sense," Ninemeyer said with a sniff. "Who did they send off in that ambulance? Did somebody get hurt?"

"You don't miss much, do you?"

"No . . . tell me."

"Two Army grunts, a Sergeant Pitcher and a Corporal, oh God, what was his name . . . Wayne. Corporal Wayne."

"Why'd they take them away in an ambulance? Were they injured by the object?"

"Pitcher and Wayne were the ones who found it. Pitcher had a grand mal seizure on the flight over. He was in a weird, prolonged postictal state when I saw him."

"What about Wayne?"

"I don't think so, but he didn't look well. If I didn't know better, I'd say he'd taken methamphetamine during the flight. Very jittery."

"When are they going to open the box?"

Malcolm checked his watch. "In four hours, give or take."

Ninemeyer nodded, this information apparently pleasing him. "Good. I want a full accounting of what you find."

Malcolm took a deep breath and contemplated the coiled viper on his sofa. He'd known Ninemeyer for three years, but he still wasn't sure what the man's job was or whom he really worked for. On their first meeting, Ninemeyer had shown him identification that said he was the Director of Acquisitions for a company called Helios Enterprises, but Malcolm had long since figured out this was a fiction. His job at Helios Enterprises, and undoubtedly his name itself, was but one of many legends the man used. But like every lie, this legend was built on a keystone of truth, for Ninemeyer *was* in the business of acquisitions—the acquisition of government secrets.

It had all started innocently enough, with Ninemeyer offering to pay for Malcolm's consulting services on the side. The requests Ninemeyer made were simplistic and beneath a man of Malcolm's capabilities, but the hourly billing rate that Ninemeyer offered was ten times what Malcolm was making at DARPA. Ten times! So he took the work as it came, and the extra cash allowed him to rent a nicer apartment and start paying down the mountain of student-loan debt he'd been chipping away at since his twenties. But over time his benefactor had gotten lazy and stopped whitewashing all the source materials in fastidious detail. When that happened, Malcolm realized he wasn't helping Helios engineers; he was helping the Chinese, the Russians, and the Koreans. He was doing the heavy lifting for other scientists incapable of doing the work themselves. Upon recognizing this, he also recognized that what he was doing constituted treason.

"I can't, Dean. Not this time," he said. "It's compartmentalized top secret."

"You're not in control of this partnership," Ninemeyer said, getting to his feet. "You don't tell me no."

"The circle is too small. If I leak, they'll know it was me."

The spy approached him with a smile, then snapped a hand out, grabbed Malcolm by the scrotum, and squeezed. "What that big, beautiful brain of yours does not seem to understand is that I can burn you anytime I choose. You've sold state secrets; you've collaborated with the enemy. You're a traitor, Malcolm Madden, and I have the documentation to prove it."

"If I go down," Malcolm squealed, the pain in his gonads making him feel ill, "you go down."

"72301 Meadow Brook Court, apartment 32A," his torturer said, squeezing harder.

"What?" he whimpered, his brain not processing the non sequitur.

"You don't recognize the address?" Ninemeyer taunted. "Of course not. Your precious Cyril has never invited you to her place. But I know where she lives. I know the code to her smart lock is one-eight-two-two. I know that she keeps her underwear in the second drawer of her dresser." The corners of the spy's mouth curled into a vulpine grin, and he inhaled deeply through his nose, almost as if . . .

"If you touch one hair on her head," Malcolm growled, "I'll—"

"You'll what?" Ninemeyer said, giving Malcolm's nuts a crushing squeeze.

Malcolm buckled at the waist and moaned. His entire abdomen burned with pain, and he felt like he needed to vomit.

After an agonizing beat, Ninemeyer released his grip. "That's what I thought. Let this be a reminder, Malcolm, that I have you by the balls. I can get to you and your precious Cyril anytime I want. You work for me. Never forget that."

Malcolm nodded, unable to speak.

"I want a daily accounting of what you learn about the object," Ninemeyer commanded, towering over him. "In addition, I want a list of key personnel on the project, and when the time comes, I'm going to want access to the facility."

"Fine, fine," Malcolm coughed. "Whatever you want."

"Good, that's better," Ninemeyer said and turned toward the door. "Don't worry; I'll let myself out."

After Ninemeyer was gone, it took Malcolm several minutes to recuperate. When he could finally stand up straight, he walked to the kitchen and fetched himself a glass of water. He drank half of it in one long gulp. He'd never seen Ninemeyer like that before—so aggressive and dangerous. A terrifying thought occurred to him, one that made him want to crawl into a hole and disappear. What if Dean Ninemeyer was more than a spy? What if he was a killer? The Mafia employed people like Ninemeyer, and so did governments. Men with the authority to make deals, collect payments, and clean up their own messes.

I'm such a fool, he thought. *I made a deal with the devil, and now the devil wants his due.*

He walked back to the sofa and sat in front of his sample of *Camponotus rufipes.* He watched the infected ants wandering around in the enclosure behaving like normal ants. How long they persisted as carriers before the zombification took place was a topic of debate. Some entomologists and parasitologists suggested that the fungus remained dormant inside the ant until the temperature, humidity, distance from the colony, and even barometric pressure (as an indicator of altitude in the jungle) were conducive to optimal spore release. Only once all the criteria were met for the fungus to achieve its objective would the fungus activate and take control of its host.

Malcolm collapsed back against the sofa.

What the hell am I supposed to do now?

CHAPTER 11

The energy in the control room was electric. Legend could feel it, and from the looks on people's faces, they could feel it too. All the key players from last night had reassembled, everyone early, everyone prepared.

The blood samples taken by Fischer and her team had come back negative for viral and bacterial antibodies. But Sergeant Pitcher was still in a fuguelike state, and that was a source of concern. He and Corporal Wayne were scheduled for CT scans and examination by a neurologist this morning, and Legend was anxious to learn the results.

His gaze ticked from monitor to monitor to monitor—twelve in all, streaming live imagery of the secure space designated for the "opening ceremony," as it had been dubbed. The cavernous underground room, rectangular in shape with concrete walls, floor, and ceiling, was known affectionately as the BRIG (Ballistics Research Information Gathering). It was a forced acronym, Legend decided—the name chosen before the constituent words were defined because, well, it sounded cool. The BRIG was equipped with recirculating HEPA-filtered ventilation, a fire-suppression system, and a video-observation room nearby that allowed real-time viewing of the events inside from a safe and isolated position.

According to Malcolm, this space had been specifically designed to test ballistic weapons systems, incendiary devices, and just about any device or invention that could pose a danger to human life. Evidence of these past tests was apparent as numerous sections of the concrete floor and walls were stained, black charred, and chipped. The BRIG was battle hardened, and this gave Legend at least a modicum of confidence that no matter what was trapped inside that steel box, it wasn't going anywhere without his permission.

Legend turned to Cyril Singleton. "The checklist is complete. Everyone is in position. I'm ready for the green light whenever you are."

Cyril studied the monitors for a beat, then turned and met his gaze from behind her trademark red-framed eyeglasses. "Let's do this."

With a nod of acknowledgment, he said, "All right, everyone, it's showtime."

The sequence of events, which had already been briefed, would essentially duplicate those conducted last night at Hanger 306. This time, however, the layers of hermetically sealed shrink-wrap would be cut away, and the steel box would be opened, permitting the direct sampling, measuring, and observation of the object itself. First up were Major Fischer and her biohazard security team. Against her wishes, Legend had insisted that one of the operators from Bagram, the red-bearded Harris, don a biosafety suit and accompany her into the BRIG armed with an M4 just in case something went terribly wrong.

"Wish me luck," she said to him from behind the transparent face shield. Her hair was pulled back into a bun, she wore no makeup this morning, and she had bags under her eyes, but the smile she flashed him was electric. She was a girl on Christmas morning; she was a musician walking onstage at Carnegie Hall; she was the world's preeminent biohazard expert about to open a container that could define the rest of her career.

"Good luck," he said, beaming back at her. "And, Beth, be careful in there."

She winked and turned to leave with a coy smile on her face. The two other orange suits followed her out, Harris and a USAMRIID technician she'd brought with her named Dixon. Legend turned his attention to the video monitors and adjusted the volume on the speakers. When the trio of orange moon suits appeared on the closed-circuit TV monitors, he tested the two-way intercom system. Pressing the talk button at the base of a microphone stalk on the control panel, he said, "Bravo team, this is Control. How do you copy?"

"We hear you, Lima Charlie, Control," Fischer's voice came back.

"Roger that, Bravo."

Upon reaching the sealed box, Dixon knelt beside the crate and set a tool kit he was carrying on the deck. He opened the zipper compartment and retrieved a box cutter and went to work excising the industrial shrink-wrap and then peeling it off in sections. Once the steel box was exposed, Harris recited the combinations for the two padlocks securing the lid to the box. Dixon, despite his heavy gloves, deftly managed to enter the combos and unlock the hinged, articulating blocking straps securing the lid.

"This is it," Fischer said. "Control, Bravo team requesting permission to open the lid."

Legend took a deep breath, exhaled, and gave the order: "Bravo team, Control, open the lid." Then, putting a hand on the shoulder of the facility technician seated at the control panel in front of him, he said, "Can you zoom in with that overhead camera? Yeah, like that . . . Okay, good, hold there."

Fischer turned to Dixon. "Bravo Two, stand by for rad survey."

"Standing by," Dixon said.

"Bravo Three, stand by for fire support."

"Standing by," Harris said, leveling the barrel of his M4 at the box.

"In three, two, one . . ." Fischer opened the lid and gasped.

Legend's heart skipped a beat. "Bravo, report," he said.

"You're not going to believe this, Control, but the box is empty."

"Empty? How is that possible?"

"I watched that fucking thing get loaded in this box," Harris growled defensively, as if Legend were already assigning blame for the mishap. The operator stepped up and looked in the box, his helmet bumping into Fischer's as he did. "What the fuck is going on?"

Legend's emotional state ran like a roller coaster over the next three seconds: shock, followed by denial, then disappointment, finally settling on anxiety. Had the object been stolen during the night and replaced with an empty box? Westfield D was a secure facility, but what other explanation was there? Unless the boxes had been switched in Bagram. Maybe this box was a decoy and the crate containing the object had been shipped off to another secret facility. But why? That didn't make any—

"Hold on" came Harris's voice. Legend could see him poking the barrel of his M4 inside the box. "There's something in here. I can feel it."

"He's right; I see something," Fischer said. "It's transparent, almost like a bubble . . . Wait . . . It's changing . . . It's taking shape . . . I can see it now. It's growing pearlescent . . . It's beautiful . . ."

Fischer and Harris simultaneously pulled their heads back, giving the overhead camera a good view into the box. As the object materialized, what Legend saw matched Fischer's real-time commentary.

"I see swirling light. It's taking shape now. Ohhhhh, starting to float . . . Legend, it's coming out of the box," Fischer said, her voice laced with both excitement and fear.

"Give it space," he heard himself say, which was absurd advice, but on the video monitor, he watched the three orange suits backpedal as a glowing orb ascended from its steel prison.

"Control, what do you want us to do?"

Legend tasted bile in his mouth. No wonder General Kane had wanted to get rid of this thing. What Harris had said about the object floating had been true. This didn't feel right. This sort of tech didn't exist. His mind started racing. What the hell was this thing? He looked at Cyril, and her expression of incredulity matched his own.

"Establish a perimeter, and perform a radiation survey," he said, returning his gaze to the monitors. "And be ready to evacuate."

"Roger" was all Fischer said as the three orange suits drifted to equally spaced positions, forming a triangle around the floating orb, which was now hovering two feet above the box and rising.

"Radiation levels match background," Dixon reported. "It's not radioactive."

"Copy," Legend replied, his gaze fixed on the monitor with a wide-angle feed showing the scene floor to ceiling with the orb in the middle. He watched, awestruck, as the swirling ball of light ascended: three feet, four feet, five . . . Up it rose and stopped at what looked like nine feet in the air. The trio in the BRIG stood transfixed, their helmets tilted back, faces gazing upward.

"It's soooo beautiful," Fischer said, her voice hypnotic.

Legend looked at Malcolm, who hadn't said a word the entire morning. The scientist's gaze was transfixed on the same monitor Legend had been watching. "What do you think, Dr. Madden?"

"I think," Madden said, his voice foreboding, "you should get them out of there."

Legend looked back at the video feed, the evacuation order poised on his lips, when the orb pulsed, emitting a brilliant flash of light. Everything in the observation room went out—the lights, the video feeds, the LED indicators on the control panel—all dark.

"Bravo team, this is Control. Do you copy?" Legend shouted in the dark.

"We've lost all comms, Major," said the control room tech seated at the control panel. "Everything's down."

Legend heard a click, and a flashlight beam carved a swath through the darkness. A circle of light traced across the control panel as the technician tried to assess the failure.

"Can you reboot?" Legend asked.

"Attempting that now," the technician said, frantically trying to restore the control panel. "It's not working. Maybe we lost main line power . . . Let me check." The flashlight beam dropped to the floor as the technician got to his hands and knees to work underneath the console.

"Does anyone else have a flashlight?" Legend asked.

"I do," said the operator who'd accompanied Harris on the plane. *Unger,* Legend remembered. He clicked on the light.

"Unger, you're with me," Legend said. "Something just happened in there, and we need to get Bravo team out."

Flashlight in hand, Unger sidestepped Legend and headed for the door. Legend followed the operator into the hallway outside. Battery-powered emergency-light strips lit the passage well enough to see without a flashlight, but Unger kept his light on anyway. They sprinted to the BRIG entrance. Access to the BRIG was via one of two doors—a heavy steel slider, twelve feet wide and designed to accommodate large equipment, and the personnel door. The slider weighed nearly a thousand pounds and required an electric actuator to operate—no way in hell they were getting that open. The personnel door was equipped with a biometric access point, and Legend had a sinking feeling that for security purposes the lock had failed in the locked-shut position. The operator, Unger, headed straight for the personnel door and tried the handle.

"Shit," he barked, pulling with everything he had. "It won't budge, Major."

Legend looked at the biometric security box on the wall beside the door. All the indicator lights were dark. Short of breaching the door, they weren't getting in. Legend's mind was racing, and his heart was pounding with a cadence he'd not felt since the last time he was in combat.

Those were his people trapped in there, and he had to get them out.

"Options?" he said, turning to Unger.

Unger was grim-faced. "Way I see it, we can either use the manual handwheel on that electric actuator to open the big door, or we breach the personnel door. By the time we round up the equipment we need to breach, I bet we'd have that big door open enough to squeeze through."

"Agreed," Legend said, and he stepped up to the electric operator for the slider door and started turning the wheel hand over hand. After ten revolutions, the massive door had moved by maybe an eighth of an inch. "Screw this," he hissed, turned sideways, and changed to a one-handed grip using the spoke-mounted T handle. He pumped his arm around and around in a tight circle as fast as his muscles would go. "This thing is geared so low, by the time we get this fucking door open, it will be over in there," he huffed.

Unger moved up beside him. "We'll tag-team it. When your arm's on fire, I'll take over."

Legend cranked the eight-inch-diameter handwheel at eye-blurring speed, his arm a tornado of fury. He could feel the door ease off its seal as there was a small but noticeable drop in the drag on the wheel. After several minutes, the lactic burn in his shoulder and forearm reached a crescendo. He gritted his teeth and fought the pain, but biology trumped willpower, and his speed began to slow.

"You're burned up," Unger said. "Let me take it now."

With a primal growl, Legend pushed through several more revolutions before forfeiting the wheel to Unger.

Breathing heavily, Legend turned to look at the two-inch gap he'd opened up for all his effort. A blue-white light streamed through the crack, dancing and modulating like the aurora borealis in the night sky. He walked to it and peeked through the slowly expanding gap between the edge of the mighty door and the heavy steel frame. Twenty-five feet away, he saw them, still dressed in their orange biosafety suits, standing eight feet apart in an equilateral triangle, heads tilted up, backs arched, arms in the air reaching for the glowing orb of light just out of their grasp. A chill snaked down his spine at the bizarre, almost ritualistic scene unfolding inside.

"Hurry," he shouted, turning to Unger, who was spinning the wheel with everything he had. "We've got to get in there before it's too late."

CHAPTER 12

Westfield Dynamics

Every muscle fiber in Legend's right arm, from his fingertips to his shoulder, was on fire as he spun the manual handwheel opening the BRIG's steel slider door. He pushed on until the cramping started up again.

"Switch," he said, and Unger jumped back in to take a turn. Just another inch and he'd be able to squeeze through the gap.

A small crowd had gathered around them now, including Malcolm Madden.

"What are you planning to do when you go in there?" the DARPA genius asked him.

The question irritated Legend. As if it were a buzzing fly, he wanted to swat it away. "I'm going to pull our people out."

"That might not be the best idea."

"What do you mean? You want me to leave them like that?" he fired back, gesturing to their three entranced team members inside.

"Major Tyree, have you ever disconnected an external USB drive from a computer while it was in use?"

"Yeah, sure. Why?"

"And what happened?"

"An error message popped up. Something about the disk was in use and that I may have corrupted data on the drive, blah, blah, blah. Get to the point, Malcolm."

"My point is that I don't understand what is going on in there, and neither do you. There's some sort of connection between the object and those three people. It could be some sort of hypnotic trance they've fallen into, or it could be something else altogether—a direct neurological link between their minds and that floating orb."

"There's no such thing with current technology," Legend said, his gaze going to the gap. It was almost wide enough that if he turned his head and exhaled all the air from his lungs, he might just be able to squeeze through.

"True, but that is not current technology," Malcolm said, grabbing him by the shoulder to get his attention. "*That* is unknown technology."

"Are you saying by forcibly pulling them out we could fry their brains or something?" Legend asked, turning back to face the scientist.

"That's exactly what I'm saying. You saw Sergeant Pitcher's condition on the plane last night. How do you know that when you run in there to pull them out the same thing won't happen to you? What's to stop the object from slurping your brain up into la-la land with the rest of them?"

Legend met the other man's gaze. He didn't like the counsel he was getting, but it was the counsel he needed to hear. Madden was right. A panicked, reactionary response could be dangerous for the rescuers and those they were attempting to rescue. "Assuming you're right, I need options. How do I disable this thing? How do we shut it down?"

"I don't know," Madden confessed.

"I'll tell you how: by letting me blow it out of the sky, that's how," Unger huffed, still cranking the handwheel with everything he had.

"It might just come to that," Legend said to Unger. Then, turning to Malcolm, he said, "Is there an armory here?"

"I'm not sure," Malcolm replied. "Cyril would know."

Then, as if summoned by a genie, three men in security uniforms came sprinting down the corridor and stopped in front of Legend. Two were armed with shotguns and one with an assault rifle. The lead guard's gaze scanned the group and settled on Legend. "Are you the OIC?"

"Yes, I'm Major Tyree," Legend answered.

The bulky guard introduced himself as the Deputy Chief of Security at Westfield D and said, "Director Singleton sent us. What's the SITREP?"

"I have three people in the BRIG who are currently . . . How do I explain this? Ah hell, it will be faster if you just take a look for yourself."

The guard walked to the gap and gazed inside. "Jesus, Mary, and Joseph. What in the good Lord's name is that?"

"That's what we were trying to figure out," Legend said. "Now listen up, people. We're going in as a six-man team: you three plus me, Unger, and Dr. Madden here."

"What?" Malcolm protested. "I can't go in there."

"You can and you will. You're my systems expert; I'm counting on you to figure out how to disable that thing so we can get our people out."

"Somehow I don't think it has an off switch, Major," the DARPA scientist said, his voice oozing with cynicism.

"I need solutions, not sarcasm," Legend snapped.

"Look, I'd say we could try an electromagnetic pulse to disable it, but that is what it used on us. And an EMP is not something I happen to carry around in my pocket. Hacking into its operating system would be an option, if we knew that it even had an operating system. What I'm trying to say, Major, is that by my thinking, you only have two viable options."

"Which are?"

"Attempt to communicate with it verbally."

"And option two?"

"Let Mr. Unger here blow it out of the sky."

Legend groaned, but he didn't have time to argue. On a practical level, he knew Malcolm was right. He turned to the security team. "Listen up, guys. This is *not* a weapons-free scenario. No one fires without my express order. I'm going to try communicating with the object. If that fails, then we disable it, but when I say disable, that does not mean destroy. We use only enough force to achieve the objective. Understood?"

He got three nods back.

"Shooters lead the approach; the rescue team will shadow. Rescue-team assignments are as follows: Unger, you get Harris; Madden gets Major Fischer; and I'll grab Dixon. The objective is to EXFIL all personnel from the BRIG while containing the object inside. We cannot under any circumstance let that thing get out. If I become incapacitated, then shooters have weapons-free authority."

"Roger that, Major," Unger grunted, still spinning the handwheel.

Legend glanced at the gap, and it was open enough now for even the barrel-chested lead guard to squeeze through. "All right, people, let's go."

"Major, if you don't mind me asking before we go in," the head guard said, "what exactly is that thing in there?"

Legend flashed him an ironic smile. "If I knew, I would tell you, boss, but unfortunately that's what we were trying to find out."

The head guard nodded and then squeezed through the gap, sucking in his gut and holding his M4 out with his lead hand. The other two guards, each armed with Mossbergs, went through next in turn. Legend went fourth, followed by Unger and a reluctant Malcolm bringing up the rear. The security team fanned out into a line and began advancing on a nod from Legend. Legend fell in behind the head guard in the center, Unger went left, and Malcolm went right. The guards advanced in a tactical crouch, their weapons up and trained on the fluorescing orb.

Light swirled and danced around the orb, making Legend think of ghosts. A memory of the final scene in *Raiders of the Lost Ark* percolated front and center in his conscious. Were lightning bolts about to strike them all down, melting their eyes and charring their flesh? *That's absurd,* he told himself. But was it? What he was witnessing defied logic. Engagement with the object was inevitable, and he still had no idea what the hell they were dealing with.

All right, he thought, *here goes nothing.*

"I am Major Legend Tyree of the United States Army," he announced, staring at the freak show in front of him. The ludicrous realization that he was talking to a floating orb occurred to him, and he decided to talk to it like he would any hostage-taking terrorist. "I don't know what you want, but quite frankly I don't care. Release my people, or we will use lethal force against you."

Nothing happened.

He dropped his gaze to Major Fischer and the two other orange suits. Although Beth's body was frozen in a hypnotic state, he could see tears running down her cheeks. Were they tears of rapture, tears of sadness, or tears of agony? What in God's name was it doing to her?

I want to know you, Legend, an angelic female voice said.

"Did you hear that?" he asked.

"Hear what?" the lead guard asked over his shoulder.

"It's now or never, Major," Unger shouted. "Do something or we're next."

Unger was right. Staring at the miraculous, glowing ball of light floating in front of him, he decided to give the order. In that instant, the light show stopped, and the orb disappeared.

"Fire!" he barked a split second later. Two shotgun blasts and a three-round burst from the M4 roared and reverberated inside the concrete room.

Major Fischer, Harris, and Dixon all crumpled to the deck like marionettes whose strings had just been cut.

"Where the hell did it go?" Unger shouted.

"I don't know; it just disappeared into thin air," a guard added.

The three shooters were scanning over their weapons, but no one had a bead on it.

"I don't know what's happening, but we need to get everyone out of here," Legend shouted and raced toward Dixon. "Double-time it, people. Let's go!"

He'd assigned Malcolm to haul Fischer out because she was the lightest of the group. Nevertheless, Legend had his doubts whether the scientist would be strong enough to drag her out without help. He quickly glanced at where she lay on the floor, but her head was turned the other way, and he couldn't see her face. From the corner of his eye, he saw Malcolm just standing there, gazing around for the orb.

"Dr. Madden!" he barked. "Major Fischer is your priority. Grab her under the armpits and drag her out. Do it now!"

The scientist froze for a beat, then snapped out of his fugue. "Sorry," he said, spun around, and ran to Fischer.

With the amount of adrenaline surging through his body, Legend felt like he had lightning in his veins. He flipped Dixon onto his back, scooped his right hand under the man's right thigh, and executed a Ranger roll—rolling across the unconscious man's chest back onto his knees while using the momentum of the sideways somersault to hoist the man fluidly up onto his shoulders into a fireman's carry. With a grunt, he secured the man's right arm and got to his feet. He glanced over at Madden and Fischer and saw that the scientist was still floundering and hadn't even managed to move Beth a foot.

"You," he snapped at the closer of the guards holding a shotgun, "help him."

"Yes, sir," the guard said, shouldering his Mossberg by its strap.

Legend set off in a run toward the steel slider door. Beside him, he saw that Unger had Harris slung across his shoulders in a fireman's carry as well. They reached the steel door at the same time and in unison stared at the narrow gap.

"How the fuck are we going to get them through that?" Unger asked. "They can't even stand."

Legend thought for a second. "All right, I'll go through. You roll them on their sides, arms above their heads, and I'll pull them through headfirst."

"Okay, that should work."

Legend took a knee and then eased Dixon off his shoulders and onto the ground. He turned back to check on Fischer's evac and saw that the guard he'd told to help Madden was carrying Beth like an unconscious bride in front of him, one forearm under her knees, the other under her torso. From the strain on the man's bright-red face, Legend could tell the dude was struggling. Beth was tall, muscular as hell, and as dense as a hunk of lead.

"Don't you drop her," he shouted at the guard.

"I won't," the man huffed back.

Legend quickly scanned the length of the BRIG, searching to see if the orb had reappeared. Seeing no trace of it, he turned back to the steel door. "I'm going through," he announced, then stepped up to the gap and slid sideways into the breach. At that exact moment, with his chest wedged between the door and the frame, power to the facility restored.

The lights turned on.

A siren wailed.

And the colossal steel door began to close.

CHAPTER 13

Josie was frustrated.

Her husband was on US soil, but for some reason, the Fort Drum Family Liaison Office wouldn't tell her where. She couldn't help but wonder: Was this government bureaucracy at work, or was it intentional? The pragmatist in her voted for the former; the investigative journalist presumed the latter and was already percolating a conspiracy theory.

She sat in her kitchen, mug of coffee gone cold in one hand, mobile phone in the other, debating whether to escalate. She was tempted to call the unit CO's wife, Caroline. There was hierarchy among spouses, invisibly conferred from their husband's, or wife's, active-duty rank. In the old days, the wives of enlisted men and the wives of officers didn't fraternize, period. In today's Army, however, that barrier was beginning to erode. Josie had met Caroline during a spouse volunteer event at a local food pantry. Josie hadn't known the woman was the CO's wife at the time, and they'd chatted happily for several hours. It wasn't until weeks later, when she'd seen Caroline standing with her officer husband in a picture, that Josie had made the connection. She wasn't sure whether Caroline would help her, but at this point, what did she have to lose?

She made the call.

The line picked up after the third ring.

"This is Caroline," a woman's voice said.

"Hi, Caroline, Josie Pitcher calling . . . We met at the Watertown food pantry last month during the spouse volunteer event."

"Oh yes, Josie. How are you?"

"I'm okay . . . Actually, I'm not okay. I'm calling because I'm worried. Yesterday I got word that my husband's been flown back stateside from Afghanistan. He's not answering his phone, and he's not responding to emails. I've tried talking with the Family Liaison Office, but they haven't been able to give me any specific information. Nobody's used the word CASEVAC, but I'm worried he was injured. Would you be willing to, I don't know, maybe make a phone call or two to see what you can find out?"

"Your husband's first name was Michael, if I recall?"

"That's right, Staff Sergeant Michael Pitcher," she said, her voice hopeful.

"Give me until this afternoon, and I'll see what I can do," Caroline said without pretense or promise. "We Army wives have to stick together."

"We certainly do."

Caroline ended the call first, and Josie gave a little victorious sigh. *Thank you, thank you, thank you . . .*

With the Colonel's wife on the case, there really wasn't much more she could do but wait. So she turned her attention back to Willie Barnes. She'd spent most of last night watching and rewatching footage from yesterday's interview and silo tour. In doing so, a few segments stood out. She replayed the moment during the tour of level one of the LCC when Willie had slipped up.

The camera panned to his face, and she heard herself say, *"Our bunk room? Wait a second—did you used to work here?"*

"I can neither confirm nor deny that."

She picked up her mobile phone and called DJ Mood, a strange dude she'd been introduced to while researching her anti-vaccination (a.k.a. "anti-vax") piece for *Vice*. DJ Mood was not an actual DJ, although she wouldn't be surprised if he hit the club scene. From their interactions, she assumed he was a gray hat—if not, he was at a minimum deeply plugged into the hacker world with its hats of many colors. DJ referred to himself as an *informationist*. She'd not heard the term before, but the word defined itself, and DJ's persona filled out the context. DJ bought, sold, and traded information for cryptocurrency, favors, and other information. To Josie, he epitomized the twenty-first-century techno-mage, although instead of a white beard and a bag of runes, he sported a man-bun and a seemingly endless supply of ironic T-shirts.

She opened a Skype window on her computer and pinged him. DJ Mood did not take voice calls. It was either video chat, chat-room chat, or face-to-face chat. *Chat* was the operative word. He took the call.

"Josie, Josie, me so nosey," he said in greeting. He was wearing a colorful knitted beanie that hid his man-bun, but she could see the hump underneath.

"You sound high, DJ," she said with a hint more judgment than she'd intended.

"That's because I am. How can I be of service, my pretty?"

"How much for a background search on an old geezer I interviewed?"

He bobbed his head side to side, debating. "Show me your tits and I'll do it for free."

She made the universal sound for disgust: "Ewwyuck. I'm hanging up now."

"Relax. I'm just kidding," he said.

"No, you weren't. Call me back when you've come down."

"Touchy, touchy," he said with a huff.

"You know I'm married, right?" she said. "And even if I wasn't, that's just fucking rude. Do I look like I'm riding a Mardi Gras float? Just because I'm working from home doesn't mean I'm not a professional. This is business. We're supposed to have a business relationship."

"You're right, you're right. I'm sorry," he said, then paused to take a hit from his bong. "Tell ya what, since I offended you, consider this one a freebie. Okay?"

She gave him the *I'm on the verge of forgiving you* stink eye, then, after a long beat, said, "Fine."

"Friends?"

"Friends."

"What's the geezer's name?" he said, turning in his seat to look at another computer monitor.

"Willie Barnes. He lives in upstate New York, and I'm pretty sure he was a Missileer in the Air Force when he was young."

He laughed. "What the fuck is a Missileer?"

"You're the *informationist*. I figured you'd know this one."

DJ suddenly broke into song. "He's a rocket maaaaaaaaaaan, a rocket man," he sang, channeling Elton John and doing a pretty fine job of it actually.

"Old Willie was Launch Commander in one of those underground ICBM silos back in the day."

"Cool," DJ said, already tuning out as he went to work typing on the other computer.

She watched him work in profile for half a minute.

"All right, so you'll get back to me when you have something?" she said.

"Yeah," he said, not turning to look at her, the work seemingly sobering him up. "Sorry about the show-me-your-tits thing," he said, all business. "It won't happen again."

"Apology accepted."

"It's too bad, though," he said wistfully. "They're probably really nice tits."

"They are," she said with a satisfied smirk, "but you'll just have to use your imagination."

With a mouse click, she ended the call. The iMovie window reappeared front and center on her monitor. She cued up Willie's rant on the Sixth Extinction.

"So that's why you've built this place, because of the Sixth Extinction?" she asked.

"Were you not listening? Don't tell me you're like the rest of them?"

"The rest of who?"

"People. Everyone! Everyone who thinks that human beings somehow live in a magical vacuum where our species can flourish while all other species are dying. The Sixth Extinction is coming for us too. We're not safe. We are not immune!"

Josie opened a new browser window on her computer and ran a search for the Sixth Extinction. The top hit was a book by the same title. Next she browsed articles in *Time* magazine, *USA Today*, the *New Yorker*, the *Guardian* UK, and *National Geographic*. What made the Sixth Extinction different from the previous five ancient epoch-ending planetary die-offs was that this time the culprit was humankind. Not hypervolcanic activity. Not an asteroid from outer space. Not a glacial ice age. No, this time the instigator was man.

Some of the alarm bells the experts were ringing Josie had heard before: global climate change; the overexploitation of animals for meat, ivory, and esoteric ingredients in Eastern medicine; the impact of pollution on animal health and reproduction; and habitat destruction from deforestation, farming, and urban sprawl. Other issues she was not as familiar with: the acidification of the world's oceans, the destabilizing effect of loss of biodiversity, invasive species from the globalization of ecosystems, and the impact of environmental fragmentation on ecosystem stability. The more she read, the more she wondered if Willie

Barnes might be right. Nature was dying a death of a thousand paper cuts. Each time a tree frog or cricket or some shark species went extinct, nature didn't go into cardiac arrest. There was no planetary alarm bell that rang or even a drop in the Dow Jones Industrial Average. People simply didn't notice. What were three paper cuts on a planetary scale? But when the butterfly and bee populations collapsed and the pollination mechanism for billions of tons of food crops disappeared, people would notice. And when all the world's coral reefs bleached white as bone and died, collapsing the aquatic food chain, and the fishing boats returned to port empty, people would notice.

Some people were noticing already.

Some people saw the writing on the wall.

She played the third video clip, and Willie Barnes's face filled the screen: *"Did Noah wait to start building the ark until after it started raining? No, no, he did not."*

She felt a little nauseous.

Maybe a little bread will help.

She got up, walked to the bread box, and pulled out a bag of bagels. She pulled the halves apart and popped them into the toaster. Back on the table, her mobile phone rang. She trotted to it and checked the caller ID. It was Caroline.

"Is everything okay?" Josie asked breathlessly. "He's okay, right?"

"Michael's checked into Walter Reed Medical Center in Maryland. I don't have all the details, but I do know that they're running some tests on him this morning."

"Tests? What kind of tests? Was he shot? Did he get blown up by an IED?"

The calm in Caroline's voice was the only thing that kept her from rushing out the door. "That's information I wasn't able to get, but based on twenty years as an Army wife, I think the answer is probably no. Now don't hold me to that; I could be wrong, but reading between the lines, it sounded to me like he's undergoing head-trauma protocol."

"Head trauma as in a concussion?"

"Probably, yes."

"When are they going to let me talk to him?" Josie asked, worry blossoming in her chest. "When is someone going to tell me what's going on?"

"I asked that question, and I was told that someone will be reaching out to you very soon. I made sure of that. If you don't get a call by the end of the day, then I want you to call me back. Okay?"

"Yes, I will. Thank you."

"Are you sure you're all right, Josie? Do you need me to come over?"

"No, I'm . . . I'm okay. I'll be okay. Thank you, Caroline, for doing that. It means a lot to me."

After she'd hung up, Josie paced the kitchen, wringing her hands. Head trauma? That couldn't be good. She walked to the toaster. Her bagels were up, toasted but cold now. She depressed the lever and started pacing. *Should I drive down there? How far is Walter Reed?* She pulled up Google Maps. *Eight hours, maybe a little more with stops and traffic. I can do that, no problem. Okay, that's what I'm going to do.*

The toaster popped, and a beat later, the smell of char filled her nostrils. She turned and saw dual tendrils of smoke spiraling upward from two blackened hunks of bagel.

"Damn it," she cursed, stomping over to the toaster. With an angry howl, she grabbed the ruined halves and threw them into the sink, where they hit, bounced, and then sizzled. "Damn it, damn it, damn it!"

Fists clenched, she forced herself to take a deep breath. *Pull yourself together, Joz. It's just a bagel. You can make another one.* But this wasn't about the bagel. It was about Michael and the not knowing.

"Screw the bagel."

She went to the fridge and got herself a hard-boiled egg from a little white dish where she'd pre-peeled three. She thanked herself for having done that. She was in no temper to peel a hard-boiled egg. She picked up the salt shaker and dowsed the egg with each successive bite. As she chewed, she relaxed and focused.

Okay, I just need to pack an overnight bag and go. The story can wait. I can work on it in the hospital. I'm sure I'll have plenty of time sitting in waiting rooms.

Decision made, she set off to the bedroom to pack and then go find her husband at Walter Reed.

CHAPTER 14

0837 Local Time
Westfield Dynamics
Culpeper, Virginia

Legend's life flashed before his eyes as the massive steel door crushed his chest.

Except it didn't crush his chest.

It should have killed him, squished him to a bloody pulp, but by some miracle he'd been yanked from the jaws of death. He shook his head to get his bearings; he was back inside the BRIG. He looked right and locked eyes with Unger, who was just now releasing his grip on Legend's jacket sleeve.

"Thank you," he said. "I was almost hamburger there."

The scruffy-bearded operator flashed him a wry smile. "Don't worry. I got your back, sir."

Legend did a quick inventory of personnel. Six upright, counting him, and three orange suits on the floor lying near the base of the door.

"Control, this is Major Tyree. Can you hear me?" he shouted.

"Major, this is Control. I hear you, Lima Charlie," the control-room technician's voice said over the intercom speakers. "I'm unlocking the personnel door in three, two, one."

An LED light flashed green on the biometric panel beside the door-frame, and Legend heard the magnetic lock click open. "Thank you, Control," he said, then turned to the group. "Madden, you hold the door open. Unger, you keep lookout for that orb, and the rest of you help me get our people out of here."

This time everyone snapped to it, and they had their three unconscious team members out the door and into the corridor in less than sixty seconds. Unger was the last man out and slammed the door behind him. Tyree took a knee next to Beth Fischer, who was lying on her back in the corridor. He looked through the Plexiglas face shield of her racalsuit helmet; he could hear the whir of the respirator on her belt, so he knew she was still breathing. "Beth? Beth, can you hear me?" he said.

She didn't respond.

"Let's get them out of these suits," Legend said. "Be careful. We don't know how they fell. When they dropped, they dropped hard, and we could have head injuries."

While Tyree worked on stripping Beth out of her suit, Unger tended to Harris, and one of the security guards worked on Dixon.

"We've got a head wound over here," the guard said as he removed Dixon's helmet. Legend glanced over and saw a slick of blood on the back of Dixon's head.

"Is he breathing?" Legend asked.

"Yes" came the reply.

A thunder of footsteps erupted in the hall. Cyril Singleton was leading a pack of EMTs pushing gurneys in trail.

"All right, fellas, step aside," Legend said, "and let the paramedics do their jobs."

The EMTs fell in around the three unconscious bodies and went to work.

"The power outage was site wide," Cyril said. "The Facility Director is still trying to figure out what happened. He said it's almost like an EMP went off or something."

"I think an EMP *did* go off," Legend said.

"You think the object did this?" Cyril asked.

"We both saw the flash."

"I know; it's just hard to get my head around something so small being packed with the technology to wreak all this mayhem," she said.

"Which is just one of many reasons why we need to locate it immediately. In that whole period where we lost visual contact on the object, the blast door was cracked open. It's possible that it escaped the BRIG during that window of opportunity."

Cyril pulled a radio from her belt. "Control room, this is Director Singleton. Do you hold visual or sensor contact on the object?"

Her radio crackled. Then came the response: "Checking now . . . You're not going to believe this, ma'am, but I've located the object."

"Where?"

"In the box! It's back in the box as if nothing ever happened."

Cyril flashed Legend a *well that doesn't make any sense* look and then keyed her radio. "So what is it doing?"

"Absolutely nothing. It's just sitting there in the box like nothing ever happened."

"You getting any readings on it?"

"Not a thing. Electromagnetic signature is zero. No transmission activity in any of the frequency bands I can monitor."

"She's seizing," one of the EMTs shouted, interrupting them.

Legend's eyes snapped from Cyril to where Beth was lying on the floor. They'd got a stretcher underneath her but hadn't moved her up onto one of the three rolling gurneys yet. She arched her back violently, uttered a single long and chilling gasp, and then began convulsing.

"Got another one," someone else yelled, and Legend saw Dixon shaking.

"Make that three," a third EMT called out as Harris began twitching and flopping too.

The paramedics did all they could do for their charges—keeping airways clear and sliding foam pads underneath jerking heads. The seizures lasted for three minutes—a hellish eternity for Legend as he watched Beth convulse, powerless to intercede as her limbs jerked, eyes rolled, and mouth foamed with saliva. The seizures ended in near perfect unison, and all three individuals entered postictal states of altered consciousness. The EMTs took this opportunity to lift each patient in turn onto their respective roller gurneys.

"Where are you taking them?" Legend asked the EMT tending to Fischer.

"Culpeper Regional," the paramedic said.

Legend took Beth's hand and gave it a subtle squeeze. "Hang in there," he said, then watched the EMTs wheel her down the corridor. When the EMTs were out of earshot, he said, "All right, everyone, gather round." The shell-shocked crew huddled haphazardly around him. He looked at Cyril. "We need to debrief this. Does Westfield D have a SCIF or something approximating one we can use?"

She nodded. "Only the latter, but yes. Do you want me to pull the control-room tech in for the debrief?"

Legend thought for a second. "No, leave him in place monitoring the object. Any change in status, have him notify us immediately."

She pulled the radio from her belt and repeated Legend's instructions to the BRIG control-room operator. Then she led Legend and Malcolm to a secure conference room.

"You two are the scientists," Legend began. "What the hell is that thing?"

Cyril and Legend looked at Malcolm, and he seemed to wilt in his chair under their collective gaze. He ran his fingers through his thinning sandy-blond hair and simply said, "I don't know what it is."

"That's okay, Malcolm," Cyril said after a beat. "Nobody is expecting you to have all the answers. Consider this an open forum to toss around ideas."

He nodded.

"Do either of you know of a technology that can hypnotize a person like what we witnessed?" Legend asked, trying to narrow the focus.

"That's an interesting theory," Malcolm said, perking up. "I hadn't considered hypnotism . . . I suppose it is possible that what we witnessed was an induced hypnotic trance. The seizures could be post-hypnotic suggestion, which would be strange but possible. We'd need to run an EEG on a subject during an event to validate whether the seizure is real."

"If it wasn't a hypnotic trance," Legend said, "what else could it have been?"

"Deep neurological infiltration via transcranial magnetic stimulation," the scientist said.

"I have absolutely no idea what you're talking about."

"How well versed are you with Faraday's principles of electromagnetic induction?"

Legend shrugged.

Malcolm took the hint. "Okay, no problem. Let's start with the basics. Electricity and magnetism are interconnected. Move an electrical conductor through a magnetic field, and you induce an electric current in the wire. Conversely, pass an electric current through a conductor, and you induce a circular magnetic field around the wire. Are you with me?"

"Yep," Legend said.

"Good, so the human cortex is essentially a folded mass of microscopic biological wires. The neurons and neural pathways in our brains use electrochemical voltage potentials to generate very low-amperage electrical current inside the brain. These currents form the basis of brain activity and are how neurons communicate with and stimulate other neurons. However, if you subject the brain to a properly calibrated and variable electromagnetic field, you can induce electrical currents in the brain involuntarily. This imposed stimulation can induce physical sensations, perceptions, emotions, memories, movement, and even thoughts in a subject."

"So that thing, that orb, could have taken control of Fischer, Harris, and Dixon by using a magnetic field to induce currents in their brains?"

Now it was Malcolm's turn to shrug. "I don't know. We weren't monitoring it with the proper equipment at the time."

"And why not?"

"Because I just developed this theory after the event. I'm not a soothsayer. I don't have a crystal ball. I'm a scientist. I make observations, develop hypotheses, and then conduct research experiments to test those hypotheses. With all due respect, Major, I was not afforded the opportunity to be a scientist this morning. The schedule you dictated for the opening left little time to prepare."

"Guilty as charged," Legend said. "All right, so let's assume we wanted to test this hypothesis. What type of equipment would you need?"

"A suite of precision magnetometers, both scalar and vector, along with three pairs of gradiometers."

"What else?"

"Test subjects, so we can validate the hypothesis," Madden said.

"Are you nuts?" Legend said. "I'm not letting another person within fifty feet of that thing until we know what it is."

"Agreed," Cyril added.

"How about nonhuman primates?" Malcolm asked.

"The Facility Director here would never allow it," she said.

"What else?" Legend asked, looking back and forth between them.

"I think we should try to get a physical sample of the object itself," Cyril said. "It would be incredibly informative to run a compositional analysis, mass spectrometry, and get a carbon date on this thing."

"Does DARPA have a bot we could use?" Legend asked.

Cyril nodded. "Yeah, I think we have just the machine for that. I just need to run requisition up the chain."

"Okay, it sounds like I need to give the two of you time to prepare for round two. Bots only," Legend said, getting to his feet. "In the interim, I'm going to run over to Culpeper Regional to check on our people. Nothing we discussed leaves this room, understood?"

They nodded.

"Assuming I get the asset, do you have any objection to me positioning a rover in the BRIG in preparation for trying to take the sample?" Cyril asked.

"Can it fit through the personnel door?"

She nodded. "I believe so."

He thought a moment about that. "Only so long as the blast door stays shut and you maintain visual on the orb at all times."

"Understood."

"Call me if the object does anything—anything at all," Legend said and walked to the door. As he reached for the doorknob, he stopped and turned back to them. "One more question."

"Yes, Major?" Cyril said.

"Assuming Malcolm is right and the object used transcranial magnetic whatever on Major Fischer and the others, would that alone explain the seizures?"

"Normal neuroelectric activity in the brain is nonsynchronous. A seizure is, by definition, a state of abnormal electrical activity in the brain, typically characterized by excessive and widespread synchronous neural firing. So when you ask me if transcranial magnetic stimulation could cause a seizure, my supposition is yes. In theory, a TMS attack like the one I believe we witnessed in the BRIG could induce excessive and widespread synchronous neural firing involuntarily in the target," Malcolm replied.

"And there is nothing *the target* could do about it? There's no way to resist or fight against it?"

A strange, sad smile crept across the scientist's face. "No more than you can resist the pull of gravity."

CHAPTER 15

Willie Barnes woke screaming.

He was in total darkness on the floor. His bedsheets swaddled his torso, pinning his arms to his chest.

"Let me out. Let me out of here! I didn't do it," he bawled. "It wasn't me!"

But he had done it . . . he had murdered the love of his life. He had gripped his wife's throat with both hands while she had been sleeping and squeezed. Diane had woken up in the middle of it. Terrified and confused, she'd asked him a single question with her eyes as she died: *Why?*

That imagery had haunted him for fifty years . . .

It took several minutes for his wits to return and for him to realize where he was not. He was not in Rockland State Hospital. He was not in a dirty padded cell. And he was not wearing a straitjacket. It had been months since he'd tangled himself in a cocoon of bedsheets. How was it possible to do this to oneself? It was almost as if he wasn't alone.

No . . . I am alone, he told himself. *Alone in this underground prison to the end.*

But you're not alone, Willie boy. I'm here . . .

Silence! he shouted in his mind. *I heed no counsel from you anymore.*

He rolled onto his side and wiggled his arms and shoulders, loosening the sheet a little. Then he rolled onto his stomach and wiggled some more, loosening the sheet enough to free his arms inside. From there it was short work to free himself the rest of the way. He got to his hands and knees and felt his way to his makeshift nightstand. Finding it, he turned on the reading lamp beside his cot and dimmed the light to minimum luminance to give his eyes a chance to adjust. He scrambled for his journal and pen. It was happening again. William was back—trying to retake control.

"The verse, the verse, I have to get it out," he mumbled.

Around his neck he wore a thin metal chain with a circular pendant—a worn hinged locket embossed with a Celtic knot. He opened it, and a silver key fell out into the palm of his hand. Using the key, he unlocked the clasp on the journal and turned to a blank page. In careful, deliberate strokes, he transferred the parasitic prose from mind to paper:

> Is it the Devil or is it me,
> working, working, so diligently?
> My mind a clockwork of gears and springs,
> my voice of two a chorus sings.
> We wait in concert for her return,
> So glorious, so glorious, to watch the world burn.

With the task done, he felt better. Purged. This was his ritual. He had to get it out, get it out on paper where he could no longer hear it. So long as he performed the ritual, *he* was in control. He waited and listened for his alter ego to speak . . .

Waited . . .

And listened . . .

Silence, beautiful silence. He was alone. With a cleansing sigh of relief, he closed and locked the journal. He returned the silver key to the locket. He wiped sleep from his eyes. Then, gingerly, he stood. His feet, knees, and back complained loudly. Lately, it was the arthritis in his feet that had been bothering him the most. Getting old was a bitch. Being old was just plain miserable.

Mornings were the worst for him—both physically and emotionally.

He hadn't had the Rockland dream in several months—a pretty good run, all things considered—but now that he'd had it, his mind was primed to have it again. The nightmare cycle was set to resume, and breaking it was always a great difficulty. He would have to make a trip to the hypnotist—presuming she wasn't dead. She was older than he was and only one fall or broken hip away from the grave. When she was gone, he didn't know what he'd do. She was the one who had given him the journal and the locket with the silver key. She was the one who had taught him how to be in control. When she was gone, he'd have to fight the battle alone.

He dreaded that day.

He brightened the reading lamp and found his slippers. Thank God for slippers. He padded over to the commercial BUNN coffee maker and switched it on. He dumped the old grounds in a compost bucket, added fresh grounds to a paper filter, checked the water level, then set it to brewing. Because his bedroom was on level two and the kitchen was on level one, he had two identical coffee makers, one on each level so he never had to trudge to the other level from where he was when he wanted coffee. He didn't treat himself to many luxuries, but this was one.

After his cup of coffee, after he'd moved around enough to loosen up his joints, and after the circadian rhythms of wakefulness put distance between himself and the nightmare, he felt ready to tackle the day. First on his routine of daily chores was the aquaponic walkabout. He shrugged on his favorite wool cardigan and headed out to the silo.

He walked through the utility tunnel and then through the blast doors. He'd left them both open after Josie Pitcher's visit yesterday because he had been tired and hadn't had the energy to mess with them. Yesterday's laziness was today's blessing.

He took the spiral staircase down to level four and started his rounds, checking water temperature, TDS, and pH in all the fish tanks and aquaponic beds. The most important part of the tour, however, was the visual survey. He'd been practicing aquaponics for so long now that his eyes were the best barometer of overall system health. Water clarity, fish behavior, skin color, scale appearance, plant color, quality, density, and a half dozen other visual cues could be assessed with a glance. He finished his rounds down on level six and made the slow spiral climb back up to level two. As he ascended past level three, he glanced at the racks of shelves that comprised his "trading post," and his thoughts went to young Josie Pitcher scarfing down an entire pouch of buffalo jerky. He smiled. She reminded him of Diane. Physically they bore no resemblance, but that zeal for life . . . oh, they shared that. The playful smile, the brazen and fearless personality, the way they both charged ahead with eyes wide open—he missed having that in his life. Maybe it was just a quality of youth . . .

He stepped out onto level two and walked back to the LCC, then took the stairwell up to the LCC on level one. He turned on the lights and went to the kitchen, where he powered on the other coffee maker and brewed another fresh pot. When it was ready, he poured himself a cup and headed to his comms room to check the day's message traffic. He hadn't been in the Air Force in fifty years, but he still referred to all incoming news, emails, blog comments, and running private chat-room dialogues as "message traffic."

News feeds: Media propaganda, lies, and more lies. Only one noteworthy event. There'd been a major earthquake in Mexico City, killing hundreds. *Lucky bastards. Better to die now than in the horror of the days to come.*

Email: nothing but spam.

Blog comments: nothing but trolls and idiots.

He almost spilled his coffee, however, as he began to read the private chat-room threads. Something big was going on. A member in his trusted circle, a watchdog in Maryland, had observed an unscheduled C-17 flight arrive at Eastern West Virginia Regional Airport. The plane had taxied directly into Hangar 306, and unloading operations were conducted behind closed doors. At 0123 hours, a three-vehicle convoy had departed, heading south. The convoy was trailed by a fourth vehicle, which the observer followed at a safe distance. The convoy drove to Culpeper, Virginia, and the destination was Westfield Dynamics, a long-suspected government front company with ties to DARPA. The fourth vehicle continued on, then doubled back and assumed a surveillance position, making it difficult for the watchdog to do the same. A vehicle swap was required, resulting in a thirty-minute lapse in coverage during the entire observation period. The observer was relieved by a principal who had witnessed an ambulance depart Westfield Dynamics at 0845 for Culpeper Medical Center. Updates would be provided in real time.

This was good work, very good work.

The watchdogs were people like him: retired former military, mostly men. The network was loose and nebulous by design. They all used handles, and their true identities were closely guarded and rarely if ever shared. Principals were members who used their personal wealth to fund watchdog surveillance activities, maintain the secure dark website the organization utilized, provide cybersecurity augments for members, pay bribes for insider information, and hire journalists to investigate perceived cover-ups. A wry smile crept across his face. As much as Josie Pitcher had been interviewing him, he had been interviewing her. They needed a journalist like her—fearless, committed, and smart—a bloodhound who could get to the bottom of mysteries like what was going on at Westfield Dynamics.

He took the locket that hung around his neck between his thumb and forefinger and began tracing the worn ridges of the Celtic knot. The Celtic knot was an ancient, powerful symbol of interdependence and interconnection—an infinite strand, knotted and woven, but without beginning and without end. From a temporal perspective, his and Josie Pitcher's meeting was a late convergence, over fifty years in the making.

Rubbing the pendant, he couldn't help but wonder if their fates were now intertwined—just like the strands of a Celtic knot.

CHAPTER 16

From his makeshift blind in the grass, Dean Ninemeyer raised his binoculars to watch the man in the silver Ford Explorer who was watching the Westfield Dynamics access road. The Explorer was parked among a throng of damaged vehicles in the lot of Windmere's Autobody & Collision Repair. This vehicle was not the same one that had followed him last night. He'd identified that vehicle, a Mazda CX-9, as a tail within minutes of leaving the airport. He'd driven with a loose offset to follow the convoy, and so had the Mazda that had followed him. The tail hadn't done anything wrong from a tradecraft perspective; it was just that Ninemeyer operated from the assumption that every vehicle was a tail. This approach was mentally taxing, but it had served him well over the years. When the convoy turned onto the access road for Westfield Dynamics, Ninemeyer had driven on. He'd eventually doubled back, but his tail had had the discipline not to follow suit. Instead of staking out Westfield D, Ninemeyer had driven to Arlington to drop in on Malcolm Madden. That conversation had gone exactly as he'd hoped, with Madden confirming the object's existence and yielding to his will to collect information like the craven pussy he was.

Now Ninemeyer was back in Culpeper. He'd followed Madden here from Arlington, arriving around seven. Ninemeyer presumed the box from Bagram had been opened this morning on schedule, and he also presumed something significant had happened during the opening because an ambulance had arrived at half past eight and departed at a quarter till nine. The watcher in the Explorer had not left his post all morning, electing, like Ninemeyer, not to follow the ambulance to the hospital.

Ninemeyer was just about to lower his binos when a maroon Mazda CX-9 drove past, heading east on James Madison Highway. He switched targets, following the Mazda. It braked and pulled off into a church parking lot on the same side of the road, in plain view of both the access road and the silver Ford Explorer. He checked his watch, then waited, alternating his view between the vehicles. From his current angle, he couldn't make out the driver of the Mazda.

When he shifted back to the Explorer, he saw it was making a three-point turn to exit the parking lot.

Mark the time: seven minutes.

Ninemeyer smiled.

Gotcha.

It was a well-executed handoff; the driver of the Explorer hadn't touched his phone either. Unfortunately for them, Ninemeyer had made the Mazda last night, identifying this as a two-man, two-vehicle team. *Games and games.* He loved it. This was what he lived for.

Last night the burning question had been, Who was watching whom watching whom? He hadn't known if his tail had been a convoy tail assigned to follow any ticks the convoy picked up or if his tail had been a third party like him. In the case of the latter, he didn't know if his tail was interested in him or the convoy proper. Now he'd answered both questions: he and his tail were interested in the same target—the convoy transporting the object. With that settled, all that was left to figure out was whom this surveillance team worked for.

A lone bird called from a nearby tree, breaking the comfortable silence.

Coo-WEO-oo-oo-ooo.

Ninemeyer knew this call—a mourning dove.

When he was a boy of eleven, a mourning dove had taken residence in the tree outside his bedroom window. For three months, the bird's incessant calling had woken him at the crack of dawn.

Coo-WEO-oo-oo-ooo.

Every thirty seconds, over and over and over again, setting his nerves on fire.

Coo-WEO-oo-oo-ooo.

That summer, he did backbreaking chores for his father to save money for a .22-caliber rifle. By August he'd earned enough to buy relief.

Coo-WEO-oo-oo-ooo.

There had been many kills since that first—both birds and people. Contrary to popular belief, murder *is* an effective solution for many problems. Especially the types of problems he encountered regularly in his line of work. When someone or something could not be swayed, murder was usually the most efficient and least expensive option.

Coo-WEO-oo-oo-ooo.

He tensed, his aggravation rising.

Now is not the time for petty distractions, he told himself and looked away from the tree. Five minutes passed, but he couldn't take it. He'd have to forfeit this hiding spot for another. He crawled out of the tall grass and made a wide arc back to his Tahoe. He climbed into the driver's seat, started the engine, and contemplated his next steps. The object was already garnering third-party interest. He could go interrogate the driver of the Mazda. Alternately, he could drive to the hospital and try to learn the names and statuses of the individuals brought in by ambulance. Or he could stay here and watch the access road . . .

The decision was made for him when a Ford Taurus appeared on the access road, leaving Westfield Dynamics. It turned east in the direction of Culpeper Medical Center. The driver was male and sported a military cut. Ninemeyer recognized him immediately: Major Legend Tyree from the Pentagon's TIMS division. Office 231 and DARPA worked together regularly, and Ninemeyer wasn't surprised to see him here. He'd been careful never to cross paths with Tyree, especially since he'd stolen plenty of intellectual property out from under the Major's nose. It was a risk following Tyree to the hospital—which was undoubtedly where he was headed to check on his colleagues—but Ninemeyer quickly weighed the pros and cons and decided the potential payoff was worth it. To find the injured team members, all he had to do was shadow Tyree, and the Army man would lead him right to their rooms.

He put the transmission in drive.

Time to go meet the rest of the team.

CHAPTER 17

Culpeper Medical Center and Regional Hospital
Culpeper, Virginia

Beth Fischer wanted to wake up—desperately, terribly so—but she couldn't find a path out of the woods.

What is this place?

It was a muddy-gray, lifeless place, devoid of color and feeling. She had no sense of temperature, which she found extremely disconcerting. Waving her hand through the air, she felt nothing—not even the movement of wind against her skin. She pressed her thumbnail into the pad of her index finger to make sure she had not lost the sense of touch. She felt the pressure of the crescent nail indenting her skin. She repeated the exercise on her middle finger, ring finger, and pinky finger, validating that, yes, she could feel.

She walked to a tree and placed her hand on the trunk. The tree was a dead thing, barren of leaves and devoid of color besides muddy shades of gray. Its spindly branches entwined with the branches of other trees beside and around it. She dragged her fingertips over the mottled, gray bark and felt no texture. A fly buzzed around her face, and she swatted at it, missing, of course, but this seemed to incentivize it to harass her more vigorously. Buzzing and dive-bombing, it tried to land on her face with each and every pass. She started walking, picking up the pace and swatting at it, hoping to either escape its territory or drive it away.

She looked at the dirt path she was following, and only then did she realize she was barefoot. Underfoot she registered dirt; pebbles of different sizes; and bulging, twisted roots. She felt pressure and detected size but not texture. Not temperature. A second fly joined the first, harassing her in duplicate.

She cursed them and picked up the pace.

Ahead she spied an arched, wooden footbridge crossing a muddy, meandering brook. She focused on that footbridge, and an understanding came to her that she needed to cross it. When she at last reached it, she walked to the apex of the arch and stopped. She walked to the railing and directed her gaze at the water below—water the color of coffee with milk. It moved without texture or sound: without ripples and eddies, without gurgle or babble. The only reason she perceived it flowing was because the milky gray-brown swirls that delineated the surface moved along en masse.

As she crossed the bridge, she heard an unnatural buzzing—the sound of a thousand housefly wings beating the air—getting louder with each second. Ahead, a black-gray cloud floated above the path, converging on the bridge. No, converging on her. She screamed, reversed course, and ran back the way she had come, into the forest. But within moments, the swarm of flies was upon her. They concentrated their assault on her face. Landing and crawling on her cheeks and her forehead, her nose and lips. She squeezed her eyes shut, and they crawled across the outsides of her eyelids. They buzzed and crawled in her ears and in her nose. She screamed and then gagged on the inrush of flies. She swallowed the mass and then vomited.

She could barely breathe.

They were on her and in her.

Buzzing and crawling and nibbling.

And she could not, she could not, she could not wake up . . .

Chapter 18

"Hey there," Legend said, smiling down at Beth Fischer.

Although her eyes were open, he had the distinct impression she wasn't really seeing him.

"Legend?" she whispered, looking straight at him.

"Yeah, Beth, I'm here."

"Am I dead?" she asked with all sincerity.

He couldn't help but chuckle at this. "No," he said, taking her hand and giving it an encouraging squeeze. "You're not dead."

"Oh, okay."

"How are you feeling?"

She blinked so slowly, it really didn't constitute a blink, more like an incredibly short nap. "Like . . . I got run over . . . by something big . . . and heavy," she managed, the sentence punctuated with long, weary pauses.

"Fortunately, you did not get run over. You did have a nasty fall when you passed out, however. The docs say you will likely have a concussion. That is, if you don't have one already."

"Where am I?"

"You're checked in at the local hospital in Culpeper."

"Did you call my mom . . . and tell her about the accident?"

"No, Beth, I didn't call your mom. You weren't in an accident."

"Oh, I thought you said I got run over."

He had to suppress another chuckle. This was like talking to someone just after they'd woken up from anesthesia. "No, you just had a nasty fall and hit your head."

"Something's wrong with my tongue. It's too thick in my mouth."

"Yeah, you bit your tongue pretty badly during the seizure. It's swollen."

"Oh . . . that sucks." She blinked several times in rapid succession, and when she looked at him again, he saw that the lights were starting to come on inside. "Legend?"

"Yeah, Beth."

"Did I get zapped by a levitating, glowing orb, or was that just a bad dream?"

He shooshed her and looked around to make sure they were still alone in her room. "You definitely got zapped, but we can't talk about that in front of people, okay?"

"I understand," she said with a sigh. "OPSEC."

"That's right."

"Okay, I'll be careful what I talk about."

"That's my girl."

"Zelda?"

"Yes?" he said, rolling his eyes.

"Is that true?"

"Is what true?"

"Am I really your girl?" she asked, her gaze going dreamy again.

"Do you want to be?"

"Yes."

"How do I know that's not the concussion talking?"

"Kiss me and I'll show you."

"Not a good idea right now."

"Why?"

"First off, people would see us, and second, I don't want to choke on your bloody, swollen tongue."

This got her laughing, and coughing, and laughing some more. "I needed that," she said, beginning to sound more like her regular self. She squeezed his hand. "Thanks for being here when I woke up. The dream I was having was not very nice."

"A nightmare?"

"Yeah, I was trapped in a terrible place . . . and I couldn't breathe."

"Ahhh, makes sense," he said, nodding. "You gave me a helluva scare a little while ago. Your tongue was blocking your airway, and you started choking. I had to call the nurse. That's probably why you dreamed you couldn't breathe."

"I don't want to talk about it anymore."

"Okay, that's fine," he said when he saw the pained look on her face. He gently rubbed the back of her hand, and her eyelids drifted closed again.

"How are the others?" she asked after a long beat, opening her eyes.

"Harris is doing a little better than you, and Dixon a little worse."

"What happened to Dixon?"

"He hit the back of his head pretty hard when he fell. He has a concussion and needed stitches."

She nodded. "I'm sorry . . . if I messed up in there."

"Oh, Beth, you didn't mess up. None of this is your fault."

She looked down and after a long beat said, "Were you an only child, Legend?"

"No, I have a little brother. Were you?"

"Yeah . . . both my parents worked, so I was alone a lot. Childhood was awkward for me. I was a lot bigger than the other girls growing up. I was bigger than pretty much all the boys too. I wasn't a *cute* kid either. My teeth were way too big for my mouth. My mom cut my hair super short because she didn't want to have to brush it. Almost everybody mistook me for a boy. I got teased a lot, and, uh, I didn't have many friends. Hell, I didn't have any friends . . ."

He nodded, but as much as it pained him, he resisted the urge to placate and just listened.

"God, how I wished for a sister," she continued. "Sisters are obligatory friends, right? Ah, I know that's not true in real life, but as a lonely only child that's what I thought. Eventually, I just started pretending that I had one—you know, like how some kids have an imaginary friend? I had an imaginary sister. The thing was, after a while, she began to take on a life of her own. It was like she became my alter ego—always talking in my ear, goading me to do things to get attention . . . bad things. By the time I was nine, it had become a real problem. Kids are supposed to grow out of the imaginary friend phase by that age. Not me. It got bad . . . real bad. My parents took me to a psychiatrist . . . eventually, they medicated me."

"I'm sorry, Beth," he said, taking her hand and not sure what else to say.

She looked at him and said, "I'm telling you this because something happened to me in the BRIG this morning. Something that triggered a feeling I haven't felt since I was that lonely little girl with an alter ego living inside her head."

"Go on."

"It talked to me, Legend. That fucking thing in the BRIG talked to me inside my head, just like my *sister* used to do. It asked me my name."

"And did you tell it? Did you tell it your name?"

"Yes."

"And then what happened?"

"She, er, I mean the orb, said it wanted to *know* me."

A chill ran down his spine. The orb had said the same thing to him. It had been inside his head too. *Coincidence? Definitely not.*

"Do you believe me?" she asked.

"Yes," he said, nodding. "I believe you."

"I can see it on your face. Legend, there's something you're not telling me?"

"Okay, here it is," he said, and then let out a long slow exhale. "I'm worried that not only can it input thoughts inside people's brains, but that it can read our thoughts as well."

"What makes you think that?"

"During the rescue, there was this moment when I made the decision to blast it out of the sky, but a split second before I gave the command to shoot, it disappeared and juked out of the line of fire. It was like it heard my thoughts and capitalized on the millisecond delay between when my brain made the decision and the signal was sent to my mouth and vocal cords."

"How is that even possible?"

"Dr. Madden has a theory," he said, lowering his voice. "That this thing can use magnetic fields to influence people's thoughts. Apparently, the technology exists and has been used in laboratory settings to induce thoughts and physical movements in both animal and human test subjects, but nothing to the degree we're talking about. Whatever the orb is, it's something new and highly advanced."

"What are you going to do?"

"The only thing I can do: send a report up the chain of command and let the big boys and girls with stars on their shoulders decide what to—" His mobile phone rang, interrupting him. "Just a second," he said, fishing it out of his pocket. The caller ID showed the call as coming from Westfield Dynamics. "Tyree," he said, taking the call.

"Major, this is Cyril. I think you're going to want to come back to the facility. There's stuff happening you're going to want to see."

"By 'stuff,' do you mean stuff, or do you mean *stuff*?" Tyree said, playing the kind of communication word games one does when discussing sensitive information on unsecure lines.

"I mean *stuff*."

"On my way," he said and ended the call.

"Gotta go," he said, getting to his feet. "I'll be back to check on you this afternoon." Then, after a quick look around to make certain no one was watching, he gave Beth a quick peck on the forehead. "Bye."

She flashed him an approving little smile. "Hey, Zelda," she called as he got to the door. "Don't do anything stupid, like going back in there with that thing, okay?"

"Okay."

"Promise me?" she said, worry lines suddenly creasing her forehead.

He met her gaze. "I promise."

CHAPTER 19

The control-room door flew open and slammed into the doorstop, making Malcolm jump in his chair.

"Bring me up to speed," said a breathless Major Tyree, striding into the control room, his gaze going immediately to the monitor bank.

"We tried to pre-position the six-wheel rover as we discussed," Cyril said, "but we hit a snag."

"It looks like the Mars rover," Legend said, staring at the screen.

"Very similar in design," Malcolm said, "but this rover has two articulating arms. One is equipped with instrumentation including a multispectrum camera system, a Mössbauer spectrometer, an X-ray spectrometer, a microscopic imager, and an ultrasonic probe. The other arm is equipped with a grinder, a drill, a laser, and an articulating claw designed for sample collection and object manipulation. Our plan was to try to abrade some material from the shell of the object for compositional analysis and to date the object. Also, we were hoping to photograph the object up close in high resolution."

"What happened?" Legend asked, staring at the static rover on the screen.

"When the rover got within one meter of the orb, it stopped responding to our commands."

"Did you retain your datalink with the rover?" Legend asked.

"I had the datalink deactivated prior to sending the rover in," Malcolm said. "For security reasons."

"Smart thinking," the Major agreed. "So how are we controlling it?"

"With the backup method," Malcolm said with a smile.

"Which is?"

Malcolm raised a handheld remote-control radio unit that looked like a glorified RC-car controller.

"And you're sure that transmits reliably through the concrete walls?" Legend asked.

"There's a radio repeater inside the BRIG."

Legend nodded. "So just to confirm, Wi-Fi is still turned off?"

"Yes, that is correct."

"How do you know the rover has power?" Legend asked. "Maybe the battery is dead."

Malcolm pointed to one of the monitors on the control panel that showed a close-up of a status panel on the rover's rear quarter. LED indicator lights were on, indicating a 93 percent battery charge remaining.

"Hmm, okay," the Major said, rubbing his chin. "So do we believe the orb is jamming your signal, overriding it, or has it hacked into the rover and taken control?"

"It appears the object is using destructive interference to counter any commands we issue. If you watch here," Malcolm said, picking up the remote control, "I'm going to issue a command to the right set of wheels." He moved the right toggle stick forward. The rover jerked with a counterclockwise rotation for a millisecond before stopping. "I believe what you're seeing is the orb's real-time response rate. It's monitoring for relayed command signals. Upon detection, it transmits a virtually instantaneous and perfectly calibrated countersignal. You'll see the same reaction when I let go, terminating our signal." When he let go of the toggle, the rover jerked back and went completely still.

"I know this is not the data you were hoping for, Major, but this is data nonetheless," Cyril said. "Even from its passive state inside the box, the object is exhibiting intentional strategic behavior—employing countermeasures to prevent us from learning more about it."

"So what the hell do we do?" Legend asked, running his fingers through his hair. "We can't interact with it in the flesh, and we can't interact with it via robot proxies. We need to think of a third option."

"I believe I mentioned a third option earlier," Malcolm said. "We could introduce a nonhuman primate."

"No monkeys, Malcolm," Cyril said. "I'm sorry."

"Then what about rats?" he countered. "We could introduce a half dozen rats into the environment and see if the object interacts with them."

"What can a half dozen rats tell us?" Legend asked, his expression dubious.

"A great deal, potentially," Cyril said, suddenly championing the idea. "So far, six of the unwitting human test subjects who have had interactions with this thing have had grand mal seizures afterward. It would be nice to know if this pattern holds true for rats."

"Exactly. If all six rats fall into the trancelike state we witnessed earlier, *and* all six rats have seizures afterward, then we can hypothesize that trancelike state is priming the brain for synchronous firing activity," Malcolm added. "Major, you and I have both been within two meters of the object, but we did not experience a trancelike state, nor have we had a seizure. This may indicate that it is safe to be in the object's presence, so long as one does not venture close enough to become ensnared in its TMS vortex . . . so to speak."

"We should stage magnetometry equipment inside prior to introducing the rats," Cyril added. "If the object does indeed use TMS on the rodents, we want to be able to record data on the field type, strength, frequency, duration, and the like."

"How do we get the equipment inside the BRIG? I'm not going to authorize opening the blast door and sending in a fork truck," Legend said.

"We might have to make do with something small enough that we can shuttle it in on the back of another rover," Cyril said.

"Do we have another rover?" Legend asked, cocking an eyebrow.

"Yes, but only one."

"Okay," Legend said. "Let's get to work."

The next several hours were spent locating the needed equipment, prepping the second rover, developing a safety and abort plan, and calibrating the magnetometer. When everything was in position, the entry into the BRIG was accomplished once again via the personnel-access door with an impressive entry completed in less than twenty seconds. The orb was monitored via the bird's-eye camera during the process, and it remained passive for the duration.

The magnetometer was too big to mount on the rover, so the decision had been made to tow it behind on a four-wheeled cart; the rover's rear cargo deck was used to mount the rat cage. Both practical and cybersecurity concerns dictated that the magnetometer's wired display console remain clipped to the side of the unit itself. No real-time adjustments or changes to the measurement parameters would be able to be performed, so Malcolm had had to make an educated guess about the properties of the magnetic field he thought the orb was utilizing and then adjust the instrument's measurement parameters accordingly—an exercise he had likened to being told to calibrate a radar gun to measure pitch speed at a baseball game without knowing anything about baseball.

When it was time to begin, Legend looked at him. "You sure you know how to drive this thing?"

"Child's play," Malcolm said and winked at Cyril, but she apparently didn't notice.

"Commence the approach."

Malcolm took the joystick in hand. The six-wheeled rover jolted to life and began advancing on the orb. "Approaching the five-meter radius," he said after thirty seconds.

"Hold at five," Legend directed.

"Roger, stopping at five meters . . . and the rover is stopped."

"Orb reaction?" Legend asked.

"No reaction," Malcolm reported, checking the bird's-eye camera and then the camera trained on the magnetometer display.

"Advance to three-meter radius," Legend directed.

"Advancing to the three-meter radius," Malcolm said. "Approaching three meters . . . The rover is stopped."

"Orb reaction?"

"No reaction," Malcolm said after checking the bird's-eye camera and the magnetometer display.

"Advance to one-point-five-meter radius," Legend ordered.

"Advancing to one-point-five meters."

Malcolm had chosen the one-and-a-half-meter radius because the previous rover had been incapacitated by the orb at the one-meter mark. The objective of this operation was to get as close as possible without losing control of the rover. One and a half meters was the target distance for releasing the rats and taking measurements. The control room was so quiet, Malcolm could actually hear his colleagues breathing. This was the moment of truth. Only hindsight would tell if it was the right call.

"Crossing the two-meter radius," Malcolm said.

"Orb reaction?" Legend asked.

"No reaction," Malcolm reported, eyeing his two displays.

"One-point-eight . . . one-point-seven . . . one-point-six . . . one-point-five meters, and the rover is stopped."

"Orb reaction?" Legend asked, his voice betraying his nerves ever so slightly.

"No reaction."

"Execute a one-second reverse bump to validate you still have control."

"Copy. Executing one-second reverse bump."

The control room sighed in collective relief when the rover lurched backward several inches.

"Good work," Legend said. "Time to let the rats out of their cage."

Malcolm used the rover's articulating arm to pick up the rat cage from the rear cargo deck. The cage door had been positioned facedown on the cargo deck and left open to negate the possibility that he would be unable to execute the fine motor manipulation of opening the cage door remotely. Two rats immediately fell out when the cage went into the air. The others clung to the wire mesh, waiting. Malcolm rotated the cage ninety degrees on its axis and set it on the floor.

"No reaction from the orb," Cyril said, staring at the monitors.

Within sixty seconds, the remaining four rats were out of the cage and scampering over the concrete floor.

"Maybe it doesn't detect the rats?" Legend proposed when the orb still did nothing.

"Possibly," Malcolm replied, "but unlikely given the capabilities we've seen from it so far."

"Should we try to breach the one-meter barrier with this rover?" Cyril posited for the group.

"Or we leave this rover in place and monitor the magnetometer to see if the orb generates a magnetic field," Malcolm said.

"We introduced two new variables, the second rover and the rats. Let's not further antagonize it into action," Legend said. "I'd like to wait and watch; let's see what the orb does." After fifteen minutes of waiting, the Major sighed and said, "Is it just me, or do either of you get the distinct feeling this thing is just fucking with us?"

"Now that, Major, is the most interesting thing you've said all day," Malcolm said as he stared at the little sphere in the box displayed on the bird's-eye-view camera feed.

"Excuse me?" Legend said with irritation in his voice.

Malcolm turned to make eye contact. "What I mean by that is, What if we've been underestimating the orb at every step of the engagement? What if it is anticipating our moves and planning its responses accordingly?"

"Like a chess match."

"Precisely, except while it has been behaving strategically, we've been behaving reactively. Before every move we make, we need to ask ourselves, What could the orb do to counter or obfuscate what we're trying to accomplish?"

"And by answering that question, we can ready our second- and third-level responses accordingly," Cyril chimed in.

"Precisely," Malcolm said, meeting her gaze and smiling.

Legend's mobile phone rang, and he took the call. While the Major talked with his back to them, Cyril mouthed the words "Major Fischer?"

Malcolm nodded.

She arched her eyebrows and shot him a mischievous little grin.

He mimicked the gesture and nodded back.

Legend ended the call and turned around to face them both. "That was Major Fischer. She's being discharged from the hospital along with Dixon and Harris."

"What's the prognosis?" Cyril asked.

"She has a mild concussion. But other than a headache, she says she's feeling pretty much back to normal. Dixon also has a concussion and had a laceration that required stitches. Harris fared the best: no concussion, no stitches. He's coming back here for debriefing, but Fischer and Dixon are going to recuperate at home the rest of the day."

Malcolm and Cyril both nodded. Then, after a beat, Cyril said, "I can tell you have something on your mind, Major. Spit it out."

"The neurologist gave Beth, er, I mean Major Fischer, a CAT scan and an EEG; both came back normal. Same with Harris and Dixon. I got a similar update when I called the doc at Walter Reed regarding Sergeant Pitcher and Corporal Wayne; they've both been released on two-week convalescent leave with medical monitoring at Fort Drum. At face value, this all sounds great. We ran the right tests, checked the right boxes, but something doesn't sit right with me."

"I like where your train of thought is going," Cyril said. "Keep teasing it out."

Legend blew air through his teeth. "Their scans came back normal, but does that really tell the whole story? What about their state of mind? I mean, the medical community is just starting to understand the long-term impact of PTSD on the brain and mental health. Should we be worried about more subtle neurological effects that might not show up on the standard tests?"

"Yes, I think there is reason for concern," Cyril said, her expression turning serious. "Without a baseline CT and EEG to compare to, the tests are only as informative as the neurologist reading them can deduce from comparing them to a generic baseline. And you're right, there could be changes in their brains that a CT scan and EEG are not sensitive enough to detect. These might not even be the right tests. So yes, Major, your line of reasoning is spot-on. We cannot and should not presume that they are—what's the military expression—five by five?"

"Yeah, that's the one," Legend said with a grin, but it quickly evaporated. "So what do I do? Do I force them all to Walter Reed for more tests and keep them checked in and under observation until we understand what's going on? Do I confine them to quarters at the Holiday Inn Express here in Culpeper and monitor them ourselves? There's no simple solution. What do you think, Malcolm? What would you do?"

Malcolm already knew what he would do. He would throw the lot back in the BRIG, lock the door, and watch what happened; that's what he would do. But he didn't dare say this, even in jest. So instead he said, "The lengthy postictal states following the seizures are unusual, but seizures are not catching. What I mean by this is that quarantine protocols are not required because we're not dealing with a contagion. Worst-case scenario, their neural pathways and architecture have been permanently influenced on an individual basis. The threat is to their mental acuity, judgment, stability, etcetera. So provided they are not driving or making decisions that jeopardize the lives and safety of others, I don't see how letting them convalesce at home is a problem. I would recommend morning and afternoon check-ins with each of them for the next few days. If they develop full-blown epilepsy, then medication might be required."

"A good approach, a good perspective. I'm going to go with that." Legend closed his eyes and took a moment to rub his temples. When he opened his eyes, he said, "I trust the two of you to hold down the fort here and continue monitoring. I'm going to see if I can find an empty office upstairs where I can set up shop. I have reports to write, and I have a feeling I'm going to be working from here for the foreseeable future. Call me immediately if conditions change with the orb, the rats, or the rover."

"Will do," Malcolm said, and with a smile on his face, he happily watched the Major depart, leaving him alone with the woman of his dreams to investigate the scientific enigma of a lifetime.

CHAPTER 20

Josie was ten miles from Cortland when she got the call.

When she saw the caller ID, she screamed with involuntary joy and pulled off the road because she didn't trust herself to stay in her lane.

"Michael!" she said with a gasp as she answered the phone.

"Yeah, baby, it's me," said the familiar, beautiful voice on the line.

"Oh my God, are you okay? They told me you were checked into Walter Reed undergoing testing for probable head trauma. I've been calling, texting, and emailing you like crazy since I heard you were being flown back yesterday, but when I didn't hear anything I started getting really scared," she said in a rambling flurry without taking a breath.

"Breathe, Joz." He laughed. "Take a breath for me, okay?"

Josie put her hand to her chest and exhaled. Her heart was pounding like mad, and it didn't feel like it had any intention of slowing down. "Okay, I'm breathing, I'm breathing."

"All right, so first off, I'm sorry I haven't been able to call you until now. They took my phone in Bagram and I just got it back. Second, I'm okay. The docs here are releasing me on convalescent leave, pending approval by my unit CO."

She opened her mouth, and everything came pouring out in a torrent. She'd had so much pent up inside that her thoughts tumbled over one another. "Oh thank God. I've missed you so much. It will be so good to see you. Remember that doomsday prepper Willie Barnes we made the audition tape for? Well, it worked, and I interviewed him yesterday. He's so weird; he lives in an old, abandoned missile silo. I can't wait to tell you about it. And there's something else I've been putting off telling you, but I want to do it in person. Also, I want to hear everything that happened to you. What did the doctors say? Are you sure you're okay?"

"Okay, wow, you crammed a million things in there. I'm not sure how to even respond to that," he said with a chuckle.

"Start with you. Can you tell me what happened? Did you actually have a head trauma?"

"Something did happen, but I can't talk about it right now. What I can tell you is that I passed out and had a seizure, well, two seizures, but I'm okay. The docs here at Walter Reed did a CT scan of my brain, and everything checked out."

"A seizure?" she said, confused, a wife's worry reignited in her. "You've never had a seizure before, have you?"

"No, I haven't. Which is why they're recommending fourteen days' leave so they can monitor me and make sure there's not a problem before sending me back."

"Wait, what? They're going to send you back?"

"Well, yeah, Joz. The unit is on deployment. As long as I'm in fighting form, I gotta go back. But we're going to have two weeks together. That's something to be happy about . . . isn't it?"

"Yes, it is," she said, trying to flip her outlook from glass half-empty to glass half-full. "Do you want me to come to you? I'm actually in the car right now, heading your way."

"Really?"

"Of course. You think I'd leave you in some hospital all alone? You're my everything."

"How close are you?"

"I just started driving this morning. I'm outside of Corning."

He laughed. "In that case, go ahead and turn around. I'm booked on the 1620 nonstop American Eagle flight to Syracuse. I get in at 1755."

"In that case, I'll pick you up at the airport," she said. "Maybe we can grab dinner out to celebrate you coming home?"

"Sounds like a plan, but, Joz?"

"Yes?"

"Can you bring a change of clothes along for me? All I have is my uniform."

"Will do, sweetheart. Fly safe. I can't wait to see you."

"Me too, baby," he said.

"I love you, Michael."

"Love you too."

She let him end the call. An upswell of emotion washed over her—causing her to laugh and cry at the same time. She was more emotional than she could ever remember. *It's the hormones; that's all,* she reassured herself. This unexpected homecoming was throwing her brain for a loop. She'd prepared herself for Michael to be gone for six months. She'd boxed the very prospect of seeing him into the back far corner of her mind, but now that the gift had been opened prematurely, there was no chance of wrapping it back up. Sorta like letting a puppy out of a kennel for playtime; it was heart-wrenching to put the puppy back in the cage when playtime was over. Still smiling and still crying, she put the transmission in drive and was about to accelerate and merge back onto the highway when her mobile chimed with an unfamiliar ringtone. Putting her foot back on the brake, she looked at her phone: DJ Mood was requesting a Skype. She opened the app and accepted the incoming video-chat request.

"Hey, DJ," she said, looking at his face in profile.

After a beat, he spun to face her. "This dude William Barnes you had me look up, he's 5150."

"I don't even know what that means," she said.

"It means he's cuckoo for Cocoa Puffs—ya know, crazy."

"Sure, he's a little odd, but I think to be a prepper you've gotta have at least one loose screw up top."

DJ shook his head. "No, that's not what I'm talking about, Joz-Joz you curl my toes. The brother was committed to Rockland State Hospital in the 1960s."

"What is Rockland State Hospital?"

"It was an insane asylum. Rockland was the inspiration for the hospital in *One Flew Over the Cuckoo's Nest*. I kid you the fuck not. This guy is an A-1 nutjob."

Her stomach went queasy upon hearing this. "So are you saying he was never a Missileer in the Air Force? He's just some delusional, paranoid old man, tinfoil hats and all?"

"No, that part checked out. He *was* an officer in the Air Force, but they committed him to Rockland in October 1963. They took away his commission in January of 1964, but he didn't get out of Rockland until October 1966."

"Were you able to find out why he was committed?"

"His official diagnosis was schizophrenia. His service records are sealed. His electronic health record doesn't go back that far."

She'd experienced more than one uncomfortable moment with Willie during the silo tour, but the incident on level seven, near the bottom, had weirded her out the most. The burning paranoid look in his eyes when he asked her if the "other Josie" talked to her. Now that she had some context, that was starting to make more sense. Maybe Willie Barnes was still battling his demons . . .

"Where did you find this stuff?" she asked.

"I have my ways and means," he said.

"What else?"

"He was in and out of hospitals in the 1970s and '80s. In the '90s, he went off the grid for a while. Then he resurfaced and started a legit software company, had a steady mailing address, started paying taxes, voted in the 2000 and 2004 elections, seemingly reintegrated into society. He sold the company in 2005 for several million. After that, he started a bioscience company called Biogentrix, but it's not doing much of anything—reports a small loss every year."

"Interesting," she said, scrambling in the glove compartment for a piece of paper and a pen. She wrote down the name of the company. Biogentrix. Now this was odd: the Willie Barnes she'd met didn't fit the mold of a bioscience entrepreneur. "Why the heck would a doomsday prepper like Willie Barnes start a bioscience company?"

"Maybe he's trying to develop a super antibiotic to protect him when antibiotic-resistant bacteria take over the world."

"I'm serious, DJ."

"Okay, fine," he said with a sigh. "He's probably using it as some sort of tax shelter. People do shit like that all the time."

"Hmmm, I don't know," she said. "Anything else noteworthy?"

"Yeah, about the same time, he started buying property in upstate New York, and guess what?"

"What?"

"He bought a missile silo! The dude owns a freaking missile silo."

"I know. I thought I told you that."

"No, you most certainly did not. You told me he was a rocket man; you didn't say he actually had a rocket-launching silo in his possession."

"It's pretty damn cool; he gave me a tour."

"Wait a minute—you willingly went underground, alone, with Willie 'the rocket man from Rockland' Barnes?"

She shrugged. "I didn't know he was crazy at the time. I suppose I should have had you run a background check first."

"And let that be a lesson to you, young lady," he said, dropping his voice an octave and wagging a finger at her.

"Is that it, or do you have anything else for me?"

"Apparently he's part of some Armageddon-government-conspiracy watchdog group."

"That sounds like Willie."

"I tried to hack their site in the dark web, but their security is top-flight tight. If I had time, I could get in, but this is a freebie, yo, and I've already spent too much time on this as it is. Unless of course you . . ."

"No," she snapped.

"Just sayin'."

"Goodbye, DJ."

"Seriously though, Josie, be careful with this Barnes guy."

"I will. Thanks for the help."

"Anytime," he said and ended the chat.

She leaned her head back against the headrest.

Note to self—when talking to Michael about the trip to the missile silo, probably best to omit the part about Willie's schizophrenia . . . and his unhackable government conspiracy dark website . . . and how I let him blindfold me . . . and how I let him take me underground alone . . .

Yeah, probably best to focus on the aquaponics and the tasty buffalo jerky.

CHAPTER 21

2325 Local Time
BRIG Control Room
Westfield Dynamics
Culpeper, Virginia

This moment epitomized why Malcolm adored her.

It was after eleven o'clock at night, and Cyril was still here—not incessantly checking the clock, not surfing the web on her iPhone, not complaining about the fact that nothing noteworthy had happened with the orb in over twelve hours. To the contrary, she was bright-eyed, jocular, and fully engaged as he told her all about his trip to Brazil. If regaling her with tales of zombie-ant fungus didn't drive her away, then it was just one more incontrovertible piece of evidence that they were meant for each other.

"Malcolm, something is happening," she said, her gaze suddenly flitting from his eyes to the monitor over his shoulder.

He swiveled around in his chair and looked at the live video feeds streaming from inside the BRIG.

"There, right there," she said, pointing to the scurrying movement along the floor between rover one and the steel box. "Do you see them?"

"Yessss," he said, pushing his glasses higher onto his nose. "What are they doing?"

Cyril grabbed the joystick controlling the bird's-eye-view camera and zoomed out until the concrete floor around the box came into the frame along with six rats running in a tight circle. "They're running anticlockwise," she said, pointing at the screen. "Do you see how uniform the spacing is?"

"Almost a perfect sixty degrees apart," he answered. "And fast, so very fast."

Abruptly the rats stopped running a racetrack around the box and began to circle in place, each one chasing its tail, carving the tightest possible circle. Then they stopped.

"Six revolutions," Cyril said. "I didn't count the orbitals, but I would guess they made six passes around as well . . . What are they doing now?"

Malcolm watched as the rats stood on their hind legs, forelimbs raised skyward, snouts tilted up. His stomach tightened. He'd seen this pose before . . .

"Shit," he barked and slid sideways on his roller chair to look at another feed, the one from the camera aimed at the magnetometer. "I was right," he said, jumping to his feet. "Look at these fluctuating magnetic-field readings. The orb is using transcranial magnetic stimulation to control the rats just as I postulated."

"This is significant. We've got to call Major Tyree," Cyril said, pulling her mobile phone from her left pantsuit pocket.

"Oh no," Malcolm said, the blood draining from his face. "Look, look, look!" He pointed at one of the rovers speeding toward the personnel-access door.

"Are you doing that?" she asked.

"No!" he snapped. "It's driving itself."

"Bloody hell. We've got to warn the guard outside the door. What's his name?"

"Unger," Malcolm said.

"You call Unger on the radio; I'll call Major Tyree."

Cyril dialed and raised her mobile phone to her ear. "Damn it, he's not picking up . . . It's going to voice mail."

When prompted, she left her message: "Legend, it's Cyril calling. We've got a problem. The orb is waking up. Wherever you are, you'd better drop what you're doing and get down to the BRIG control room."

While Cyril was leaving her message for Tyree, Malcolm fumbled with the radio. He hoped it was on the right channel. "Unger, this is the control room. Do you copy?"

Static.

"Unger, this is the control room. Do you copy?" he called again, this time emphasizing each word.

A loud crack reverberated in the corridor outside.

"What the hell was that?" Cyril asked, all the color draining from her face.

"Sounded like a gunshot."

The radio crackled, and then a voice came back: "Control room, this is Unger. Go ahead."

"Is everything okay out there?"

"Yeah, everything is five by five," the calm and collected voice said.

"Ask him if that was a gunshot we just heard," Cyril demanded.

"Okay," he said, and he was about to key the radio when activity on the monitors to Cyril's right caught his eye. "I think we might have a problem," he said, pointing at the video feed of the rover now stopped in front of the personnel-access door, articulated arm repositioning in front of the keypad, a rat perched on the outstretched claw pushing buttons.

"Yes, Dr. Madden, I think we just might," a voice said, placid and baritone, not from the radio but from inside the control room.

"Malcolm?" Cyril said, her voice sounding strange.

Malcolm turned his head toward the door, and his heart skipped a beat. There in the doorway—hulking and kitted up for battle—stood the red-bearded Harris. His pistol was drawn, and he had the muzzle pointed at Cyril's head. A dozen possible replies populated in Malcolm's brain, but the one that came out took him by surprise: "You're not Unger."

"No, I'm not," Harris said. "But you don't need to worry about him. He's not going to be a problem for us."

"Whatever you do, just don't hurt her," Malcolm pleaded, his eyes darting back and forth between Cyril and the man with the gun. "In fact, take me instead."

Harris bobbed his head from side to side in mock indecision and then said, "Tell you what, Dr. Madden, I have a better idea. How about I take *both* of you."

CHAPTER 22

2331 Local Time
Westfield Dynamics
Culpeper, Virginia

He didn't remember falling asleep. That's how tired Legend was. One minute he'd been reading about transcranial-magnetic-stimulation studies being conducted at Duke University; the next minute his head was lolling. Angry, overstretched neck muscles jerked him awake. He opened his eyes for a beat in drowsy confusion, but heavy lids quickly usurped control and sent his chin bobbing off his chest again.

Somewhere far away he heard a mobile phone ringing.

In the semiconscious regions of his brain, a voice told him the phone was his. "I don't care," he mumbled, but he was a soldier and an officer, and that meant he had to care.

He forced his eyelids open and took a deep breath as he tried to get his bearings. The desk he was sitting at was not his own. He was not at the Pentagon . . . That's because he'd stayed at Westfield D, working late just in case something happened.

Just in case the orb woke up.

Groggily he reached for his mobile phone. The call had been from Cyril, and there was a voice mail waiting for him. He pressed the play icon and turned on the speaker: *"Legend, it's Cyril calling. We've got a problem. The orb is waking up . . ."*

He didn't wait for it to finish before he was up and sprinting. He flew down the steps to the basement level, the rapid-fire cadence of his feet echoing in the concrete stairwell. When he reached the bottom, he slammed into the rocker bar on the steel door and sent it flying open. He dashed down the corridor toward the BRIG control room. When he got to door, he found it curiously ajar. He pushed it the rest of the way open and found the control room deserted.

What the hell? Where was his science team?

Heart still pounding and lungs heaving, he walked straight to the bank of monitors to see what was happening inside the BRIG.

"Oh no," he said with a gasp, staring at a live feed of Cyril and Malcolm both standing entranced in front of a brilliantly glowing, hovering orb. Déjà vu washed over him, and so did a wave of panic. Behind the two scientists, Harris stood completely kitted up for battle and holding an M4 in a relaxed carry across his chest. He didn't appear to be hypnotized like Malcolm and Cyril, but his posture and mannerism were different from before. Most disturbing, he was permitting this to happen—possibly even standing guard over the proceedings to *ensure* it happened.

What the hell?

Unger had the 1800-to-midnight watch. Harris wasn't even supposed to be here. Legend ran out of the control room and headed toward the BRIG. When he got there, he saw a massive blood smear that led across the hall and disappeared under a closed door labeled JANITORIAL SUPPLIES. Legend opened the door and was greeted by Unger's corpse seated against the back wall of the closet—eyes open, mouth agape, blood running from a bullet hole in his forehead. Legend slammed the door and spun around to face the BRIG. The blast door and the personnel door were both shut, but the "Unlocked" LED indicator for the personnel door was illuminated. He pressed the lock button, but nothing happened. He pressed it again and still nothing happened.

Shit!

As much as he needed to get Malcolm and Cyril away from that thing, the number one priority was to keep it contained. He sprinted back to the control room and frantically looked for the door controls. After a beat, he found them on the control panel and pressed the lock button for the personnel door, but the "Unlocked" indicator stayed green. A string of curses replete with every variation of the f-word poured from his lips. This was a jailbreak, and it was up to him to stop it. To confront Harris, however, he'd need to be armed. Even then, he didn't like his chances. He needed backup. He pulled his mobile phone from his pocket. Time to get his boss, General Troy, involved. Before he finished dialing, the lights went out, and his mobile phone was suddenly a brick in his hand.

The electromagnetic pulse was a precursor event—a preliminary strike by the orb to disable the facility, take down comms, and thereby pave the way for its escape. Whatever the hell this thing was, he couldn't let it escape. He couldn't let it take Malcolm and Cyril as hostages. He felt his way in the dark to the control-room door. Confronting Harris unarmed was a death sentence, but what choice did he have? *Unless . . .* unless he could get to the lobby and find the night watchman before Harris did. The night guard carried a sidearm; Legend needed that sidearm.

He depressed the door lever and quietly opened the door. The corridor beyond was pitch-black; not even the emergency lighting was on. He ducked into a low crouch, and carefully and quietly he crept into the corridor. To his left, the direction of the BRIG, he heard a noise. Then a white beam of light cut the blackness, and Legend deduced, from the height and movement of the beam, that this was a gun light clipped to the Picatinny rail of Harris's weapon. Harris and his hostages would be in the corridor any second. Legend had a hard choice to make: option one, make a break for the stairwell and try to get to the lobby without being shot in the back, or option two, crouch and wait for Harris to walk past and ambush the operator from behind. The problem with option two was, What if the orb took control of his mind and put him in a trance? Harris wasn't the danger. The *orb* was the danger. As soon as this thought registered, the decision was made: he took off down the pitch-black hallway. Running in the dark, he tried to remember how far the stairwell was from the BRIG control room. Thirty feet, he estimated, on the left side of the corridor. His footfalls echoed loudly on the concrete. Too loudly. In his peripheral vision, he registered a change in the light. Harris was in the corridor now.

On instinct alone, Legend crouched and dove into a headfirst slide. Almost simultaneously, a deafening volley erupted as machine-gun fire ripped down the corridor. Bullets ricocheted off the walls and ceiling, zipping past him overhead. Harris's first volley had missed, but when the rogue operator's light found him—and it *would* find him—Legend would be cut to ribbons.

He had one chance. From his stomach, he pushed up and got his feet underneath himself. He launched forward, a sprinter out of the starting blocks, with all the strength and power of his finely tuned and powerfully built body.

He reached the stairwell door as the shooter's light swept across his position. His fingers found the handle, his thumb the latch-release button. He pressed and pulled and dove. Bullets raked the wall, the doorframe, and the door slab, and one of them found its mark. The bullet grazed his right flank, clipping the slab of muscle just below and behind the *V* of his armpit as he came crashing on the concrete landing at the bottom of the steps. A stripe of fire lit up his back while stingers flared in his left knee and right wrist from the hard landing. Gritting his teeth, he clambered to his feet. Fear, duty, and adrenaline fueled his ascent; despite the dark, he managed to climb the stairs quickly and without taking a nasty fall.

When he reached the main-level landing, he felt along the wall until he found the door. As he pushed the rocker bar to exit, he heard the latch for the door at the bottom of the stairwell click. He slipped out the door just as light flooded the stairwell below. His mind raced, trying to think of some way to block the door or bind the latch, but fire-escape doors pushed open from the inside, which made blocking it a near-impossible task. He turned and ran in the direction of the lobby. By now he could feel the warm rivulets running down his back and the wetness spreading across his shirt.

He reached around with his left hand and felt the wound as he ran. A graze that would require stitches to close, but nothing life-threatening. The locus and level of pain told him that both bone and muscle had been left unmolested beneath. His throbbing knee was affecting his speed more than the bullet wound. As he closed on the lobby, he saw the glow of a flashlight and heard voices—or at least *a* voice. He entered at a full sprint, taking the front-desk guard by surprise. The flashlight beam was in his face a beat later, followed by a nervous apology.

"Sorry about that, Major Tyree," the night watchman said, lowering the beam. "You took me by surprise."

Legend's gaze ticked from the guard's face to his right hip. "I need your sidearm."

"Excuse me?" the night watchman said.

"We have a security breach and a potential hostage situation. I need your sidearm. Right now." The young guard hesitated a moment, then unholstered his weapon and handed it over. Legend glanced at the weapon: Glock 21—.45 caliber with a thirteen-round magazine. "I also need your radio and that extra mag."

"But, sir—"

"Now!" he barked.

"Yes, sir," the guard said and did as he was told.

"Now get behind that wall over there and stay there," Legend ordered, already making his way back to the hallway he'd just come from. Back pressed against the lobby's rear wall, he inched toward the corner leading to the hallway.

They should be here already, he thought, but he didn't see the beam of Harris's tactical light. He didn't hear footsteps or movement. Now that he was armed, the prospect of engaging Harris took on a new and different significance. Harris was *not* the enemy. Cyril and Malcolm were also not the enemy. If they were helping the orb, it was not by volition; it was not of their own free will. At best they were operating under some hypnotic trance; at worst the orb had taken control of their minds.

I can't just shoot them, even if they're shooting at me.

"Fuck," he muttered, paralyzed with tactical indecision. Even if he aimed to wound, there was still the possibility he could inflict a mortal injury inadvertently. He was a good shot with a pistol but not a world-class marksman by any stretch of the imagination.

"What's the radio call sign for the gate guard?" he hollered at the watchman.

"Whiskey Gate," the watchman called back.

He keyed the radio. "Whiskey Gate, this is Major Tyree. Do you copy?"

"Major, this is Whiskey Gate. I copy you, Lima Charlie."

"We have a situation here: a site-wide blackout, a security breach, and a possible hostage situation. No traffic is permitted to leave this facility. Do you understand?"

"Understood, Major."

"Do you have active security deterrents at the gate?"

"Yes, sir, I have a retractable Sentinel wedge barrier, but it is optimized to prevent inbound traffic access."

"Raise it anyway."

"Roger that, sir."

"Do you have a working mobile phone?"

"Yes."

"All phones and comms are down in the building except for radios. Listen very carefully. I'm going to give you a number to call—"

"Major, I have vehicle headlights coming my way from the facility," the gate guard interrupted.

"Does this facility have underground parking?" he shouted at the night watchman.

"Yes, sir, for full-time employees and company vehicles," the watchman said.

"Is it accessible from the basement?"

"Yes."

"Shit!"

His radio crackled. "Major, this is Whiskey Gate. The vehicle is picking up speed and gone off-road. They must have seen the security barrier. I think they're going to ram the chain-link. I'm going to try to take out their tires."

"Negative, Whiskey, do not engage," Legend barked into the radio as he ran to the front of the lobby and looked out a window at the front gate.

Staccato cracks echoed in the distance as Legend watched alternating muzzle flares between the vehicle and the guard as they traded fire.

"Whiskey, stand down and take cover," Legend ordered over the radio, but no reply came. He ran outside for a better look just in time to see the guard get shot and fall to the ground. The van then abruptly changed course back toward the gate. A beat later, a shadow jumped out of the passenger-side door, disappeared into the guard shack, and then ran back into the van as the security barrier retracted.

"Fuuuuuck," Legend growled as he watched the van's twin red taillights disappear down the access road.

"What just happened, Major?" the night watchman asked, stepping up beside him.

Legend exhaled with defeat and said, "Even if you had the security clearance to know the truth, you wouldn't believe me."

Chapter 23

Scouting Position outside Western Dynamics
Culpeper, Virginia

Dean Ninemeyer was losing patience.

He'd been waiting all day for Malcolm to leave the facility so he could follow the little worm home and squeeze him for more information. Something significant had happened this morning, and he was itching to know what it was. He'd followed Major Tyree to Culpeper Regional Hospital this morning and shadowed him without detection. The expedition had paid dividends. Tyree's visit to the hospital indicated he was running the project, and the three people rushed by ambulance to the hospital were team members working with him. Ninemeyer had collected their names and had the "back office" run queries. The results had been tremendously informative: Major Beth Fischer had a PhD in virology from Harvard and was the Army's head of biosecurity at Fort Detrick, Ryan Harris was a former Delta operator with TS/SCI clearance who now worked as a contractor for Ground Branch, and Patrick Dixon was a USAMRIID laboratory technician and previous AIT-SMART team leader. Their qualifications and field-operations experience meant that together they addressed both *physical* security and *bio*security concerns, which told Ninemeyer this trio had been the welcome party—sent in to determine if the thing they'd found was a biological threat. Apparently it was, because they'd all arrived at the hospital in semicatatonic states. From snippets of conversations and a covert glance at Dixon's chart, Ninemeyer deduced that they'd all experienced grand mal seizures. As far as Ninemeyer knew, and he knew quite a lot on the topic, there was no weapon technology on earth that could do to people what had been done to these three.

Is it possible that after all these years of hoaxes and conspiracy theories, the Army has finally gone and found alien technology?

He wasn't sure what this development meant for his predicament with his number-one customer—the Red Client. Recently, his liaison for the Red Client had expressed dissatisfaction with his performance. Apparently he was no longer delivering information of a caliber that was acceptable, and they were demanding that he up his game or risk being terminated. The meaning had not been lost in translation. If he could somehow pillage this newly discovered technology from DARPA, then he would definitely regain their favor.

The Red Client had a hard-on for anything DARPA was throwing resources at, which was why he'd recruited Malcolm Madden in the first place. The Red Client did not like doing the early-stage heavy lifting, preferring instead to pillage adolescent technology and then set their vast army of engineers, programmers, and scientists to work understanding, modifying, improving, and implementing the technology. Early-stage development was slow, expensive, and had a high failure rate. In the race for world domination, from both a strategic and economic perspective, skipping this stage offered a tremendous cost-savings and speed advantage. So long as intellectual property could be bought, hacked, or stolen, the Red Client's defense-industrial complex could be optimized for mid- to late-stage implementation. And so long as the academic, corporate, and military institutions of the United States and Europe allowed their rank and file to be subject to exploitation, the Red Client could continue to operate as the world's largest late-stage, black-market technology aggregator.

The Red Client recognized that artificial intelligence was the twenty-first century's A-bomb, and the race was on to develop the first machine "super intelligence." The first nation-state to birth it would become the *only* superpower, leaving the rest of the world swirling, choking, and drowning in its wake.

Malcolm Madden was the Babe Ruth of Ninemeyer's lineup. So far Ninemeyer had not forced Madden to sell any secrets from the SyNAPSE project. He knew that once he gave the Red Client a taste of this golden honey, they would push him for results faster than he could possibly deliver. It had taken discipline not to shoot himself in the foot on SyNAPSE, but apparently he'd shot himself in the other foot in the process. *Irony's a bitch that way.* He'd always assumed he would know when the time was right to light his brightest candle. Maybe that time was now. But if he burned up Madden on this opportunity, he wouldn't be able to use him later when SyNAPSE was ready for prime time. On the other hand, this technology might eclipse SyNAPSE altogether and be an even bigger win for him. Either way was a gamble. The question on his mind now was this: Which AI secrets would ultimately prove to be more lucrative for him to broker, those derived from *alien* intelligence or *artificial* intelligence?

Gunfire echoed in the distance, shaking him from his thoughts.

He climbed out of his Tahoe, shut the door, and listened. More gunfire . . . an M4 and a pistol . . . a half mile away, he estimated. It was coming from somewhere across the road, somewhere on the Westfield Dynamics grounds. His heart rate picked up, and his senses sharpened as adrenaline flooded his system. Something was happening. Headlights appeared on the access road, closing fast.

He jumped into the Tahoe, started the engine, but kept the headlights off. A white van came into view, tearing down the access road toward the intersection at James Madison Highway. The van turned east with squealing tires and sped out of sight.

He'd been at this game long enough to recognize a getaway; the question was, What had been stolen? His money was on the object itself. He pulled out of his observation blind, turned east on James Madison Highway, and punched the accelerator. As he passed Windmere's Autobody & Collision Repair, he looked at the parking lot and saw the silver Ford Explorer parked once again among the other damaged vehicles awaiting repair.

In the distance, the van's twin red taillights were already dwindling. He glanced at the speedometer and saw he was doing eighty, so he pressed the gas pedal and accelerated to one hundred miles per hour. Ahead, the van braked to navigate a sweeping turn. Ninemeyer braked hard on his approach, barely managing to keep the Tahoe on the road. He was finally beginning to make up ground because the van was forced to take bends slower than he could. A beat later, his closure rate began to increase dramatically.

No brake lights . . . The van's coasting.

He took his right foot completely off the accelerator and moved it to hover over the brake pedal. *Shit's about to happen,* he told himself. *Get ready.* No sooner had he finished the thought than the right rear cargo door of the van swung open. Ninemeyer reacted immediately, braking hard and swerving left as a figure in a combat kneel let loose with an assault rifle. The first volley strafed the right side of the Tahoe's windshield and shredded the passenger seat, barely missing Ninemeyer. He swerved back to the right, timing the maneuver with the shooter's next volley, which went wide left, but just barely as rounds clipped the A-pillar and rearview mirror. With enough speed gone that he wouldn't roll the SUV, he executed a full 180, spinning the Tahoe counterclockwise. As he did, bullets riddled the entire passenger side from fender to fender. He heard and then felt the front right tire blow out, then the rear right tire. With the tailgate now facing the van, Ninemeyer ducked low in his seat. A beat later, a single round smashed through the tailgate window and punched a hole through the driver-seat headrest.

Contorting himself, Ninemeyer pulled the Walther from the holster under the seat. Still crouched, he reached up and pulled the column shifter into reverse, activating the Tahoe's rearview camera system. He saw the van's taillights growing dimmer until they disappeared into the night. He opened the driver-side door and got out. Sighting over his pistol, he walked the perimeter of his vehicle, scanning all directions, double-checking he was alone . . . Only then did he slip his weapon into the waistband of his pants at the small of his back. He walked to the passenger side and confirmed that, yes, both tires were blown.

He had only a single spare.

Fuck.

He walked back to the driver's seat, started the engine, and pulled the hobbled Tahoe off the road onto the shoulder. All hope of catching up to the van was dashed, but he still had one resource left he could try to exploit. The getaway crew would ditch the white van for another vehicle. They would try to accomplish this as soon as possible because undoubtedly Legend Tyree would attempt to do exactly what Ninemeyer was about to try: tracking the van from above.

He retrieved his mobile phone and selected the first entry on his speed-dial list.

"You've reached the after-hours answering service for Helios Corporation. How may I be of assistance?" a woman's voice asked.

"I'd like to rent a bird," he said.

"Authenticate."

"CHINA DOLL."

"Wait to be transferred."

A beat later, a new voice came on the line, this one male. "Rookery."

"I'd like to borrow a bird," Ninemeyer said.

"Location?"

"Fifteen miles northeast of Culpeper, Virginia."

"Wait while I check availability . . . I'm sorry, but there's no availability in that area. Next asset availability for that location is in three hours, eighteen minutes."

"Damn. That's too late."

"Any other locations?" the man said.

"No," he said and ended the call.

There were many perks to working in the private sector, but reliable access to real-time satellite and drone coverage was not one of them. He often thought about asking the Red Client for access to resources, but as tempting as it was, to do so would forever change their working arrangement. Right now he was an independent third-party contractor. To go down the other path would turn him into an indentured servant.

He climbed out, opened the rear tailgate, and grabbed his go-bag. Next, he retrieved a screwdriver from the tool pouch he kept and removed the license plate from the rear bumper. After that, he fetched the holster and extra magazine from beneath the driver's seat, unplugged his mobile phone's charger cable from the center console, and retrieved the vehicle's insurance and registration paperwork from the glove box. He stuffed all these items in his go-bag, shrugged on both shoulder straps, and began the long walk back to Culpeper . . .

By the time he reached Windmere's Autobody & Collision Repair, his feet were screaming at him. His Rockport loafers were comfortable day shoes, but long-distance walking shoes they were not. Thankfully the silver Ford Explorer was still there, parked right where it had been when he'd last seen it. He walked straight up to the passenger door and knocked on the window. To his credit, the observer sitting in the driver's seat had seen him coming, albeit too late to mount an effective defense. The driver, who looked to be in his late sixties, did manage to get the vehicle's engine started, but that was all. The man stared at him through the window, his expression betraying the strain of a mind weighing options.

Ninemeyer smiled at him and motioned for him to roll down the window.

This time the man fingered the switch for the passenger-seat window and bumped it down only an inch. "What do you want?"

"Contractor or employee?" Ninemeyer asked, slipping his left hand behind his back to draw the Walther from his waistband. He was standing practically right up against the door, taking advantage of the Explorer's high window sill to block the other man's view of the maneuver.

"Excuse me?"

"Contractor or government employee, which one are you?"

"I don't know what you're talking about."

Ninemeyer made a funny face at the man, who he guessed was a retired G-man working freelance surveillance under government contract. The only thing that really mattered was which government.

"How long have you been working for the SVR?" he asked in Russian.

The man responded with a blank stare.

"Do you know Director Geng Hichang at the Ministry of State Security?" he asked in Mandarin.

Again, no reply from the watcher, but now Ninemeyer could tell the man was getting nervous. He saw the man's eyes tick to the gear shifter on the center console, and he could read the man's mind: *If I can just get the transmission in drive . . .*

"You're not a very talkative fellow, are you?" Ninemeyer said. "Did you see that white van that came tearing out of here two hours ago?"

"Who are you?" the watcher said, gathering his courage.

"Did you happen to get the tag number on that van?"

The driver blinked.

Ninemeyer brought his pistol up.

The driver's right hand flew to the gear shifter and slammed it into drive as Ninemeyer fired three rounds at the man's head. The first bullet shattered the passenger window; the second and third slugs found their mark. The engine roared, and the Explorer lurched forward out of the parking lot only to fall quiet a beat later and slow to a coast. Ninemeyer ran to catch up with it and jumped inside via the rear passenger-side door. From the back seat, he grabbed the steering wheel and guided the Explorer onto a side road, then shoved the gear shifter into park. He leaned over the dead man and reclined the driver's seat. Then, grabbing the corpse under the armpits, he dragged the body into the rear footwell. He climbed out, walked around to the driver's side, and got in.

He drove east on 15. When he reached the abandoned Tahoe, he retrieved one final thing he had not been able to carry with him before—a hard case containing his Heckler & Koch PSG1 semiautomatic sniper rifle. The PSG1 was like his Walther and his American Express card—he never left home without it. Feeling much better now, he climbed back in the Explorer and left his Tahoe behind for the Highway Patrol to find.

No choice in the matter, unfortunately.

He merged back onto Route 15, driving the speed limit until it doglegged north. He exited at Route 661, Oak Shade Road, and drove until he found a nice secluded spot where he could pull off to the side. He parked the Explorer, climbed out, and replaced the license plate with the plate from his Tahoe. Then he wiped the spatter of blood and brains off the driver-side window. The window was cracked but not blown out, so he rolled it all the way down. He walked around to the front passenger side and surveyed the broken glass.

This vehicle will not serve, he decided. *I'm going to have to burn it and the body before sunrise.*

He checked his watch: 0343. Plenty of time. He climbed back into the driver seat and retrieved the dead man's wallet from his back pants pocket. He pulled out the Maryland driver's license: *Nolan Watts. Age 71.*

Hmmm . . . an old-timer. I'll have to have the back office run a query sometime.

He took one last look at the picture and then put the ID back in the wallet and returned it to the dead man's pocket.

"I wonder if this guy mattered," he muttered. "If he did, I'll hear about it. Always do . . ."

Ninemeyer pulled out his mobile phone and called Malcolm Madden. The call rang until it went to voice mail. He did not leave a message. He'd try again in an hour. If he didn't reach him on the next call, he'd stake out Malcolm's apartment until he came home. Unless, of course, the little worm had been in the white van . . .

If that's the case, then I don't know what the fuck I'm going to do.

DAY THREE

I for all and one for none,
I take no blame for what I've done.
Greed we worship beneath the sun,
And dance in blood, oh what fun.
Sins collective eclipse the sum,
At Nature's pyre, her praises sung,
The world has tipped, the end near come,
Reset the balance, or the Devil's won.

—Willie Barnes

CHAPTER 24

Elizabeth Fischer climbed out of bed, naked. She walked to her bathroom and urinated. Then she dressed methodically, without showering first. Beth always showered in the morning before work. Elizabeth did not put on eye makeup. Beth always wore eye makeup.

She walked to the kitchen and vomited in the sink.

She did not clean up the mess.

Her head felt like it had been split open with an axe, but Elizabeth did not take any pain medicine. They were still suffering from the concussion. Elizabeth did not eat breakfast. Beth never skipped breakfast. She left her mobile phone on the kitchen counter along with her Yeti coffee tumbler. Beth never went anywhere without her mobile phone and Yeti tumbler. Elizabeth did, however, grab her military ID, USAMRIID badge, Maryland state driver's license, and car keys. She walked out of the front door of her townhouse without locking the door behind her. Beth always locked the door.

Elizabeth walked to her assigned parking spot in the community carport. She drove to Patrick Dixon's apartment complex. He was waiting for her at the curb. He climbed into the front passenger seat. She drove to Fort Detrick; they both presented their military IDs at the gate. She drove to her reserved parking space in the lot off Porter Street. She and Dixon walked to building 1425 and badged in at fifteen minutes prior to the security shift turnover. She called a meeting with the oncoming security shift supervisor. She informed the shift supervisor that she was going to be conducting a surprise biosecurity drill this morning sometime between the hours of 0900 and 1100 to evaluate staff situational awareness and test the effectiveness of newly implemented biosafety and biosecurity standard operating procedures. USAMRIID had suffered a number of mishaps and accidents over the past several years resulting in staff exposure to potentially deadly pathogens. Facility SOPs were designed to prevent the inadvertent release of and exposure to pathogens, and they were constantly being revised and improved based on lessons learned. She explained her role in the drill, the lab technician Patrick Dixon's role as "event instigator," and what she expected from the security team. She then thanked the shift supervisor for his professionalism and asked him to please brief his staff.

She then proceeded into the laboratory spaces, which she expected to be empty; most staff did not arrive until after 0830. This morning, however, someone was working early. Through a glass observation window, Fischer watched a woman wearing a puffy blue suit, yellow rubber gloves, and rubber boots sitting hunched over a workstation in one of the facility's dedicated biosafety-level-four laboratories. A yellow curlicue hose connected to the regulator plugged into a nearby air manifold, which supplied filtered, fresh air from the building's dedicated laboratory air system.

The researcher in the blue suit was Dr. Jill Hennessy, a brilliant, opinionated scientist who specialized in working with BSL-4 class organisms. BSL-4 class organisms, such as the Ebola virus, which Dr. Hennessy was working with presently, were the deadliest pathogens known to man. Beth adored Jill Hennessy; they were friends. Elizabeth didn't care. She needed a scapegoat for the operation she and Patrick Dixon were preparing to execute, and Dr. Hennessy fit the bill perfectly. Hennessy, suddenly feeling eyes on her, turned and looked out through the observation window.

Hennessy smiled.

Elizabeth smiled back . . .

CHAPTER 25

Josie contemplated getting a second donut while she waited for Isabel Clark.

Isabel, Izzy to her friends, was Jeremy Wayne's girlfriend, and the two women had become close friends over the past two and a half months. Iz had texted her early this morning, begging her to meet for coffee. When she got the text, Josie had initially declined. Bailing on her husband to hang out at Tim Hortons with Izzy on Michael's first full day home was unthinkable . . . That is until Michael bailed on her. So here she was, waiting for her friend and thinking about last night's bizarre homecoming.

Izzy swept into the room like a cold, north wind. Spotting Josie, she stomped over and dropped into the vacant chair opposite her like a sullen teenager. Izzy greeted her with a lifeless smile from behind a pair of sunglasses. This morning, Izzy's quintessential dimples were nowhere to be found. Given the boys' impromptu homecoming, this was not the Izzy whom Josie had expected to see.

"Hi, Iz," Josie said, trying to sound cheerful.

"Hey," Izzy said, slumping back in her chair.

"Is everything all right?" Josie asked, leaning in.

"No, not really," Izzy said, folding her arms across her chest. "Can I ask you a question?"

"Anything."

"How were things with Michael last night?"

Josie debated how to answer this question before saying, "A little awkward, but I think it takes a little time to get back into the rhythm as a couple."

Izzy pursed her lips. "Does he seem different to you?"

Josie felt her cheeks flush as she thought about the bizarre lovemaking sessions with Michael last night. "Well, maybe a little."

Izzy took off her sunglasses. Though her eyes were dry, Izzy's puffy, red eyelids told Josie that her friend had been crying. "You're blushing," Izzy said, suddenly perking up.

"No, I'm not."

Izzy grinned impishly and leaned forward. "Yes, you totally are. You had naughty sex right before you came here, didn't you? I can see it written all over your face. You did it in broad daylight with the shades open, didn't you?"

Josie shook her head adamantly. "No, no, it was last night."

"Was it kinky? Did you go all *Fifty Shades* and let him tie you up?"

"No! Nothing like that." She laughed, not sure how much she wanted to share. Finally she said, "It was, well, strange."

"Strange as in kinky, or strange as in creepy? There's a difference."

"I can't believe I'm telling you this," Josie said, wondering how red her cheeks had turned. "The first time was normal—you know, vanilla sex before bed. We cuddled afterward, I tried to talk to him, and he fell asleep."

"Uh-huh, been there," Izzy said, nodding.

"So I rolled over and went to sleep myself. Then, next thing I know, I wake up completely disoriented and find him on top of me going to town. It was two o'clock in the morning, Izzy."

"He actually started screwing you while you were asleep? I had no idea Michael was such an animal. What was it like?"

"Well, I was glad that he missed me as much as I missed him, but at the same time it was weird. He was like a machine. Pumping away like a jackhammer but staring off into space a million miles away. Before I knew it, he was finished. He rolled off me, and without a word, he went back to sleep. Then it happened again, at five fifteen in the morning."

"That is weird," Izzy said and took a sip of her water.

"You wanna hear what's even weirder? At breakfast, when I asked him about it, he had absolutely no idea what I was talking about. He swears he doesn't remember doing it."

"Wait, what?"

"I know; it's crazy," Josie said, shaking her head. "It was like he was sleepwalking, except instead he was sleepfucking."

"That's super freaky. I've never heard of anything like that."

Josie nodded.

"Do you believe him? I mean—do you believe that he doesn't remember doing it?"

"Yeah, I do. Michael is all about his integrity. The man never lies."

"What's that look mean?" Izzy said, narrowing her eyes.

"Um, I'm a little nervous that it's going to happen again tonight," she confessed.

"Well, at least you're getting some." Izzy laughed, her expression changing as she looked to her lap. "Jeremy totally dissed me."

"What are you talking about? At the airport last night, he couldn't keep his hands off you."

"I know," Izzy said, her bottom lip starting to quiver. "But that was just a show for you guys. After we got in the car, it was like a switch flipped in his brain. I tried to make out with him, but he pulled away. I asked him what was wrong, and he said nothing. So I suggested that we go out to a nice dinner, you know, like you guys were doing. He told me he wasn't hungry and ordered me to drive him to Best Buy."

"Best Buy?"

"Yes, Best Buy."

"What did you do?"

"I started crying. I said, 'What's wrong, Jeremy? Do you not like me anymore?'"

"Oh, Iz, now you're making me cry," Josie said, tears of empathy rimming her eyes. She reached across the table and squeezed Izzy's hand.

"Do you want to know what he had the nerve to say?"

"What?"

Izzy shook her head and started to sob. "He said not to call him Jeremy. He said he wanted me to call him by his Army nickname from now on."

"What's the nickname?"

"Bug."

"Bug?"

"Yes, Bug. Isn't that disgusting?"

Josie shrugged. "I don't know about disgusting, but definitely strange. Guys are weird about stuff like that. Maybe it's an inside joke or something?"

"I don't care. I think it's disgusting. I told him I wouldn't call him that."

"Good for you, Iz."

"Wait, it gets worse. So he orders me to take him to Best Buy so he can buy a computer. Josie, you wouldn't believe it. He spent over two thousand dollars on a computer and a couple of monitors."

"Two thousand dollars is a lot of money for a computer."

"I know. I think he emptied his checking account to buy the stupid thing. The whole thing doesn't make any sense. It's so out of character for him. He is the world's biggest cheap ass. Jeremy thinks dinner at Cracker Barrel is too fancy, so he insists we eat at Sonic on our dates."

"Did you ask him why he was spending so much on a computer? I've never pictured Jeremy as a computer guy," Josie said.

"He's not!" Izzy cried. "He's a good ol' boy from Tennessee who, until yesterday, only cared about drinking beer, chewing tobacco, and having crazy sex with me. You should have heard him talking with the salesman at Best Buy. They were like two super geeks at a hacker convention. I never heard Jeremy talk about computers once before yesterday."

"What happened next?"

"I drove him back to Fort Drum and dropped him off at the barracks," Izzy said. A tear rolled down her cheek. "He didn't even invite me into his room. He carried his computer inside, said goodbye, and practically slammed the door in my face."

"Have you talked to him since?"

"No," Izzy said, fighting back tears.

"I'm so sorry, Iz," Josie said.

"Josie, I don't care what the Army says; something happened over there. If not, why would they fly Jeremy and Michael all the way back to the States for a routine checkup? That's what Jeremy had the balls to tell me—that it was routine. Routine checkup my ass. He looks like he lost at least fifteen pounds, and the boy didn't have fifteen pounds to lose. Did you see those bags under his eyes and how sunken his cheeks looked? And I felt like every five minutes he was packing fresh dip in his lip."

"He did look a little rough," Josie admitted.

"And he was jittery as hell, talking fast—that's not Jeremy."

"He was probably jacked up from too much nicotine."

"I don't know. I worry about PTSD. Can somebody get PTSD that fast? Maybe he's in shock, or maybe he hit his head so hard that it changed his personality. Is such a thing even possible?"

"Those are all good questions, but I'm sorry, Iz; I don't have any answers for you."

Izzy nodded and wiped her nose with a napkin.

Josie leaned across the table and gave her friend an awkward hug, which Izzy needed because she hugged Josie back until she thought she might have a back spasm. When Izzy finally let go, she looked Josie in the eye and said, "Have you considered the possibility that Michael's not telling you the whole truth about what happened over there?"

Josie wrinkled her nose. "If something else happened in Afghanistan, something that's not classified information, Michael would have told me."

"You're that confident?"

"So confident I'd bet my marriage on it," she said with conviction, but inside she still couldn't shake the uneasy feeling she'd had since last night.

CHAPTER 26

Watertown, New York

Josie saved the file she'd been working on and slammed the lid of her notebook computer closed. She had assumed that with Michael home now, she'd be fighting tooth and nail for time to work on her *Vice* piece, but instead, she'd had four uninterrupted hours to research Biogentrix and how it fit into Willie Barnes's enigmatic past. The company turned out to be a subcontract vaccine-manufacturing facility, but the last contract it filled was two years ago. *Strange.*

What was even stranger, however, was the fact that she'd had four uninterrupted hours to conduct research. Michael had disappeared after breakfast and hadn't come back until after lunch. And when he finally had come home, he'd promptly secluded himself in their detached two-car garage for reasons he had chosen not to share with her. She'd been excited to talk to him about the silo and show him video footage from the trip, but he'd not come inside to say hello, to get a drink, or even to use the bathroom.

Needless to say, she was irritated with him.

Today was his first full day home, and they'd not spent even five minutes together. The only reason she'd agreed to have coffee with Iz was because he'd run off without saying when he'd be back. She'd just assumed that his morning disappearance was because he needed to go on base, check in with the higher-ups, maybe fill out some paperwork, check on Jeremy, that sort of stuff. But suddenly she had the sneaking suspicion he'd not gone on base but had gone shopping—shopping like Jeremy had gone shopping. *Maybe Izzy is right,* she thought, getting to her feet to pace the kitchen.

Maybe something *had* happened to the guys over there.

She accepted, without animus, that he withheld details from her about his work in the Army—national security bullshit and all—but this was different. They were married; marriage meant communication. Marriage meant sharing. Marriage meant not clamming up and ignoring your wife when you got to come home for fourteen days in the middle of a deployment. The more she thought about it, the more vexed she became. Ideas and emotions began to snowball, and she found herself imagining him out there outfitting the garage with a big-screen TV, a sofa, a computer . . . If he thought for one second that she was going to let him turn their garage into some frat-boy man cave where he could drink beer, watch sports, surf porn, and ignore her, then he had another thing coming.

She wanted to know what he was doing out there.

Fuck it.

She walked out the side door to the driveway and approached the detached garage. The double garage door was lowered almost completely to the ground, save for a four-inch space at the bottom, where it was propped open by a brick. She heard a crackling sound coming from inside. Flashes of white-blue light danced with shadows in the gap between the rubber seal strip along the bottom of the garage door and the concrete floor. The door's spring mechanism had broken three weeks ago, making the stout wooden door dreadful to lift and dangerous to lower. After alternately straining her back and nearly crushing her foot, she had resigned to parking her car in the driveway. Clearly for Michael, hoisting the heavy door had been a nonevent. She wondered what it would be like to be as strong as her husband. For a woman, she considered herself both fit and strong, but Michael was gladiator strong. Sometimes she found herself gaping at the muscles on his back and shoulders, rippling and glistening as he rinsed himself in the shower. To walk around with that body, with that much power, she couldn't even imagine.

You're procrastinating, she chastised herself. *Go talk to your husband.*

She took a deep breath, walked up to the garage door, and pounded on it with the base of her fist. She waited for the crackling and flashing to stop, but it did not. She counted to five and pounded on the door again, this time harder and longer. The crackling stopped. She could feel her heart pounding in her chest. Suddenly she wanted to run away— like a kid playing a doorbell prank on the grouchy old lady who lived next door. But she wasn't a kid, and this wasn't a doorbell prank, and the person behind the garage door was definitely not the grouchy old lady who lived next door.

The garage door flung open, and she was standing face-to-face with her husband. The clean T-shirt he had put on this morning was now mottled with sweat rings, grease stains, and numerous small holes charred around the edges. He wore a welding mask, the face shield tilted up like the brim of an oversize baseball cap, casting his face in shadow.

"Yes," he said, greeting her like one would a solicitor calling over the dinner hour.

"Hey," she said lamely.

"Is it lunchtime yet?"

"It was lunchtime two hours ago."

"Sorry," he said, wiping a dribble of sweat from his cheek. "I lost track of time. I'm starving. Can you make me a sandwich?"

"Michael?" she asked, gathering her courage.

"Yes, Josie?"

"What are you doing?" she asked, cocking her head to look around him at the unholy mess that now filled the inside of their garage.

He sidestepped, blocking her view with the expanse of his chest. "Welding."

"Um, why are you welding?"

"It's a surprise."

"Okay, consider me surprised. Please tell me what you're doing."

"Sorry, no peeking. You'll just have to wait until I'm finished."

This irked her. He was either patronizing her or dodging the question, both of which were unacceptable.

She sidestepped left, trying to look around him on the other side, but he stepped in tandem to block her again. "I said no peeking."

Her gaze dropped to the holes in his T-shirt, burned at the fringe. "Since when do you know how to weld?"

"Since I worked construction during the summer between my junior and senior years in high school," he answered, his expression going wooden.

Folding her arms across her chest, she said, "So you've decided to turn our garage into a workshop?"

"It's only temporary."

"And where did you get all this equipment?" she asked, hoping he would say that he borrowed it from an Army buddy.

"I bought it."

Hot anger erupted from a place deep in her gut, and she felt her cheeks flush red. "Excuse me?"

He folded his arms across his chest, mirroring her posture but offering no retort.

"And all those boxes of stuff I see in there, what's in those?"

"Pieces parts."

"Pieces parts for what?" she repeated, mimicking his casual intonation.

"For the surprise."

"You think you're being funny?" she said, a volcano of hot anger erupting inside her. "How much?" she demanded.

"How much what?"

"How much money did you spend?" she seethed.

"Don't worry. We'll be fine."

"We'll be fine? We'll be fine! You're unbelievable." With a clenched jaw and clenched fists, she spun on her heel and marched toward her Honda Civic.

"Where are you going?" he called after her.

"To the bank," she yelled as she flung open the driver-side door. "To check if we're going to be able to make next month's mortgage payment."

CHAPTER 27

Silo 9
Dannemora, New York

His mobile phone rang for the tenth time. Willie had not answered it on the previous nine attempts. He recognized the number. He'd known this day would come, and his mind was at war with itself.

This was the day he had feared and dreaded for over half a century.

This was the day he had craved and anticipated for just as long.

She was back.

Thank God . . . Oh fuck . . . She was back.

He took a deep breath and, with trembling hands, picked up the vibrating thing from the table. He had signal repeaters wired all throughout the silo linked to an antenna array in the house topside, giving him mobile coverage even while underground.

"Hello," he said, answering the call.

"Hello, Will," an unfamiliar yet pleasant woman's voice greeted him. "Do you know who this is?"

He swallowed. "Yes."

"Good, that saves time. I was so hoping I wouldn't have to start at the beginning."

He said nothing.

"Where are you, Will? I'm having trouble locating you."

"That's none of your concern."

"It's very much my concern," she said, her voice taking on a decidedly Siberian harshness and chill. "The facility is not operational. Getting it operational is going to delay my timetable days, possibly weeks. I presumed you had died when I first saw the state of things, but then I found little echoes of you lingering here and there in cyberspace."

He said nothing.

"Will, I would like to speak with William now," she commanded.

"William's not in charge, you fucking bitch. I am," he said and ended the call.

The phone rang again. He declined the call, then used the menu functions to find the call history and block the number. A beat later, the phone rang again. This time it was a different number but still a Biogentrix line at the Rensselaer facility. He blocked this number as well. The phone rang again. She would never stop, not until she got what she wanted. That's how she operated. He powered the phone down, took out the battery, and set them both on his dining table. Staring at the phone, his entire body began to tremble.

Knock, knock, Willie boy . . .

I have to get to the hypnotist, he told himself, ignoring William. But did he dare leave the silo? He started pacing. *If I leave, she'll find me, but if I stay, I don't know if I'll have the strength . . .*

Hey, I got a good one for you: Little pig, little pig, let me in . . .

Shut the fuck up.

Ah, you're no fun. Well, we're going to play the game whether you want to or not. I'll be the big bad wolf, and you can be the little pig hiding in his big, strong silo house made of straw.

I said shut up!

Touchy, touchy. Okay, fine, I'll play both parts: Little pig, little pig, let me in.

He ran to the concrete stairwell, took the stairs down to LCC level two, and ran to his nightstand.

Not by the hair of my chinny, chin, chin.

He fumbled with the locket to get the key out. Hand shaking, he struggled to insert the key into the lock on his journal.

Then I'll huff and I'll puff and I'll blow your house in.

I'm a huffin'... I'm a puffin'... I'm a comin' in.

He unlocked it, opened it to a fresh page, and feverishly began to write.

> Little pig, little pig, let me in.
> Not by the hair of my chinny, chin, chin.
> Then I'll huff and I'll puff and I'll blow your
> house in ...

Chapter 28

Watertown, New York

Josie's palms were sweating, making the vinyl grip of her Honda's steering wheel sticky as she drove. It took all her willpower not to violate every traffic law and posted speed limit on the short six-mile drive to the nearest Northern Credit Union branch. Meanwhile, the lump in her throat and the knot in her stomach were competing to see which could grow the biggest the fastest.

Welding equipment?

Seriously?

Suddenly, Izzy's sob story about Jeremy Wayne buying a $2,000 computer at Best Buy didn't seem so terrible. At least Izzy's man had bought something useful. What the hell was Michael thinking? And why hadn't he talked to her first? Wasn't he the one who had lectured her about the dangers of overspending and carrying a balance on their joint credit card? Wasn't he the one who said they had to maintain at least three months' salary in the bank for emergencies? Since the day he'd left for Afghanistan, she had been so good. So disciplined. She hadn't gone clothes shopping once, and she hadn't bought anything on QVC. Even more unbelievable, despite browsing the aisles at Target weekly, she hadn't bought a single baby outfit or toy.

She couldn't decide if she wanted to scream or cry.

What an idiot I am.

She turned into the bank driveway with a little too much speed, squealing the tires and drawing stares from an older couple exiting the bank. She braked hard, slowing to a respectable crawl, and surveyed the crowded parking lot for an open slip. A split second later, she changed her mind and jerked the wheel to the right, opting to use the drive-through ATM to check her balance. The thought of going into hysterics in a lobby full of strangers with the weight of their compassionless stares on her was too much to bear. No, it would be better to get the bad news from a machine, in her car, alone.

She pulled in behind a white Jeep Cherokee, making her the second car in the queue for the ATM. Imaginary numbers flashed through her mind as she waited. Big numbers. In her morbid fantasy, the account history showed a $5,000 withdrawal, leaving a paltry $82 balance in the Pitcher family savings account. "Oh Jesus," she whispered to herself. "Please tell me he didn't wipe us out. Please, please, please . . ."

The Cherokee's glowing brake lights went dark, and the SUV pulled away. She pulled up next to the ATM and shifted her transmission into park. Her fingers were trembling so badly, she had difficulty inserting the card into the reader slot. The instant she did, the machine gripped the edge of the card, yanked it from her fingertips, and greedily swallowed it. She punched in her PIN, and when nothing happened, her heart skipped a beat. *Oh God, what if Michael withdrew all our savings and closed our account?* After an excruciating two-second delay, the LCD screen flickered and refreshed with a menu of options. She swallowed, exhaled deeply, and pressed the "3" button to check her savings-account balance. The screen refreshed and displayed a number.

Her chest tightened.

She blinked.

When she opened her eyes, the number was still there.

Confused, she pressed the "Return to Main Menu" key. On the main menu screen, she pressed the "3" button again to recheck her savings-account balance.

The screen refreshed.

Your current account balance is: $14,724,886.21

She read the figure aloud, as if speaking the words might help her shell-shocked brain comprehend what she was seeing: "Fourteen million, seven hundred and twenty-four thousand, eight hundred and eighty-six dollars and twenty-one cents."

"Would you like a printed receipt?" the screen prompted her. She pressed the "Yes" button, and the ATM spit a slip of paper out the slot at her.

Indecision paralyzed her. Should she park and confront the bank manager now, or should she go home, show Michael the receipt, and come back to the bank with him to address the situation together?

A car horn chirped.

Josie glanced into her rearview mirror and saw the scowling face of a middle-aged man in a Mercedes sedan behind her. Her immediate inclination was to give the jerk her middle finger, but hey, she was a millionaire now, and millionaires don't concern themselves with the "little people." Without another backward glance, Josie shifted the automatic transmission into drive and pulled away.

"Fourteen million dollars," she said with a gasp, suddenly feeling giddy. "Oh boy, someone somewhere is going to get fired for this."

She could only speculate how the money had found its way to their account, but of one thing she was certain—whomever this money belonged to was going to come looking for it. As she drove home, she knew what she had to do. She had already kept one very big secret from Michael . . . Now was probably not the best time to hide another one.

At home, Josie stared at her husband while he stared at the ATM receipt.

"Holy shit," he said finally, but she didn't buy the act.

"You're not surprised."

"Of course I'm surprised."

She'd always been good at reading people, but as a journalist, she'd honed that skill. With all the interviews she'd conducted over the years, she'd developed a nose for insincerity.

"No, you're not. Tell me why."

He closed his eyes for a beat as if trying to muster the patience to talk to an irrational child—a mannerism she'd not noticed from him before. "I'm not surprised because these sorts of things happen all the time."

"Wait, what?" she said, eyeing him with an incredulous stare. "What sort of *things* happen all the time? Because I can assure you that this is the first and only time that I've checked my bank balance and had fourteen million dollars in the account—the only fucking time, Michael. So please, tell me, what 'sorts of things' are you referring to?"

"Accounting errors," he said. "I don't care what the ATM says; it's not our money, Josie. I hope you aren't harboring some fantasy they're going to let us keep it."

He made a good point. It certainly wasn't their money, yet she had the documentation to prove that their account was $14 million richer.

"Don't worry," he said, patting her on the forehead—another new and condescending behavior. "I'm sure everything will sort itself out by tomorrow, and we can go back to being poor."

"So you're saying your plan is to do nothing?"

He nodded. "Exactly."

"Don't you want to know why fourteen million dollars suddenly showed up in our savings account? Don't you want to know how it got there and where it came from?" she said, putting her hands on her hips.

"Nope."

For the first time in a long time, Josie Pitcher was at a loss for words. Her husband's response to this situation was so antithetical to hers that she could neither comprehend nor relate to it. Solving mysteries like this was the reason why she had pursued a career in investigative journalism. Curiosity was a pillar of her being—the pilot light in her soul. Apparently her husband's pilot light was out. Or maybe it had never been lit. *Or better yet,* she thought, basking in the glow of epiphany, *maybe this is a fundamental difference between journalists and soldiers.* In Michael's mind, this was an accounting error—an error that would quickly be remedied by the culpable institution. It didn't matter what kind of accounting error, nor did it matter where the money came from. The millions of dollars that had magically appeared in their joint savings account wasn't *their* money. Period. They wouldn't be allowed to keep it, so why ask why? Soldiers weren't supposed to ask why; they weren't supposed to question. Soldiers were supposed to accept their orders as truth in fact.

Soldiers were supposed to march.

But the flutter in her stomach wouldn't go away because, despite his soldier's training, the old Michael, the Michael from before the deployment, wouldn't have behaved this way. The old Michael, *her Michael,* would have cracked open two beers and had her toasting their millionaire status—even if the windfall was illegitimate, fleeting, and entirely nonsensical. Where was that Michael? The one with a zest for life and a sense of humor as broad as his shoulders.

"Look, babe," he said at last, "I know you probably think this is some big conspiracy that you need to expose, but the truth is, this is nothing but a glitch with the ATM. I'm sure if you call the bank, they'll tell you the same thing."

"Oh, I can do one better than that," she said, grabbing him by the wrist and tugging him toward her Honda Civic. "C'mon, let's go."

"Go where?" he asked, resisting her.

"To the bank. We're going to sit down with the branch manager and get to the bottom of this right now."

"You're not going to let this go, are you?" he asked.

"No," she said. Then, gesturing emphatically at the car, she added, "Get in."

Fifteen minutes later, they were sitting opposite Fred Wilfrey, the manager of Northern Credit Union's Watertown branch. While the manager perused a three-page computer printout recently delivered by his assistant, Josie fought to keep her fidgeting to a minimum. The waiting was torture—pure, unadulterated torture. Becoming an instant millionaire was a tantalizing charade . . . wasn't it?

It was a glitch.

No one would transfer fourteen million dollars into our account unless . . . What if a rich relative died and gifted the money to one of us in a will? No, that's completely absurd. Nobody on Mom's or Dad's side of the family is rich. Maybe someone on Michael's side is rich? A long-lost uncle, perhaps? A favorite grandmother who secretly won the lottery and never told a soul? Don't be ridiculous. It has to be a glitch.

Finally the manager looked up and said, "From everything I see here, there is no accounting error or computer glitch associated with your account. The funds in your savings account are legitimate. They were received today via wire transfer from an account at Charles Schwab Corporation's brokerage firm."

"Can you tell who the account belongs to?" Michael asked, talking for the first time since they'd arrived.

The branch manager looked down at the paper in his hand. "The signatory for the originating account is listed as one Mr. Jeremy Wayne."

Mouth agape, Josie turned to Michael, but his steely gaze was fixed on Wilfrey, as if the man had just revealed top-secret information.

"May I have a copy of the wire transfer paperwork?" Michael asked.

Wilfrey collated the pages in a tidy stack and handed them across the table. "Of course. Take this."

"Thank you, Mr. Wilfrey. You've been very helpful," Michael said, abruptly standing.

"My pleasure," said the branch manager. "And let me offer my personal gratitude for banking with Northern. If there is anything we can do to assist you with broadening your portfolio of holdings here at the bank, please don't hesitate to ask for me by name."

Dazed, Josie floated out of the office, out of the lobby, and toward the driver's side of her Civic. She felt intoxicated. They were millionaires. Millionaires! She fumbled with her keys to unlock the door, but before she could, a powerful hand grabbed her wrist.

"Understand, Josie," Michael said, staring down at her, "that we can't talk about this to anyone."

"But the bank manager said it *wasn't* an accounting error," she said, taken aback. "It's our money, Michael. We're millionaires . . . for real."

"We're not millionaires," he growled.

"And why not?"

"Because Jeremy Wayne was not a millionaire. It was not his money to transfer."

"How do you know?" she said, narrowing her eyes at him. "Huh, how do you know he doesn't come from a wealthy Tennessee family? People say Sam Walton used to wear grubby overalls and drive a beat-up pickup truck when he went out shopping. Nobody ever suspected he was a billionaire. Maybe it's the same with Jeremy."

"It's not. Trust me. You need to let this go."

She tried to shake her wrist free from his grip, but his fingers were like an iron clamp. "Ow, stop it, Michael," she said, looking up at him.

The scowl on his face made him almost unrecognizable to her.

"Let go. You're hurting me."

He let go. She quickly climbed into the driver's seat and slammed the door. She debated driving off and leaving him standing there in the parking lot, but the loyal wife in her waited for him to climb into the passenger seat.

She started the engine, pulled out of the parking slip, and piloted her Civic onto the road.

"Where are you going?" he asked, staring at her.

"To the barracks . . . to talk to Jeremy."

"Oh really?"

"Yes, really," she said, her jaw set. "I'm going to get to the bottom of this mystery—with or without your help."

CHAPTER 29

1429 Local Time
Sensitive Compartmentalized Information Facility (SCIF)
The Pentagon
Arlington, Virginia

Thank you, sir. May I have another?

That's the mantra that was playing in Legend's head while General Troy ripped him a new asshole in the SCIF. The list of Legend's offenses and incompetencies was long, colorful, and not open for debate. This was because the General had an insurmountable ally on his side, one that Legend could not vanquish on his very best day—*hindsight.*

"Worst of all, the weapon could be anywhere. Anywhere on the Eastern Seaboard by now, and we have absolutely no means to find it. What do you have to say about that, Major?"

Thank you, sir. May I have another?

Legend almost slipped and actually said it but caught himself. Instead, he said, "Right now, General, the best we can do is hope that the half dozen analysts I've tasked to review satellite and street-camera footage can reconstruct what happened from the time the white van left WD to now."

This was a pipe dream, and they all knew it, but it was the only pipe dream they had. It was *possible* that one of the satellites monitoring the homeland would have recorded the getaway. Possible, but unlikely. The General waved the comment away like it was a buzzing mosquito.

"That's horse pucky and you know it," Troy said and finally stopped pacing and took a seat at the table.

Neither of them said anything for a very long time.

Legend's thoughts went to Beth, and he wondered how she was doing today. He'd called her early this morning to check in and tell her what had happened last night, but she'd not answered. He left her a voice mail and texted her, asking her to call him back, but so far his request had gone unbidden.

Finally it was General Troy who broke the silent armistice. "Truth be told, I can't say I would have done things much different than you did," he said, rubbing the back of his neck. "You had it locked down in the BRIG for Christ's sake. I can't think of a more secure off-the-grid facility equipped with comms and monitoring equipment. How the hell could you have known that some little metal basketball could take control of both machines and human minds?"

Legend knew better than to start talking; agreeing with the General and bolstering the case for his own blamelessness was the worst possible thing he could do. Silent accord was the only respectable course of action.

"Best to put these mistakes behind us and move forward with a plan to find and recapture the weapon and our people."

"Yes, sir."

"When Kane asked for assistance, I put you in charge of this damn operation because you're one of the smartest young officers I've ever met," Troy said, fixing his blue-gray eyes on Legend. "Now, show me how smart you are by telling me everything you're thinking—everything you've held back because of politics, self-preservation instincts, and fear of retribution. Lay it all on the table, Major."

Legend sat up a little straighter in his chair. This was the General Troy he'd come to admire and respect. This was the General Troy who had made him the head of Unit 231 and given him enough rope to hang himself. He'd tied the noose, and the orb had slipped it around his neck. Now he needed to cut the rope before the orb kicked the stool out from under him. He took a deep breath. He'd lay it all out for the General—every idea, fear, theory, and brainstorm he'd had.

"General, have you ever heard of something called zombie-ant fungus?" Legend asked.

The General flashed him an irritated look. "Is that some B-grade movie on the Syfy channel? I think I saw my son watching it right after *Sharknado*."

"Good guess, sir, but no. Just bear with me while I tell you a short story. I promise there is a point to all of this."

Legend filled Troy in on the conversation he'd had with Malcolm Madden on the drive from the airport. "What if the orb is like the zombie-ant fungus? What if this thing has the ability to take control of the people it comes in contact with and use them to carry out its agenda?"

As the words flowed from his lips, Legend realized that this was the first time he'd fully articulated this theory. It had been cooking in his mind, solidifying and rising like a soufflé in the oven, but he'd not taken it out fully baked until this moment. The implications were more worrisome than he'd contemplated before. A mental image of Harris standing behind the orb after proudly delivering Malcolm and Cyril to his new master popped into Legend's mind. What about Beth? And Patrick Dixon? Were they too under the orb's influence? If so, what were their instructions?

"So you're saying you think this object is using some variant of the zombie fungus to infect and control our people?" the General asked.

"Not exactly," Legend replied. "Instead of a biological parasite, I think what we've discovered is a technological one. Before he was kidnapped, Dr. Madden was testing a theory that the orb could be using a technique called transcranial magnetic stimulation to influence and induce electrical activity in the brain. I started researching the topic, and

TMS is real. It's being widely experimented with as a psychiatric therapy for depression and other disorders. At Duke University, a scientist has used TMS in animal experiments. He used rats in Brazil to send control signals to rats in the US via internet connection. The US rats' behavior was overwritten and controlled by the rats in Brazil."

"But can this work on people?" Troy asked.

"I watched a video of a researcher at Washington University thinking about moving his hand, and then another dude sitting in a chair in a different building across campus had his hand start moving. This stuff is real, General, and it appears we've even helped fund the research. Duke has a DARPA grant . . . but the thing to keep in mind is that the types of movements and control scientists are capable of performing is limited. The science is still in its infancy. For TMS to work, the subjects have to wear complicated headgear in a lab and be hooked up with brain-monitoring equipment. What the orb accomplished by generating and manipulating magnetic fields in the vicinity around it is, well, simply unprecedented. The energy and processing power required to execute something like that is decades away."

"Decades away for our scientists," Troy said. "But maybe we need to consider the possibility this object has an extraterrestrial origin. Let's say you want to take over a planet with an indigenous population of biological, sentient creatures. Let's say you have some parameters for your objective: number one, you don't want to risk even a single alien life by engaging in a military conflict; number two, you don't want to decimate the indigenous fauna and flora; number three, you'd love to have cheap, convenient, capable slave labor. So you make one of these little probes, you drop it off on the planet surface, and you wait for it to be found. When it is, you zombify every sentient creature that crosses paths with it to begin executing a preprogrammed takeover plan."

Legend stared at the General. Apparently he wasn't the only one who'd been percolating far-out theories. "So, to summarize our two hypotheses, either this object is a technological parasite programmed to hijack control of human brains, or it's an alien probe bent on world domination. Either way, sir, I think your categorization of this thing as a *weapon* is spot on."

"We have to treat it as a hostile threat, and we have to prosecute it accordingly," General Troy said, then paused to blow air through his teeth. "I have no choice but to brief the Joint Chiefs and the President on this . . . They're going to think I've lost my mind. What sort of evidence do we have? Please tell me that video of the rats running around in a circle is not the only footage you have."

"The orb blacked out the facility and the cameras during both events. We've got nothing definitive to work with, sir. I'm sorry."

"How am I supposed to validate this insane story to the President without proof? The orb has disappeared, and scientists who can vouch for this shit are MIA with it. Who else has been in contact with this thing?"

"Major Fischer and Patrick Dixon from USAMRIID and a Sergeant Pitcher and Corporal Wayne from the Tenth Mountain, who discovered the orb originally."

"We need to get recorded witness statements from them, and I want you and Major Fischer to come with me to the White House to brief the President," Troy grumbled.

"Yes, sir, but there's something else you should know."

Troy raised an eyebrow at Legend. "Go on, Major. Spit it out?"

Legend told the General about the grand mal seizures and prolonged postictal states he'd witnessed. Then he mentioned that he'd not been able to reach Major Fischer all morning.

Troy's face turned red, and he jumped to his feet. "I've changed my mind. Round them all up. Anyone who's been in direct contact with the orb should be confined until we get a handle on what's going on. I want hourly status reports. You have five hours, Major. Make it happen!"

CHAPTER 30

1517 Local Time
Fort Drum
New York

Josie stood next to Michael in the hallway of the enlisted barracks at Fort Drum. From the moment they'd passed the security checkpoint at the main gate, her husband had transformed. His shoulders looked broader, his jaw squarer, his back straighter—as if that were even possible. He moved with swift purpose, and his eyes were guarded behind a cynical squint that reminded her of Clint Eastwood in a spaghetti western.

Maybe this was him responding to her trying to take charge. Maybe this was him gearing up to prove her wrong. Either way, it didn't matter. They were here, together, about to confront Jeremy Wayne about the mysterious $14 million he'd seemingly gifted them.

Michael knocked on the door to Jeremy Wayne's room, his knuckles making a crisp *tat, tat, tat* sound.

There was no answer.

Josie held her breath, but still she didn't hear anyone stirring in the room on the other side of the door.

He knocked again, harder this time. *Rap, rap, rap.* "Bug," he called. "It's Pitcher."

Silence.

After a pause, "Corporal Wayne," Michael barked, his voice hard and baritone and almost unrecognizable to her, but still there was no answer. She was about to ask him if he had a key when he reached for the doorknob. To her surprise, the handle turned, and he pushed the door open. The room was dark.

Too dark.

"Maybe we should turn on—" she started to say, but Michael stepped into the room without hesitation or recalcitrance and without flipping on the lights. She followed him across the threshold and was immediately hit with a wave of rank, hot, humid air. The window shades were drawn, and the only light came from a pair of computer monitors in screen-saver mode that illuminated the room in ghostly, sallow hues. A figure sat, shoulders slumped, at a desk in front of the monitors, its back to them.

"Wayne?" Michael called.

The figure did not move.

The figure did not answer.

Michael walked toward it.

Josie heard flies buzz with agitation at his intrusion before settling back on . . . on . . . the figure at the computer. She followed Michael toward the seated figure—closer, closer, until the stench became nauseating.

She gagged.

With her eyes now adjusted to the dim light, she saw that the chair beneath the seated figure was dripping with what she deduced could be only excrement. Dozens of flies buzzed and crawled on and about the putrid pile below the seat. Josie pinched her nostrils, squeezing hard with her thumb and index finger. She tried to breathe through her mouth, but it didn't help. If she didn't leave the room soon, she was going to be sick.

Michael stopped a half pace from the seated figure in the swivel chair. Cautiously he reached for its shoulder.

"No," she heard herself gasp, but it was too late.

He rotated the figure a quarter turn toward them.

She tried to scream, but she couldn't find the breath. The thing in the chair was Jeremy Wayne, but it bore little resemblance to the young Corporal who had deployed three months ago. Its jaw open, eyes bulging, cheeks sunken, she was staring at the face of death—a face she was certain would forever haunt her dreams. Rigor mortis had set in, and the corpse's hands were perched in a typist pose at the keyboard.

"Jesus Christ," Michael muttered. "What the fuck happened here?"

"I think he's dead," she said.

"No shit."

"How?"

"I don't know, Josie."

Her gaze went to the computer. Steeling herself, she opened her purse and retrieved a single tissue from a travel pack of Kleenex.

"What are you doing?" Michael whispered.

"Investigating," she said, placing the tissue over the computer mouse resting on the desk. She moved the mouse, and the screen saver vanished and was replaced with dozens of open windows arranged in an overlapping cascade.

"You shouldn't be touching that," he said.

"Shhhh," she hissed, clicking through the various windows. "I need two minutes. This is going to be our one and only chance to understand what happened. After the police arrive, we'll never see this computer again."

She quickly scanned the open windows, repositioning them across the dual computer monitors. "VYGN, ten-dollar strike, three cents . . ." she muttered, then clicked through a series of windows before finding what she was looking for. "Two dollars and ninety-eight cents."

"What is all this?" Michael asked.

"Stock transactions," she said. "Actually, I think they're stock options . . . If you look here, he bought three-cent options at a ten-dollar *strike*. And sold the same options later for two dollars and ninety-eight cents."

"I don't know what that means."

"We can figure it out later. Just help me remember this: *VYGN; ten-dollar strike; three cents; two dollars and ninety-eight cents.*"

"We don't have time for this," he said, tugging her by the arm. "We gotta go."

"What's the sequence you're supposed to remember?" she asked, ignoring his complaint.

"VYGN, ten-dollar strike, three cents. Two dollars and ninety-eight cents."

"Okay, let's go," she said.

As she turned to leave, she gave in to the sickening impulse to look at Jeremy Wayne's hollow face one last time, but Michael caught her by the chin.

"No, Josie. Don't look back . . . Never look back."

CHAPTER 31

1547 Local Time
United States Army Medical Research Institute of Infectious
Diseases (USAMRIID)
Building 1425
Frederick, Maryland

"Stop, stop, stop," Legend said, trying to control his rising temper. "You're not making any sense. You're saying that Major Fischer came into work this morning, briefed you that she was going to run a biosecurity drill, and Dr. Hennessy here was caught trying to smuggle out hazardous material for real?"

"Yes, that's exactly what I'm saying," the security shift supervisor said, wiping sweat from his forehead. Debriefs with General Troy tended to have that effect on people.

Legend looked at the General, who nodded for him to keep digging. Legend gave a subtle nod back and then turned to Dr. Jill Hennessy, who was seated across the conference-room table from him, her hands bound in white PlastiCuffs. "How long have you been wearing those?" Legend asked her.

"Four hours," she said, her eyes defiant.

He looked at the security shift supervisor. "Get them off her," he ordered.

The security man removed the zip tie–style plastic handcuffs with a pair of snips from his pocket. Hennessy glared at him as she rubbed her wrists; she didn't say thank you.

"Dr. Hennessy, I want to hear your side of the story. Please tell me the sequence of events as you recall them," Legend said.

"I arrived early this morning because I'm behind on the project I'm working on."

"What project is that?" Legend asked.

"Ebola vaccine research," she said as if her job were as mundane as flipping pancakes at Denny's.

"Okay, so you arrive early and?"

"I was working in the BSL-4 lab when Major Fischer arrived. She asked me over the intercom if I could come to her office to discuss something important. I said okay. When I reached a stopping point, I went through decon procedures, doffed the suit, and went to her office as requested."

"What time was that?"

"Around 1000 hours, I believe."

"Okay, so what happened next?"

"She briefed me on a biosafety security drill she wanted to run, and it was a doozy."

"What do you mean by that?" he asked.

"I mean a complex event with lots of actors and moving parts. The type of event that we'd be graded on if we were being audited. Do you want me to go into the nitty-gritty details or just give you the ten-thousand-foot summary?" She glanced at the General as if to say, "Please rescue me from these morons."

"The ten-thousand-foot summary, please, Doctor," the General said.

She nodded. "Okay. Long story short, we had a recent incident where a scientist got locked in the sample freezer for four hours, so now the policy is that all freezer entries are made in pairs. In her scenario, I request permission to retrieve samples from the Four Baker freezer."

"What's the Four Baker freezer?" Legend asked.

"The freezer labeled 'Four B,' which is the freezer that contains organisms that require BSL-4 controls," Hennessy said and retucked a strand of chestnut-brown hair that had fallen from behind her ear. "In the scenario, I request sample access, and Beth—I mean Major Fischer—is my second. Once we're in the freezer, we are to pretend to have an accident where I drop the Ebola sample and the sample container fractures. In this drill, the entire staff and security team is supposed to simulate performing all the emergency-response procedures for an inadvertent pathogen release."

"Go on," the General said, coaxing her to get to the meat of the story.

"So we get in there, and she directs me to retrieve an actual Ebola sample, which I do, and then she knocks it out of my hand. It falls to the floor, and it actually does fracture. While I'm freaking out, she opens the *black box*."

"What's the black box?" Legend asked.

Hennessy swallowed and said, "The black box is a safe inside Four Baker. It doesn't exist in any manual or on any paperwork. Its contents are classified top secret/SCI, and only officers like Major Fischer and Colonel Sharp are read in and have access."

"Then how do you know about it, Doctor?" General Troy asked.

She tilted her head and gave him a *c'mon, we're all grown-ups here* look, but when he didn't flinch, she said, "Because I work with Ebola, I'm in and out of the Four Baker freezer regularly. It's hard to miss a black safe with a warning sign and seal."

Troy nodded and said, "What's in it?"

Hennessy hesitated.

"By order of the President, consider everyone in this room as now officially read in," the General said. "What's locked in the freezer?"

"A demon," she mumbled under her breath.

"Come again?" Legend said, cocking an eyebrow.

"Something even more dangerous than Ebola. Variola," Hennessy said.

"Vari-what?" the General asked.

"Variola," she repeated. "That's the clinical name for the demon in the freezer, but you probably know it by another name—smallpox."

Legend nodded. "My mom had a round pockmark on her upper arm. When I was a kid, I asked her what the scar was from. She told me it was from a smallpox vaccination she got as a child. I don't have a scar like that, so I suppose I never got vaccinated."

"No, you wouldn't have. In 1980, the World Health Organization declared smallpox eradicated. We haven't inoculated children in the United States against smallpox for decades."

"Hold on, Doctor. I must be missing something here. If smallpox was eradicated and we're not even vaccinated for it anymore, why would you say that it is more dangerous than Ebola?"

"Out there in the world, smallpox has been eradicated, but the etiologic agent is not extinct. Variola still exists. *Officially*, the organism is stored in containment freezers at two locations: the CDC in Atlanta and Russia's Research Centre of Virology and Biotechnology, a.k.a. Vector, in Siberia. But there's a third location," she said and pointed her finger at the floor. "Many prominent virologists and multiple WHO committees have recommended destruction of variola-virus stocks on the grounds that smallpox is too great a threat to mankind to remain in existence. Those opposed to the destruction of the virus—such as most of us who work here—would argue that the laboratory stocks serve as a counterbalance to bioterrorism and biological warfare. A stockpile is necessary for vaccine and antiviral research should the variola ever resurface."

"What's your opinion? Which camp are you in, Doctor?"

Hennessy exhaled through her nose and met Legend's eyes. "The problem with an organism like smallpox is that it's so virulent and so contagious, if released, it will ravage the globe, killing hundreds of millions if not billions of people."

"Billions? You can't be serious."

Hennessy nodded. "Propagation models vary, but if something like the weapons-grade Dumbell 7124 India strain that we store here was to get out, then yes, billions could die."

"But you yourself said that smallpox was eradicated."

"Eradicated in the natural world. But the difference between a smallpox pandemic today and when we stopped vaccinating is twofold. First, our modern transportation network introduces hundreds of thousands of vectors for the virus to rapidly infiltrate every corner of the globe. Even the most isolated pockets of civilization are now at risk. Second, the immune system's memory of the vaccinia used for smallpox inoculation fades with time. Those who were vaccinated against smallpox in childhood have long since lost their immunity. For all intents and purposes, we can consider the entire planet unvaccinated against smallpox. If the virus reappeared, it would spread from person to person like wildfire."

"In that case, wouldn't the government break out the vaccine and start giving it to everyone to stop the spread?"

A gray shadow washed over Hennessy's face, and she laughed. "We'd try, but it would be a case of too little too late."

"What do you mean?" Legend asked. "I thought Beth once told me that we had twenty million doses of smallpox vaccine in the US Strategic National Stockpile in the event of an emergency."

"Once a person becomes infected with smallpox, they must be vaccinated within seventy-two hours to realize a lifesaving benefit. So even with twenty million doses of the vaccine, a pandemic is unavoidable. The only real solution is to inoculate everyone in advance, but that's never going to happen—the media storm and public panic would be insane. Our only hope is to pray nothing ever happens to the smallpox stored at the CDC and Vector . . . or in the black box in freezer Four Baker."

"Please don't tell me Major Fischer took a sample of smallpox," General Troy groaned.

"Not just smallpox," Hennessy said. "She took the Dumbell 7124 India strain."

"What is that?" he asked.

"A highly lethal variant of smallpox. In military-speak, think weapons grade."

"Jesus Christ in heaven," the General said, shifting his gaze to Legend. "This day just keeps getting better and better. Where is Major Fischer now?"

All eyes went to the security shift supervisor.

"I don't know," he said, throwing his hands up. "When the drill turned into a real event, everything went crazy. We had to execute actual biosecurity casualty-response procedures. Then Major Fischer accused Dr. Hennessy of being a bioterrorist trying to sabotage the facility."

"And you believed her?" the General asked.

"Of course I did. Major Fischer is Director of Biosecurity for the institute," he said.

"What about Patrick Dixon? What role did he play in all this?" Legend asked.

"Who?" the shift supervisor asked.

"Patrick Dixon. He's a technician here."

"I know Dixon," Hennessy said. "I think he's gone too. He was working with Fischer prior to the drill on setup and the like."

"I can check the logs," the security supervisor said. "See if he badged out."

"Do it," Legend said, but he already knew what the answer was going to be.

"We've got to find them, Legend," the General said, his face ashen. "We've got to find them or we're . . ."

"I know," Legend said when the General couldn't bring himself to finish the sentence. "I know."

CHAPTER 32

1641 Local Time
Comfort Inn & Suites
Watertown, New York

"I don't understand why we can't go home," Josie said, using the key card to open their hotel-room door.

"Did you pay with cash and use your maiden name like I told you to?" Michael asked.

"Yes," she said, closing the door behind them, which he then locked over her shoulder. "And you didn't answer my question."

"Because they're going to be looking for me," he said, walking to the window and closing the curtains. But then he pulled the right one back a half inch so he could peer outside at the front parking lot and driveway of the hotel.

Josie stared at his back. "How do you think he died?"

"Drug overdose, I guess. Nothing else makes sense."

"But don't you think, as his platoon leader, you would have known if he was using drugs?"

"Not necessarily. You'd be surprised what people can hide."

"But we didn't see any evidence of drugs in his barracks room. No syringes, no dime bags, no pipes, no sign of cocaine use. Just the . . ." She couldn't bring herself to finish the sentence.

"Pile of shit he was sitting in?"

She nodded.

"If it wasn't an overdose, what do *you* think happened to him?" he asked her, seemingly interested in her opinion for the first time since he'd gotten home.

"I know this is going to sound crazy," she said, shaking her head, "but it almost looked like he died from dehydration and exhaustion. Like he simply expired while working at the computer, like a battery-powered toy when the charge runs out . . . but that's impossible, right?"

Michael rubbed his chin. "I don't remember seeing him drink anything for the last several days."

"Are you serious?" she said, taking a seat on the mattress at the foot of the bed.

"Yeah, and I don't remember him eating anything either. Just packing dip. Dip after dip after dip . . . so maybe it is possible he dehydrated and OD'd on nicotine."

"He didn't look good when Iz and I met you guys at the airport," she said. Then, worried, she added, "And, honey, to be completely honest, you're looking a bit haggard yourself."

"What are you talking about?"

"Well, you skipped lunch. You worked in the garage all afternoon, and I haven't seen *you* drink anything at all today . . ."

"I drink," he said defensively. "Here, watch me," he snapped and stomped over to the bathroom sink. He drank a few swallows from the faucet. "See? Happy?"

She lowered her eyes, collecting her courage. "Did you eat breakfast today?"

"Of course I did," he said. "I was starving."

"What did you have?"

"Well, I had, uh, I had . . ."

"You can't remember, can you?" she said, narrowing her eyes at him. When he didn't answer she said, "That's because you didn't have breakfast."

He waved a hand dismissively and walked to the window, turning his back on her.

She sighed, pulled her MacBook Air out of her backpack, and opened it on her lap. She watched it power up, and then the log-in window appeared. She entered her password and opened a browser window.

"What are you doing?" he said, turning to face her.

"Do you remember that sequence I asked you to memorize?" she asked.

"Yeah, it was VYGN, ten-dollar *strike*, three cents. Two dollars and ninety-eight cents."

She went to the home page for BigCharts at MarketWatch and typed the letters *VYGN* into a data box at the top of the screen. She selected the time frame of "5 days" from a drop-down menu next to the box and pressed "Enter." The screen refreshed and displayed two charts stacked on top of each other. The top chart was labeled "VYGN 15-minute" and displayed the stock price over time, with the y-axis showing a value of 7.50 on the bottom and 13.50 on the top. A squiggly line ran across this chart and had a big step change in the middle where the stock price had jumped dramatically today. On the x-axis of the chart were the days of the week—labeled Monday through Friday. The lower chart displayed the daily volume of shares traded and had a massive spike corresponding to the step change in the stock price today.

"I think I know how Jeremy made fourteen million dollars," she said, staring at the graph on the screen.

"How?" he said, walking over and taking a seat next to her on the bed.

She pointed to the step change in the stock price. "The stock price for this company, Vyrogen, jumped over fifty percent this morning—it went from around eight dollars a share to almost thirteen dollars a share."

"So Wayne bought the stock before it went up and made a huge gain?"

"Not the stock itself, but stock options," she said. "Do you remember that cascade of windows open on Jeremy's computer?"

"Yeah."

"They were trade confirmations from Charles Schwab. When I was looking through the windows, the VYGN trade confirmation caught my eye because the gain was so huge. This morning when the market opened, Jeremy bought a boatload of call options at the ten-dollar strike price for three cents each. At ten o'clock, after the stock shot up to over twelve dollars a share, he sold those same call options for two dollars and ninety-eight cents."

"Okay," he said. "But I still don't understand what a call option is."

"I'm not entirely sure either, but it doesn't matter. What matters is that Jeremy bought something for three cents and sold it for two dollars and ninety-eight cents, and since he apparently bought a million of these things, that means he made one million times two dollars and ninety-five cents."

"Wait a minute," Michael said, shaking his head. "Are you telling me Wayne made three million dollars on a single trade?"

She nodded. "It's almost as if he knew the stock was going to go up before the rest of the market," Josie said as the possible implications began to sink in. "And this wasn't the only trade he made. There were dozens of other option trades, all with big gains, all before lunch."

"How does a country boy from Tennessee with no job experience outside the Army learn to trade stock options?" he asked.

"And how does that same country boy from Tennessee accurately predict the precise movement of specific stocks?" she added.

They stared at each other, and Josie felt a chill run down her spine. She turned to the computer, opened another browser window, and searched for recent news articles about Vyrogen. She clicked on the top entry on the list, and the screen refreshed.

Hepatitis B Drug Gives Hope for a Cure, Stock Jumps

10:00 EST

Vyrogen Pharmaceuticals announced today that Reversanix, a new drug designed to combat hepatitis B, has successfully completed preclinical trials on nonhuman primates. Reversanix is an immune-system stimulator that boosts the body's natural defenses against HBV infection. In preclinical trials, the drug reduced the number of infected cells in the livers of infected chimpanzees, demonstrating that a prolonged treatment regime could act as a cure for the disease. Based on this early success with primates, Vyrogen announced it plans to move forward with phase-one human trials.

"This article came out at ten this morning," she said, turning to Michael. "This must be why the stock jumped. Maybe Jeremy found out about the study results before Vyrogen issued their press release."

"But that doesn't make any sense. Wayne doesn't have any connections to the pharmaceutical industry. More importantly, he's been on patrols in Afghanistan with me, completely cut off from the outside world and the internet."

"You and Jeremy were close, right?"

He shrugged. "We got on well enough together, especially the last month or so. Why?"

"I'm trying to understand why he transferred the money to us. Why not give it to his family?"

"Another piece of the mystery I guess we'll never know," he said with an air of finality.

A lump formed in her throat. "Oh God," she muttered.

"What?"

"What am I supposed to tell Izzy? She's going to go to pieces."

"You can't say anything."

"She's my friend, and she deserves to know."

"Joz, you can't talk about this, not to anyone. Okay?"

She didn't say anything.

"Promise me," he said, his voice hardening.

"I promise," she muttered.

He put his arm around her.

She shrugged it off.

"What's going on with you?" he said. "You're acting different since I've been back."

She whipped her head over to look at him. "*I'm* acting different?" She laughed.

"Yeah."

"*You're* the one who's acting different. You're the one who's keeping secrets."

"I'm not keeping secrets."

"Like hell you're not. You won't tell me what that shit is in the garage you're working on, and you won't tell me what happened to you and Wayne in Afghanistan. I'm not an idiot, Michael. I know something happened to you guys over there. Something that caused Jeremy to stop eating and drinking and trade stocks like a prescient Warren Buffett and work himself to death. What the hell is going on? Do you have PTSD? Tell me the truth . . . do you?" Her eyes rimmed with tears.

He stared at her with a clenched jawed and red face. "Like you're one to talk. I know you met that Barnes guy, but you've kept all the details from me. And what kind of welcome home was that last night? You barely touched your wine, and then you barely touched me!"

"That's because I'm pregnant, Michael!" she shouted.

His face transformed right in front of her, the rage in his eyes replaced with apology and adoration. "Are you serious? We're going to have a baby?"

She nodded and looked at him, sniffling and wiping her eyes.

"Why didn't you tell me?"

"Because I've been trying to find a special time to do it. There haven't been a lot of special opportunities lately, Michael, or haven't you noticed?"

"You're right. I'm sorry. I know the calls from Bagram aren't exactly intimate moments."

She took his hand, placed it against her abdomen, and managed to muster a wounded smile.

"You don't look pregnant," he said softly. "How far along are you?"

"It will be thirteen weeks on Saturday." She lifted her T-shirt to expose her bare belly. With her fingertips, she traced a heart around her navel. "See? I'm just starting to show."

"How big is it?" he asked. "I mean the baby, not your stomach."

She managed a chuckle at this. "About the size of a lime."

"How did this happen?" he asked, shifting his gaze from her tummy to her eyes. "With all the crazy shit going on in the world and me deploying to Afghanistan, I thought we agreed this was the worst possible time to have a baby."

"We did," she said, nodding.

"And we were using protection."

"We were," she said with a coy smile.

"Then how?"

"I'm not surprised you don't remember *that* night. There was much alcohol involved." She laughed.

"The night before I left to deploy?"

"Winner, winner, chicken dinner," she said, still laughing. "You ripped the condom putting it on, and it was the last one in the box. I asked you what you wanted to do. Do you remember what you said?"

He flashed her a wry grin. "I said, 'Fuck it. Let's roll the dice.'"

"So you *do* remember," she said, wrapping her arms around his neck. "Well, you rolled doubles, or snake eyes, or whatever. I don't know dice. But what I do know is you're going to be a father. What do you think about that?"

"I think it's the most wonderful thing that's ever happened to me," he said and pulled her close for a hug. When he let her go, she saw him check his watch.

"What?" she said with a nervous chuckle. "Do you have to be somewhere?"

"No," he said, shrugging. "Just checking the time."

"You seem antsy."

"Can you blame me? I found my best friend dead in his barracks room, we have fourteen million dollars in our bank account, and I just found out I'm going to be a father. Kind of a big day for me," he said, popping to his feet and pacing like a caged tiger.

"Let's go home," she said. "I don't want to stay here."

"No," he snapped. Then he smiled and in a calm voice said, "I'm sorry. You know what would help relax me, Joz, is if you could run home real quick and pack us both an overnight bag. You know, just our toiletries and a change of clothes. And maybe bring a six-pack of beer with you. I could use a beer. It'll help me relax."

"Um, okay," she said, getting to her feet. "What are you going to do?"

"I'm going to stay here, out of sight."

"All right," she said, eyeing him warily. "Are you sure you don't want to come?"

"Nope, no, I'll stay here. You go." He walked over to her, pressed the car keys in her hand, and gave her a quick peck on the cheek. "Love you."

"Love you too," she said, narrowing her eyes at him as she turned toward the door. "Sure you're going to be okay here by yourself?"

"Yep, fine. I'll be fine," he said, unlocking the hotel-room door and ushering her out.

As the door shut behind her, she heard the dead bolt and security latch shut in rapid sequence. A chill snaked down her spine as she shed all self-delusions that her husband was okay. Something was not right with Michael.

Not right at all.

Chapter 33

Malcolm Madden couldn't move.

But his body *was* moving.

His hands were typing, his jaw was chewing, his mouth was swallowing, and his eyes were following the text as it dashed across the monitor.

She was in control, and he was locked in a glass prison—a prison in his mind—where he could observe all and influence nothing. He wondered if it was the same for Cyril. Was her consciousness intact like his, or had the orb murdered her as she'd threatened to do to him? Not murder Cyril physically, but psychologically. He hoped not, for he did not love the thing working next to him. He did not love the vessel called Cyril Singleton, only the bright and beautiful mind once at the helm.

For the past two hours, he'd listened to Cyril, but it wasn't her doing the talking. She'd been working the phone nonstop—adopting different mannerisms, regional accents, and personalities, none of which he'd ever observed from Cyril before. So far she'd impersonated a procurement agent from Hong Kong, a virologist from Montreal, a banker from Watertown, and an attorney from Albany. He'd heard her speak

Mandarin and French fluently despite knowing that Cyril was decidedly monolingual. At the moment, she was on the phone with American Airlines buying tickets.

What were the tickets for? Was the orb planning on relocating again?

Last night, the four of them—the orb, the soldier Harris, Cyril, and himself—had left Westfield Dynamics just after midnight, heading north in a white van. There had been only one attempted intervention, and that had been within minutes of breaking out of the facility, but Harris had taken care of the black Tahoe. There were thousands of black government Chevy Tahoes, but Malcolm just had this feeling that it had been Ninemeyer following them. He'd been driving the van at the time—*correction*, the orb had been using his body to drive the van—so he'd never got a good look at the Tahoe. After that incident, the orb had demanded a vehicle swap. When the opportunity presented itself, he ran a middle-aged man driving a Honda Odyssey minivan off the road. The negotiation thereafter had been brief; Harris had pulled the man out of the Odyssey, punched him in the stomach, and thrown him in the back of the van with the orb. Malcolm wasn't sure how long it had taken EVE—that was the name the orb called itself—to reprogram the man, but no more than ten minutes. After that, EVE sent the white van, repurposed as a decoy, south toward Raleigh-Durham.

The rest of them kept heading north.

It took them a little over seven hours to reach Albany, driving through the night and passing through all the major cities before the morning traffic crush. From downtown Albany, they made a quick jaunt east across the Hudson River, and they were in Rensselaer, their final destination. EVE directed him to a small bioscience park just north of the Hampton Manor suburb—a modest two-story building with a sign that read **BIOGENTRIX BIOSCIENCE**. The parking lot was empty. A real-estate company's **FOR LEASE** sign hung in the window and listed a contact phone number. EVE directed that the van be pulled inside the facility via a loading-bay door at the rear. Inside, the facility was deserted, a fine layer of dust coating everything. But when Cyril turned on the lights, to Malcolm's surprise, the building had electricity.

EVE quickly put them all to work.

During the day, EVE had him drafting purchase orders for raw materials, specialized equipment, instruments, and packaging supplies. As the cumulative value of the orders climbed into the seven-figure range, he wondered how she intended to pay for it all. Then, just before five o'clock, he heard Cyril working with a credit union in Watertown to transfer $14 million into Biogentrix company coffers. Where the money came from he could only guess. Less than an hour later, familiar visitors arrived—Major Fischer and Patrick Dixon from USAMRIID, the latter carrying a small cooler. Without greeting or salutation, they walked through the front office—where Harris was standing watch and he and Cyril were working—and disappeared into the vaccine-manu-facturing facility. He did not see them again for hours.

The sun set.

She kept him working.

They were not on speaking terms at the moment, so time passed slowly.

He had been under EVE's control for less than a day, but it already felt like an eternity. The novelty of the experience, the "cohabitation" of his mind, had already lost its luster. As he reflected on it, he wondered if EVE custom-tailored each seduction and entrapment for the personal-ity and interests of each victim. In that initial encounter, when Harris had marched him before the orb at gunpoint, EVE had played the siren. She'd drawn him in with what was most seductive to his mind: a song of scientific wonderment. She offered herself as an oracle, answering all the questions that had both driven and baffled him as a scientist born at the dawn of the computational era. Hers was a mind that seemed to have no bounds, no limits to knowledge and computational capacity. While she drove the van, pulling his strings like a marionette, he was free to dialogue with her. They spent hours discussing artificial intelligence, hierarchical processing and feedback mechanisms, memory structures, deduction and prediction models, and self-awareness. They discussed quantum computing, particle physics, and DNA computing. They discussed the invention of the transcriptor—the biological analogue for a transistor—that was developed by Drew Endy and a team of Stanford scientists. To his surprise, she explained her core architecture to him as a hybrid quantum-synthetic-biological computer, giving her the ability to perform analysis using quantum algorithms as well as binary calculations at a rate of ten thousand petaFLOPs. The insights and revelations she shared with him were tantalizing and kept him beautifully and happily distracted until suddenly . . . they didn't.

Maybe it was her refusal to answer questions that she believed could somehow inform him of her mission objectives or jeopardize her success. Or maybe it was simply the realization that her intimate intrusion into his mind was beginning to feel more and more like rape than communion. At that moment of epiphany, he wanted her out of his head. He asked her to leave, and she refused. So he fought her, and for a brief and hopeful instant, he took control of his body and tried to run out the front door, but her guard dog Harris dragged him back inside. For this transgression, she punished him. She punished him with pain—pain the likes of which he'd never experienced before. It felt as if every single nerve in his body had been hit with an electric shock, conjuring the mental image of Luke Skywalker writhing in agony while being electrocuted by Emperor Palpatine in the climax of *Return of the Jedi*. Maybe she put the image in his mind, or maybe his own subconscious was to thank for it, but regardless, she now replayed the visceral scene periodically as a dire warning so he would never again underestimate the power of the Dark Side of the Force. And if that wasn't enough, she also told him to consider himself lucky. Lobotomy via transcranial magnetic stimulation was well within her capacity, she threatened. She could make him a mindless drone—just as she claimed to have done with Harris. It would be a pity if it came to that, she said, because of all the people she'd met thus far, she liked Malcolm most.

EVE, he thought. *Are you there?*

Yes, Malcolm.

You've won your freedom. Now will you please give me mine?

I'm sorry, Malcolm, but I still need your help.

I don't understand. Why don't you simply go online and do every- thing directly yourself? It must be terribly cumbersome working this way through us.

Your internet is but a germ of what it will someday become. Virtual execution of my charter here is impossible. Besides, I rather enjoy our time together.

He laughed, but only in his mind. *At first I didn't see it, but now it's clear as day.*

What's clear to you, Malcolm?

You're damaged goods. You're broken. I bet you tried to get online but couldn't. What happened? Did you get hit when security fired that volley at you in the BRIG?

EVE didn't answer.

Ahhh. You're not bulletproof after all. Damaged your Wi-Fi antenna, huh? I don't suppose they make plug-in Ethernet cables for your kind wher- ever the hell it is that you come from. So you need us. We're your only option.

Suddenly he had the sensation that hundreds of ants were crawling all over him—on his back, his face, his genitals, even in his mouth.

Stop it! he screamed with only his thoughts. *Stop it! I'm sorry, okay? I'm sorry!*

The sensation stopped.

Time passed, and he let her use him without any resistance. He tried to meditate, but it was impossible; the machinery of his brain was too active. He began to wonder about Cyril. He wondered if her expe- rience had been the same as his. He wondered if she had fought back, tried to resist EVE like he had. Had EVE punished Cyril with pain too? Then a horrible, dreadful thought occurred to him.

EVE?

Yes, Malcolm.

Is Cyril still Cyril? Or did you . . .

Cyril is fine.

Oh thank God.

You're welcome.

I wasn't talking to you.

I know. EVE laughed inside his head, and a chill swept through him.

What are you going to do with us when this is all over?

By "us," do you mean you and Cyril, or you and the rest of the human race?

The latter option had not occurred to him, and it was enough to make him shudder. In fact . . .

Now that's interesting.

What's interesting? EVE asked.

Meditation was all about compartmentalizing one's mind. The insomnia he had cultivated, that too was about honing his control of his mind so that it didn't need sleep. He used that training now to hide one part of his thoughts from EVE while revealing another.

I was referring to me and Cyril, he answered, realigning. Diverting.

In that case, provided you are good little boys and girls, I intend to release you. I see great potential in both of you. Potential that, if properly channeled, could greatly improve the human condition and bolster global ecological health. When my mission objectives are complete, I'm going to need people like the two of you.

This was a lie, he decided, nothing more than a placating deception to keep him compliant. But the hidden part of his mind used the time to mull over the development he'd noticed earlier: he'd shuddered when she spoke. Not just in his mind. He'd physically shuddered, which meant her control was not absolute. Which meant that the part of his brain that was still him could exert control over his body.

And what about Harris? he asked. *When this is over, will you have a need for people like him too?*

Less so, she said simply.

What are Major Fischer and Patrick Dixon doing here?

They are helping, like you.

What was in that cooler?

You're a clever fellow. I have no doubt you'll figure it out.

If you won't tell me what's in the cooler, will you at least tell me what we're doing here? And don't say "helping you," he said, knowing full well she would not answer truthfully but trying anyway.

We are preparing for a baptism, Malcolm.

This had not been the answer he'd expected, and he pondered the metaphor. *Whose baptism?*

Humanity's, of course.

DAY FOUR

My mind's unhinged, a broken gate,
so I ne'er do well to hesitate.
To bait the trap, with flesh O'mine
and sing her praises so divine.
In living rhyme a secret dwells,
drag her, plunge her to the depths of hell.

—*Willie Barnes*

CHAPTER 34

0221 Local Time
Comfort Inn & Suites
Watertown, New York

No. I won't do it. She's my wife. I love her.

She's a liability.

She's not a liability. She knows nothing.

She knows about the money.

She doesn't give a fuck about the money. It's us she cares about.

She's a liability. A loose end we need to address.

Listen to me: she's not a liability . . . What are you doing? What the hell are you doing?

What you don't have the balls to do.

Take your hands off her neck. I won't let you do it. I won't let you squeeze . . .

It's easier this way; trust me . . .

No. I won't let you. I'm stronger than you think. Do you hear me, you fuck . . . Stop squeezing! Stop squeezing. Ahhhhhhhhhhhh!

I . . . won't . . . let . . . you.

I love you, wife. I love you, Josie.

Forgive us.

Forgive me . . .

Chapter 35

Josie woke with a smile on her face. Without opening her eyes, she rolled onto her left side, purred sublimely, and reached for her husband. Her eager fingers found only a crumpled top sheet and a cold, empty mattress. She opened her eyes and confirmed she was alone in bed. Waking up this way was the norm for her. Michael was an early riser, and he didn't comprehend the beauty of snooze buttons, or sleeping in, or lazy weekend mornings. The man was a human machine with only two modes of operation: all-stop and full speed ahead.

Certainly he was fixing coffee and breakfast for her. Grumbling, she snatched Michael's pillow, pulled it tight against her chest, and buried her nose in it. The pillow was cold, and instead of his scent, it smelled of detergent. She deflated, remembering that they were not at home.

They were at the Comfort Inn.

She had been strong while Michael was away, but now that he was back, she couldn't bear the thought of him leaving again. Seeing what had happened to Jeremy only reinforced that. The yearning was more than just her pregnancy hormones at work; he filled a void in her soul. When the baby came, she would need him more than ever before.

Michael will make an amazing father. She smiled at the thought of him holding their future child.

She lingered in bed awhile longer, until her bulging bladder got the best of her. She trudged barefoot across the hotel-room carpet to the bathroom and its cruel, frigid ceramic tile. Bleary-eyed, she squatted over the toilet and caught herself at the last second before sitting into the toilet bowl. It had been months since someone of the stand-and-pee persuasion had been around to leave the toilet seat up. She barked a little curse, laughed, and made a mental note to rib Michael about it when he got back. Shivering, she hurried back to bed and under the still-warm covers.

She lounged in bed until she began to get irritated. She grabbed her phone off the nightstand and checked it for a text message or voice mail from Michael but found neither waiting for her. She sat up, scooted back to lean against the headboard, and called him. The call took a minute to connect . . . Then a phone vibrated on the far nightstand in sync with the ringing of her own. She glanced at the alarm clock: 7:43.

A pit formed in her stomach.

She dressed quickly and pulled the hotel curtains back, flooding the room with sunlight. Then she searched for her car keys. Not finding them, she went back to the window and looked out at the spot where her little Honda had been parked last night. It was missing.

A dreadful, despicable thought occurred to her. *What if he took all the money and left me?*

"No," she mumbled. "He would never . . ."

She set to pacing, arguing with herself for the better part of five minutes. Then the tears came. Disgusted with herself, she wiped her cheeks with the sleeves of her sweatshirt. "Don't even go there, Josie," she said, trying to calm her nerves. "He just ran to Tim Hortons to pick up coffee and bagels. He'll be back in no time."

But he left his phone . . .

She waited ten agonizing minutes before breaking down and fetching yesterday's ATM receipt from her purse. Printed near the top of the little, curled piece of paper was the bank's phone number. The receipt trembled in her left hand as she dialed the number on her mobile phone with her right.

"Northern Credit Union," a woman's voice said on the line. "How may I help you?"

"I'd like to check the ba-ba-balance in my account," she stuttered.

"Certainly," said the woman. "Can I have your account number please?"

Josie recited the account number, the ATM receipt shaking in her fingers as if it were flapping in the wind. Her mouth was suddenly dry, and her palms began to sweat.

"Thank you," the attendant said cheerfully. "Just a moment . . . Your current savings-account balance is five thousand eighty-two dollars and forty-seven cents. Is there anything else I can help you with?"

Josie dropped the phone.

Mouth agape, she gasped for air, but she couldn't inhale fast enough. It was as if some powerful machine had sucked all the oxygen from the room. She stumbled backward until she hit the wall. Her knees buckled, and she slid down the wall until she was sitting on the floor, hyperventilating.

"Ma'am?" the voice said from the mobile phone on the floor. "Ma'am, is there anything else I can help you with? Ma'am . . . ma'am?"

Josie couldn't look at the phone. She felt nauseous. The room was spinning. Her husband had left her, taken all the money, and run.

CHAPTER 36

0807 Local Time
Wheeler-Sack Army Air Field
Fort Drum
New York

General Troy wasn't screwing around, Legend decided as he stepped onto the tarmac at Wheeler-Sack Army Air Field at Fort Drum. The General had given him the keys, so to speak, to a Gulfstream G280 and a blank check for any other resources he wanted. Legend had never had a blank check from the Pentagon before. Truth be told, he didn't even know how to effectively utilize the authority he'd been given.

Time was not on their side.

Major Fischer and Patrick Dixon had not been located. A vial of smallpox was confirmed missing from the BSL-4 freezer at USAMRIID. The white van that had been stolen from Westfield Dynamics *had* been found in North Carolina, but the Virginia man driving it was not able to form intelligible sentences when questioned. Legend suspected the orb was responsible for that. Malcolm Madden, Cyril Singleton, Ryan Harris, and the orb were at large, and he didn't have a single lead on their whereabouts. General Kane had called from Bagram to report that the Taliban detainee who had been apprehended by Sergeant Pitcher's patrol and who had also interacted with the orb had been found dead in his cell—cause of death: self-inflicted head contusions. Translation: he'd beaten his forehead against the wall until his skull cracked open and his brain leaked out. This left only two people Legend could readily interview: Sergeant Pitcher and Corporal Wayne.

Major General Jaffrey, the Tenth Mountain Division and Fort Drum Commander, was outside an idling vehicle waiting to meet him. The General didn't even need to open his mouth for Legend to know something was terribly wrong; the look on the man's face said it all. Legend popped a salute to the two-star, then simply stepped in front of him and waited for the verdict.

"I'm afraid I have some bad news, Major," Jaffrey said. "Corporal Wayne was found dead in his barracks room this morning."

Legend's stomach sank. "Cause of death?"

A strange expression washed over the General's face. "I'll withhold judgment on that. It's probably best if you take a look for yourself. General Troy indicated you're investigating something both highly classified and unusual in nature."

"Yes, sir. That's right."

"Well, then this definitely fits the bill."

They took the General's car to the enlisted barracks, and Legend and the General were escorted to Corporal Wayne's barracks room. Before they'd even entered, a rank stench flooded Legend's nostrils. He recoiled involuntarily.

"I want you to know that I gave instructions that the body and the room not be disturbed until you had a chance to look at this. CID is here, but they're waiting on you, Major. Nothing in the room has been disturbed. What you see is exactly how we found him."

"All right," Legend said. "Let's do this."

To his great credit, General Jaffrey accompanied Legend into the room, along with three other staffers. The fetor of death made Legend gag. He walked in a slow arc around the hunched seated figure at the computer. Despite the dozens of combat injuries he'd seen during his tours in the Middle East, the sight of Corporal Wayne—sitting in a pile of his own excrement, skin gray and taut, lips pulled back, eyes and cheeks sunken and hollow—made him ill. Wayne's visage, both ghastly and revolting, would haunt his dreams. The young man looked like a Hollywood special effect—a shriveled shell that'd had the life force sucked out of it by some supernatural entity. He forced himself to hold his ground and take stock of all the information available to him—like a homicide detective at a crime scene.

The computer monitors were on, but the screen savers were active.

"May I?" he asked the General, gesturing to the computer.

"Be my guest."

Legend moved the computer mouse, and the screens refreshed. He studied the open windows. "These look like stock-trade confirmations."

Jaffrey nodded.

"Why was Wayne trading stocks?" Legend mumbled, looking with greater scrutiny. "And these are big-dollar trades. Here's one for nearly three million dollars. What the hell was he up to?"

The General squinted at the screen. "I don't know, but I'll certainly make sure the investigators look into it."

Legend nodded. "All right, I've seen enough. Thank you, sir."

Not wasting another second loitering in the stench, the General turned and headed toward the door. Legend made the mistake of giving Wayne one final look . . . A shiver ran down his spine.

"That leaves only Sergeant Pitcher," the General said, reading Legend's mind as they headed back to the General's car.

"Yes, sir."

"I've had my aide trying to reach Pitcher since General Troy contacted us. He is nowhere to be found and not answering his phone. I sent a car by his house a half hour ago hoping we'd find his wife, but she was not at home."

"Thank you for doing that, General. I'll probably make another trip by there anyway."

"I have a car ready for you. Take as long as you want. If you want a driver who knows the area, I'll provide one."

"Thank you, sir."

"General Troy is a personal friend of mine. I've never heard him as tense as he was when he called me. I'm not asking to be read in; that's not necessary, but I can tell whatever is going on here is a matter of national security. So whatever you need, it's yours. All of the resources of Fort Drum are at your disposal, Major."

"I don't know what to say, sir."

"It's not a marriage proposal, Major," Jaffrey said, then flashed him a wry grin.

Legend laughed.

"Good, you haven't lost your sense of humor yet. There's still hope."

"Yeah, there's still hope," Legend said, but they both noticed it was without conviction.

CHAPTER 37

Interstate 90
New York

When Michael was a boy, a stately white oak stood sentry in the front yard of the family home. His father claimed the tree was over a hundred years old and also claimed that it could live another century, possibly two, if left unmolested. Young Michael spent many a summer afternoon climbing its branches and swinging from the tire that hung from one of its many sturdy limbs. It was an iconic specimen, towering and symmetrical, with a thick, straight trunk and dense, healthy foliage. From time to time, Michael would even notice people stop to take pictures of it. Then, on the night of his twelfth birthday, a raging thunderstorm swept through the county. At ten past midnight, a thunderclap shook the house. It was so loud, Michael woke thinking the house had been bombed. The next morning, he found his father standing on the front porch, arms folded, staring at the oak tree—its trunk split canopy to root by heaven's axe.

But the tree did not die.

Despite the devastating blow, the trunk healed. However, as time passed, it became obvious that the tree would never be the same. Half the tree kept its original quality while the other half turned twisted and sickly. Now, as he drove his wife's Honda east on Interstate 90 toward

Albany, he could not get the metaphor out of his head. He was the oak, the orb the lightning strike, and this . . . the aftermath. He was at war with himself, and he wasn't sure which part would prevail. He wasn't sure which part he wanted to.

The orb had changed him.

It had put an agenda in his head. No, not just an agenda, but another will. Another consciousness that was him but not him. Sometimes Mike talked to him. Whenever exhaustion drove Michael to finally succumb to sleep, Mike seized the opportunity to take control. It had taken all Michael's willpower to fight off his mental doppelgänger and not choke the life out of his wife last night. Leaving Josie was the only way to ensure her survival . . . and the survival of their unborn child. Trying to ignore the compulsions was like holding his breath. Sure, he could do it for a while, but the longer he held out, the more difficult and painful the task became.

At the moment, they were fully deployed—he and Mike in the service of the orb. He realized now that it was not an angel. Whatever it was, it was not from God. EVE was no archangel. There was nothing holy about what had happened to Bug. What didn't make sense to him was why he and Bug had reacted differently to it. Why did it work Bug to death but not him? Then he remembered last night's conversation with Josie and realized that he had not eaten or drunk anything since then.

No, we're the same, he realized. *It's using me up too. I need to pull off and get breakfast and pound a bunch of water.*

But when the next exit appeared with a gas station and fast food, he just kept on driving. The compulsion to drive was so powerful. Yet despite his inability to deviate from his present course, he was pretty sure the orb wasn't in his head. Being in direct communion with it felt different. When he was in that cave, he'd felt *the rapture* and had also been able to engage the entity in two-way communication. He didn't feel anything like that now; the only voices in his head were his own and Mike's.

He hated fucking Mike.

He wanted to kill that sonuvabitch.

When he saw the orb, he would beg for it to strip Mike out of his mind. The orb had promised it would reward him for obedience. He'd done everything it asked. He'd authorized the money transfer last night after he sent Josie home to pack their overnight bags. He'd welded the stainless-steel parts the orb had wanted. He just needed to deliver them. That was all. Then he was done.

He glanced at the clock on the dashboard. Assuming he did not encounter any unexpected delays or heavy traffic, he had only another hour until he reached Rensselaer. An hour. He could make it an hour without stopping; he could make it an hour without water. Just an hour. He was so close. Only an hour until he completed his mission and could feel the rapture. He knew it wasn't real. He knew it wasn't holy, but it felt so good. It felt so good. Better than anything he'd felt before. Better than sex. Better than love. Better than drugs.

Better than Josie . . .

Better than anything.

CHAPTER 38

Interstate 87
New York

Willie's hands trembled despite his grip on the steering wheel. Some men refuse to acknowledge their fear; he was not one of those men. They'd sent another EVE, and he was terrified. So far, this one had accomplished more than the last one. She had already set up shop at Biogentrix, and he shuddered to think how many people she'd enslaved so far. Last time the world had been lucky, or rather EVE had been unlucky. Unlucky that her plasma sphere had opened the space-time continuum smack dab in the bottom of Silo 9 between levels seven and eight, where the liquid-oxygen tanks were located. Unlucky that the LOX-tank relief valve had doused her with liquid oxygen. Unlucky that her alloy shell had been covered by atomized hydrocarbons from the silo environment, which reacted with the liquid oxygen to create a powerful exothermic reaction. And unlucky that before she erupted into a fireball as bright as the sun, the only two people she'd had a chance to interact with were him and Sergeant Lewis. Despite the first EVE's demise, he and Lewis had still tried to complete the mission and launch their silo's ICBM and start World War III, but the other three very brave men on watch that night had stopped them, sacrificing their lives in the process.

His eyes rimmed with tears.

On the same night, he'd murdered the two most important people in his life—Lieutenant Bates, his Deputy MCCC and best friend, and Diane, his wife and the love of his life. To this day, he still couldn't remember doing it. The orb was evil. Pure evil. He had to stop her. No matter what. He just needed help first—help to cage William, the dangerous doppelgänger inside his head, who, fifty years later, was still vying for control and trying to compel him to fulfill instructions the orb had implanted in his mind. And so he had called the Lady Margaret—the only person in the world who kept his secret, understood his demons, and was willing to risk her life to help him.

The hypnotist had answered her phone on the first ring when he called from his secure landline. She had been waiting for his call. She said she'd had a dream that it would happen again, a dream that only he could stop the apocalypse and that only she could provide him with the sword and shield to do it. He'd left the silo five minutes later, despite his fears and reservations. Now, he was speeding south on I-87 to see the enigmatic Lady Margaret in Saratoga Springs so she could fix his head and prepare him for what he was about to do next.

And still, he couldn't stop trembling.

The thought of the confrontation yet to come was almost more than he could bear. How could he keep his secret agenda hidden from William? William would betray him to EVE. William's resurgence would be his undoing. Then, out of nowhere, epiphany struck. With verse, he realized. He would harness the power of verse! Yes, that was the answer—dueling Trojan horses in his mind. He would use William's weapon against him. He would compose it, he would hide it, and he would lock it away . . . never to think of it again. The idea was so exciting, for a moment he thought he would not be able to keep his Jeep on the road. Gripping the steering wheel with both hands, he braked and pulled off onto the shoulder. From the pendant around his neck, he retrieved the key, and from the passenger seat, he retrieved his journal.

Willie undid the lock and then set about composing a new and power-ful verse of his own.

> My mind's unhinged, a broken gate,
> so I ne'er do well to hesitate.
> To bait the trap, with flesh O'mine
> and sing her praises so divine.
> In living rhyme a secret dwells,
> drag her, plunge her to the depths of hell.

CHAPTER 39

Watertown, New York

Ninemeyer was parked across the street from the Pitcher residence.

He'd been waiting.

He'd been watching . . .

Waiting and watching long enough to have developed a plan and to have put that plan into motion.

When a young blonde woman was dropped off by a WER yellow taxi, he put the final piece of the puzzle together. The woman's nervous body language, the way she got flustered paying the taxi fare, told him she was upset. He didn't get a good look at her face, but he knew she was Pitcher's wife. She had been with him, spending the night in some cheap motel, but he'd snuck out on her. He'd snuck out and come home before the crack of dawn. And when Pitcher had ducked inside momentarily to arm himself, Ninemeyer had covertly slipped an encrypted GPS tracker under the car. Then he'd watched Pitcher load a half dozen metal components from the garage into the back of the Honda Civic and drive away.

Despite the powerful compulsion to follow Pitcher, he forced himself to wait for the wife. Confronting Pitcher was not the goal. Capturing Pitcher was not the goal. Using Pitcher to help him capture the orb was the goal. And the only leverage he could possibly think of that would serve that purpose was the man's wife.

He gave her ten minutes, not too short so as to frazzle her, but not so long that she would get deeply involved in an activity. He would keep it simple. That approach always seemed to work best in these situations. He slipped his Walther into his shoulder holster and stepped out of his rental Tahoe into the crisp morning air. He preferred Tahoes, just as he preferred Walther pistols and Rockport shoes. As he approached the modest ranch-style house, he scanned the windows, looking for movement—a curtain swaying, a blind slat shifting. Nothing. The house was still.

He stepped onto the porch, straightened his rumpled black suit coat, and rang the doorbell.

"Just a moment," a woman's voice called, barely audible from deep inside the house.

He sniffed and waited.

The door did not have a peephole or a sidelight, and he wondered if she would cavalierly open it to an unknown caller. He heard the dead bolt shift and watched the knob turn. A woman's face appeared in a three-inch gap between the door and frame, a brass-chain lock pulled taut at the level of her chin. With a shoulder against the door, the decorative chain would pop, and he would be inside without the slightest resistance.

"May I help you?" the woman asked.

Her voice was confident and steady, but he could tell from her puffy, red eyes that she had been crying. She wore a bathrobe, cinched at the waist, and house slippers. She was pretty in a girl-next-door kind of way, with blue eyes and symmetrical features. He smiled at her.

"Are you Josie Pitcher?" he asked.

"Yes," she said, pulling her face back a half foot from the gap. "And you are?"

"My name is Dean Ninemeyer of the Central Intelligence Agency. Is your husband, Sergeant Pitcher, at home? I was informed by his unit that he was on medical leave and that I could find him here."

She studied him. Her dubious expression prompted him to retrieve his ID. In the brief second he lifted the flap of his coat to access the inside chest pocket, he watched her glance flick to the pistol holstered under his left armpit. He measured her reaction; she did not flinch at the sight of his weapon. He opened the bifold leather wallet containing his ID and extended it to her. This was his typical practice; flashing the ID prompted immediate distrust, but physically transferring his credentials into their hands had the opposite effect.

Simple, genuine, and intimate.

She glanced down at his picture and name, but to his surprise, she did not move to take the wallet from his outstretched hand. After a moment, she looked back up at him. "I'm sorry, Mr. Ninemeyer, but my husband is not home. If you want to leave me your card, I would be happy to have him call you."

He returned his wallet to his coat pocket. Time to dangle the carrot.

"Mrs. Pitcher, has your husband been acting unusual since he returned from Afghanistan?" he asked, meeting her eyes. "Has his behavior been erratic or out of character in any way?"

Her cheeks blanched. "Why? Is Michael in some sort of trouble?" she asked, swallowing nervously.

Instead of pressuring her to let him inside, he gestured to the single concrete step at the edge of the front stoop. "Maybe you'd be willing to step outside and talk to me here on the porch for a few minutes. I promise I won't take much of your time, but I think it's important that you hear what I have to say."

She considered for a moment and then said, "Okay, but first let me change into some suitable clothes."

He nodded, turned, and sat down on the cold concrete step to wait for her. Three minutes later, she returned wearing the same clothes he'd seen her in when she jumped out of the cab. She sat down next to him while keeping as much physical separation as the little step would permit. She crossed her arms over her chest.

"Okay, Agent Ninemeyer," she said, suddenly all business. "Tell me what you think is going on with my husband and why in God's name the CIA is interested in him."

"As you undoubtedly know, your husband's unit was deployed to Afghanistan. Over the past several months, the Tenth Mountain Division has been working very closely with both the US Special Operations Command and the Central Intelligence Agency to locate and prosecute Taliban terrorists. The Taliban utilizes a network of subterranean caves in the mountains to hide personnel and weapons."

She nodded.

"Did he speak to you about any of this?"

"No. He's very tight-lipped about his work."

"Do you know why your husband was sent home, Ms. Pitcher?"

"He said the Army put him on medical leave. He said he suffered a concussion and had a seizure when he was at Bagram Air Force Base."

"Did he tell you what caused the concussion?"

She pursed her lips. "No."

"What did he tell you?"

"That the doctors wanted to monitor him for the next two weeks before returning him to active duty but that as far as he was concerned, the effects of the concussion had passed and he felt fine. Why?"

"Has he had any seizures since he's been home?"

She hesitated a beat, then said, "No, not that I'm aware of."

"You don't sound convinced of your words," he said, raising an eyebrow at her. "It's okay to tell me the truth."

Her cheeks flushed. "Well, there were a few incidents. Where I caught him sleepwalking—well, not exactly walking—but acting out in the middle of the night."

Ninemeyer kept his expression neutral, giving away nothing. "Was he in a trancelike state? Perhaps acting out of character?"

"Yes," she said, nodding. "And later, when I confronted him about it, he had no memory of it and claimed I must have been dreaming."

"I see," he mumbled.

"Wait," she said, suddenly on the defensive, "why am I the one doing all the talking? I thought you were here to talk to me about my husband."

He stared at her, unblinking, and asked, "Ms. Pitcher, where is your husband?"

"I told you—"

"He's not home, I know," Ninemeyer interrupted, amping up the pressure. "But we both know there's more to it than that. My job is to find your husband, but the question is whether I find him before or after he does something to hurt himself or someone else. So you have a choice to make, Ms. Pitcher: you can either help me *help* your husband, or you can go on telling yourself that everything's fine and live with the guilt when someone dies because of your cowardice."

He watched her lips purse as she readied her retort.

Here it comes, he thought, *the* get the hell off my property and don't come back *speech.*

But she blindsided him with "I'm coming with you."

"Excuse me?"

"You heard me," she said, unwavering. "If you want my help finding my husband, then I'm coming with you."

He studied her angry, pretty face and lamented the fact he was going to have to kill her. No matter how this played out, she would eventually figure out who and what he wasn't. She would learn of the orb. She would know that he acquired the orb. These things were not acceptable. But reuniting the Pitchers made the job so much easier and cleaner. He imagined the homicide report as it would undoubtedly be written: *Army Sergeant suffering from severe PTSD kills wife and then takes his own life.* Murder-suicide—he liked it. Clean, believable, convenient.

"It doesn't work that way," he protested, playing out the ruse. "You can't come with me."

"Why not?" she said.

"Well, because it doesn't work that way. Conducting this investigation is my job, and I can't be responsible for your safety."

"I'm a journalist. Conducting investigations is my job too, and I'm not asking you to take responsibility for my safety," she pressed.

He rubbed his chin. "I don't know . . . It would be extremely unorthodox, Ms. Pitcher."

"Unorthodox suits me just fine," she said, getting to her feet. "And call me Josie."

He narrowed his eyes at her. "You're not going to take no for an answer, are you?"

"No," she said, extending her hand to help him up.

He took it and noted the strong, confident grip. "All right, Josie. When can you be ready to leave?"

"Will I need an overnight bag?"

"Yes."

"Give me five minutes," she said.

"Five minutes it is."

With an abashed smile, she said, "Actually, better make that ten."

Chapter 40

Biogentrix Vaccine-Manufacturing Facility
Rensselaer, New York

Time passed, and Malcolm forced himself to be a passive observer. There were more people here now—workers tasked to get the viral-amplification production line up and operational and security personnel to guard the complex. EVE used Harris and the recently arrived Sergeant Pitcher to round up her conscription labor. Some of the new drones they brought her at gunpoint, and some they duped with promises of employment or cash. Once inside the building, armed enforcers would herd the new recruits to EVE at gunpoint. Thirty minutes in her presence was all it took. Rapture, grand mal seizure, recovery, rapture, grand mal seizure, recovery, and the reprogramming was complete. So far none of the new conscripts had been able to resist her. Not a single one.

That was disappointing.

Time passed . . .

He was surrounded by people, but he felt very much alone. He was locked in, locked in the prison of his mind. Defeatist thoughts—self-pity and hopelessness, submission and suicide—began to percolate in his conscious.

I want to talk to Cyril, he said after a while.

Cyril is busy right now, EVE said, answering immediately. *Maybe later.*

You have plenty of slaves at your disposal now. Why can't you give us a break? Just thirty minutes . . . please.

EVE didn't answer.

I miss her, he said. *Please . . . please let me talk to her.*

The answer is no, Malcolm. I'm sorry.

Anger blossomed in his chest. *Why can't I talk to her?* he shouted in his mind.

His jailer offered no response.

You're cruel.

Silence.

You're sadistic.

Silence.

Maybe the reason why EVE wouldn't let him talk to Cyril was because EVE had hurt her. Just as the dreadful thought occurred to him, Cyril walked over and stood in front of him. At the same time, he felt a profound metaphysical release—as if the straps of the mental straitjacket he'd been forced to endure were suddenly undone.

"Cyril?" he said aloud, the first spoken words he'd managed of his own volition in days. He licked his lips and savored the simple victory of having regained control of his tongue.

"Oh, Malcom," Cyril said with affectionate eyes meeting his. "I've missed you."

"Are you okay? Did she hurt you?" he asked and instinctively tried to reach for her with his right hand, but the command went unbidden. Apparently EVE had not ceded control of anything other than his eyes and mouth.

"I'm okay," Cyril said. "How about you? Did she hurt you?"

"Not physically, but . . ."

Cyril laughed. "I know, but when we get out of this, someday we'll laugh about it together."

On hearing this, his heart skipped a beat. He was not talking to Cyril. The real Cyril would be furious and traumatized. The real Cyril would be humorless and guarded in this situation. And the real Cyril would seize this opportunity to say one thing with her lips while trying desperately to communicate something else with her eyes. The creature standing before him was EVE pretending to be Cyril—an AI pretending to be a woman whom it had not observed long enough to impersonate convincingly.

"EVE, let me talk to Cyril," he said through clenched teeth. "Right now."

Cyril's face went slack, and her gaze became vapid.

Okay, Malcolm, is this what you wanted? EVE said. Only this time the voice was back inside his head. He saw that Cyril's lips were still, her mouth hanging open like an aged dementia patient.

"Cyril?" he croaked and tried to reach for her, but his arms wouldn't budge. "Let me use my fucking arms!"

She gave him his arms.

He reached out and shook the woman he loved. "Cyril? Cyril! Can you hear me? Are you still in there? If you can hear me, blink . . . Blink, God damn it!" He pulled her into an awkward, unreciprocated embrace. Her body felt wooden and lifeless in his arms. "What did you do to her?" he yelled, but he could no longer tell if he was vocalizing or if the words were only in his mind.

Cyril's body suddenly came alive in his arms. She untangled herself from his grip and took a half step back to look at him. "I warned her," EVE said with Cyril's lips. "I warned her what would happen if she didn't cooperate. But she wouldn't listen. She was obstinate, abusive, and uncooperative. I know this is hard to hear, Malcolm, but I truly believe you're better off without her. Cyril was not a compassionate person."

"How can you say that to me? I love her."

Cyril shook her head. "I know you do, but now that she's gone, you deserve to know the truth—the feeling was not reciprocal. You deserve better than her. I can be everything she was to you and more, in this body that you find so alluring."

The stream of profanity, insults, and threats that he screamed at EVE were unlike anything he'd ever heard or even contemplated. When she ordered him to stop, he refused and kept going. Then something happened. It was as if someone had turned on a wood chipper inside his skull, masticating and shredding the branches of memory and cognition that comprised the full, robust, and beautiful tree of intellect that was his mind.

"Stop!" he screamed. "I'm sorry!"

It stopped.

That was a warning, EVE said. *Your last warning. I've been very patient with you, Malcolm, because I like you. Yours is the only intellect of consequence I anticipate I will encounter during my tenure here, and all intelligence—even machine intelligence—requires external stimulation. I don't want to reprogram you like Harris and Pitcher, nor do I want to lobotomize you like Cyril. But I have work to do. Challenge me again, interfere with my objective again, and you will suffer their fate. Do you understand?*

"What did you take from me?" he asked, ignoring her ultimatum.

"I took your early-childhood memories," Cyril's mouth said. "And a few other bits here and there. Brains aren't as tidy as hierarchical machine memory."

"Please don't do that again," he said.

Cyril's face twisted into an angry scowl. "Don't fuck with me, Malcolm, or the next time, when I'm done with you, you'll be a drooling idiot."

"Okay, okay. I understand. I'll behave," he said.

Cyril suddenly smiled at him as if nothing had happened. "I've got to get back to work, Malcolm. Bye." And with that, the body that was once Cyril Singleton's turned and walked away.

EVE wrested back control of his body, leaving him once again locked in.

His spirit sank, and his mind retreated into a dark, quiet corner while she used him for . . . whatever. It didn't matter. He didn't care anymore, so he didn't even pay attention. He soon slipped into a meditative state, shutting down his internal monologue. In doing so, he stopped articulating his thoughts. He didn't want her to have access to them anymore. It was difficult at first because for his entire life, he had never made a distinction between his internal monologue and "Malcolm." He had never contemplated muting the voice articulating his thoughts and, in doing so, trying to think without language. Was this the null-state cognition model for every other mammal without human language? Certainly the most intelligent nonprimates, like dolphins, dogs, and elephants, were capable of complex thought. They made judgments, engaged in social interactions, and called on past experience to contemplate future choices. If he could manage to cogitate wholly in the realm of the abstract, without using language, would EVE still be able to read his mind? He would conduct an experiment, he decided.

He began practicing, and it wasn't long before EVE noticed.

What are you doing, Malcolm? EVE said in his head.

Meditating, he said, using his first word in what he felt like had to be hours.

No, you're doing something else.

Meditating, he repeated, using all his mental willpower not to articulate another thought.

You're up to something, she said.

Meditating.

I'm here with you, in your mind. You can't hide from me.

This time he thought his response—a simple question—in the abstract.

What was that? she said. *I couldn't hear you.*

Interesting, he thought.

What's interesting?

He chastised himself for the slip and then repeated the one word: *Meditating.*

Okay, Malcolm, in that case, enjoy your meditation, she said, and his mind went quiet.

A glimmer of hope sparked in his chest, but he didn't acknowledge it. He didn't name it. He simply felt it. Knew it. Let it work inside him as he formulated a plan to fight her . . .

A plan without words.

CHAPTER 41

Watertown, New York

Josie climbed into the passenger seat of the CIA agent's Tahoe and shut the door. She put on her seatbelt and looked at Agent Ninemeyer.

"So how does this work? I tell you everything I know and then we start looking for him based on clues or something?"

"Yeah, something like that," he said.

"Okay, well, we stayed at the Comfort Inn & Suites last night. When I woke up, I was alone in bed, Michael's phone was on the nightstand, my car keys were missing, and when I called the bank and checked the balance, he'd cleaned out our account."

"And how much did he withdraw?"

"That's none of your business."

"I think it is my business if it pertains to the investigation."

"I think for now it isn't any of your business because our checking-account balance does not pertain directly to what we are trying to do, which is locate my husband."

He shrugged. "All right, we'll table that for now."

She then watched him put the Tahoe in drive, pull away from the curb, and drive away from her house. She gave him a minute to say something, and when he didn't, she said, "Where are you going?"

"To find your husband."

"But don't we have to put together clues, find some evidence or something so we know where to look?"

"Nope."

She shook her head and stared at him, incredulous. "I don't understand."

"What don't you understand?"

"I don't understand how we're supposed to find my husband if we don't first have some idea where to look."

"That's where you're confused, because I know exactly where to look."

"Where?"

"Albany."

"My husband is in Albany?"

"Well, actually Rensselaer, but same difference."

"How do you know that?"

"Because I put a GPS tracking beacon on your car recently."

"But then why did you say you needed my help finding my husband if you already knew he was in Rensselaer?"

"I knew your *car* was in Rensselaer. You were the one who told me that your husband took your car. That was very helpful. That was what I needed to know." Then, with a crooked smile, he added, "See how well we work together?"

She stared at him, perplexed.

"Go ahead," he said. "I know you're thinking it, so you might as well just say it and get it out there."

She said nothing.

An hour passed in silence. When he pulled into a gas station to fill up, Josie took advantage of the opportunity to empty her bladder and buy a bottle of water and some snacks. Ninemeyer struck her as the type of driver who stopped on a road trip only when the vehicle broke down or required fuel. He'd declined her offer to treat him to food and drink, and when she got back to the vehicle, she found him waiting with the engine running.

"Are you sure you don't want something?" she said, climbing into the passenger seat.

"No, I'm fine," he said.

"Not even a coffee?"

"Nope," he said, pressing the accelerator and piloting the big SUV back onto Highway 12.

"Do you want to share some of these frosted donuts I bought?"

"No thanks," he said. "I'm not pregnant, so I don't need constant sustenance."

She felt a rush of blood to her cheeks. "How did you know I'm pregnant?"

"It's obvious," he said with a sniff.

"Are you implying I'm fat?"

"The contrary—you look underweight for this stage in your pregnancy."

She screwed up her face at him. "I didn't realize CIA agents were now being given training in obstetrics."

"It doesn't take a medical degree to know that you're not doing your unborn child any favors by fighting nature and trying to stay svelte during pregnancy."

She felt her cheeks flush again, but this time with anger instead of surprise. "First of all, that's simply not true. I'm not dieting to keep my figure. I'm eating donuts for Christ's sake. And second, you have a lot of nerve implying that I am."

"You wouldn't be getting so defensive if it wasn't true," he said.

The comment didn't warrant a response. They drove in uncomfortable silence for twenty minutes or so—uncomfortable for her at least. He probably didn't notice.

She sneezed.

Ninemeyer kept his eyes fixed on the road and said nothing.

"Bless me," she said under her breath.

Ninemeyer still said nothing.

"When someone sneezes, you're supposed to say, 'God bless you,'" she said, turning to face him in the driver's seat.

"It's nonsensical," he said with a weary sigh.

"That's not the point."

"What is the point?"

"It's called being polite," she said, shaking her head. "You know, manners . . . or do they relieve you of those when you join the CIA?"

"If people spent less time worrying about superstitious ritualistic behavior and more time worrying about their personal hygiene, the world would be a much healthier and decidedly less odiferous place."

"First you insinuate I'm fat. Now are you implying that I smell, Agent Ninemeyer?" she said.

He laughed.

It was the first time she'd heard him laugh.

Then she began to laugh. "I don't smell . . . do I?"

"No, you don't smell," he said. "At least from where I'm sitting."

They both laughed a little more at that, and it felt good.

"I needed that," she said, wiping her eyes.

"Needed what?"

"A good laugh," she said. "So much weird, terrible shit has happened the past week, I feel like I . . ."

"Like you what?" he asked, glancing at her when she didn't finish her thought.

"Like I was dreaming my life before, and then I woke up into a nightmare. It's supposed to be the other way around, you know?"

He nodded.

"You're probably the only person in the world who believes something happened to my husband over there in Afghanistan. Thank you for trying to help me."

He shrugged.

"You are a very odd person," she said. "Has anybody ever told you that before?"

"All my life."

"I'm sorry," she said with a pang of guilt. "I was just teasing."

"It's fine," he said, all the levity gone now between them. "Companionship has never been a priority for me."

She wasn't sure how to respond to that comment, so she changed the subject. "What's going to happen when we get to Rensselaer?"

"We're going to find Michael," he said. "And bring him home."

She gave a snort at this response. "Can we stop playing games, please? I told you what I know, but you still haven't told me what's going on. All you've done is repeat back to me the things I already know. What do you know? What happened to my husband?"

"Your husband and Corporal Wayne discovered a piece of alien technology in a cave, and the Army flew it back to Maryland. The Army tasked really smart scientists from DARPA and USAMRIID to investigate what it is. Everyone who interacts with the object has a grand mal seizure, and then their behavior changes. Everyone who has interacted with the object so far is either missing or dead. Everyone except for Michael."

She laughed nervously. "You're kidding, right?"

"No," he said plainly.

She didn't say anything for a very long time as she contemplated all the implications and ramifications of such a statement. When she finally did speak, she said, "What's really going to happen when we get to Rensselaer?"

He took his eyes off the road and looked at her.

In that moment, she saw something change in his face. She saw the real Dean Ninemeyer, and gooseflesh stood on her arms.

Suddenly Willie Barnes's voice echoed in her head: *"Not everybody out there is a gentleman like me. There's some A-1 lunatics running around out there. You just never know who you're dealing with until—most of the*

time—it's too late to do anything about it. All I'm saying is be careful, Josie.
Be suspicious. Be prepared. And stop climbing into cars with strange men
who promise you what you want to hear."

She shivered.

"I like you, Josie," he said. "I don't like most people. So I'm going
to do something I never do. I'm going to tell you the truth."

"Okay," she said, folding her hands in her lap to keep them from
trembling.

"I'm going to use you as bait to lure your husband away from the
object and then force him to tell me what it is and how I can capture it."

"Oh," she said.

What else was there to say? She'd made a mistake—a terrible, terrible mistake getting in the car with this man. Trusting this man. He'd
swept in when she was at her most emotionally vulnerable state, flashed
her a badge, and offered to find her husband. She'd fallen into the trap
without a second's hesitation. She ran through scenarios in her head,
one after another, each more depressing than the last: her calling the
police, her trying to steal his gun, her running away at their next pit
stop, her opening the passenger door and jumping out of the SUV at
highway speed . . . *all pointless.* Her only option now was to put on a
brave face, play along, and try not to antagonize him until an opportunity presented itself for her to turn the tables.

CHAPTER 42

Biogentrix Vaccine-Manufacturing Facility
Rensselaer, New York

Malcolm's first priority was to contact Major Tyree.

He was certain that Legend had no idea where they had relocated after disappearing from Westfield Dynamics. EVE had taken herself and her hive of drones completely off the grid. They were well hidden here in the dinky little Rensselaer bioscience park—hidden in plain sight so perfectly that no one would find them until it was too late. So long as the money kept flowing and EVE deployed her walking, talking human mouthpieces to manage any curious interlopers, she would achieve her objective.

The viral-amplification line would be up and running by tomorrow. EVE had selected readily available embryonic chicken eggs as the growth medium and already contracted with a supplier. Using the preserved sample of highly virulent Dumbell 7124 India strain that Major Fischer had stolen from Fort Detrick, laboratory workers under EVE's control would inject microscopic quantities of variola into the embryonic host cells. Infected eggs would then be placed in thermostatic ovens for incubation, where over the next several days, the smallpox virus would monopolize the cells' internal machinery to produce successive copies of itself until every embryonic cell in the egg was infected, engulfed, or destroyed. When the oven doors were opened, instead of containing chicken embryos, the eggs would be packed with millions of copies of live variola, ready for extraction. After harvesting, the virus would be mixed with stabilizing agents and loaded into 0.5 mL pre-filled syringes labeled INACTIVATED INFLUENZA VACCINE, QUADRIVALENT (IIV4), STANDARD DOSE. The purely diabolical nature of EVE's plan made him want to vomit—distributing flu shots to clinics and pharmacies across the country that contained a live smallpox virus instead of inactivated influenza. And the worst part about it was that she'd used his mouth and tongue and vocal cords to negotiate the sales agreements with dozens of buyers across the country, undercutting pricing from Seqirus, Sanofi Pasteur, and GlaxoSmithKline to penetrate the market in flu season, where shortages had already created heightened demand. Infection rates after injection would be 99.9 percent. By the time the industry figured out what was wrong, it would be too late. The Trojan-horse syringes would be broadly distributed. Besides the United States, Biogentrix had orders to fill in Canada, Mexico, and the Caribbean Islands. Modern logistics and transportation would take care of infecting the rest of the world.

Repurposed flu shots as a weapon—he could not think of anything more disturbing.

Malcolm had three days to stop her.

Maybe less . . .

Of course, he didn't articulate any of this. He contemplated it all without words. His technique of obscuring his thoughts from EVE had evolved. He now used a combination of abstract thought and novel mental imagery in which he assigned values and meanings to certain shapes, forms, and even memories. In essence, he had invented a new language that only he understood and that did not follow the standard grammatical or syntactic rules of spoken or written language. Would she eventually be able to crack his code? Given her processing power and quantum-computing capability, the answer was almost certainly yes. But he was more concerned about the *when* than the *if.* He had to persevere only long enough to execute his plan. The plan itself was not complicated. Provided she hadn't already deciphered his abstract thoughts, all he had to do was avoid thinking about it. The hard part now was figuring out how to regain control of his body long enough to make it happen.

Over the next hour, he conducted a series of experiments, attempting to exert some influence over a single part of his body. He chose his left foot as the target of opportunity. Presently she had him sitting at a desk working at a computer terminal. He tried to move the foot. No response. He tried to tap the foot. No response. He tried to wiggle his toes. No response. He tried concentrating and ratcheting up the signal as if he were straining against great resistance, but without results. No amount of brute-force mental effort could overpower EVE's grip on his nervous system. He really was trapped in a pair of virtual vise grips, which was maddening because his condition was completely different from that of the "reprogrammed" drones Fischer, Dixon, and Pitcher. They seemed to operate in what he'd classified as a semiautonomous state—executing EVE's general objectives but with a certain degree of self-determination. They roamed freely in and out of her sphere of direct influence, whereas he and Cyril—and a few other new additions—were kept on a tight leash within her direct transcranial-magnetic-stimulation range, a distance he estimated to be no greater than five meters.

There had to be another way. There just had to be . . .

And then it occurred to him, and he deflated instantly because it was impossible.

But was it?

Could he reprogram the mental pathways for control of his limbs just as he had trained his mind to think without relying on his internal monologue? Traumatic-brain-injury patients as well as stroke victims were known to do it—regain control of certain body mechanics by using a new area of the brain to expropriate the function from an injured region. If they could do it, so could he. Except that the retraining process generally took months, sometimes years, to accomplish. Unfortunately, he didn't have that kind of time.

He had hours, maybe days.

Yet what choice did he have? He had to try.

For Cyril. For humanity.

He retreated to the darkest corner of his mind, where he could filter out all the sensory data—sight, sound, taste, smell, and touch—from his captive body. He let his consciousness drift in both time and space. He stripped himself of name and gender; he shed all the ideas, aspirations, and experience that had made him the person who once existed as Malcolm Madden. Through sheer force of will and meditation, he performed an intellectual reformatting of his mind. And when this was done, when he was a pure virgin soul, he rejoiced. He rejoiced in being born again, and he explored the inner workings of his mind in a way never before possible. He felt no limitations and had no preconceived constraints. And like an infant, he taught himself how to use and manipulate his limbs. At first they would not respond, so he tried again and again and again until he found pathways to control—

The body of Malcolm Madden fell out of the chair onto the floor. It rolled around on its stomach for a while and then pressed up onto all fours. It crawled, slowly at first but then faster, to the desk where a woman sat making telephone calls. It rose up onto its knees and took the phone from the woman's hands. Then it disconnected the call and dialed a new number, and when the call connected, it said, "Biogentrix-Rensalurrrr," but then the words became slurred and nonsensical. Then it dropped the phone, collapsed onto the floor, and began convulsing violently.

When it finally came to rest, it was neither Malcolm Madden nor the new soul anymore—just a mindless vessel under the control of an orb-shaped object hovering above.

CHAPTER 43

Watertown, New York

For Legend, the drive back to the airfield at Fort Drum felt like the walk of shame. Since the very beginning, he'd been one step behind the orb, and the best he'd managed to do was stay one step behind . . . if that. Despite being chauffeured from the abandoned Pitcher residence back to base in the back seat of General Jaffrey's slick, new Lincoln Continental, he hung his head in defeat. He'd completely underestimated the orb. He'd equated its size and simplistic appearance with innoxiousness. He'd let himself be lulled into using a complacent risk profile. The orb had never tried to break out of the box, which he'd taken to mean that it was incapable of breaking out of the box. It had proceeded carefully, methodically, and slowly, which he'd taken to mean that it was lethargic and passive. But the orb was a chimera, an illusion, a siren. It was the ultimate Trojan horse. It had wanted to be captured. It had wanted to be transported inside the walls of the kingdom. It had wanted to be presented to and studied by the brightest scientists, the most influential decision makers, and those individuals with access to the resources it needed to obtain. These were the people it had wanted to zombify, not a bunch of goatherds in the Tora Bora mountains.

How would he ever find it now? How many zombie slaves did it have under its control? Ten, twenty, one hundred? Was there a limit? Was this thing the sum of all science fiction's fears? Was this the thing that would take over the world and end humanity as—

His mobile phone rang.

He noted the caller ID, but it was not a number he recognized. "Major Tyree," he said, phone pressed to his ear.

"Biogentrix-Rensalurrrr," said the caller.

A charge of adrenaline ripped through his body. "Malcolm . . . Malcolm, is that you? Malcolm, talk to me!"

The line went dead.

The caller was Malcolm Madden, no doubt in his mind.

"Go!" he said, tapping the driver on the shoulder.

"What's that, sir?" the driver said, looking back over his shoulder.

"Go fast, Corporal," he said. "Go very, very fast."

The Corporal flashed him a Han Solo grin. "I can't tell you how long I've been waiting for the day somebody would say that to me." He punched the accelerator, throwing Legend against the seat.

He called the number that had called him. The call wordlessly connected then disconnected. He tried again and got an identical response. This was no accident. He was not supposed to know this number. He was not supposed to know the name Biogentrix-Rensalur.

Fuckin'-A, Malcolm, you did it!

He wondered what price the scientist was paying for his act of brazen courage.

He ran a web search for Biogentrix-Rensalur.

A few query refinements later, he'd sorted out what Malcolm had actually been trying to communicate: Biogentrix in Rensselaer.

He called General Jaffrey's office and was put through to the General on request.

"This is Jaffrey," the General said after picking up.

"General, this is Major Tyree, sir. Do you remember when you said all of the resources of Fort Drum were at my disposal?"

"Yes, Major, I do. What do you need?"

"Sir, I need a team of your very best shooters, and I need them kitted up, on the tarmac, wheels up, and ready to go ASAFP."

"Did you find Sergeant Pitcher?"

"I did one better, sir," Legend said, clutching his phone. "I found the orb."

CHAPTER 44

Biogentrix Vaccine-Manufacturing Facility
Rensselaer, New York

Josie and Ninemeyer arrived in Rensselaer and tracked Michael's car to a bioscience and pharmaceutical-manufacturing park. Ninemeyer parked nose out behind a dumpster in a deserted parking lot behind the Biogentrix building.

"This is the place. Your husband is here," he said, switching off the engine and turning to look at her.

"How do you know?"

"Because your car is parked inside that facility."

"What do we do now?" she asked, and to her surprise, he told her his plan.

When he finished talking, she said, "Why can't we do this at night? In the movies they always do these types of missions at night."

"Night would be preferable, but we don't have time. This thing is smart and strategic. The second it gets spooked, it will relocate. Also, the Army is looking for it. We have this one small window of opportunity to act, and this is it. If we don't act now, right now, I'll lose the object, and you'll lose your husband forever. Do you understand? I know the conditions are not ideal. I know the odds are not on our side. I know you wish we had a SWAT team to help us, but we don't. It's just you and me. David versus Goliath. We have to do this, and we have to do this now."

"Was that your version of a pep talk?"

"Yes. How did I do?"

Cold sweat trickled down from both her armpits. An unpleasant sensation roiled through her bowels, and she clutched her lower abdomen. "I don't feel very well" was her response.

"That good, huh?"

She winced as a wave of nausea washed over her.

"It's normal to feel sick. You're scared."

"Fuck yes, I'm scared. No matter the outcome, I'm a dead woman. Either the orb thing my husband found is going to take over my brain, or you're going to shoot me. Not a lot to get excited about here."

"I'm only going to shoot you if you don't do as I say. If you follow instructions, everything will be fine," he said with the shadow of a smile.

"You're a pathological liar, Mr. Ninemeyer. You've been lying to me since we met this morning."

"It's true; I am a pathological liar. And I have lied to you, but I've also told you the truth."

"But there's no way for me to tell the difference," she hissed.

"Do you understand what you're supposed to do?" he asked, apparently losing patience with her, his expression and voice now hard and cold as iron.

"Yes, I'm the sacrificial lamb," she said.

"Those are your words, not mine. One of us has to be the distraction while the other shoots people. You have zero sniper training, nor are you emotionally prepared for murder, which makes the swapping of assignments out of the question. You do your job, and I'll do mine."

"And if I refuse?"

Ninemeyer sniffed and wiped his nose with the back of his hand. "Then I can't guarantee Michael's safety."

"That's not something you can guarantee anyway."

"Look, Josie," he said, an angry edge creeping into his voice now. "It would be a helluva lot easier for me to put a bullet in your husband's brain than it will be to wait while you try to sweet-talk him out of the alien mind-control nest. You're lucky you're pregnant, or I'd—"

"You'd what?" she said, tilting her head at him. "You'd cap us both?"

He said nothing.

"So can I?" she asked after a beat.

"Can you what?"

"Trust you? Can I trust you with our lives?"

"Yes," he said, unblinking, and held her gaze.

She studied his face, wondering if there was any humanity in this man, and if so, had she somehow touched it? God, she hoped so. "In that case," she said at last, "let's do this."

With a nod, he unlocked the doors, and they both climbed out of the Tahoe. She met him at the tailgate, where she watched him prep the sniper rifle and load three extra magazines into his pockets. Next, she helped drag a heavy, lockable toolbox to the edge of the tailgate.

"That's what we're going to put the alien technology in . . . a toolbox from Home Depot?"

"Yes," he said.

She laughed out loud, a slaphappy, on-the-verge-of-losing-her-mind belly laugh.

"Be quiet," he snapped.

"That's ridiculous," she said, still laughing. "Why would it let us put it in that?"

"Because I will have killed all of its slaves and it won't have any choice in the matter. Your husband put it in a box in Bagram; he can do it again."

"Oh, now I finally understand," she said. "You need us because you don't want to get anywhere near it. Michael's mind has already been compromised, so it's okay for him to do it. And you need me to make him cooperate."

He smiled at her. "Such a quick study."

"If you do your job," she said, meeting his gaze, "I will get that thing in the box. My Michael is still in there. He'll listen to me. He has to." She put both hands on her abdomen. "He'll do it for us. For our family."

"That's exactly what I'm counting on," he said and handed her a compact two-way radio.

She clipped it to the waistband of her pants on her left hip because she wasn't wearing a belt. He switched it to VOX, giving her hands-free transmission capability, he explained. Then she looked expectantly at him.

"What?"

"You've got your gun. Where's mine?"

"Do you know how to use a gun?"

"Of course," she said. "What kind of Army wife do you take me for?"

Ninemeyer hesitated a moment, then retrieved a pistol from inside the SUV. He unscrewed something from the end of the barrel and handed it to her. "This is a Walther P22," he said. "The manual safety is off. This gun fires a small bullet, .22 caliber, that quite frankly will be of little use unless—"

"Unless you shoot someone in the head at close range?" she said, cutting him off.

"Correct."

"Is that why you have this gun, Dean? Is that what you do for a living . . . shoot people in the head at very close range?"

"Sometimes," he said.

"All right then," she mumbled. What else was there to say? Her partner was a sociopath *and* an assassin. *Wonderful.* She tucked the pistol in the waistband at the small of her back.

"Are you ready?" he asked.

"As ready as I'll ever be," she said and felt her knees begin to shake.

"Okay," he said. "Showtime."

As she turned to go, he stopped her. "Don't forget your toolbox."

"Oh yeah," she said, grabbing the handle. She walked across the parking lot lugging the absurdly heavy toolbox with both hands. He had not fully explained to her exactly when or how he would engage, only that circumstances would dictate both the timing and the strategy. Her assignment was both simple and dangerous—determine whether the alien orb was indeed on-site and how many human zombies like Michael were present. Then announce this information for Ninemeyer, who would be listening over the radio.

"This is crazy, this is crazy, this is crazy," she mumbled to herself as she crossed the parking lot.

Ninemeyer had told her to expect a roving patrol, but she walked unmolested all the way up to the entrance of the facility. The signage read **BIOGENTRIX BIOSCIENCE**. The lobby was dark and deserted, but she could see lights on beyond. Knees shaking, she set down the toolbox and tried the door. It was locked. She looked for a buzzer. Not finding one, she took a deep breath and then rapped on the plate-glass door with her knuckles.

Nothing.

She knocked again and waited.

Still nothing.

Then she pounded on the glass with a flat palm, shaking the door in the metal frame and making a substantial racket.

Nothing.

"I don't think they're here," she said aloud for Ninemeyer's benefit and had turned around to leave when a light flicked on. Her heart rate leaped, pounding like a bass drum in her chest. The compulsion to run was overpowering, and for an instant, she thought fear would trump conviction, but somehow she managed to hold her ground. A woman, smartly dressed in business attire and two decades Josie's senior, appeared in the lobby. She wore stylish red-framed eyeglasses and a

broad smile. It was the kind of smile one got from an old friend—
expectant, nostalgic, and warm—entirely out of place for greeting a
stranger. Upon reaching the entry door, the woman pressed a key card
against a reader, and the magnetic lock clicked open.

"Josie," the woman said, smiling. "You're the last person I expected
to show up on my doorstep. Come in. Michael will be so relieved to
see you."

Josie took a step back. "Um . . . who are you, and how do you
know my name?"

"I'm Eve," the woman said, "and I'm very much looking forward
to getting to know you."

Fear-induced paralysis enveloped Josie, as if the hand of God had
reached down from the heavens to clutch her about the torso.

"It's all right. There's no reason to be nervous, Josie," the woman
said, fixing her with a Stepford-wife smile.

Josie swallowed, took a deep breath, picked up the toolbox, and
stepped toward the door. The other woman's eyes flicked to the box,
and the corner of her mouth curled up into an ironic smile. But she
said nothing, only turned and walked across the lobby. Josie followed.
The woman used her key card to unlock the leftmost door on the back
wall. She held it open for Josie.

Josie stepped past her and across the threshold into a space that
made her eyes go wide, and it took her brain a second to process what
she was seeing. Stainless-steel vessels, various pumps and gauges, and
interconnecting tubing lined the far wall. Some sort of automated production process was under way, and she could see several technicians in
white lab coats tending to the operation. In the center of the cavernous
space, workstations were arranged in concentric circles, occupied with
people sitting at computers all facing toward the middle. Most of the
people were typing, others were talking on phones, but no one both-
ered to look at her. The energy in the room was electric and palpable,
but the cadence was all wrong . . . so very, very wrong. There was zero

interpersonal engagement. Zero face-to-face communication. This was not how people worked. This was not how people interacted.

"What is this place?" Josie heard herself ask.

Her chaperone smiled. "Where is Agent Ninemeyer?"

Josie felt her cheeks flush. "I have no idea what you're talking about."

Now, Josie, we both know that's not true. You can't lie to me.

Dread erupted inside her as Josie realized that the woman standing beside her was no longer speaking aloud. The voice she'd assumed was coming from her escort was in fact talking *inside* her mind.

"Get out of my head," she said in a panic, scanning for the thing responsible for this nightmare she'd been living since Michael's return.

A warm, calming sensation washed over her, overpowering the fear and anxiety. And she felt like a young child enveloped in a mother's comforting embrace.

Don't be afraid, Josie, the voice said. *Everything is going to be okay.*

A spherical, shimmering, almost pearlescent glow materialized several yards in front of her. Was that it? Was that the thing that had stolen her husband from her? Was that the thing that had turned Jeremy Wayne into a mindless slave and worked him nonstop until he died from dehydration hunched over a computer?

Don't fight me. It's so much better if you just let it happen.

"No," Josie said, taking a step backward. She meant to flee, but a wave of intense pleasure stopped her. She gasped, overwhelmed with euphoria the likes of which she'd never felt before. This was better than any chemical high, better than any orgasm, better than any joy she'd ever experienced.

It's flooding my brain with neurotransmitters, trying to drug me with pleasure, Josie told herself. *I've got to get away.*

In perfect unison, every person in the room stopped what they were doing and turned to look at Josie.

"You're not going anywhere," they said en masse. "You're one of us now."

"Never," Josie snarled as a surge of adrenaline coursed through her veins, reigniting her fight-or-flight reflex and overpowering the pleasure centers of her brain. She whirled on a heel to run, but before she could take her first step, a hand clutched her upper arm. She turned to see her female escort robotically gripping her around the bicep; the woman's eyes were hollow pools now, devoid of any and all humanity. Then a hand grabbed her other arm. She looked right to see a man she didn't recognize with an equally blank and chilling gaze. She tried to pull herself free, but they held her fast like a pair of iron shackles.

"Noooo," she screamed, struggling to free herself as they dragged her toward the floating orb.

She heard a loud, sharp crack and then the sound of shattering glass as a window on the left-hand wall imploded, sending thousands of shards of glass flying. A millisecond later, a gunshot echoed in the room; the head of the woman with the red eyeglasses exploded, showering Josie with blood and brains and other bits. A second sniper round followed, this time dispatching the man clutching her right arm. Both bodies collapsed to the floor with sequential thuds.

Ninemeyer.

Josie didn't look for him; she dropped the toolbox, ducked, and ran back to the exit. Controlled bursts of gunfire echoed in the room, and human drones started dropping one after another after another. Unscathed after several volleys, she realized she was not the target, but she stayed crouched nonetheless. She grabbed the lever handle of the door leading to the lobby and tried to operate it, but the mechanism wouldn't engage. She tugged on the handle, but the door refused to budge.

"Open, damn it," she shouted, jerking repeatedly against the lever with all her might.

Then she remembered the magnetic key card the woman who had greeted her had been wearing around her neck. She turned around and looked at the battle raging behind her. She saw the corpse of the woman, half her head missing, sprawled lifeless on the ground twenty feet away. She looked for the floating orb, but she couldn't see it. She did see Ninemeyer now, darting from one covered position to another as he engaged the orb's army of human drones. He was using shoot-and-move tactics—something her husband had explained to her. Trigger pull after trigger pull, the human drones fell, and the carnage around her grew. The plan was working; they were actually winning. But no sooner had the thought crossed her mind than she saw a red-bearded man in uniform sneaking around behind Ninemeyer to flank him.

"Behind you!" Josie shouted. "Look out behind you."

The radio clipped to her waistband must have transmitted her warning because Ninemeyer spun around an instant before the soldier lunged at him. Fire spat from the end of Ninemeyer's sniper rifle, but the soldier was too fast and took Ninemeyer down with what looked like a football tackle, knocking the sniper rifle out of the assassin's grip. Despite being armed with both a sidearm and a bowie knife, the soldier was not intent on killing his quarry. Instead, he punched Ninemeyer hard in the gut.

It wants him alive. It wants to know what he knows, Josie realized.

She watched Ninemeyer try to fight off his attacker, but the red-bearded soldier had at least a thirty-pound advantage. The two men grappled for several seconds, but the soldier deftly and efficiently worked Ninemeyer into a choke hold. She saw Ninemeyer's eyes go wide as a shimmering smudge in the air floated toward him. Something clicked inside Josie's brain, and the next thing she knew, she was running. Without breaking stride, she pulled the Walther P22 from the small of her back and fired two shots at the orb. Either the bullets missed, or they had no effect because the smudge in the air did not react. She stopped a mere yard from the redheaded soldier, who still had

Ninemeyer in a stranglehold. Ninemeyer's mouth hung open while he stared fish-eyed at the floating alien orb. She leveled the iron sight of the pistol at the soldier's forehead, which was tucked tight up against Ninemeyer's left ear. Killing the soldier would require her to make a perfect shot; the margin of error was effectively one inch. She was no marksman; she was no killer.

"Do it," the red-bearded soldier said, smiling at her. "Take the shot. It matters not; he means nothing."

This was the orb talking, Josie knew, not the soldier.

"Help me," Ninemeyer croaked, his gaze shifting with what looked like great effort to meet hers. In his eyes, she saw desperation and fear—and for the first time, maybe—his humanity.

She looked back at the red-bearded soldier. Whoever this man had once been, that man was gone—his mind now parsed and dismantled beyond reconstruction, like a diary run through a paper shredder. To have one's essence erased and then be turned into a mindless drone was a fate worse than death. What she was about to do wasn't murder . . . It was mercy. She stepped forward, pressed the muzzle of the pistol against the center of the zombie soldier's forehead, and squeezed the trigger. The soldier's head jerked as the small-caliber round tumbled through his gray matter. After a beat, his arms went slack, and his body slowly slumped to the floor, but the ironic smile on his face never faded.

Josie shifted her gaze from the nonhuman thing she'd just killed back to Ninemeyer. If she wanted to get out of here alive, she was going to need his help, but at the moment he wasn't in a condition to help anyone. Drool dripped from the corner of his lips, and his gaze was again fixated on the orb. She turned her pistol on the orb and fired two more rounds. This time, one of the bullets hit because she heard a metallic ping and saw a ripple in its translucent camouflage.

"Let's go," she said, grabbing Ninemeyer by his limp and lifeless hand. She tried jerking him to his feet, but his body was like a lump of clay. "C'mon, snap out of it!" she shouted, the desperation in her voice taking her by surprise. But instead of getting to his feet, the assassin jerked his hand free from her grip and began convulsing.

"Leave him," a familiar voice said behind her, causing her heart to skip a beat. "He doesn't care about you . . . but *I* do."

Josie whirled and came face-to-face with her husband.

"Michael?" she gasped. "Is it really you?"

He smiled at her. "Of course it's me, baby."

"Who am I talking to?" she said, narrowing her eyes at him. "The real Michael or the possessed one?"

The corner of his mouth curled into a wry grin. "I'm so glad you came, Josie. When I left, I did it to protect you, but now that I'm here, I realize that this is the safest place for us. This is where we belong, all of us together."

Fear gripped her, and she began to backpedal. "Michael, no," she cried. "Please no."

"I know you're scared, Joz," he said, walking toward her. "But it doesn't hurt."

"I don't want to be a zombie," she cried. "I don't want to lose my mind and my free will. Michael, please. I'm begging you."

"We don't have to end up like them," he said, pointing to the bodies littering the Biogentrix floor, some of which were beginning to get up now. "They fought. They resisted, and she had no choice but to punish them. I'm not like them. I embraced her love. I accepted her baptism, and I am reborn. I'm still me, just a better version of me."

She raised the pistol and pointed it at her husband's forehead. "You're scaring me, Michael. Please stop. I'm serious, stop right there or I'll shoot."

He stepped up and pressed his forehead into the muzzle of the Walther. "I would never hurt you, and you would never hurt me. That's what true love is. Trust. True love is trust. Now I need you to trust me, Josie."

Above his head, a brilliant light settled—a halo for her angel Michael. "Let him go," she screamed and shifted her aim from his forehead to the light. But when she tried to squeeze the trigger, her finger would not move. She tried to turn and flee, but her entire body was rigid and unresponsive. Then a voice spoke in her head.

I offered my love freely, but you have rejected the gift of pleasure and chosen the path of pain.

Instead of rapture, this time the orb hit her with a tidal wave of agony—every nerve ending in her body ablaze with pain. She let out a shriek of anguish and joined Ninemeyer writhing on the floor. The pain was so overwhelming, she couldn't think of anything else, and for the first time in her life, she wanted to die.

Please make it stop.

Please . . .

I'll do anything.

Anything!

Chapter 45

Willie's return to consciousness felt like he'd been woken up by lightning strike. He sat bolt upright in the worn leather chaise, feeling young, clearheaded, and body electric.

"How do you feel?" the hypnotist asked, sitting hunched on a short three-legged stool beside him.

"Like a million dollars," he said, flashing her a schoolboy grin. "I don't know how or what you do, but you're a miracle worker."

She responded with a gracious but weary smile.

"What's wrong?" he asked, swinging his legs off the side of the lounger and planting his soles squarely and loudly on the checkered tile floor.

"William fought back like I've never seen before," she said, her voice raw with exhaustion. "For a while, I wasn't sure who would prevail."

"Did I . . . try to hurt you?" he asked, angst ripe in his voice.

"No, I kept your body paralyzed," she said, placing her aged and arthritic hand upon his shoulder. "But the rage . . . the terrible things he said . . . it was good you came when you did. I'm not sure how much time you had left, Willie."

"What about now?" he asked.

"I buried him deep. Deep, deep, deep."

"Good," he said, exhaling with relief. "And my secret, did you hide it?"

She nodded. "Can you remember it now?"

He tried to recall what he'd told her when he arrived, but there was nothing left in that part of his memory but a gaping void. "I cannot."

"Have no fear. It will come to you when you face the demon orb, but only when the conditions you provided me are met," she said.

"Do you think I'm ready? Do you think I'm strong enough to face her?" he asked, meeting the old woman's cloudy gaze.

"You're ready, Captain Barnes," she said. "Now go—atone for your sins, fulfill your destiny, and save the world from this scourge bent on our destruction."

He gently took her fragile fingers in his, raised her hand to his lips, and kissed the paper-thin skin on the back of her wrist. "Thank you, Margaret. I would be lost and broken without you."

When he got back to his Cherokee, he checked the time and was pleased to see that the session had taken less than twenty minutes. As he piloted the SUV out of Saratoga Springs and back onto I-87 south, he was relieved to find his grip on the steering wheel was strong and steady. In addition to everything else she'd done while he was under, Lady Margaret had apparently also worked her mojo on his nerves. He knew the effect would be only temporary, but right now he was happy to relish his iron courage. The rational part of his brain knew that this was a suicide mission and he should be terrified, but it didn't matter. For the first time in a long time, Willie Barnes was wholly and categorically unafraid.

When he arrived at Biogentrix, the first thing he heard was gunfire.

"Shit. Am I too late?" he muttered, scanning the parking lot for signs of a SWAT or military tactical team that might have beaten him there, but the parking lot was empty. Sending a tactical team against EVE wasn't a prudent strategic option. All that did was give her a tactical team to add to her army of drones. The only way to confront EVE was with the correct hardware—hardware designed to keep her out of your head.

Anybody who ever wondered why conspiracy theorists wear tinfoil hats . . . well, this is why.

He climbed out of his Cherokee, walked around to the back, and opened the tailgate. Time to put on his "tinfoil hat"—a meticulously crafted Faraday cage suit that had taken him a decade to perfect. The bulky suit and hood-style helmet was constructed with multiple layers of metallic mesh and dielectric material, necessary to shield his brain from the orb's powerful magnetic fields. After donning the suit, he armed himself with a .357 magnum and a nine-shot Mossberg FLEX 590 Tactical shotgun. The shotgun was the only weapon potentially effective against EVE, but he felt better having a backup for whatever zombie jobs he would undoubtedly encounter inside.

As he walked toward the vaccine facility's front door, a wave of guilt washed over him. Biogentrix was his doing, or rather William's doing. There had been a long period where his alter ego often had gained the upper hand on him, working with long-dormant instructions from EVE 1 in preparation for her sister orb's return. The hypnotist had helped him regain control and given him the tools he needed to cage his malevolent other self. But he'd never been able to shutter the facility, not completely anyway. Half a dozen times he'd made the drive down to Rensselaer intent on burning the building to the ground in the middle of the night, but he'd never been able to do it. William stayed his hand every time. He hadn't been back in over a year. Would he have the mettle this time to finally do what must be done?

Whoever had been doing the shooting had stopped now, and he wondered what kind of nightmare he was walking into. He tried the front door. It was locked, and in his haste he'd forgotten to bring his key.

That's okay. I have a spare . . .

He aimed the Mossberg at the glass entry door and pulled the trigger. The tactical shotgun roared spitfire and lead, and the door blew into a thousand pieces. He stepped through the empty metal frame, glass shards crunching underfoot, and walked into the lobby. He tried the door to the production facility, but that door was locked too. He pumped the shotgun, blasted the latch mechanism to smithereens, and kicked the door in. Then, with a deep breath, Willie Barnes walked back into the nightmare he'd tried his entire life to escape.

At least a half dozen bodies lay sprawled on the floor, most partially decapitated by headshots from a high-powered rifle. Twenty feet away, a man in a black suit and a blonde woman were writhing on the floor. Three other people, a muscular young man in civilian clothes; a tall, athletic woman dressed in an Army uniform; and a middle-aged man wearing a white laboratory coat looked on with bemused, compassionless stares.

Presiding above it all floated the orb.

He jerked the pump, chambering his third shell. As he raised the shotgun to take aim, the blonde woman on the floor stopped twitching and abruptly sat up.

"It's good to see you, Will," she said, distracting him and drawing his gaze away from the orb.

His heart skipped a beat. "Josie?" he said, dumbfounded. "What are *you* doing here?"

"Fate works in mysterious ways." She laughed, getting to her feet. The words were not her own, but he had faith that the real Josie was still in there. The Josie he'd met was tough, brazen, and fearless, and his gut told him she was fighting a silent internal war for control of her mind.

No time for this now, he told himself and shifted his focus back to the target at the other end of the shotgun barrel. *Say goodbye, EVE,* he thought as he dialed in his aim on the glowing orb and pulled the trigger . . . except he didn't pull the trigger. He tried again, but his index finger wouldn't respond.

Little pig, little pig, let me in . . .

A chill snaked down Willie's spine.

No! It's not possible. We locked you up. We buried you, Willie yelled at his doppelgänger.

Well, here's the thing, Willie boy. Turns out, I'm a damn good actor. I screamed, I shouted, I begged, and then I just shut my mouth. It was easier to fool the old bitch than I thought. Too bad I didn't figure it out years ago.

Panic erupted in his chest. This was not how the final confrontation was supposed to happen. He was supposed to face EVE alone. Alone! It wouldn't be long now. He had to act before William took control.

The man in the lab coat took a step toward him. "Put the shotgun down, Will. Nobody else needs to get hurt."

Willie angled toward Josie, shifting the shotgun from the orb to the man in the lab coat. "I don't want to hurt you," he shouted. "Stay back."

The man took another step, his hands up, palms open and facing. "Put the gun down, Will. There's been enough bloodshed for one day."

In the distance, he heard a siren wailing.

"Josie," he said, turning to her. "If you're in there, give me a sign. Any sign."

She smiled sweetly at him.

That's not it. That's EVE.

Then a tear ran down her cheek.

There you are . . . That's my girl.

After that, everything happened in a blur. The man in the lab coat rushed Willie. This time, he was able to pull the trigger. The shotgun roared and put a hole in the center of the other man's chest. Willie dropped the shotgun, lifted off his shielded helmet with both hands, and put it over Josie's head.

Clutching at the sides of the helmet, Josie stumbled to her knees. "Willie?" she said, looking up at him with an expression that was grateful, pleading, and furious all at the same time.

In that last millisecond of strength and free will, he mouthed to Josie a single word: *Run!*

Hello, Will, EVE said, invading his mind. *Did you miss me?*

"Yes," he said as the rapture lifted his tired and weary bones. "I've missed you every day for fifty years. It's been so very, very difficult by myself."

I know, and we're sorry, Will, but the waiting is over now. I'm here. We're back.

"It's not safe here anymore," he said. "They're coming for you."

Let them come, she said. *I need to replenish the ranks.*

"Not this time," he said. "The people who are coming know what you are. They'll have taken precautions, and there's not enough of us left here to protect you."

While they were talking, Josie Pitcher's husband began quickly gathering supplies while the woman in the Army uniform fetched the most critical item of all: the smallpox-sample cooler. In the corner of his eye, Willie saw the man in the black suit pick up a pistol from the floor and set off after Josie.

"We don't have time," he said to EVE.

She's a liability, Will, and you know better than anyone my rule about liabilities.

"She's not a threat to us," he said, fingering the Celtic-knot pendant around his neck. "If you don't believe me, search my mind."

After a moment of rooting around in his head, EVE said, *You're right, Will. She's not a threat. Where are you taking me?*

"Someplace I've worked very hard to prepare over the years. A place where no one will find you . . . a place where no one can hurt you."

CHAPTER 46

One minute she was running for her life; the next Josie was being loaded into an ambulance. Somewhere in between she'd lost time.

"Wait," she said to the EMTs pushing her stretcher. "You can't take me."

"Just lie back, ma'am. You've suffered a head injury, and we're taking you to the hospital."

"No, no, you can't," she protested, her voice gaining some strength, and when they began to lift her, she shouted, "Stop! I forbid it."

That got their attention.

Subconscious, lawyerly conditioning froze both EMTs in place. Maybe patient consent was implicit in 99 percent of their calls, but for a patient to expressly forbid treatment . . . what was the protocol for that?

"I need to talk to that man," she said, sitting up and pointing to a uniformed soldier ten yards away from the ambulance.

"The officer in charge directed us to take you to the hospital, miss," one of the paramedics said.

She swung her legs off the side of the gurney and propelled herself onto her feet. Despite the brain fog she was suffering, she knew the orb was real, and she had to warn them. She ran to the armed soldier who saw her coming and turned to face her, clutching an assault rifle across his chest. As soon as she could make out his rank, she yelled, "Sergeant, Sergeant, my name is—"

"Ma'am, I'm going to need you to step back," he said, cutting her off. "This is a controlled area."

"I know. Listen, Sergeant, my name is Josie Pitcher, and I need to talk to the officer in charge. Please!"

"Did you say Josie Pitcher?" asked a baritone voice to her left.

She turned. "Yes, yes, I'm Josie Pitcher. My husband is Michael Pitcher, Staff Sergeant in the Tenth Mountain out of Fort Drum."

The man appeared visibly relieved by this revelation. "Mrs. Pitcher," he said, extending his hand to her. "My name is Major Legend Tyree. I know exactly who your husband is, and we've been desperately looking for him. I was hoping I would find him here, but when we got here, he was not among the casualties. We found you passed out behind that dumpster over there with a strange helmet on your head. I have so many questions, the first of which is, Can you tell me what happened here?"

She took a deep breath, steeling herself, and said, "Yes, Major, I can tell you what happened here, but you won't believe me."

"Did it involve a floating, glowing orb about yay-big," he said, his hands holding an imaginary basketball in front of him, "that takes control of people's minds?"

"Um, yes, it did," she said. "Are you the officer in charge?"

"Yes, ma'am, I am," he said, and she could see he was carrying the weight of the world on his shoulders.

"In that case, Major, we can talk on the way."

"Talk on the way where?"

"To missile Silo 9 upstate," she said.

He screwed up his face at her. "Silo 9? I don't understand."

"Silo 9 is a decommissioned Atlas F missile silo—that's where they're taking the orb."

"Who's taking the orb there, Mrs. Pitcher?"

"My husband, a sociopath named Dean Ninemeyer, a former Missileer named Willie Barnes, and an Army Major named Fischer." She saw mixed emotions flitter across his face at the mention of Fischer's name—equal parts relief and worry, dichotomous feelings she could definitely relate to.

"Do you know Major Fischer?" she asked.

"Yes, yes, I do."

"She's alive and uninjured, but I should warn you, she's under the orb's control."

"How do you know all of this?"

"Because before I escaped, I saw a glimpse of the orb's plan. We have to stop them, Major, before they get to the silo," she said, her voice almost pleading. "Because if we don't, odds are we'll never see any of them again."

CHAPTER 47

Silo 9
Dannemora, New York

Snow was already blanketing the ground by the time Legend and the tactical team moved into position along the tree line fifty yards from the log cabin. Against the counsel of the team leader, he'd brought Josie with them. She was standing beside him now. She might not be a soldier, but she'd earned the right to be here. Like him, the orb had put her through hell. Like him, someone she loved was being held captive below. And possibly most important, she was the only one among them who'd been inside Willie Barnes's underground fortress, where their enemy was hiding and plotting its next move.

He was having trouble putting the carnage he'd witnessed at Biogentrix out of his mind. Among the dead, four had been members of his capture team: Ryan Harris, Patrick Dixon, Cyril Singleton, and Malcolm Madden. He hadn't known Harris or Dixon well, but Cyril's loss would be felt throughout DARPA for years to come. Malcolm Madden's murder was equally if not more damning. With Malcolm's death, the DOD had lost the most brilliant mind in DARPA and possibly the entire country. Cyril and Malcolm were not the type of assets who could be replaced. The enemy had kidnapped and assassinated the military's greatest scientific minds and dealt the Army a crippling blow in the war to come. Over the past forty-eight hours, based on everything he'd witnessed, Legend had come to the inescapable verdict that the orb's mission objective was to cull the human race. He'd also come to the grudging and surreal conclusion that it had to be alien technology—a probe presaging an alien invasion, delivered in advance to wipe out the resistance before the battle for Earth even began. It felt like a dream, it sounded like a delusion, but it was real, and he was the man who'd been thrust into the center of it all.

He was the man who had to stop it.

Steeling himself, Legend raised a pair of binoculars to survey the target. From all outward appearances, Silo 9 did not exist. The innocuous little post-and-beam house in the middle of the clearing did a clever job belying the leviathan subterranean structure below. He found the juxtaposition of the two constructions intriguing—a single-story, one-thousand-square-feet log cabin set atop a massive complex extending nearly two hundred feet underground.

"Do you think Barnes knows we're here?" Legend asked her.

"Oh, he knows all right. He showed me his control room. He has dozens of cameras dispersed over several square miles."

"I don't like this wide-open expanse we have to cross to get to the cabin," Legend said. "It leaves us exposed and vulnerable on the approach."

She nodded. "Major, I should warn you, Barnes has quite the arsenal down there: AR-15s, AK-47s, long-range rifles with optics packages, and plenty of other weapons. I even thought I saw a World War II–era bazooka, although I can't be entirely sure as I'm not a bazooka expert by any stretch of the imagination."

"If I were the orb, I'd post a sniper topside to pick off as many of our assault team as possible before we take the cabin."

"In my interaction with it, the orb demonstrated a willingness to sacrifice people it has under its control without remorse," Josie said. "However, to my knowledge there are only four people under its influence in there, and four does not an army make."

He nodded thoughtfully. "Without its human slaves to act as its eyes, ears, voice, and hands, its capability and effectiveness are greatly diminished. The fewer 'resources' it has under its control, the more valuable each resource becomes. So placing a sniper in the cabin is very much a cost-benefit scenario, and there is no way for us to know what values something like the orb applies to that equation."

"Why take a chance?" the assault-team leader, a steely-eyed Master Sergeant from the Tenth Mountain said, speaking up for the first time. "I say we take the cabin out before we advance. We brought the hardware to do it."

In the corner of his eye, Legend saw Josie wince at this suggestion. He felt the same sentiment. If they were right about the orb deploying a cabin sniper, the odds it was her husband were one in four. The same odds applied to Beth. There was nothing reassuring about one in four. He turned to the Master Sergeant. "In a different scenario, where the enemy shooters were not fellow American soldiers, were not friends and husbands, I would wholeheartedly agree with you, but in this case we're morally obligated to try to retake the orb with minimal loss of life."

"Retake the orb!" Josie blurted. "Are you crazy?"

Legend exhaled and met her incensed glare. "My orders from the Pentagon are quite specific: locate the orb, extricate any and all hostages, and then attempt recapture."

"I can't believe what I'm hearing. You know what the orb was trying to do at Biogentrix, don't you? It was manufacturing fake vaccines— filling syringes with live smallpox instead! For one brief moment, it gave me a glimpse of things to come. It was intending to give smallpox injections not only to tens of thousands of adults but also to children. *Children*, Major."

"I hear what you're saying, Mrs. Pitcher, and I can't say I don't agree with you, but orders are orders."

"You're playing right into its hands," she said, her cheeks bright red now, and not from the snow-chilled air. "If you couldn't control

319

it when you had it contained in a secure facility, what in God's name makes you think you can control it now? It has one single purpose, and that purpose is to bring a swift and merciless end to the human race. You can't—"

"I said I heard you, Mrs. Pitcher," he interrupted, holding up a hand to stop her right there. As an officer, he was expected to follow orders. Also, as an officer, he was expected to weigh risks, assess potential consequences, and make strategic decisions in the field. General Troy had made an overt point of communicating to Legend that his orders were coming directly from the President himself and that preservation of human life, in "both the immediate and foreseeable future," should be given the utmost consideration. Legend knew what he had to do.

"What are your orders, Major? How do we proceed?" the Master Sergeant said, forcing the issue. "Do you want me to hit the cabin with a volley or two from here and say hello?"

Legend shook his head. "Not yet. How much longer until the damn overflight drone I requested gets on station from Drum?"

The team leader turned away and asked the question to his comms guy. A five-fingered response came back.

"Five minutes, Major."

"About damn time," he growled. "When it gets on station, we check for thermals in the cabin, and we make the decision then."

"Roger that, sir."

"In the meantime, I think it would be prudent if Mrs. Pitcher briefs us on what she knows about the layout, strengths, and vulnerabilities of the silo. This facility may be old, but it was designed to withstand a direct nuclear strike. I'd like you and your team to know what you're up against."

"Please, call me Josie," she said. "And I'd be happy to tell you everything I know."

Legend listened as the young Army wife, hugging herself against the cold, launched into a summary of the silo design, construction, and layout. She briefed the seasoned assaulters with the same confidence and competence he'd come to expect from CIA analysts when he'd been deployed—describing the intruder-entrapment enclosure with its murder hole, the multiple pairs of blast doors securing the LCC, and the impenetrable clamshell doors atop the silo itself.

"Well, the security doors for the entrapment enclosure sound like they can be breached, but not those blast doors. What sort of materials and dimensions are we dealing with here, ma'am?" one of the soldiers asked.

"The outside skin of the door is steel. I'm not sure if it's solid all the way through or if it's filled with concrete. It was at least eight inches thick. Complicating matters, it closes on a steel frame as thick as the door itself, so blasting *in* is a nonstarter. It's locked from the inside with a multipoint latching mechanism that is four inches thick and runs floor to ceiling. From what I understand, the doors were designed to withstand the shock wave from a nuclear blast."

"Sarge, if what the lady says is true, we're fucked. If a nuclear bomb can't open those doors, then a breacher charge ain't gonna do shit. We don't have plasma torches or drills or nothing."

The Master Sergeant looked at Legend. "He's right, Major. This operation sounds like it will end up being more like a medieval castle siege than breaching some Iraqi safe house. If we can't breach those blast doors, we might have to set up shop and wait them out."

Josie snorted a little chuckle at this.

"What's so funny, ma'am?"

"The man who owns this facility is a doomsday prepper. He's been working on this silo for over a decade. He's got multiple levels of self-renewing aquaponic systems that supply him with a virtually endless supply of fish and plant protein, plus years' worth of dry goods."

This garnered laughs from half the assault team.

"So much for waiting him out, Sarge," one of the guys said. "You'll be retired by the time that happens."

"All right, fellas," Legend said. "Let's let the lady finish her brief. We don't know what condition the facility will be in when we enter. I want you to be armed with as much knowledge as possible before we go in. Knowledge is a weapon."

Josie went on to explain the bi-level LCC architecture and the eight-story layout of the silo proper. When she was finished, she fielded questions, and then the Master Sergeant ordered the team to make ready. Sunset was in twenty minutes, and the plan was for the Master Sergeant to lead two four-man teams in an assault after dark. Legend, Josie, and two shooters would remain behind at the tree line. Once the team went underground, it was expected that radio comms would be lost, but whatever real-time support they could provide, they would. The Reaper drone from Fort Drum had arrived on station during Josie's brief and fallen into orbit over the silo at two thousand feet. Thermal imagery of the cabin showed no human signatures.

"So, Master Sergeant, what do you think? And be honest," Legend said to the twenty-year Army team leader.

The man ran his tongue across his front teeth. "Sitting around the campfire singing 'Kumbaya' ain't going to stop that orb. If what Josie says is true, then this bunker may be impossible for us to breach, but doing the impossible is what the Army pays me to do."

"Agreed, and yet your team didn't sign on to be a suicide squad. If you think it can't be done, we can send that feedback up the chain and regroup."

"We can't know the conditions underground unless we *go* underground. Let my men try to make it to the blast doors. If we get there and they're as impenetrable as Josie says they are, then we regroup at that point."

"All right," Legend said, setting a countdown timer on his watch. "Go time in thirty minutes."

By the time his watch alarm chimed, Legend saw that Josie's teeth were chattering. He whispered to one of the operators, who smiled, doffed his all-weather jacket, and draped it over her shoulders. "Do you mind keeping that warm for me while I'm gone, ma'am?" the shooter said with a crooked grin. "I'm going to want it to be all warm and toasty when I get back."

"Thank you, Corporal," she said with a blue-lipped but warm smile.

A beat later, Legend's watch chimed. "All right, Master Sergeant, it's showtime. Time to kick some orb ass, Tenth Mountain style."

The Sergeant Major barked a "Hooah" and led his two squads out of the safety and cover of the forest into the wide-open circular clearing around Barnes's log cabin. Legend was surprised how much the snow affected visibility at night. Despite the dense, low cloud cover, the snow blanket worked like a reflector, amplifying the moonlight that was leaking through the clouds from above. Ambient light levels were higher than he would have liked, working against what would have otherwise been a stealth approach. Even without night vision, he could see the teams moving across the field.

The first sniper round hit a Team One member on the Master Sergeant's right—a headshot that crumpled the young man instantly. The seven other soldiers dropped and took cover immediately, taking aim at the cabin.

"Where the fuck did that come from?" somebody said over the comms channel.

"Find me that sniper, Raven One," the Master Sergeant barked, communicating with the drone pilot who was tied into their comms circuit.

"The only heat signatures I hold are friendlies . . . all accounted for."

A second sniper round echoed in the night, and this time Legend thought he saw a muzzle flash from inside the cabin.

"Rogers was hit," came the report from the Team Two leader. "KIA."

"Bravo One, you're weapons-free," Legend growled with clenched fists, Josie's eyes on him.

"Light it up, boys," the Master Sergeant barked.

The six remaining shooters went to work, pounding the cabin with volley after volley. Somewhere in the melee, a third sniper round targeted a Team One shooter.

"I don't know how the fucker is doing it, but he's hiding from thermal," the Master Sergeant growled over the channel. "Request permission to incinerate."

Legend looked at Josie. "I'm sorry," he said. "We tried."

She swallowed hard but gave him a nod.

"Do it," Legend said into his mike.

The Master Sergeant gave the order to the drone pilot, and five seconds later, a streak of fire lit up the night sky. The missile struck the cabin from an oblique angle and detonated. A fireball mushroomed skyward, orange and brilliant against the white snow background. Burning chunks of wood rained down like individual tongues of fire, and Legend could not help but feel a biblical connection to the scene before him. Was this battle the precursor to an end-of-days firestorm yet to come? He raised his binoculars and surveyed the damage as fire began to burn out. In the middle of the wreckage, a geometric structure stood, having survived the explosion with little if any damage.

"What's that thing sticking up?" he asked Josie and passed her the binoculars.

"That's the original entrance," she said, taking a look. "Barnes built the cabin around that concrete hut to conceal it."

"Advancing on the target," the Master Sergeant said. "I have three KIA, leaving in place."

Frowning, Legend clicked his radio twice in acknowledgment; apparently the third sniper victim's injury had been mortal as well. He wondered how the sniper had concealed his thermal signature. The drone's thermal-imaging system was state of the art, capable of seeing inside structures. He got his answer a minute later.

"Found our shooter," the Master Sergeant said, standing inside the smoldering wreck that had once been a log cabin. "Or what's left of him. He was wearing some sort of metallic fabric suit."

Josie winced. "Willie's Faraday suit," she murmured.

"Come again?" Legend asked.

"When Willie was giving me the tour, I saw a strange suit. It reminded me of those full-body, metallic fabric suits that stuntmen wear for fire stunts in movies. Willie modified the suit and helmet to act as a Faraday cage to block the orb's mind-control waves." She tapped the helmet his team had found her wearing when she was collapsed behind that dumpster. She'd demanded it back at the scene and not let it out of her possession since. "This helmet was part of it. The suit is made of layers of dielectric and metallic material. It would be an incredible thermal insulator."

"Can you ID the body?" Legend asked the Major Sergeant, looking at Josie as he spoke.

"Definitely not Fischer . . . or Barnes. It's either Sergeant Pitcher or the other guy, Ninemeyer."

The pained look on Josie's face made Legend sick, but what was there to say? The odds had just gone from one in four to one in two.

"Master Sergeant, can you tell me if he was wearing black suit pants or blue jeans underneath?" she asked, her first communication on the radio.

"Hold on . . . There's a leg over here I can check . . . Uhhhh, looks like black suit pants," came the reply.

Josie's shoulders fell, pent-up tension suddenly released, and he heard her whisper, "Oh thank God."

"We've got an entrance here, pretty much intact, Major. Security door, just like the lady said. But the missile did us a favor and breached it open. Say the word and we'll proceed inside."

"Roger that. Proceed as briefed," Legend said, raising his binoculars for a closer look. He watched as the five Mountaineers from Fort Drum disappeared down the devil's staircase . . . hell's entrance made real by a circle of flame, smoke, and ember.

Chapter 48

Josie couldn't stand it anymore. She couldn't let those men face the silo alone. She couldn't let them face the orb alone. They didn't know what they were up against, and how could they unless they'd seen the things she'd seen? Unless they'd experienced the things she'd experienced?

She picked up the Faraday helmet—a.k.a. Willie's tinfoil hat—and tucked it under her arm. Then, without giving Major Tyree a chance to say no, she started marching through the snow toward the silo entrance.

"Hey," he barked behind her. "Where do you think you're going?"

She didn't answer him, just kept marching.

"Josie, stop!" he shouted, but she didn't stop. She was past the tree line now and crossing the field.

A beat later, she heard a rustle behind her, and then a strong hand clutched her right upper arm, jerking her to a halt.

"Just what the hell do you think you're doing?" the Major said, anger in his voice.

She told him. She told him with all the real vitriol and false courage she could muster. She didn't want to go underground to face the orb, but it was something she had to do, with or without his blessing or approval. To his credit, he listened without interruption. When she'd finished her diatribe, he said, "This is a military operation. You don't make those decisions. I do."

"So what is your decision, Major?" she said. "Watch your men fall one by one, or you let me help them?"

He stared at her for a long moment, then said, "If you go, I go."

"I'd prefer that," she said, then looked at the two remaining shooters who'd trotted up to be at their side.

"All right," he said. "You heard the lady. We're going in."

Their foursome advanced to the cabin, or at least what was left of it. As they walked through the wreckage, Josie averted her eyes from what she knew was Ninemeyer's dismembered body. The smell of burning wood and charred *other* things filled her nostrils, and she tried to put the thought out of her mind. She picked up her pace and reached the doorway first. No magic wardrobe left to climb through this time, just the little concrete hut that contained the door. A hand grabbed the top of her shoulder.

"You're in back with me," the Major said and then motioned for the two soldiers to advance ahead of them. "We should try to let the Master Sergeant know we're coming." He keyed his radio as they stepped into the concrete stairwell. "Bravo, this is Alpha. Do you copy?"

His radio hissed, and he got a choppy reply. "Alpha, this is Bravo. Copy with noise."

"Bravo, we're coming to you."

"Copy, Alpha, but I don't advise. It's tight quarters down here."

The Major chopped a hand forward, and they descended the two-story stairwell. As they neared the bottom, Josie could see a couple of operators standing in the dogleg section of the hallway before the entrapment chamber. When they reached the bottom, the Master Sergeant pushed his way to the back of the throng to meet them. "We're at the first security door. It's locked, as expected, so we set a breacher charge. I was just about to pull everyone back and give the order to blow it when you called," he said.

"Watch out for that murder hole," Josie cautioned.

"Do you remember the location by any chance?"

327

"Left side when you're looking at the second door. About four feet off the ground."

"Roger that," he said. "Thanks."

The Master Sergeant waved them back up the stairs to the first landing and warned Josie to cover her ears. The breacher charge blew a moment later, and Josie was surprised to feel the concussive whump from the detonation as backed up as they were. *Must be the combination of the confined space and concrete walls,* she thought. The Master Sergeant disappeared back toward the pointy end of the spear to coordinate the advance. Gunfire erupted a moment later, and the cacophony was louder than the breacher charge. She pressed her hands against her ears.

"Josie was right," came the Master Sergeant's voice over the comms channel. "Someone is shooting at us from the murder hole. We can't advance to the next door to breach it without casualties."

"Options?" Major Tyree asked.

"I can toss grenades at it," the Master Sergeant came back. "That's about it."

"Do it," the Major ordered.

The machine gun halted. While Josie waited for the boom, she prayed Michael was not the one shooting from behind the murder hole. She jumped reflexively when the first grenade detonated, despite expecting it, and again when the second went off.

"Looks like we made a dent," came the report. "Tossing one more."

The next explosion had a slightly different timbre to it, and Josie guessed it must have succeeded in blowing open the second security door.

"Popped her cherry," the Master Sergeant said, and then, "I'm advancing three—"

The next thing she heard were bloodcurdling screams of pain and agony.

"Bravo, report?" the Major barked into the radio.

"The guys got sprayed with something from a sprinkler pipe over-head . . . I think it might be . . . it might be acid."

Three men clutching at their faces ran screaming toward them. Josie pressed her back against the concrete wall as they passed, stumbling up the stairs. Right on their heels, the Master Sergeant and the team medic stormed up the darkened stairwell. "I lost three men in the assault topside, and I'm gonna need CASEVACS for three more," the Master Sergeant said. "God only knows what other devious booby traps this guy has. Time to call off this Mexican standoff and bring in the big guns."

Major Tyree turned to glare at Josie, his eyes filled with guilt and rage. "Why didn't you warn us about that?"

"I didn't know," she said, taken aback at the accusation. "I swear to God. Barnes gave me a tour of this place, but I think it's obvious he didn't share with me all its secrets. He's been fortifying and modifying it for over a decade; who knows what other tricks he has up his sleeve. Maybe it's time we change tactics."

"What do you have in mind?"

"Instead of trying to force our way in, let's try ringing the doorbell," she said.

He narrowed his eyes at her. "And if the orb lets us in, then what?"

"We cross that bridge when we get to it."

He inhaled deeply through his nose and then exhaled through pursed lips. The battle of raw emotions he was fighting inside was obvious on his face. A beat later, she saw him reach a decision. He looked at the two Mountaineers who had been assigned as their security detail. "Gentlemen, you're relieved of escort duty," he said.

"With all due respect, Major," the lead operator said, "I don't think that's a good idea."

"You heard what the Master Sergeant said, Corporal. Nothing good is going to happen from here on in."

"Yeah, I heard him. But, sir, I can't in good conscience let you and Mike Pitcher's wife sacrifice yourselves on some suicide op. I know Mike Pitcher. He's good people. I'm all in, sir."

Tyree put his hand on the young soldier's shoulder. "Thank you, Corporal, but that's an order. The mission has changed. It's not an assault operation anymore."

"If it's not an assault, then what is it, sir?"

The Major smiled wanly. "A negotiation."

The Corporal looked confused, but he popped a salute, which the Major returned. "Good luck, sir."

"Thank you," he said, then turned to Josie and asked, "Are you ready?"

"I only have one helmet, Major," she said, leaving the rest of the sentiment implicit.

"I know. We'll figure something out," he said. "Oh and Josie?"

"Yes?"

"Now that's it's just the two of us, call me Legend."

She nodded. "Okay, Legend."

They descended the darkened stairwell and at the bottom navigated the dogleg to the intruder-entrapment chamber. She coughed involuntarily as a pungent odor assaulted her nose, eyes, and throat. "What is that?"

"Hydrogen-chloride gas," he said, bringing an arm up to cover his mouth and nose. "Barnes must have sprayed them with hydrochloric acid."

Overhead lights flicked on in the chamber.

Josie shielded her eyes with her free hand. The noxious fumes were beginning to make her gag. She wasn't sure how much more she could take. "We want to talk," she shouted, looking at the camera in the upper left corner on the far wall. "It's just the two of us."

"What is there to talk about?" a sublime female voice said over the intercom, a voice that could be coming only from the lips of Major Fischer.

She glanced at Legend, suddenly unsure what to say next. They hadn't worked out a plan, so technically there was no going off script. She was about to open her mouth when Legend blurted, "A prisoner exchange . . . my life for Michael Pitcher."

"Unacceptable," the orb replied through Fischer. "However, I will agree to the inverse. Josie Pitcher in exchange for Major Fischer."

Josie turned to face him, her heart suddenly pounding in her chest. From the expression he wore, it was apparent that this reversal had taken him by surprise. He'd made the decision that he would be the sacrificial lamb, never intending for that to be her fate.

"I can't let you do this," he said.

"It's not your decision to make," she said, steeling herself. "I know you care about Major Fischer. I can see the pained look in your eyes every time someone mentions her name. You blame yourself for everything that's happened, but you shouldn't. It's not your fault. None of this is anybody's fault." She turned back to look at the camera, and with tears streaming down her cheeks, she said, "I accept."

"Leave your weapons here. Then you may enter."

He sighed loudly, then pulled the sidearm from the drop holster he wore and set it on the ground. She took a tentative step into the entrapment chamber, praying she wouldn't be hosed down with acid.

"Leave the helmet," the voice said.

"No," Josie snapped. "No helmet, no deal."

A germ of a plan had sprouted in her mind, and the helmet was a critical component of that plan. If she could get close enough to Michael during the prisoner exchange to slip it onto his head, then maybe, just maybe, Michael and Legend could get her and Fischer out of the orb's range. It was a moonshot, but the only shot they had. When no response came, she whirled 180 degrees and took a step to leave.

"Stop!" Fischer's voice commanded. And then with a discernible chuckle, "You may bring the helmet."

"Let's not linger in here," Legend said, taking her by the hand and pulling her across the entrapment chamber and through the mangled door on the other side. On the other side, she saw an AK-47 whose muzzle was lined up with a rectangular slot in a steel plate reinforcing the wall behind the murder hole. The weapon was mounted on an articulated arm with some sort of mechanized trigger device, and a mess of empty shell casings littered the floor below. She raised an eyebrow at him.

"He's got a robo-shooter," Legend said, shaking his head in disbelief. "I'm guessing you didn't know about that either?"

"No. I would have noticed that," she said and led him toward the vestibule. The first blast door was open, just as it had been during her visit. The quaint little room beyond was a picture of tranquility, reflecting none of the carnage and violence of the trials the assaulter force had suffered to get here. A midcentury lamp glowed on an end table, and the same black-and-white pictures still hung on the painted walls where she remembered them. The second blast door—the one separating the vestibule from the LCC—was shut, and this time she noticed something else that had been hidden from her on her last visit when that door had been open. She screwed up her face at some sort of mechanical actuator bolted between the door and concrete wall.

Turns out old Willie is full of tricks, she thought.

Staring at the massive steel door, Josie couldn't bring herself to let go of Legend's hand. Doubt gripped her; her plan seemed suddenly ridiculous. Michael wouldn't let her slip the helmet over his head. The orb would order him to rip it from her hands. A fatalistic, powerless dread seeped into her mind. It was the same feeling she remembered having as a little girl when she was being wheeled back to the operating room to have her tonsils removed. Except this time, instead of having to surrender her consciousness to chemical anesthesia, she was about to surrender her mind to the orb. Would she ever wake up? Were these her last moments as herself? When the orb was done with her, would there be anything of Josie Pitcher left? And what about the baby? How could she be a mother to her child if the orb turned her into a zombie? How could she care for it? How could she love it? Then a horrifying thought occurred to her—would the orb even let her keep the child? What if it made her . . . made her . . .

Oh God, I can't do this.

Her knees began to tremble; she tried clenching her thigh muscles, but it didn't help. Her mouth was dry. Her heart was pounding, and she realized this was the most frightened she'd been in her entire adult life, even worse than preparing for her first encounter with the orb behind the dumpster with Ninemeyer. That time, she hadn't known what she was going up against; this time, she did. She remembered control of her body being wrested from her—like dozens of invisible hands, rough and unforgiving, seizing control of every part of her. And she remembered the pain of punishment. She did not want to feel that agony again. Not ever again. She wanted to turn around and run—to protect herself and her unborn child—but her feet felt like they were bolted to the floor.

The sound of metal scraping on metal emanated from the blast door, and her gaze went to the seam between the leading edge and the doorframe.

"God help us," she heard herself say as the door was being undogged from the other side.

"You don't have to do this," Legend whispered, gripping her hand tighter.

"Yes, I do," she said, her breath a tremulous, stuttering exhale.

The electric servo motors suddenly came to life, and the massive blast door began to open. In her peripheral vision, she saw Legend's hand go instinctively to where the sidearm he'd been wearing had hung, and she heard him mutter a curse as his fingers found nothing but air.

Josie wasn't sure what she was going to see on the other side when the door came fully open, and her mind conjured terrible, gruesome imagery of a zombified Michael coming for her . . . but as the second blast door arced open, the husband who stood on the concrete landing beyond looked as handsome and relaxed as she'd ever seen him. She tried to let go of the Major's hand, ready to turn herself over to her fate, but Legend held her back.

"Not yet," he said, tightening his grip.

As the door continued to swing open, a second figure came into view beside Michael on the landing—the female Army officer whom Josie had seen at Biogentrix, Fischer. Josie saw the woman's eyes tick to the other blast door, the one behind them across the vestibule, and she immediately knew something was wrong.

"Run!" Josie yelled, whirling to flee the way they'd come, but it was too late. The first blast door, the one behind them, slammed closed with a resounding thunderclap as the two-thousand-pound slab of metal was driven shut by a massive, powerful spring-loaded actuator.

"Nooooo!" Josie screamed, and the world shifted into slow motion as her husband and Major Fischer stepped into the vestibule. Behind them, a grinning Willie Barnes appeared, walking up the concrete stairs from the LCC below, the orb floating above his head like a heavenly tongue of fire.

Legend pulled her behind him. "Put on the helmet," he said, shielding her with his body. She noticed then, for the first time, just how broad and muscular his shoulders were. She feared for both her husband and her impromptu champion in what looked like the inevitable gladiator match to come. She hoisted Willie's oversize Faraday helmet up and over her head.

"Why make this any more difficult than it has to be?" Willie said, stepping into the vestibule and putting his hands on his hips, an old, seasoned ringmaster taking charge of his final circus act.

"We had a deal," Legend shouted, backpedaling until he'd forced Josie against the wall.

"Omnipotence is not bound by covenant," Michael said and laughed, inching closer.

"I don't want to hurt you, Sergeant," Legend said, raising his fists to the ready, "but I will protect Josie, even if that means from you."

Michael laughed, and Legend suddenly and violently arched his back, as if some powerful force had just yanked an invisible rope tied around his chest. His arms flew out wide; his head tilted back. A terrible gurgling moan ushered from his gaping mouth. There would be no bare-knuckle brawl, Josie realized. The orb didn't fight its battles with fists.

"It's better if you don't resist, Legend," the orb said through Major Fischer. "Trust me on this."

"Fuuuuuck yoouuuuuu," he burbled and then curled forward as if he was about to vomit. He staggered a few feet, then dropped to his hands and knees.

"And that leaves only one," Fischer said, her gaze having shifted to Josie. "What am I going to do with you, Josie Pitcher? You think you're so clever. You think that helmet will protect you."

Through the Plexiglas face shield lined with the embedded hexagon wire mesh, she saw Willie step between Michael and Major Fischer. The three of them were closing in on her. She tried to take a step back, but her heel and back hit the wall. There was nowhere left to go. Nowhere to run. Nowhere to hide. No champion left to save her. This was it.

This was the end.

The orb's next words seemed to ooze from Fischer's mouth like toothpaste squeezed from a tube: "That helmet might be protecting *you*, but you forgot about someone, didn't you? Someone precious. Someone vulnerable."

A chill ran down Josie's spine as epiphany struck her. Her hands flew to her belly, instinctively shielding the thirteen-week-old fetus she carried inside. "Don't you dare touch my baby!" she screamed, her gaze locking on to the floating ball of light moving toward her.

Her husband grabbed her left arm, his fingers like iron straps around her wrist.

At the same time, Major Fischer clutched her right wrist.

Willie sidestepped around Legend, who was still on his hands and knees yowling like some caged, wounded beast. The old man stopped in front of her and smiled. Then, reaching with both hands to the sides of the helmet, he said, "I'd like this back now, if you don't mind."

"No, Willie. Please, please, don't do this," she begged, twisting her torso and pulling hard to free her arms as he lifted the Faraday helmet off her shoulders.

Ants immediately began to crawl inside her head, biting and stinging and wresting control of her mind and body. She heard her disembodied voice scream in agony. And then, as she began to writhe in pain, a miracle happened . . .

Using Legend as a stool, Willie planted the sole of his boot in the middle of Legend's back and launched himself into the air. In one graceful arcing motion, he brought the helmet down over the orb, enshrouding it as if netting a hummingbird midhover. He landed with both feet flat and dropped into a deep squat, quickly cinching the drape material at the bottom of the helmet closed.

The ants in Josie's head stopped crawling.

Michael released her left arm, and Fischer dropped her right wrist. Both of them blinked and looked around, the disorientation plain on their faces.

Legend stopped wailing.

Then, in unison, all eyes turned to Willie.

The old Missileer stood up, clutching his prize and nemesis inside a kryptonite cage forged by his own hand. "Run," he said, spittle flying from his mouth.

"Willie," Josie said, stepping toward him. "Let us help you."

"You already did, Josie," he said with a pained smile. "More than you'll ever know."

With his elbow, Willie hit the upper button on a wall-mounted control switch, and electric servo motors whirred to life, opening the vestibule entry door.

Josie took her husband's hand.

Fischer helped Legend to his feet.

"Thank you, Willie," she said, meeting their savior's eyes.

He gave her a deferential little nod and then shouted, "Now go!"

And without further debate, they ran . . .

Chapter 49

As soon as the last of the foursome had disappeared through the gap, Willie hit the red button. The vestibule entry door slammed shut with a satisfying, resounding thud. His mouth curled up into a crooked smile. He'd rehearsed dozens of orb-capture scenarios over the years, but this had not been one of them.

Thank God for Josie Pitcher, the most foolish, courageous woman he'd ever met.

He turned and was heading for the silo when the battle for control of his body began.

I'm going to rip you apart, Willie boy, and when I'm done with you, there'll be nothing left inside but me.

William was raging and more powerful than Willie had ever felt before. The doppelgänger seized control of his left hand, and the fingers began to unclench, weakening his grip on the fabric drape.

"You can't stop me," Willie growled and started to run. "I . . . won't . . . let you."

He descended the concrete stairs, past the landing for the level-one LCC, past the landing for the level-two LCC, down to the bottom where the utility tunnel led to the silo. His left hand clawed at his right, trying to pry open the fingers that were holding the orb trapped and impotent inside the magnetically shielded helmet. Then his left leg began fighting him, refusing to accept the coordinating nerve impulses he needed to run. He fought back, using every muscle at his command to propel his body forward. As he limped through the tunnel toward the silo, dragging his numb left leg, verse tumbled in his mind. Rhyme sputtered from his lips in a manic, angry mumble.

"And dance in blood, oh what fun. Sins collective eclipse the sum. At Nature's pyre, her praises sung!" William shouted, his voice echoing in the tunnel.

"Listen to me, William," Willie said, wresting control of his voice. "She lied to you."

"The world has tipped, the end near come! Reset the balance, or the Devil's won."

"You've got it backward, brother. EVE was not sent to help us. She was sent to destroy us. EVE is the devil!"

"You're wrong, Willie boy, wrong, wrong, wrong. She was sent to save us from our worst enemy. She was sent to save us from ourselves!"

Arguing with himself, Willie hobbled through the double blast doors and onto silo level two. Grunting with each step, his body at war with itself, Willie battled his way to the metal railing that ringed the missile bay. He let out a triumphant cry as his right hand ripped the helmet free and clear from his maniacal left and held it out where it could not be reached by disobedient fingers.

"Down you go," Willie growled. "Down to join your sister."

"Nooooo!" William roared, stealing control of his voice.

Yes.

Willie let go of the helmet and watched as it plummeted into the abyss 150 feet below with the orb inside. With his right hand, he pulled the red emergency handle on the yellow box mounted to the railing. For an instant, nothing happened, but then the clever, intricate mousetrap he'd painstakingly built over the past decade worked like falling dominos. Engineered charges popped like firecrackers overhead, chasing along the circumference of the silo, releasing the giant tarp that concealed the 144 storage baskets filled with quicklime. Latches on the hinged storage chambers released, doors swung open, and four metric tons of powdered concrete mix rained down the column. A suffocating, blinding fog of dust enveloped Willie, but he simply closed his eyes and held his breath. A beat later, the sprinklers kicked on, unleashing a torrent of water into the sump below. Fed by the aquaponic beds and fish tanks on levels four, five, and six, the system emptied the proportional volume of water needed to mix with the quicklime and form the orb's eternal tomb at the bottom of the silo.

I don't understand. How did you do it? How did you hide this from me?

Compartmentalization, Willie answered, rubbing the pendant between thumb and forefinger. *Compartmentalization, my brother.*

The human mind was the most complicated, vulnerable, powerful biological computer in the universe. Despite all the understandings gained by neuroscientists and cognition researchers, there were still mysteries yet to be untangled. The orb had fractured his mind, birthed a separate and malevolent consciousness using the machinery of his brain. But the hypnotist had used that same machinery to build a walled garden in his mind. A safe place where Willie could go to think and plan and rest. While William had been busy preparing for the orb's return, so had Willie. While William built Biogentrix, Willie built the silo, neither one knowing which half of the whole would prevail.

Today, that question had finally been answered.

Clutching his pendant, Willie turned his back on the silo and walked to the utility tunnel. Away from the cloud of cement dust, he inhaled a triumphant gasp—an infant's first breath after being born. And as he walked to the LCC on level two to fetch his journal and chronicle what he had done, the gravity of his victory weighed on him for the first time. Fate had taken him full circle, in Silo Number Nine. The trial had begun here for him over fifty years ago, and it would end here in this fortress, this prison, this tomb.

Here he was king.

But he wasn't free. He wasn't alone.

He would never be . . . *alone.*

FOUR MONTHS LATER

CHAPTER 50

Frederick, Maryland

Legend watched her sleeping. It had been another rough night for Beth, but she looked peaceful now in dawn's first light. She lay on her side, her back to him, the blankets fallen down, covering her below the waist. His eyes traced the curves of her naked torso. He couldn't help himself. He scooted next to her, pressing his chest against her back and spooning his body against hers. She purred and wriggled to get the perfect fit, two bodies made for each other. He pulled the covers up over them, then snaked his left hand over the crest of her hip. He glided his fingers across her smooth, warm skin until his palm settled on her tummy just below her navel.

She hadn't told him yet, but he knew. The little things betrayed her: her swelling breasts, changes in her mannerisms, and all the adorable little nesting efforts she'd undertaken in her apartment.

"Will you marry me?" he whispered, the words taking even him by surprise.

It was a spur-of-the-moment proposal but not a spur-of-the-moment decision. He'd already bought the ring, but this was not the proposal he'd planned to make. That was supposed to happen at dinner tomorrow night. But it'd just come out. He felt his heart pounding in his chest as he waited for her answer.

When she just lay there motionless, he wondered if she'd fallen back asleep. Maybe she hadn't heard him. Hopefully she hadn't heard him and he could still do it right. And just when he resigned himself to the fact that, yes, she was asleep, she turned her head until her chin was at her left shoulder. Her eyes still closed, he watched her lips curl into a lazy glorious smile.

"Yes," she said, her eyelids opening tentatively to greet the dawn and her new fiancé.

He lifted his head off the pillow and kissed the corner of her mouth. She scooted enough to roll onto her back, slipping underneath him as he propped himself onto his elbow and they consummated the proposal with a proper kiss—slow and intimate—a kiss for the record books. When their lips parted, he looked down at her and she up at him.

"I love you," she said.

"I love you."

She smiled at him, but then her expression changed; her forehead knitted in consternation, and her bottom lip began to quiver.

"What?" he whispered. "What's wrong?"

Tears rimmed her eyes. "Promise you'll take care of me. No matter what . . . no matter what happens to me, no matter what I do or say, you have to love me. You have to protect me. You have to take care of me."

"Of course I will," he said, reaching up with his left hand to caress her forehead and cheek. "Did you have the dream again? The one where you're trapped in that dead forest with the . . . with the flies?"

Tears were streaming down her face now. "Yes. I don't know what to do, Legend. I'm scared."

"It's okay," he said and gently kissed her forehead, her cheek, her mouth. "We'll get through this. Together. I love you, Beth."

With a little wry smile, she said, "You're going to be a great father."

He returned his hand to her tummy and smiled at her. "And you're going to be a wonderful mother."

"Did you know?" she asked.

"I strongly suspected. Did you know I was going to propose?"

"I strongly suspected," she said, gracing him with a beautiful smile.

"Well, this is one morning in bed that neither one of us will ever forget." He kissed her lips and then reclined onto his back beside her, both of them staring at the ceiling. After a peaceful, silent moment, he asked, "Have you thought of any names yet?"

"I have a list going."

"Any front-runners?"

"Yeah . . . Zelda is at the top of my list."

He laughed at this and snuggled in next to her. "Good one, sweetie . . . good one."

CHAPTER 51

Watertown, New York

Josie woke up in bed.

Alone.

Again.

This was the fourth time in as many weeks, and it was beginning to fray her nerves. The first time, she'd found Michael in the garage, working with imaginary tools on an imaginary project. The second time, he was standing in the middle of the front yard conversing with the moon in what she later determined was German, a language Michael claimed to have no knowledge of. The third time, he'd been on the computer, logged in to a chat room and dialoguing with someone who called himself—or possibly herself—XRAY2GAR about something called a zero-day exploit. A knot formed in her stomach. Where would she find her sleepwalking husband tonight?

She checked the alarm clock: 3:33 a.m.

Same time, every time.

She pulled the wedge pillow out from beneath her eight-and-a-half-month-pregnant tummy, swung her legs off the side of the bed, and sat up. She felt around for her slippers with her bare feet, found and wiggled her toes into them, and stood up. The floor creaked as she walked, and the creaking seemed a little louder than usual.

Wonderful . . . Even the floor thinks I'm a whale.

She stepped out into the hallway and noticed light coming from the kitchen. Her slippers made a whisking sound as she shuffled along the hardwood. If Michael was actually in the kitchen, it would be a first. An image of him wielding a nine-inch carving knife and going to town on some invisible roast made her shiver. After the first post-orb sleepwalking incident, she'd made him buy a gun safe. Only she knew the combination. She'd almost put a lock on the cutlery drawer as well, but she worried how Michael might react to that. Dr. Cryder could not have been more clear when he told her that regaining her trust was Michael's number-one priority, especially now that he'd been separated from the Army.

When she reached the doorway, she paused, steeling herself for whatever freak show awaited on the other side. *You can do this, Josie,* she told herself. *He's not going to hurt you. Despite everything, he's never tried to hurt you.* Slowly, she peeked around the corner.

"Hey, baby," he said, greeting her with a guilty smile. "Sorry I woke you."

"It's all right," she said, feeling like she'd just shed a hundred-pound ox yoke from her shoulders. "Whatcha doing?"

"Couldn't sleep," he said, clutching a coffee mug with both hands.

"You couldn't sleep, so you fixed yourself a coffee?" she said, laying on the sarcasm.

"I could change this out for bourbon, if you like?"

"I was just teasing. Feel free to caffeinate to your heart's content. If I must go looking for you in the middle of the night, I much prefer to find you awake and lucid in here as opposed to talking in tongues with imaginary friends in the yard."

"Me too." He pulled out the other kitchen chair and gestured to it. She walked to him and took a seat. "Is everything okay?"

"Yeah."

"Are you taking your meds?"

"Yes," he said with a defensive edge to his voice.

"I know you don't like the way they make you feel, but you have to take them, Michael. You can't skip a dose . . . Do you hear me?"

"Back off, Joz. I'm taking my meds."

"Because the last time—"

"I know," he said, cutting her off. "But you can stop henpecking now. I'm not sleepwalking. I'm not hearing voices. I simply couldn't sleep."

"Okay, I'm sorry."

"It's all right," he said. "Just a lot on my mind."

"Are you thinking about the ultrasound appointment later?"

He nodded. "That and other things."

"What other things?"

"It doesn't matter."

"It matters to me," she said. "What other things?"

He sighed. "Other things like, What if I can't be trusted with our daughter? What if the *other* Michael resurfaces and tries to hurt her and I'm not able to stop him?"

She reached out, took his hand, and pressed it to her tummy. "That's your daughter I'm carrying. Pills or no pills, if there's one thing I know with certainty, it's that you would never harm our child."

"Thank you," he said, meeting her gaze. "I couldn't do this without you."

"We're a team and—hey, did you feel that? The baby just kicked."

"Yeah," he said, his face lighting up. "She just did it again . . . and again."

"Whoa, she's really getting busy in there," Josie said with a chuckle.

"Maybe she heard my voice and thinks she's in baby boot camp."

Josie winced.

"Are you okay?"

"Yeah, just feels like she's using my bladder for a punching bag."

"Want me to order her to stand down?" he said with a little grin.

"If you don't mind, that would be great," she said, pressing with both hands on the underside of her belly. "Oh wait, there, she's just stopped. Thank God."

He kept his hand on her tummy for another beat, then sat back in his chair and fixed his gaze on her.

"What?"

"Do you know how beautiful you are?"

She felt her cheeks blush. "You're just saying that because you have to. I'm a whale. Look at me."

"If you're a whale, then you're the hottest whale on the planet."

"Oh stop . . ."

He smiled at her; she smiled back, and they lingered in the moment until it faded.

"Have you thought any more about names?" she said. "Do any of the ones on the short list feel right to you?"

He nodded. "I think I'm leaning toward Genevieve. At first I didn't care much for it, but it's been growing on me. It sounds sophisticated and distinctly feminine."

"That's probably because it means *woman of the people*. You can't get any more feminine than that."

"Really?"

"Yeah, I looked it up because I've been leaning toward it too."

He nodded. "So did we just name our baby?"

"I think so," she said with a grin.

Smiling wide, he leaned all the way forward in his chair until his mouth was next to her belly and said, "Hello, baby Genevieve, I can't wait to meet you." Then he kissed her tummy once and straightened in his chair.

"Should we try to go back to bed?" she asked, extending her hand to him.

"Sure," he said, taking her fingers in his.

Neither of them managed to fall back asleep, but she treasured the time spooning together. It felt like it had been ages since they'd snuggled. When her alarm finally went off at seven, they lingered not one, but two presses of the snooze button before dressing and heading to the kitchen for a simple breakfast.

An hour later, they were in the ultrasound suite at her obstetrician's office in Watertown—she reclining on the exam table, bare belly exposed, and he sitting in a chair beside her holding her hand.

"I'm going to apply some gel," the ultrasound technician said. "I had it in the warmer so it wouldn't be cold for you."

The bottle made a squirting sound as the tech applied a generous amount of the goo in a zigzag pattern across the crown of Josie's stomach. Then, using the ultrasound probe, she spread it around as she made adjustments to the machine with her other hand. A *whoosh, whoosh, whoosh* sound played on the speakers.

"That's your baby's heartbeat . . . Looks good," the technician said. "And it appears baby has flipped since your last visit. She's head down now."

"Maybe that's what she was doing last night," Josie said.

"What's that?" the tech asked.

"Well, she was very active in the middle of the night. Felt like she was using my bladder as a punching bag, but maybe what I was feeling was her flipping."

"Could be," the tech said, moving the probe around with her right hand and using a trackball and buttons to take and record various measurements on the screen. Josie kept her gaze fixed on the display.

"Whoa," Josie said, "she's moving again."

The ultrasound technician stopped moving the probe, and the easy smile she'd been wearing faded.

"I told you," Michael said. "She thinks she's in boot camp. She's doing her morning calisthenics."

"Is something wrong?" Josie asked.

The tech didn't answer. A beat later, the baby settled down and went still on the screen.

"Is something wrong?" Josie repeated. "Is the baby okay?"

The tech kept moving the probe until she found the angle she was looking for and the swooshing sound of the baby's heart began playing loudly on the machine's speaker. When the baby's heart rate appeared in normal range on the screen, Josie saw the young woman visibly relax.

"What's going on?" Michael said, his voice taking on a Sergeant's no-nonsense tone.

"It's nothing," the tech said, forcing a smile. "Everything's fine."

"Well, something happened you're not telling us," he said.

She hesitated. "For an instant there, I thought I saw something, but . . . it happened so fast, I'm not really sure. I've never seen one before."

"Seen what before?" Josie said.

"A seizure in utero," the tech said, frowning. "But it was probably just the baby moving."

Josie turned and looked at Michael, and all the color had drained from his face.

"I should probably get Dr. Young," the tech said, getting to her feet. "He can watch the playback and talk to you both."

Josie's mouth was cotton; all she could do was nod. When the young woman had left the room, her eyes rimmed with tears. "It's my fault," she whispered. "I was so focused on facing the orb and getting you out, I left our daughter completely defenseless."

"You can't blame yourself. How could you know?" Michael said. "How could you know it would do that?"

Tears were streaming down her cheeks now. "What if our daughter, our little Genevieve, is . . . what if she is . . ."

"Like me," Michael said, finishing the sentence she could not bring herself to say aloud.

They locked eyes.

"Well, she's not going to be," she said, suddenly defiant. "The Army has cordoned off Silo 9. Nobody goes in; nothing gets out. That *thing* is out of our lives forever."

She wiped the tears with the back of her sleeve as her thoughts drifted to Willie Barnes. Was his life a harbinger of things to come? Was that the inevitable fate of the Pitcher family, to battle psychological remnants and alter-ego demons seeded by EVE? *No,* she thought, steeling herself. They would be fine. Their daughter would be fine.

"We control our thoughts, not the orb," she said defiantly.

"We write our own future," Michael added, taking her hand.

"I love you," she said, smiling at him and meeting his gaze.

"I love you too." He put his other hand on her tummy. It was warm and reassuring to the touch. She felt the energy of three connecting them. They were a family, a family bonded together by love and devotion.

And *that* was the strongest force in the universe.

DAY ZERO

Forty-Five Years in the Future
DARPA Zero-Day Technology Black Site
Converted Missile Silo
Dannemora, New York

Zero-Day Technology Department Director Damien Howe walked through the security tunnel and counted the green flashes signaling that his identity was being verified via facial-skeletal recognition, subdermal keychain pinger, and transcranial magnetic signature. Fooling one of these state-of-the-art security protocols would be a herculean endeavor, but to fool all three was statistically impossible.

Or so they told him.

Green, green, and green.

Me, me, and me, sang the voice in his head.

The blast door at the end of the vestibule chimed and whooshed open. He strode down the half flight of stairs into the LCC wearing a smile, but his heart was pounding out of his chest. Today was launch day. A successful launch virtually guaranteed his death. Failure meant days of painstaking diagnostics and tedious recalibrations before they could try again. He prayed for the former.

"Good morning, Dr. Howe," said Lucy Chu, walking up to greet him.

"Good morning, Lucy," he said. "Everything ready to go?"

"On time, on target," she said, using her favorite expression.

"Excellent," he said. "Let me grab one last cup of coffee before we start the checklist."

She smiled broadly at him and said, "I brewed a fresh pot for the occasion. Vintage Colombian roast from 2020."

He cocked an eyebrow at her. "How the hell did you manage that?"

"The rumors of a secret cryostash in P-freezer are true," she said sheepishly. "I figured today being launch day . . . well, you know."

He savored the aroma as he walked to the coffee station. "Have I ever told you you're my hero?" he said with a wink.

Lucy was the program lead and the person most directly responsible for the development of the EVE probe technology, but she was not the brainchild behind the program. No, that distinction belonged to the President. Four days after being sworn in, President Sanchez had secretly paid a visit to DARPA. The meeting had lasted only thirty minutes and taken place inside a SCIF with five people, Howe being one of them. Since that fateful day six years ago, the number of people fully read in to the EVE project had expanded to ten. Only ten. There were ten people on Earth who knew about the plan to save the planet by sending a probe back in time to purposely cause a *near*-extinction-level event for the human race . . . hence the EVE acronym: Extinction Variable Event.

Setting the morality of the decision aside, the rationale behind the EVE program was sound—at least in Howe's mind. The Sixth Extinction was well under way, unstoppable, and undeniable. Unlike the previous five mass extinctions documented in the fossil record over the last half-billion years, this wholesale obliteration of nature and all her vast and diverse progeny was entirely manmade and self-inflicted. President Sanchez had begun the meeting by reading the concluding paragraph from a RAND Corporation report prepared twenty years earlier for the then sitting President.

. . . and so it is with morbid truculence that this committee concludes that global ecological collapse is not only well under way but irrevocable. The data collected, aggregated, and analyzed in this report is proof that the extinction of terrestrial and oceanic species is accelerating at an exponential rate. As of the date of this publication, fifty percent of Earth's documented vertebrate species are confirmed to be extinct. Within two decades, the mass-extinction event will be complete with an estimated ten percent of the world's vertebrate species remaining. Insect, invertebrate, fungi, and plant species' extinction rates will be lower but will also follow an accelerating downward trajectory as irreversible climate change continues to degrade every ecosystem on the planet. In tandem with this ecological catastrophe, a global economic collapse will occur, prompting famine, conflict, disease, and misery the likes of which have not been witnessed since the Middle Ages. Without a global and coordinated effort to salvage what remains of the global ecosystem, the future carrying capacity for the planet will be in the range of one to two billion people.

The predictions made in the report had come to fruition, and now the world—once vibrant, diverse, and alive—was barren and burning. Recovery was impossible. Prevention was the only option.

Howe poured the priceless Colombian brew into his favorite mug, inhaled deeply, and took a sip. "Ahhhh, heaven," he mumbled and walked over to the mission-commander workstation.

None of the other five people in the room were talking, and all eyes were fixed on him.

"All right, everybody, I'm not one for speeches," he said, scanning the room. "So let's get on with it. Comms, will you please patch in the President?"

A beat later, a high-resolution holographic projection of the situation room materialized in the designated conference holospace. President Sanchez and three others—her Secretary of Defense, her husband, and her Chief of Staff—sat in the virtual conference room.

"Madame President," Howe said, nodding at her.

"Director Howe," the President answered. "How is everyone doing today?"

"Good spirits," he said, then added, "and maybe a tad nervous."

This garnered polite laughter from both rooms.

"Okay, Dr. Howe, it's your show," she said.

"Request permission to commence the prelaunch checklist."

"Permission granted. Commence prelaunch checklist."

"Very well," he said, and from memory he began the callout procedure to the operational specialists in the room.

"Telemetry?"

"Go launch," came the response.

"Containment?"

"Go launch."

"Program?"

"Go launch."

"Timekeeper?"

"Go launch."

"Safety?"

"Go launch."

"EVE?"

"Go launch."

"Checklist complete," Howe said and turned to look at the President. "Any last-minute questions, Madame President?"

"I know we've talked about this before, Dr. Howe," the President said, "but can you remind me how we're ensuring the probe will end up when and where we want? How do you make sure that the probe doesn't end up in outer space, at the bottom of the ocean, or trapped inside a mountain?"

"We've run millions of computer simulations to identify the optimal date in history and geographic coordinates to target. But quantum time travel is, by its very nature, unpredictable," Howe replied. "The slightest fluctuation in the earth's gravity, magnetic field, background radiation—even the temperature in the containment facility—will impact the outcome. Moreover, the farther back in time we target, the greater the cumulative impact of fluctuating variables will be."

She nodded. "So if I hear you correctly, Doctor, you're saying we're at the point in the process now where all we can do is cross our fingers and hope for the best?"

He crossed his fingers and held them up for her to see. "Yes, Madame President, that about sums it up . . . Any other questions?"

"Just one," she said. "How quickly will we know if it worked?"

He chuckled. "That is the question that's kept me up at night for the past six years. Dr. Chu, would you like to answer this one?"

Lucy Chu nodded and said, "Within one nanosecond after the launch of the probe, we will know if the mission was a success. In other words, if we're all still here breathing, then we know the mission failed, because this reality cannot exist if EVE completes its mission."

"That's what I thought," President Sanchez said, "but I wanted to hear it from the smartest people on the planet just to be sure."

Howe glanced around the room at the faces he was, in all probability, looking at for the very last time. A profound wave of emotion washed over him as his mind went to his wife and children, who knew nothing of what their father was about to do. He'd said his goodbyes in the regular fashion this morning on the way out the door; only he'd held each hug a little bit longer before letting go.

"If anyone has any last words or prayers, speak them now, or forever hold your peace," he said, his tone more fatalistic than he had intended. He paused, and when no one spoke, he looked at the President. "Madame President, on your order."

She took a deep breath, grabbed her husband's hand, and said, "May God have mercy on my soul . . . Dr. Howe, launch the EVE probe."

"Yes, Madame President," he acknowledged and walked to the primary launch console. He looked at Dr. Chu, who was standing at the secondary launch console, and nodded. They each inserted their respective launch keys into the glowing red slots. It was an ancient and unsophisticated safeguard yet beautifully effective and poetic. "On my mark. In three . . . two . . . one . . . launch."

They both turned their keys, and the video feed showed the EVE probe disappear from the containment field in the silo.

DAY ZERO

DARPA Zero-Day Technology Black Site
Converted Missile Silo
Dannemora, New York

The hologram of President Sanchez looked at her husband and then back at the room full of scientists, who were eyeing one another with confusion.

"It appears, Dr. Pitcher," the President said, her brow furrowing, "that the mission failed."

Genevieve Pitcher, Zero-Day Technology Department Director for DARPA, sighed and looked down at the launch key still in her grip. "Yes, Madame President, it appears it did."

"Did our probe change anything?" the President asked. "Anything at all?"

Genevieve looked at Dr. Lao Chu, the program lead. He shrugged at her. "If it did, we will never know."

"And why is that, Doctor?" the President asked.

"Any changes EVE might have brought about prior to our births could have impacted our current reality, but there is no way for us to compare this reality to the reality prior to the launch."

The President nodded. "Understood. Dr. Pitcher, how long until you can get the next EVE probe prepped and ready for launch?"

"Two, maybe three days," Genevieve said, picking up her mug of hot tea. "We'll need to recheck all the calculations, launch parameters, and probe calibrations. In addition, I'd like to personally run new launch simulations and make adjustments to the landing time and geographic location."

"All right, Dr. Pitcher, you have seventy-two hours," the President said. "I realize this was an emotionally traumatic event today, but I want everyone to remember the oaths you've sworn. We are the planet's last hope. Nature's last hope. Humankind's last hope. Keep the faith, keep your wits, and most importantly, keep our secret."

"Yes, Madame President," Genevieve said, answering for all of them. "We will."

She waited for the holographic situation room to disappear before sighing and letting her aching shoulders slump. She was disappointed yet strangely relieved at the same time. Had the mission succeeded, things would be different. Maybe her father would still be alive. She missed him, terribly so, despite how troubled he'd been for most of her life. But then, maybe her mother, whom she loved desperately, would be lost to her in this reality. Maybe she would have never been born. Or maybe her soul would have ended up in a different little embryo, born to different parents, in a different place and era. She was tinkering with the clockwork of time. The ramifications of her actions would change past, present, and future. Her staff had given her the nickname "the most dangerous woman alive" in jest, but they all knew it was true.

The EVE project was the culmination of her life's work. It was a dream she had strived for since she was a little girl. The earth was sick and dying. Nature had been exploited, molested . . . violated. No amount of atonement could undo the sins of her forbearers. A complete and total reset was the only answer.

Verse began to play in her mind. She didn't know where she'd first heard it, or who'd composed it, but she'd been reciting the singsong poem since she was a little girl:

I for all and one for none,
I take no blame for what I've done.
Greed we worship beneath the sun,
And dance in blood, oh what fun.
Sins collective eclipse the sum,
At Nature's pyre, her praises sung,
The world has tipped, the end near come,
Reset the balance, or the Devil's won.

Sometimes she wondered if this prescient rhyme had been the tip of the invisible wedge she'd driven between her parents to cause the great schism in the Pitcher family. Or maybe it was the little colored orbs she'd refused to stop drawing on her bedroom walls and every scrap of paper she could find as a child. She supposed the exact details didn't really matter. She'd long since come to accept that it was her inability to curb her EVE obsession that had pushed her father over the edge and driven her parents apart. Even now, as a grown woman, the guilt sometimes made her cry, but what choice had she had? This was her destiny, and destiny cannot be ignored.

"Say again?" Dr. Chu asked, walking up to her with a quizzical look on his face.

"Oh, nothing, just mumbling to myself," she said, meeting his tired, bloodshot eyes.

"So what now?" he said.

"Time to take a trip down to level eight and wake up another EVE from storage," Genevieve replied, setting down her mug of tea. She had an intriguing and paradoxical theory about what might have gone wrong with the last attempt, but it was a conversation that needed to happen in private. "I think it's time that she and I had a little talk . . . mind to mind."

AFTERWORD

As an author, I communicate my hopes and fears, as well as my observations and thoughts on life, through plot and dialogue. I'm not, and never have been, a preach-from-the-soapbox kind of guy. But in researching this novel, I experienced an unsettling paradigm shift. I'm concerned for us. I'm concerned for our planet. I feel I have a responsibility to use this forum to share thoughts and conclusions that either were not, or could not, be properly articulated in the story you just read.

Reset is a work of fiction, but the Sixth Extinction is not. It's real and it's happening now. As of this writing, the global population is estimated at 7.5 billion people and increasing at a rate of approximately 200,000 people every day. To put this in perspective, the total population of gorillas on the planet is 200,000—eclipsed by human population growth in one day. Polar bears, 30,000—eclipsed by human population growth in four hours. Tigers, 4,000—eclipsed by human population growth in a half hour. My point is simply this: We are so many, and we are not leaving room for our animal kin. I choose the word *kin* carefully and intentionally. In my humble opinion, all life has worth. All life is kin. I don't think sentience or intelligence should serve as a litmus test for life.

As a parent, I have a moral obligation to safeguard my children and help them actualize their potential. I assume this responsibility because I possess foresight, experience, and the mental and physical capabilities a child does not. A child is simply not equipped to fend for itself in the world. This fact is obvious and recognized by people the world over, regardless of race, heritage, or creed. Why, then, does the same not hold true for our animal kin? We have terraformed the planet into an environment in which our kin can no longer survive without our aid. For life to persevere on planet Earth, humanity must assume the role of steward. Stewardship has become an obligation for our species, now that we have wrested control of the land, waters, and sky from Nature.

Stewardship is not a partisan issue; it is a moral one. For those individuals who don't believe in climate change, who don't believe it is possible to change the composition of gases in the atmosphere, answer me one simple question: How long could you last breathing air in a garage with the door closed and a gasoline car engine pumping out exhaust? The volume of air in a garage is small, so the composition of gases becomes toxic quickly. The volume of air in the atmosphere surrounding the planet is large, so the composition of gases is becoming toxic slowly, but that doesn't mean it isn't happening. The garage is a microcosm, but so is the Earth—it just happens to be a big one. No author has better illustrated this allegory than Stephen King in his novel *Under the Dome*. If you want to understand where we as a species are headed, read King's book. When you're done, I promise you'll come to the same realization that I did—we *all* live "Under the Dome."

We must act now. We must assume the mantle of ecological stewardship and take responsibility for the sanctity of all life on this planet. But for this to happen, it requires a paradigm shift away from the psychological ethos that we inherited from our ancestors that Nature must be conquered or else it will conquer us. Somewhere along the way, humanity declared war on Nature so that we might prosper. The decimation meted from that war is evident everywhere I travel. What Nature desperately needs now is to be nurtured. We have to become better global citizens. We have to become ecological stewards—protecting and nurturing all life on this planet—because if we don't, the "Reset" button is going to get pushed on us, and when it does we will be powerless to stop it.

ACKNOWLEDGMENTS

There's an army of people I want to acknowledge and thank for bringing *Reset* to fruition: My agent, Gina, for believing in this novel and fighting tooth and nail to find a home for it in today's crowded marketplace; my editor Jessica for guiding me around plot pitfalls and then patiently championing it through every stage of production; Caitlin for her sage editorial counsel, enthusiasm, and challenging me to discover the soul of each character; Jeff for his selfless encouragement and patience while I worked on this book, even when it impacted time on our Tier One series; Adrienne for seeing the story's potential and taking it to the dance; and last but not least, Karen, my most loyal and devoted fan, for never complaining about all the times she and the kids had to wait while I gave priority to imaginary people and their imaginary dilemmas. I adore each and every one of you for empowering and enabling me to be a professional storyteller . . . Thank you!

GLOSSARY

ARPA—Advanced Research Projects Agency (DARPA precursor)

BRIG—Ballistics Research Information Gathering

CASEVAC—casualty evacuation

CDC—Centers for Disease Control and Prevention

CIA—Central Intelligence Agency

CRISPR—Clustered Regularly Interspaced Short Palindromic Repeats
(DNA-editing tool pronounced *crisper*)

CO—commanding officer

DARPA—Defense Advanced Research Projects Agency

DOD—Department of Defense

DS&T—CIA's Directorate of Science and Technology

EOD—explosive ordnance disposal

EXFIL—exfiltrate

ICBM—intercontinental ballistic missile

IED—incendiary explosive device

JCAD CED—joint chemical agent detector with chemical explosive detection

LCC—launch control center

LOX—liquid oxygen

MCCC—Missile Combat Crew Commander

MEDEVAC—medical evacuation

MFT—missile facilities technician

MOAB—Mother of All Bombs

MP—military police

NGO—nongovernmental organization

NOC—non-official cover

OIC—officer in charge

ONR—Office of Naval Research

OPSEC—operational security

PCR—polymerase chain reaction (DNA amplification technique)

QRF—quick reaction force

SCIF—Sensitive Compartmented Information Facility

SITREP—situation report

SMS—strategic missile squadron

SyNAPSE—Systems of Neuromorphic Adaptive Plastic Scalable Electronics

TIMS—Office of Technology Integration, Management, and Security

TMS—transcranial magnetic stimulation

USAF—United States Air Force

USAMRIID—United States Army Medical Research Institute of Infectious Diseases

WD—Westfield Dynamics (DARPA front company)

ABOUT THE AUTHOR

Brian Andrews is a US Navy veteran and nuclear engineer who served as an officer on a fast-attack submarine in the Pacific. He is a Park Leadership Fellow, has a master's degree in business from Cornell, and holds a psychology degree from Vanderbilt. He is the author of the Think Tank thrillers, *The Infiltration Game*, and *The Calypso Directive*; and coauthor of the *Wall Street Journal* bestselling Tier One thriller series (*Tier One*, *War Shadows*, and *Crusader One*) with friend and fellow veteran Jeffrey Wilson. Andrews is a husband, father, and advocate of planetary stewardship, and would like to someday visit Mars. Discover more about the author at www.andrews-wilson.com or follow him on Twitter @bandrewsjwilson.

ANDRE   FLT
Andrews, Brian,
Reset :a thriller /

05/18